MINDERS

MICHELE JAFFE

razOr
bill

An Imprint of Penguin Group (USA) LLC

A division of Penguin Young Readers Group
Published by the Penguin Group
Penguin Group (USA) LLC
345 Hudson Street
New York, New York 10014

USA / Canada / UK / Ireland / Australia / New Zealand / India / South Africa / China
Penguin.com
A Penguin Random House Company

Copyright © 2014 Penguin Group (USA) LLC

ISBN: 978-1-59514-658-8

Printed in the United States of America

1 3 5 7 9 10 8 6 4 2

This book is dedicated to my friend Meg, whose awesomeness cannot be encompassed by all the adjectives in the dictionary even if you used each of them a hundred googol times.

PROLOGUE
WEEK 5

Her ears were ringing, and there was a metallic taste in her mouth.

Where was she? What had happened?

Sadie glanced around the room, the uneven stacks of boxes looming like cliffs in the inadequate light from the high windows. The sounds of someone clipping their nails and watching a nature program came from inside the office up ahead, the announcer saying, ". . . but the natural habitat of these majestic creatures is succumbing to the drumbeat of civilization."

He moved toward the office. As he walked Sadie felt his right hand tighten and realized he was holding something, something she couldn't identify. His grip felt strange, less sensitive than usual.

Gloves, she realized as he brought his hands up and she saw them. He lifted the edge of the right one just past the scar on his wrist to glance at the Mickey Mouse watch, which showed nine thirty exactly. *Why would he be wearing glo—*

She saw it then. The object in his hand.

He was holding a gun.

Her mind reeled. *No*, she thought, then yelled, *No! Whatever you are planning, stop. Don't do this. It won't get you what you want.* But he'd perfected his ability to ignore her now. She felt as if he'd built a wall between them, impervious and reflective, so everything she said just reverberated back.

He took a step forward, then another. Dread filled her. She wanted to close her eyes, look away, but that wouldn't change anything. He raised the gun, and as he stepped into the office she heard him think, *Watch this, Sadie.*

As if she had a choice.

FELLOWSHIP INTERVIEW
ROQUE MIND CORPS

CANDIDATE: SADIE AMES
INTERVIEWER: CURTIS PINTER
LOCATION: DETROIT UNION CLUB
DATE: APRIL 25
OFFICIAL TRANSCRIPT

CURTIS PINTER: Please sit down, Miss Ames.

SADIE AMES: Thank you.

CP: My name is Curtis Pinter. I am legally bound to inform you that this interview is being recorded with an Enhanced Veracity Evaluation system. Essentially a lie detector. Are you comfortable with that?

SA: I see no reason to object.

CP: Good. We'll begin with simple questions to get some baseline readings. What is your full name?

SA : Sophia Adelaide Ames. But I prefer to be called Sadie.

CP : What are your parents' names?

SA : Grace and Hector Ames.

CP : Do you have any siblings?

SA : No, I'm an only child.

CP : Where were you born?

SA : Here in Detroit.

CP : What is your favorite book?

SA : Descartes, *Discourse on the Method*.

CP : Would you say you're an introvert or an extrovert?

SA : Introvert.

CP : Do you have a best friend?

SA : Yes. Her name is Decca.

CP : A boyfriend.

SA : Yes. Pete.

CP : You know why you are here?

SA : Because I am a finalist for the Mind Corps Fellowship.

CP : Exactly. Very prestigious. There are seventy-five finalists out of a pool of over a thousand. Fewer than half of those will be made Mind Corps Fellows. So, it is exciting company.

SA : I feel lucky to have made the cut.

CP : I doubt very much that you believe in luck, Miss Ames. Unless you think all your achievements are simply your good fortune?

SA : I wouldn't say that. I work very hard. But I was lucky to be born into the kind of family that can encourage and support my hard work.

CP : What are the first three words you think your friends would use to describe you?

SA : Loyal. Driven. Analytical.

CP : What sorts of things do you enjoy doing with them?

SA : The same things everyone does. Watching movies or going out for dinner or to events.

CP : What kinds of events?

SA : At our country club.

CP : Have you ever rebelled against your parents or done anything to test your relationship?

SA : When I was five I shoplifted a Snickers bar.

CP : What happened?

SA : I got caught.

CP : How were you punished?

SA : I was so upset about having broken the rules, my parents thought that was punishment enough, so they didn't bother.

CP : That's an interesting way to put it. "Didn't bother." Do you wish they would have?

SA : That was a figure of speech. They were right. It taught me to be self-disciplined. I never stole anything again.

CP : Do you spend a lot of time together?

SA : As much as we can. We're all busy, and they go out most weeknights.

CP : They don't take you?

SA : Their events are almost always work related—dinners with my father's clients or fund-raisers for my mother's charities—so there would be no place for me.

CP : Who do you have dinner with when they're out?

SA : My homework, generally.

CP : It doesn't bother you to be abandoned?

SA : I don't feel abandoned. I'm very proud of my parents and the work they do.

CP : What kind of work is that?

SA : My father has a holistic investment practice, and my mother is on the board of several not-for-profit agencies that focus on improving conditions for children living at or below the poverty line.

CP: Here in Detroit?

SA: Yes. Mainly in City Center but wherever the need is greatest.

CP: Does she spend time in City Center?

SA: No, her work is more at the fund-raising and oversight level.

CP: You live in Lower Long Lake. That's, what, twenty-five minutes from City Center?

SA: I suppose, on the Zipway. I think it's about thirty miles. On regular streets it would probably take an hour.

CP: Have you ever been there?

SA: A busload of us went on a school photography trip this year to take pictures of the abandoned Barrington Building.

CP: What did you think?

SA: It was an excellent subject for the class.

CP: I meant what did you think of City Center?

SA: Oh. We only drove through. We didn't really spend time there.

CP: You must have had some observations, even from the window of the bus?

SA: I noticed the street names because my mother is on the mayor's steering committee for the Road Sponsorship program, so when I saw Fitness Zone Boulevard and CouponCouponCoupon.com Way, I felt like I was seeing her work.

CP: If you are accepted as a Mind Corps Fellow, you will likely to end up in an environment with a stronger resemblance to City Center than your community. It will be chaotic. You will see things that make you uneasy. Do you think you would be able to maintain your composure and objectivity?

SA: Yes. Especially if I can help change that and improve the lives of those who live there.

CP: You are finishing your junior year of high school. Where do you see yourself in five years?

SA: Spending the summer between college and medical school doing an internship at a clinic or health center in an underserved neighborhood.

CP: You're quite an overachiever.

SA: I work my hardest at everything. That's just achieving, not overachieving.

CP: You are the valedictorian of your class, the co-captain of the tennis team, the head of your school's community volunteer committee, a national debate champion, have never been in trouble, and are considered a role model by your peers and teachers alike. Your résumé makes you look perfect. Tell me one thing about yourself that's not perfect.

SA: My father would say I take things too seriously.

CP: Do you agree?

SA: Pete—my boyfriend—would.

CP: And you?

SA: It's not something I really think about.

CP: Can you always control your thoughts?

SA: Mostly.

CP: Sometimes the experience of Syncopy can trigger underlying conditions. Please answer yes or no to the following. Have you ever experienced claustrophobia?

SA: No.

CP: Depression?

SA: No.

CP: Homicidal urges?

SA: No.

CP: Animal attacks?

SA: No.

CP: Panic or anxiety attacks?

SA: Not at all.

CP: Phobias?

SA: I'm afraid of heights.

CP: What about heights, specifically? The openness?

SA: Falling.

CP: Have you ever been witness to a crime?

SA: No.

CP: What would you do if you found yourself in that position?

SA: Contact the appropriate authorities and help the victim.

CP: In that order?

SA: If possible. Alerting those with the power to do something would seem to be the prudent first step.

CP: So if you saw a convenience store clerk being held up by a robber with a gun to his head, you'd—

SA: Call Serenity Services.

CP: You wouldn't try to tackle the robber?

SA: That would most likely get us both killed. Approaching someone with a gun is far more likely to escalate the situation to violence.

CP: Interesting.

SA: The statistics are very clear on that.

CP: The statistics, yes. But what about your gut reaction? Would that really be to think of statistics?

SA: I work hard to behave according to what is most logical, rather than by listening to my "gut."

CP : I'm going to give you a hypothetical situation and ask you some questions about it.

SA : Okay.

CP : An old woman is looking at a Rembrandt in a museum when a fire breaks out. You can only save one, the woman or the painting, but not both. Which would you save?

SA : I'd ask the old woman what she wanted me to do.

CP : You didn't even have to think about that.

SA : It's the logical thing to do.

CP : And if she told you to choose?

SA : I'd send her out with the painting and stay behind myself.

CP : And if that were not an option?

SA : I would save the painting. It would benefit more people.

CP : And if instead of an old woman you had to choose between saving the painting or a kitten?

SA : The painting. Of course.

CP : What if the old woman is a Nobel Prize–winning scientist on the cusp of a breakthrough cure for cancer?

SA : If I had a chance to find all that out, I would imagine there would be time to save both her and the painting.

CP : That's a cop-out.

SA : So is continually tweaking a hypothetical problem so that it never concludes.

CP : So it is, Miss Ames. Very well, let's take a real-life example. I see that you have worked the past two summers at the snack bar at the country club. What would you do if you found out a co-worker was stealing from the cash register?

SA : I would tell our boss.

CP : What if they said they desperately needed the money and begged you not to turn them in?

SA : You're not helping them if you don't. If they need the money that badly, they need help, and stealing won't be the answer over the long term. Alerting someone in charge would be the best way to get them the true assistance they need and avert a much bigger catastrophe.

CP : What if it was a cute guy you wanted to date?

SA : I don't believe in dating at work.

CP : What if it were Decca? Your best friend.

SA : Then I would sell the Rembrandt we just rescued, take the money, and she and I would go on the run.

CP : Really?

SA : No. I would turn her in and get her the best help I could. Because if Decca were stealing, it would mean that she was gravely unhappy or deeply in trouble, and I would do everything in my power to get her happy and well again. And the best first step would be to put a stop to the destructive behavior.

CP : I thought you said your friends would describe you as loyal. Now you're turning them in?

SA : Not punishing someone and letting them "get away" with something isn't love, and it isn't friendship. It is lazy and enabling. People use loyalty as emotional blackmail for morally questionable decisions. Making the hard choice shows you are paying attention and that you care. That is true loyalty.

CP : Very rousing.

SA : I'm sorry if that was too zealous.

CP : Never apologize for showing that you have a pulse, Miss Ames. If you are accepted as a Fellow, you will be on your own in someone's mind, entirely, for nearly two months. You will have no contact with anyone, no one to talk to. And no control. Up until this point your whole life has been about control. This would mean completely yielding to someone else.

SA: That doesn't worry me.

CP: But are you sure it is what you want?

SA: Yes. Very much.

CP: So far it seems like this fellowship would simply be something else to add to your already impressive college application. Give me one reason why I should believe it means more to you than that.

SA: I just killed off an old woman—possibly a Nobel laureate—and a kitten, and turned in my best friend and two co-workers for stealing in order to persuade you to give it to me.

CP: So you did. [Laughing.] Still, tell me *why* you want it.

SA: I want to feel what pressures other people feel. Experience the world guided by someone else's moral compass. See and hear and taste with senses formed in a completely different mold than mine. I want to see what it's like to live someone else's lie.

CP: Well put.

SA: Someone else's *life*.

CP: Of course. I believe that covers everything. Thank you, Miss Ames.

END INTERVIEW

CHAPTER 1
ORIENTATION

At nine forty-five on a sunny Thursday morning, Sadie Ames took a sharp left "at the birdhouse," as directed by the instructions she'd been e-mailed, and went from a single-lane road to a rutted mud track overhung with trees. As she came around the curve, pebbles pinged against the side of her Saab convertible—red, at her father's insistence—and her tires jiggled over an uneven patch of mud.

Sadie's hands curled around the steering wheel, knuckles going white. *No no no*, she thought to herself. It was a warm June morning, but she felt a chill of apprehension. This could not be happening. She was *not* going to be late to orientation. She'd allowed an hour and a half for what was only supposed to be a forty-minute drive; even with the accident backing up things on the Zipway, everything was going fine.

Until she got lost.

"Something's wrong," she said into the speakerphone. "This can't be the place." There was no way that an elite research facility would be down an unmaintained trail barely big enough for a bike.

Pete's voice came through her earpiece: "What does your GPS say?"

"Nothing. I'm out of range."

She heard him chuckle. "No wonder you sound so panicked. You without a GPS—"

"—is like a bun without a burger," she interrupted the familiar litany. "I know."

Pete said, "I just think it's funny that a girl who knows exactly where she's going has such a terrible sense of direction. It's like one of nature's jokes."

"Hilarious." Sadie had slowed almost to a crawl now, the branches of the bushes scratching against the sides of her car.

It was true, she did have a terrible sense of direction, but he didn't have to harp on it. She secretly thought he did it because it was one of the few things he was better at than she was. She enjoyed the competitiveness of their relationship—as Pete said, it made them both sharper—but sometimes it could feel a little petty.

Not that she would tell him that. Although movies and books said being in love meant sharing everything, she'd learned early in her relationship with Pete that sharing often led to pointless drama.

His voice broke into her thoughts. "Look, tell me the address, and I'll find the directions."

"I'll be fine," she said, hoping she sounded calmer than she felt. The clock on her dashboard flashed 9:49.

"Oh, that's right." The tension in Pete's voice was palpable even through the speakerphone. "You can't reveal the location of your secret spy camp."

"It's not spy camp," she said, her jaw tight. Glancing in her rearview mirror at the narrow, brambly track she'd just come point-eight miles down, she thought that going back looked even worse than going forward.

"I still don't get why you want to do this," Pete's voice went on, as though he wouldn't have leapt at the chance to do it the previous year when he was eligible—if he'd been accepted. "It's just some glorified exchange program. You'd learn more about how other people live by going to Mexico and building houses for a few weeks like I did last summer. And we could hang out on the beach together."

Agree with him, she told herself. *There's no reason to go over this again.* "That does sound—" She rounded a curve and then stopped herself midsentence. "There's a guardhouse in front of me. I wasn't wrong after all." Relief flooded over her like a warm bath.

"Oh, great," Pete said. Did he sound disappointed? No, she was just being touchy because she was excited.

"This is it. I should probably go."

Pete said, "Aren't you going to say you'll miss me?"

"It's just orientation. I'm only going to be gone for two days," she told him, adding quickly, "Of course, I'll miss you."

"That's better. I love you, babe."

"You too," Sadie said and hung up.

Her heart was racing, and her chest was a little tight. The guardhouse was freshly painted with dark-tinted windows. As she drew even with it, a man who clearly knew his way around a gym stepped out of the door, holding up a hand to stop her.

"ID please, Miss Ames. Kindly remove your sunglasses." He held the card she'd handed him and looked at her face, then back to the card. She imagined him checking each item on it. Hair: strawberry blond (two shades darker than her father's); eyes: green (slightly lighter than her mother's); age: sixteen (seventeen in October); height: five feet, eleven inches (two inches shorter than Pete); build: average. Apparently satisfied that it was her, he slid the ID through a machine on his hip, read the license number of her car into a microphone attached to his collar, said, "Please keep your sunglasses off," and disappeared into the guardhouse.

Sadie felt a knot of panic and excitement forming beneath her rib cage as she waited. A light breeze teased a loose strand of her hair and whispered through the tall grass on either side of the road. It was peaceful, silent except for the low murmur of her engine and the sound of insects humming. A sign on her right said ROQUE BIRD SANCTUARY. RESPECT OUR FEATHERED FRIENDS AND KEEP YOUR SPEED BELOW 25 MPH. Sadie squinted at the landscape, looking for birds, but didn't see any.

The guard was back a minute later, handing Sadie a pass with a picture of her squinting, evidently shot by a hidden camera mounted somewhere in front of her. "Show this at the next gate," he said and waved her on. She'd already pulled away when she realized the guard had known her name *before* she had given him her ID.

That was some security for a mere bird sanctuary.

Of course, it was no more a mere bird sanctuary than

the orientation she was there to attend was for the "glorified exchange program" Pete described.

Sadie had first heard about Miranda Roque and the Mind Corps Fellowship from her sixth grade science teacher. Even though only juniors could apply, she had requested a brochure immediately and had read it so many times she could quote it from memory.

"Under the visionary guidance of Miranda Roque, daughter of founder Joseph Roque, the Roque Corporation has become a leader in the use of cutting-edge technology to solve complex social problems and effect real change. The Mind Corps program, the only one of its kind in existence, is the heart of this effort, giving the leaders of tomorrow the tools they need to begin effecting change today.

"Because of the rigorous selection and vetting process, few people are nominated, and fewer are chosen. Out of a pool of over a thousand, a maximum of thirty will be offered a place as Mind Corps Fellows in any year, making it the most selective fellowship in the country, if not the world."

When she got the call ten days earlier—was it really only ten days?—that she'd been chosen, it had been almost a letdown. Not because she didn't want it, but because she wanted it so badly, had been waiting and dreaming about it for so long, it was hard to believe it was actually happening.

She had been surprised by Pete's negative reaction when she told him the news, but her parents had behaved exactly the way she'd expected. Her mother had given her a rare hug and said, "Darling, how wonderful for you. I'm so glad we can give you the opportunities I was never afforded. Your father will be very impressed," before floating elegantly up the glass staircase to make sure she hadn't wrinkled the dress she was wearing to the charity dinner that night.

Her father had tousled Sadie's hair and said, "Nice work. Better rest our hands for all the waivers they're going to make us sign." Adding, as he followed his wife up the glass staircase to change, "And kiddo, don't go taking this too seriously and getting a swelled head on us."

Since then, school had ended, Pete had graduated, there had been parties at the country club and BBQs at friends' houses, vodka popsicles, and a day to recover from the vodka popsicles.

As Sadie's father had predicted, there had also been a lot of forms to fill out and waivers to sign. Sitting at the slate-topped table in her family dining room, she'd put her neat initials next to boxes indicating her acceptance of a series of rules that ranged from maintaining complete confidentiality to not wearing perfume and never attempting to meet or contact her Subject "in this or any other universe." She'd signed the bottom of every one of ten pages absolving the Roque organization from responsibility for anything, including "mental degradation or personality shifts as a result of steps taken to contain or end a failure of compliance."

"'Failure of compliance,'" Hector Ames had read aloud, chuckling, as he filled the line with his oversized signature. "Sounds menacing. Fortunately, that's not something we'll have to worry about. My girl likes nothing more than following rules."

Sadie felt a tightness between her shoulder blades and, glancing down at her speedometer, saw that she was five miles an hour over the posted speed limit. She tapped the brake and made herself take a deep breath.

The road, smooth and wide now, looped between swaths of rolling green grass, past another guardhouse, and climbed to the top of a small hill. Below it, settled between the hill and the lake, was an old-fashioned-looking cottage. It was half-timbered, with gabled windows, and surrounded by elaborate gardens. Compared with the modern glass-and-steel house Sadie had grown up in, it looked surreal and impractical, somewhere Pinocchio or Snow White would feel at home, not the kind of place that would foster cutting-edge science.

The clock on her dashboard read 9:56 when she pulled up in front of the building. It seemed substantially bigger up close, about the size of a small hotel. Another guard stopped her car in the pebbled drive. He took her keys and gave her a plastic security badge with the photo of her squinting on it. She bent to reach for her overnight bag, but he stopped her. "There are no personal items allowed inside the Manor."

"Not even a toothbrush?" she asked, immediately feeling foolish.

"Everything you need will be provided." He gave her an encouraging smile, but his eyes were cold and appraising, and Sadie felt a slight chill inch up her spine. "Please go straight in to the main reception room, Miss Ames. The others are waiting for you there."

The others, Sadie repeated as she walked down a dimly lit, green-carpeted hallway that smelled of wood polish and fresh-cut flowers, toward the sound of voices. One of her deepest secrets was that rooms full of strangers made her panic. All those eyes looking at her. It was idiotic, she knew, a sign of weakness she hated. The only person she'd ever admitted it to was her best friend, Decca, who loved attention and whose first reaction had been to laugh.

"You're pretty, impeccably groomed, and, thanks to me, well dressed. If I wasn't so self-centered, I'd totally hate you. What are you afraid of people seeing?"

"I don't know. My mind freezes up, and I can't think of anything to say."

"Pretend you're at a debate tournament," Decca suggested. "You always have plenty to say there."

Sadie had shaken her head. "That's different. We prepare for that. I know exactly what's going on, what I'm being judged on. What the rules are."

Decca shrugged one shoulder. "So make up your own rules."

Sadie remembered feeling shocked. "You can't just make rules up."

"Rule one," Decca said, holding up a finger, "breathe. Rule two, pause in the doorway and survey the scene and tell yourself you're going to have a good time. Rule three—"

"You want me to stop in the doorway so people can stare at me *longer*?" Sadie asked incredulously.

"It will make you appear quietly confident," Decca assured her. "Nothing diffuses hostility like quiet confidence."

"You should be secretary of state," Sadie said.

"Rule three," Decca went on, ignoring her, "get a beverage. And rule four, talk to the cutest guy in the room."

"I think I liked the hanging-around-in-the-door part better. You *know* there's no way I'm going to seek out the cutest guy in the room and start chatting with him."

Decca looked at her pityingly. "Of course not. You won't have to go looking for him; he'll already be standing next to you."

Sadie had laughed and said, "I think you're talking about yourself." Which was true. But the memory of the conversation made her feel a little better as she turned a corner and found herself on the threshold of a room filled with people.

It was large and square, the wood-paneled walls hung with portraits of someone's distinguished ancestors. A large brass chandelier lit a round table with an elaborate bouquet of flowers in the middle, surrounded by tiers of muffins, scones, croissants, and individual coffee cakes. There was a silver coffee urn to one side, and servers in dark pants and shirts circulated, refilling cups and clearing plates.

The other Fellows clustered around the pastries, making halting conversation and eyeing the doors cagily, watching to see if anyone important was coming in. Sadie could tell that every one of them was used to being number one and that none of them was excited to share that position. She took a deep breath and felt like she could smell the animosity in the air.

In Decca's honor she paused just inside the doorway, but she only had time to repeat "This is going to be fun" once before she heard a soft click and the doors closed behind her. A moment later someone clinked a spoon against a water glass, and all eyes swiveled toward the other end of the room, where Curtis Pinter, the man who had interviewed her, was standing.

He wore a well-cut navy blue suit and a light blue oxford-cloth shirt with no tie. He looked younger than he had at the interview, only a few years older than the Fellows, in his early twenties.

With his wavy dark hair falling forward and his eyes and skin the color of expensive honey, he also looked much more handsome. Definitely the cutest guy in the room.

As though he knew what she'd been thinking, his eyes met hers, and he gave a small, wry smile. Sadie felt her pulse speed up, and her cheeks got warm. She was relieved when his eyes moved past her, taking in the room at large.

Like a master showman he let the silence stretch until the anticipation and excitement in the air was almost unbearable. Without preamble he said, "Imagine seeing inside Picasso's brain while he was painting. Sitting in while Shakespeare thought of 'To be or not to be.' Hearing what Mozart heard as he penned *Don Giovanni*. If we'd known then what we know now, we could have. *You* could have."

He gestured around the room at them. "You are about to embark on a voyage of exploration to the only place science has yet to reach. In just a few days you will join the elite group of people to experience Syncopy, the ability to live in someone else's mind. I can't promise that you will enjoy it—in fact, there will absolutely be parts you don't enjoy. But I can promise unequivocally that after the next six weeks, nothing about your life will ever be the same."

CHAPTER 2

"What is Syncopy?" Curtis asked. "As one of our researchers put it when I asked her to boil it down to one sentence"—he read from a paper he'd pulled out of his pocket—"'Syncopy is a form of heightened interperception that allows Minders'— that's you"—he glanced up at his audience—"'to shadow the thoughts, feelings, sensations, and memories of their assigned Subjects.'" He carefully folded the paper and tucked it away, and Sadie was struck by how precise and neat his movements were. "In other words, it's like getting to play God without any of the responsibility, blame, or endless posing for portraits."

He paused for their laughter, then went on. "Syncopy is the merging of old interperception technology with new stasis technology, to create something that is far more than the sum of its parts. During Syncopy you will literally be an observer in someone else's mind. You will learn their deepest secrets and their worst fears. That's why you are prohibited from meeting your Subjects. You know things about them that would be far too easy to exploit, even unintentionally."

It was silent, everyone's attention completely riveted on Curtis. "You'll be exposed to things that make you uncomfortable, and some things that make you *very* uncomfortable. You'll be in the bathroom with your Subjects. You'll shower with them, go on dates with them, get busy in the backseats of cars with them. Some Minders choose to treat those 'intimate' moments as free time, to catalogue the impressions from their day or week mentally, giving the Subject time "alone." Others use them as a marker of their Subject's behavior at moments of intense sensation. Everyone approaches and experiences Syncopy in different ways. But one thing is universal."

Curtis's eyes met Sadie's again, and she felt like he was speaking directly to her. "The experience of Syncopy will test you. It will push the limits of your experience, comfort, and patience. It will make you feel more powerless than you ever have before. It will overwhelm you. It may terrify you. You won't be disappointed."

Around her there was a scattering of nervous laughter, breaking the spell of his gaze, and Sadie realized she'd been holding her breath.

"For all this magic to happen," he went on, his eyes moving from one side of the group to the other, "your body must be put in stasis. We'll start you in a shallow stasis for a week so we can monitor you closely and fine-tune the connection between your Subject's signal and your brainwaves."

A hand went up near the front of the room, and a girl

asked, "What is the difference between shallow stasis and deep stasis?"

"It's like the difference between ducking your head under water in a bathtub and submerging yourself in the middle of a lake," Curtis explained. "We've found that the initial jump into Syncopy can be overwhelming, so to minimize that disorientation and maximize your ability to work productively from day one, we suppress certain sensory inputs, such as taste and temperature. In shallow stasis you also have access to a panic button that makes it possible for you to exit Syncopy easily and safely if necessary."

A guy with hair that appeared to have been parted by a ruler asked, "Why would we panic?"

Curtis chuckled. "Right. You're not a group prone to panic." Sadie felt herself nodding instinctively and, glancing around, saw that everyone else was too. "That's exactly why. Syncopy is unidirectional. That means all you can do is witness. You won't be able to talk or move or advise or offer suggestions. To say that your hands will be tied is an understatement. You will not have the ability to communicate or influence events in any way. Hours can feel like days, days like years, when you are in someone else's control."

The group went completely still.

"Everyone will be brought out of stasis at the end of the first week and interviewed," Curtis went on. "If the Committee is satisfied with your performance, you will move from shallow to deep stasis for the remainder of the six weeks. At that point—"

A girl with her hair pulled into a tight bun shot up a hand. "Excuse me?"

Curtis paused. "Yes?"

"What happens if the Committee isn't satisfied?"

"You will return home."

The girl said, "You mean we're kicked out of the program." Her tone was challenging.

Curtis shook his head. "Your Syncopy session ends. You still remain a Mind Corps Fellow with all the privileges and responsibilities that entails."

Another voice, this time a guy with a southern accent standing next to the table, asked, "How often does that happen? Not making it past the first week?"

Curtis gave a weary smile, as though he'd answered all these questions before and they weren't the important ones. "About half the time."

Southern accent said, "Do you mean every other year someone doesn't make it—"

"I mean half of you will be allowed to enter profound stasis. In other words, either you or the person standing next to you won't make it for the full six weeks."

Saying it like that was like waving a scent in front of a pack of hunting dogs, Sadie thought. Every one seemed to sit straighter. Any cordiality between the Fellows vanished as they all galvanized their determination to be one of the fifteen who made it.

A guy in a brown checked oxford shirt asked, "What will the Committee be looking for to assess our performance?"

The air seemed to have thickened and become more dense. "We'll be reviewing the quality of your observations and your bond with your subject, looking for a balance between empathy and objectivity." Complete silence as everyone committed that to memory. "We need to know that the relationship is functional and appropriate. Once you enter deep stasis, you will not be able to leave for the next five weeks."

A boy to Sadie's left: "What about the panic button?"

Curtis shook his head. "While you are in deep stasis it functions only as an emergency beacon. If you push it, police will be immediately dispatched to your Subject's location. It is intended to be used only if your Subject is in the process of committing a crime. You will remain in stasis until it is possible for us to remove you safely. Coming out of deep stasis is a more complicated process than coming out of shallow stasis."

A short boy near the front asked, "More complicated how? What can go wrong?"

"There have been incidences of temporary memory loss." Curtis's eyes swept over the group. "Any other questions?"

The girl standing directly in front of Sadie swung her thick charcoal-black hair to one side as she put her hand up. Her voice was husky, and she had the confident and entitled posture of a pretty, popular girl. "You mentioned Picasso and Shakespeare and Mozart at the beginning. Why send us into the minds of poor kids? Why not into the minds of geniuses?"

How do you know they're not geniuses? Sadie asked herself.

She didn't know she'd said it out loud until a voice that seemed to come from the coffee urns said, "Indeed. How do you?" It was a woman's voice, and Sadie was surprised to realize it was one of the servers who had spoken.

The girl with the dark hair turned to lock a false smile on Sadie, ignoring the interruption from the server. Sadie saw she'd been right; the girl—her name tag read "Flora"—was pretty.

And entitled. "What I meant was, if we can go into anyone's minds, why this population? What can we learn from *them*?"

Flora had addressed Sadie, but it was the server who answered. The woman stepped away from the wall and began making her way through the group toward the front. She was tall and thin, but she moved as though she was accustomed to cutting a wide swath through a crowd. As she passed, Sadie smelled leather and roses and wood smoke.

"You might as well ask why we send snobby, self-centered teenagers instead of adults," she said. "The answer to both questions is the same. I wanted to get things done, fix things in communities that needed fixing, and I knew the old men already in office were too entrenched. Too many people sticking bills in their G-strings." The woman had reached the front of the room and turned to face the Fellows.

Sadie gasped, and a low murmur came from the group as everyone else let out a surprised breath at the same time. This was Miranda Roque, who had built her father's chemical company into a global multinational worth billions and then withdrawn from public life, dedicating all her money to aggressive philanthropic missions no one else would even consider. Miranda Roque, famously reclusive, was standing *there*, right in front of them.

Talking about G-strings.

Her hair was a silver helmet, and her eyes were cool sapphires, but there was a glint in them, and she paced restlessly, as though the contained exterior were a false front over a blazing furnace.

She talked as she moved, in a precise, clipped way, as though every sentence was an order. "I decided to empower a group of young leaders and give them a tool their elders never had. When their minds were still pliant, I'd send them into the trenches to observe their counterparts at the riskiest moments of their lives." Miranda had to be at least eighty, but she seemed to buzz with restless energy. "You, all of you, will finish high school next year, go on to college, get jobs. For you, a risk will be getting drunk the night before midterms. But these kids, a year or two out of high school, most of them are adrift. No school; boring, dead-end jobs. There are other options, of course: scholarships, gangs, everything in between. Through Syncopy you will know everything they think, everything they feel, every wish and desire and superstition. I want that information. I want to *know* them."

Her eyes moved to Flora, and she glared. "Not every one of my initiatives works. And not every one of your Subjects will live to be notable—or even live. But I can assure you, young woman, there's not a single Mind Corps Fellow who would say that his or her Subject was anything short of exceptional."

Miranda pointed toward the bouquet of flowers in the center of the table. "Every one of those flowers is a species I developed myself. Three of them shouldn't grow here, two shouldn't be that color, and four of them, like this one"—she reached through the group to pluck a white flower with a single red spot on one petal from the arrangement—"started off as weeds. Despite what my enemies say, with the right care and vision, civilization can be cultivated anywhere." The eyes beneath her high brow shone, and Sadie felt ignited by their fierce challenge. "In case you haven't figured it out, I'm Miranda Roque. This is my house. Make me proud."

She tucked the flower into Curtis's buttonhole, then made her way toward the door behind Sadie. It slid apart as Miranda approached, only now there was no sign of the thick green carpet, no scent of wood polish and flowers that had been there when Sadie entered. Instead it opened onto a sterile, cream-colored hallway with a sign that read FLOOR −14. BADGE RULES IN EFFECT.

"Where are we?" someone behind Sadie asked.

"Home sweet home. Subbasement fourteen," Curtis said. "Welcome to Mind Corps."

CHAPTER 3

A decade earlier Miranda Roque had built the finest research facility in the country, staffed it with the top scientists and academics in the world, and buried it beneath the ground. Each of the twenty subbasement floors was headed by a different researcher and dedicated to cutting-edge specialties like geocorporation, cipherlogistics, and infodemiology.

Syncopy, which grew out of late-night coffees on several different floors, now took up all of subbasement fourteen with fifty-three staff members, four state-of-the-art laboratories, and the most advanced nanochip research facility in the world.

The Fellows' tour guide, Catrina Devi, told them this as they walked from one cream-on-cream corridor into another. Catrina had dark hair styled in a pixie cut, high cheekbones, luminous brown eyes, and almond skin. She was what Decca would have called "one of those," meaning one of those women who are so naturally beautiful they could wear a piñata—or in this case an ankle-skimming lab coat and no jewelry except a single gold bracelet—and make it look like they were dressed for a chic party.

Curtis had introduced her as soon as they got off the elevator. "Catrina was one of our first Mind Corps Fellows five years ago," he told them. "Now she oversees our Stasis Center. She'll be doing this next part of the tour. For the six weeks you're in stasis, your life is in her hands."

A smattering of nervous laughter. Sadie watched Curtis give Catrina a warm smile and wondered if their relationship was more than just professional. If she'd been a Mind Corps Fellow five years earlier, she would have to be twenty-one or -two, Sadie calculated.

A tight cluster of Fellows peppered Catrina with questions as she led them down the long hallway, most of which Sadie thought were designed more to get attention than answers.

The guy with the southern accent asked, "Could stasis be used to perform surgeries without anesthesia?"

"That isn't something we've explored yet," Catrina told him.

A girl with dark hair to her waist: "How old will our subjects be?"

"They've all been out of high school for at least a year, so usually between nineteen and twenty-two. Never older than twenty-five."

The walls of the corridor curved gently, the floors absorbed the sound of their footsteps, and the light was buttery, shadowless. Everyone's voice sounded slightly more pleasant, their

movements more graceful, and Sadie was struck by the tranquility of the place. It reminded her of her home, but even more calm
and orderly. It was, she felt, a place where nothing bad could
happen.

They passed departments of bioethics, sociology, anthropol-
ogy, psychology, and chemical engineering, things she'd expect,
but there were also unfamiliar specialties like neuronutrition,
chronogeography, and bricolage.

As far as Sadie could tell, almost no one involved with Syncopy or Mind Corps was even close to thirty. Which made more
sense when the boy with the perfect part asked, "How do you
get a job here?" and Catrina answered, "By being the best in
your field or by being a former Fellow. Usually, of course, those
are the same thing."

A few Fellows laughed, but Catrina's tone made it clear she
wasn't joking.

Sadie wondered if she ever laughed.

They turned into another corridor, and Sadie was surprised
to see an old-fashioned painting hanging on one wall. It was a
portrait of a striking man dressed in nineteenth-century attire.
Pausing, Sadie saw that a little metal plaque screwed into the
frame identified the man as Judge Montgomery Prester Roque.
It would have fit in perfectly upstairs, but down here it seemed
strange, almost jarring.

When she looked at it more closely, she saw there were four
round holes in it, right over the figure's heart.

"They're bullet holes," Curtis Pinter's voice said from just
behind her. "Most people don't notice." He came and stood
next to her. "It's nice to see you again, Sadie."

"You too, Mr. Pinter."

"Call me Curtis," he suggested. "I want you to feel relaxed around me."

There's little chance of that, Sadie thought as her cheeks flushed. "Curtis, then." He was looking at her as if he was genuinely interested in what she had to say, but she found her mind had gone completely blank. Finally, unable to think of anything smart to say, she stammered, "How did the bullet holes get there?"

"It happened almost twenty years ago. After Miranda's first major philanthropic project—"

"The Perfect Garden," Sadie broke in, trying to look like less of a moron.

"I see someone overprepared for their interview."

Sadie's cheeks flamed. "I—I just didn't want to miss anything." She found herself strangely aware of his proximity. Forcing her attention away from the spicy citrus scent of his cologne, she recalled details from the articles she'd read. "The Perfect Garden was a home for underprivileged orphans, wasn't it? But there was some controversy around it."

"Gold star to Miss Ames." Curtis nodded. "Miranda swore she could take children no one wanted and educate them in such a way that each of them would become a success. The curriculum was basically an intensive study of Shakespeare and weapons training. And it worked. They were creative, aggressive, and disciplined. Every student in the first class—the only class to graduate—had made at least a million dollars by the time they were twenty-four."

"That's amazing," Sadie said reverently.

"Yes. Unfortunately, a few of them turned the same traits toward less-than-legal pursuits—and excelled at those as well. A state commission was convened and ruled that Miranda had perverted the natures of those in her care by pumping up their drive to succeed and giving them the skills to be excellent criminals."

Sadie frowned. "But they were the same drive and skills that made them successful."

"Exactly what Miranda told the commissioners." Curtis grinned at her, and she found herself thinking how nice his teeth were. "With a few mentions about looking at themselves in the mirror. None of which went over well, and the state ordered the program shut down immediately. Miranda was furious, of course. The head of the commission reminded her of Judge Monty, so . . ." Curtis cocked his finger into a gun and aimed it at the painting.

Sadie gaped at him. "*Ms. Roque* shot the painting?"

Curtis laughed. "Not what you'd expect, is it?"

"No." Sadie shook her head slowly. "But that just makes her seem even more wonderful."

"Wonderful or dangerous," Curtis said. His eyes sought Sadie's, and held them. "Of course," he went on, his voice low, intimate, "the two things aren't mutually exclusive."

There was an intensity to his gaze that made Sadie's pulse jump and gave her the feeling of playing out of her league. "No?" she breathed, unable to move her eyes from his.

"No," he said. A twinkle appeared in his eyes, and his lips curved into a sly smile. "After all, Miranda is a very good shot."

In her most earnest tone she said to Curtis, "Statistically, Miranda being a good shot makes her less dangerous."

Curtis glanced at her quickly and laughed when he realized she was joking. "Too true."

He gestured her around a corner into a wider corridor

where the rest of the Fellows were gathered. One wall was lined with offices; the other was made of panels of frosted glass. Curtis excused himself, and Sadie rejoined the group clustered around Catrina.

Catrina was standing with her back to the frosted glass, saying, "The technology that enables interperception—the ability of individuals to see inside one another's minds—has been in existence and use for nearly three decades," she said, "but it was restricted, uncomfortable, and hard to control. Until six years ago, when scientists here made a stunning breakthrough."

As she spoke, the entire wall of glass behind her sank into the floor, revealing a massive oval chamber with a vaulted ceiling. Radiating out from the center of the oval were four concentric widening circles of what looked like bathtubs, each with a number from one to thirty. A thick shank of cables and wires was coiled inside of each of them. Lab technicians in spotless cream-colored coats moved silently along the perimeter, like acolytes of a very modern cult.

"Six years ago we invented stasis," Catrina said, leading them into the room. She stepped toward one of the tubs, her face showing its first hint of emotion as she patted the tub lovingly. "This changed everything. It's officially known as the DCSS3 Dynamic Corporeal Suspension System, but around here we call it the Stas-Case. Take a good look at it, because it will be your home for six weeks."

The Fellows all pressed closer, glancing shyly into the vessels, everyone apparently apprehensive to touch too much, as though the tubs were alive. Sadie wondered if anyone else was unnerved by the thought of lying there for six weeks surrounded by twenty-nine other motionless bodies.

Catrina's voice broke the eerie silence. "Curtis gave you the philosophical overview, but I've been tasked with explaining the science behind what we do here, and I'm going to start at the beginning so there's no confusion." She pointed a finger in a semicircle at the group. "You are Minders. That means you enter stasis and go into the mind of another person. That person is called your Subject. Sometime between birth and the age of thirteen, a neuronano relay was placed at the base of your Subject's skull, where it meets the spinal cord. This is the gateway to the brain, and every thought or action originates here as a set of bioelectrical impulses. The microscopic relay collects and forwards all that brain activity in real time. Using sensors, that activity is mirrored onto your mind, letting you experience it exactly the way the Subject does. That is called interperception."

Sadie was so entranced she had to remind herself to breathe.

"If you'd done that fifteen years ago, you wouldn't have been able to keep both your thoughts and your Subject's in your mind at once during interperception. Theirs would have overridden yours, which means any kind of research or evaluation could only have happened later. But stasis changes that." Catrina's eyes lit up. "By freeing the mind from responsibility for your body, stasis increases your mental capacity enough so that all those impulses can be mirrored onto your brain with adequate space left over for your normal thought processes to occur simultaneously. You can not only observe, you can evaluate, and because you can remain in stasis safely for a long time, you can keep an uninterrupted link with your Subject for an extended period. Thus Syncopy—extended, conscious sessions of interperception—was born. We have only begun to explore the implications of this incredible process, but I'm among those who think it will be hailed as the most significant advance in a century."

A boy with dark hair spiked straight up said, "Have you ever been a Subject?"

Catrina shook her head. "To be a Subject you must have a neuronano transmitter implanted. But Minders can't have transmitters because they interfere with the ability to enter Syncopy. So you can either be a Subject or a Minder, but not both."

"Has anyone ever died during Syncopy?" the girl with the tight bun asked.

Catrina frowned, as though the question was in poor taste, then said, "No Minder has ever died."

"What about—" the girl began to ask but was interrupted by Curtis's return.

There was something about him, Sadie thought, that made the air feel more electric. He smiled and said, "Did you explain everything, Cat?"

Catrina gave him a look Sadie couldn't quite fathom. It wasn't flirtatious, although her ears had gone pink at the sound of his voice. It looked more like . . . relief. She said, "Yes. We're all done with the preliminaries."

Curtis smiled, crooked a finger at the group, and said, "Then it must be time to get naked. Follow me."

After the tour, orientation became a mix between summer camp and the most invasive physical Sadie could imagine. When Curtis had said they were going to get naked he hadn't been joking, although Sadie learned with relief it was more the kind of nakedness that involved baring your soul rather than your skin.

Sadie spent the next two days immersed in CAT scans, MRIs, fMRIs, electrocardiograms, radiocardiograms, blood tests, hearing tests, vision tests, and tests for strength, endurance, and respiratory health. There had also been basic self-hypnosis tips and a course on "Maintaining a Mental Notebook," since they would have to memorize all their observations while in stasis. Sadie and Flora had been assigned as a team in an exercise the second morning of orientation, and their tension from the first day had been overpowered by the shared goal of winning.

"Three o'clock," Flora said as they walked away from the coffee cart near the stasis chamber. "Only an hour left of orientation."

Sadie blew on her coffee. "I wish we could start Syncopy tonight, without going home."

Flora raised an eyebrow. "Come on, don't you want one more good makeout session with Pete?" She stopped herself. "Sorry, I forgot you only have eyes for Hot Curtis now."

Sadie laughed. "Speak for yourself."

Flora shook her head. "Catrina is more my type."

"I'm afraid you might not be hers," Sadie said apologetically. "I think she and Curtis are a couple."

Flora waved that away. "For expediency, maybe, but not really. Trust me."

Sadie wasn't sure. She'd gotten lost the previous night on her way to dinner and ended up in the oval room with the Stas-Cases. She'd been walking the perimeter looking for corridor G when she heard voices and realized it was Curtis and Catrina talking.

As she came up Curtis was saying, "I'm simply suggesting we consider protection."

"Protection," Catrina sniffed.

Sadie stood rooted to the floor, unable to move.

"I don't like it any more than you do," Curtis said emphatically, "but we need to be careful. Minimize the risks. I want to make sure we're safe."

"I understand. It just feels like you're pushing me away." Catrina's tone was measured and cool, but obviously it didn't mean she didn't care, just that she was thoughtful. Sadie wished Pete or her father could hear her. Maybe then they'd understand that not everyone oozed emotion.

Curtis was soothing. "You know that's not what is going on. I'm doing this for us. And it's only temporary."

Snapping back into her conversation with Flora, Sadie said, "I overheard them talking, and they definitely seemed to be involved."

"Maybe for now," Flora said with a shrug. "Nothing lasts forever."

Sadie laughed. "I'll concede if you'll tell me how to get to office D-210."

Flora turned Sadie so she was facing the direction opposite the one she'd been about to walk in and said, "Go straight past three corridors and turn left. I'll see you in the Survaillab for closing remarks."

"If I find it," Sadie said.

Flora's instructions were perfect, and Sadie was pressing the admittance bell next to D-210 at exactly three o'clock.

The appointment had appeared on her TrackUPad that morning with no explanation, so she didn't know what to expect. She felt a surge of pleasure when the door slid open and she saw Curtis sitting with his feet on a desk, in the middle of what sounded like a personal call.

"Just steer clear, that's all I'm asking." He motioned Sadie into his office. "This isn't the time for one of your little games."

His desk was sleek and modern in dark wood, the two low chairs facing it at precise right angles covered in buff suede. Three brightly colored old-fashioned tin wind-up toys in the shape of a tiger, an elephant, and a bear playing the cymbals sat on one corner of the desk, and a computer sat on the other. Behind it hung a framed vintage poster from the movie *Metropolis*. The space felt warm with a hint of edge, just like Curtis himself.

He gestured Sadie into a chair facing him as he got off the phone, then smiled an apology. "Sorry, family drama. How has orientation been? I don't think I've been lucky enough to catch sight of you since that first day."

Sadie willed herself not to blush and said, "Orientation has been somewhat disorienting, actually."

He chuckled and rubbed the back of his neck. "That sounds about right. And I'm afraid I'm only going to exacerbate that." His feet came off the desk, and he leaned across it toward her.

"Why?" Sadie asked, trying not to get distracted by the pleasantly subtle scent of his cologne.

"We don't have a lot of time, so I'll cut right to it. I've decided to start an elite program within Mind Corps, and I want you to be part of it."

Sadie suddenly had no trouble focusing. "Elite in what way?"

"We're selecting a few Fellows to be Minders for Subjects who have been tagged as high risk. Either they've been arrested and served time, or they've come close. By targeting them, we want to understand how crime can spread from an individual

to blight an entire neighborhood. But Syncopy with these Subjects exposes Minders to strains others don't face. So we're only
picking the best of the best."

Sadie's heart thudded against her ribs. "What kinds of
strains?"

"These Subjects are more likely to repress their feelings
and memories than deal with them. Repression is like a magi-
cian, using smoke screens and big spectacles to distract you
from its secrets. That takes a lot of work, so these minds may
be more unstable, more like living in a minefield." He paused.
"The other difference is that instead of being posted in an
unfamiliar community, your Subject would be here in City
Center. Only a half hour from your home. Which means we
would need to rely even more heavily on your maturity and
integrity." He leaned back. "What do you think? Would you be
comfortable with that?"

City Center.

Impressions from her photography class trip flooded Sadie's
mind. She remembered passing houses, stores, and skyscrapers
that had been completely abandoned, whole neighborhoods
silent except for ghostly wind; other streets so densely packed
with people that the sidewalks spilled into traffic and the intersections became a matted knot of cars and people, the air thick
with curses and honking.

Their bus had gotten caught in one of those intersections,
and Sadie was staring out the window when a fight broke out
between two guys. A clot of people formed around the fight-
ers, and between the heads of the crowd, Sadie watched them
pound each other. Raw, visceral energy came off them in waves

so potent that she'd felt them even through the double-paned window of the bus, making every sensation, every color, more intense.

What would it be like to experience that firsthand? she asked herself now. The sensation of knuckles cracking against bone, of fury overriding all reason, of being filled with so much powerful emotion.

She remembered the beautiful ruin of the building they'd photographed earlier that same day. Remembered standing on the edge of the seventeenth floor and forcing herself to look down, fingers of panic closing around her throat, making her struggle for breath, petrified with fear.

Not, as she'd told Curtis in her interview, because she was afraid of falling. That was a lie.

It was jumping she was afraid of. Becoming so numb she didn't care any longer.

Now, sitting in Curtis's office, she realized she was nodding. She said, "Yes. If you're asking would I be willing to go through Syncopy inside the mind of a criminal, the answer is yes."

Curtis held up a hand. "A *potential* criminal. Not hardened, not yet, but still the kind of person I'd tell you to steer clear of if you were my sister. I want to be certain you really understand what I'm asking. This person will be almost your exact opposite. Someone with no respect for rules or laws, possibly no code of conduct or loyalty, and very likely a disordered internal landscape. There's a high probability of violence. Are you sure you're prepared for that?"

"Absolutely."

"Details will be crucial. To understand the hidden power dynamics of City Center, we'll need you to pay close attention not only to your Subject's internal Mindscape but also the external landscape. Associates, friends, enemies, the strengths and weakness of alliances."

"Of course," Sadie said. She hesitated for a moment, then blurted, "Why me?"

Curtis tented his fingers on his desk and locked his eyes on hers. "Because your father is wrong. You're not too serious. You have a gravity about you, but that's different. It's what sets you apart. And why you are going to be so very good at this."

Sadie was speechless. She would have laid down her life for Curtis at that moment.

"Come on," he said, pushing back his chair and standing, "Let me walk you to the Survaillab. You're far too valuable to risk losing, and from what I hear it's statistically unlikely you'd find it on your own."

She laughed and said, "Thank you," and from the smile he gave her in return she was fairly sure he knew she wasn't just talking about the directions.

The Survaillab was a wide, raked room terraced with long tables partitioned every two feet into a series of linked cubicles. A Mind Corps technician greeted Sadie at the door, looked at her badge, and said, "You're number nine. Second row at the end."

Sadie waved at Flora and took her seat. Inside her personal cubicle was a screen that was blank except for the number nine.

When all the cubicles were filled, Curtis appeared at the front of the room. "Congratulations. You've done the hard part. Now all that's left is for you to lie around for six weeks."

There was a collective chuckle.

"Several of you have asked for information about your Subject: their name, age, basic things. I told you to wait. This is not the moment you're waiting for."

A few nervous laughs. "We've learned it's better for all of that to come out organically during Syncopy. But there is one thing you can't learn while you're on the inside." The lights dimmed, and the individual screen in front of Sadie popped to life.

She was looking at a busy city street clogged with cars and buses. An elevated train ran above it, making a clatter, and on the ground horns honked incessantly. The street was a jumble of stores, crammed together like too many teeth in a mouth—Huang's PawnIt, DollarDollarDollar, Your Neighborhood Drug—with a fenced-in playground on the corner.

"These are CCTV feeds of each of your subjects from the past week. It is the only time you'll see them from the outside."

Sadie scanned the image. The playground was empty, but the sidewalks were crowded with pedestrians and vendors selling sunglasses and toys. She was wondering how she was supposed to tell who to look at, when the camera angle began changing, pulling in and focusing on one figure. He was wearing a blue jacket and had broad shoulders, but that's all she could see because he was standing with his back to the camera, staring into the empty playground.

He'd been there all along, Sadie realized, but she hadn't noticed him because, unlike everyone else, he was standing still. Now his head came around, as though in response to someone calling his name, and the camera pulled in on his face. Almost as if he sensed it, sensed her, he looked right into the lens, and Sadie's breath caught in her throat. He had dark hair, the faintest trace of stubble on his cheeks and chin, and eyes that were incredibly blue.

And incredibly angry.

The image cut out, but the eyes seemed to hover in front of her, burned into the monitor.

As she pulled out of Mind Corps and turned toward home, Sadie kept seeing Subject 9's eyes in front of her.

"There's a high probability of violence," Curtis had said during their meeting. "Are you sure you're prepared for that?"

She'd thought she'd known what she was agreeing to. But now, having seen those eyes, she realized she had no idea. The darkness behind them was unfathomable.

And by this time tomorrow, she would be at the center of it.

CHAPTER 4

At a little before one P.M. the next day Sadie lay in the Stas-Case and took her last glimpse of the oval room. It had taken three hours to attach all the sensors and run diagnostics, but she was finally ready.

Or her body was. Because as the minutes of preparation had inched forward, she'd found herself becoming more and more convinced she was making a mistake.

She felt a hand on her arm through the stasis suit and saw Curtis to her left.

"You ready?" he asked.

No! she tried to tell him, but the mouth guard she was wearing made it come out as a gurgle.

She grabbed his hand and looked at him desperately.

"You're afraid," he said. "That's normal. Statistically speaking."

She glared at him.

"I'm not bullshitting you. More than seventy percent of Minders report having second thoughts before they enter stasis." He leaned close to her. "But there's nothing to be afraid of. This is only shallow stasis, you'll be out in a week for evaluation, and if you need to get out sooner you have the panic button. Can you feel it?"

She concentrated on her left hand, then nodded. The biohaptic gel her body was encased in made sensations harder to read.

"Good," Curtis said. "You can keep it right there in your hand the whole time. Remember, it has a failsafe built in, so you have to squeeze it three times before Syncopy will be terminated. The first time will put the system on standby, the second will set it to ready, and the third will complete the process and sever your stasis connection. That way you'll never have to worry about doing it by accident. Do you understand?"

Sadie nodded. She felt calmer.

Curtis smiled. "The computer is going to count backward from nine. As it does, let your mind wander back through what you did last night. Reviewing recent memories will help the circuits build a bridge between your mind and your Subject's. When you hear 'one,' open your eyes. You'll be there. Okay?"

Sadie nodded again. He leaned out of view, and she heard him say, "She's ready, Cat." Near her head a computerized voice announced, "*Counting down to Syncopy. In nine . . .*"

Sadie's heart rate spiked, and a monitor near her began to beep. Curtis was back, his gaze holding hers, saying in a soothing voice, "There's nothing to worry about. You're going to be great. Take a deep breath and close your eyes, and I'll see you in a week."

She let her eyelids slowly come over her eyes.

"Good. Now think back to last night. You left here and drove home. You turned onto your street, and the first thing you saw was—"

"Eight . . ."

—Cars everywhere. Sadie's normally quiet street had been clogged with cars when Sadie got home. She knew why when she pulled into her driveway and saw a girl in the burgundy uniform of her mother's preferred valet service standing under a white umbrella.

Her stomach had dropped. Her parents were having a party. They must have forgotten that they'd said they would have a quiet dinner, just the three of them. Or forgotten entirely about her coming home.

"The hostess asks that guests enter through the front door and then make their way to the pool," the valet said.

Sadie wondered which of her mother's charities this was a fund-raiser for. Not that it mattered; she had no intention of going. She would go straight upstairs to her room and call Decca.

Ignoring the valet's instructions and hearing nothing from the backyard, she turned left before reaching the stairs and followed a path lined with glossy-leafed lemon trees around the side of the house. The white globe lanterns her parent's landscape architect had designed for outside entertaining were lit, and mirror-topped café tables had been arranged beneath the arbor that ran along the swimming pool. There was a small stage for a band at the far end of the pool, but no band on it. It was like a stage set, Sadie thought—PARTY: CASUAL, EVENING—everything straining in hushed readiness, but no guests. They must still have all been inside.

Between the house and the pool were three long rectangular tables covered with white cloths. One of them was set up as a bar, and the other two looked like they would hold a buffet. Each of them was decorated with an ice sculpture of a walnut.

The sculptures aren't even very good, Sadie thought as she skirted the tables and made for the door. They looked more like brains than walnuts.

"SURPRISE!"

People burst from under tables, behind lemon trees, beneath the stage. Sadie took two steps backward and would have ended up in the pool if Pete hadn't caught her.

"I'd say she was surprised," her father said to her mother. "Guess she's not made of stone after all."

"Smile, darling," her mother said when she leaned in for a kiss on the cheek. "Everybody likes the smiling girl."

"Seven . . ."

Sadie remembered Decca appearing a quarter of an hour later, her dark skin glowing in all the candlelight. She'd thrown her arms around Sadie, and while they posed for pictures said through her teeth, "You're completely miserable, aren't you?"

"Is it that obvious?" Sadie asked, smiling.

"Only to me." Decca got serious. "Do you want me to start a fire so everyone has to be evacuated?"

Sadie suddenly felt much better. "No."

"Say 'not yet,'" Decca told her. "It's best to leave your options open."

"Six . . ."

Sadie remembered Decca disappearing "to chat with that nice man at the bar" when Pete came up and slipped his arm around her.

"Come here, there's something I want to show you," he'd said, too loud, drawing her into the shadows next to the pool house and kissing her.

The air was warm and heavy with the citrus scent of the lemon trees. She'd reached up, twined her fingers in his hair, and pulled his mouth hard against hers. The kiss was deep, intense, and long. When they separated, Pete stared at her, breathless. "It's nice to know you missed me."

"Of course I did," she told him.

"So how was spy camp? Learn all the secret handshakes? Get asked out by a lot of nerds?"

Before she could stop herself Sadie snapped, "It wasn't like that."

Pete gave her a wondering look. "I was kidding. Relax. I'm sure you were much too busy learning how to manipulate people without them knowing."

Sadie tried to keep her tone light. "If I could do that, do you think we'd be having this conversation?"

He grinned at her. "How was it really? You look great, by the way."

"It was amazing, Pete. Incredible."

He tucked a stray piece of hair behind her ear. "And you're excited to start?"

"More than I've ever been for anything in my life," she said. She'd known it was the wrong thing to say the minute the words were out, but she couldn't take them back. She braced for his reaction.

But he surprised her. He said, "I'm so happy for you, babe. Of course, I'm going to miss you."

She looked up at him gratefully. "I'm going to miss you too." She touched his cheek. "A lot."

"And miss kissing me?" he asked, his nose rubbing against hers.

"And miss kissing you," she confirmed.

"Maybe we should do something about that." His hand slid up her thigh under her skirt.

"Pete, there are people—"

His lips were at her ear. "Your parents are great hosts. No one is paying any attention to us. We could leave, and they wouldn't notice."

That was true. Apart from Decca and Pete and a few of her father's partner's kids, all the guests were her parents' friends. "I've been going nonstop today, and I haven't showered," Sadie said, reaching down to halt the progress of his fingers up her thigh.

"So?" He pulled away slightly and gave her a mischievous smile. "I wouldn't mind getting a little dirty."

Sadie rolled her eyes. "That's disgusting."

He grinned at her, his adorable grin, then took her hand and pulled her toward the stairs to the house. "Come on, let's not waste time."

She planted her feet. "What are you talking about?"

"It's our last night together for six weeks. I was thinking we should make it . . . memorable."

No, she thought, her heart sinking. *Not tonight.*

"Five . . ."

Smile, darling, Sadie heard her mother's voice in her head. "We agreed to wait until we felt ready," she said. Her voice sounded high and a little panicked.

Pete didn't seem to notice. "Until *you* felt ready," he corrected, tucking her hair behind her ears. "We've waited for a year. Isn't that enough? Come on, babe. I love you. You love me. What more do you want?"

She wanted to feel excited. She wanted to *want* it. And she didn't. But she couldn't tell Pete that. "I want it to be perfect."

"Trust me, it will be. Stop worrying. You're overthinking it," Pete coaxed. "Sometimes I wish you were a little less cerebral."

"There are plenty of airheads who would be happy to date you," Sadie said coldly.

He smirked at her and tapped the tip of her nose. "That was a joke, babe. Relax. You don't have to take everything so seriously."

Over Pete's shoulder Sadie saw Decca leaning against the side of the bar. She was telling a story, her hands cartwheeling in the air, the bartender captivated, laughing. As Sadie watched, Decca leaned toward him and whispered something in his ear, putting her hand on his chest. He took the hand and kissed it, and Decca tipped her head back and laughed.

Why couldn't she feel what they did? Why was it so easy for everyone besides her? What was wrong with her?

Her eyes moved back to Pete, looking at her earnestly.

"Seriously, babe, what are you so afraid of? It's me, Pete. Your boyfriend. Who you love. What do you think is going to happen?"

Nothing, she thought. *I'm afraid of nothing—of feeling nothing, no connection, no passion, no heat.*

She reached up to straighten the collar of his shirt. "It's just—this is a big deal," she said, calling up an argument that had worked in the past.

He made his comical frowning face. "To be clear, by 'this,' you mean sex."

"You don't have to keep saying it. Yes."

"But at graduation you said—"

"I know what I said at graduation. And that's true." She smiled at him. "Only tonight seems so rushed."

"*Rushed*? It's been a year, Sadie." His voice rose with emotion. "I've waited for a goddamned *year*."

Sadie gazed at him in shock, hardly recognizing her boyfriend in this guy with the hard eyes and set jaw. The smile felt galvanized on her face. "Are you angry? Because I won't have sex with you?"

"Yes. No. I'm—" He dropped his arms and took a step away from her, raking his hand through his hair. "I'm confused. If you loved me the way I love you—"

"I do." She *did*.

"Then you would want this too."

"You know I do. Very much."

"But not tonight," he said.

"Right," Sadie agreed hopefully, not realizing, until it was too late, that it was a trap.

He looked beyond her. "I don't know, Sadie. I just don't know." He pulled his phone out of his pocket and checked the time. "I should go."

Sadie blinked, feeling cold and confused. "Like that? You're going to leave it like that? For six weeks?"

He avoided her eyes. "No. I just—let me cool off. I'll be in touch."

"*Four* . . ."

I'll be in touch.

I'll be in touch.

I'll be in touch.

"*Three* . . ."

Torches were still casting gold light at the corners of the pool, but the party had thinned out, and the band was packing up.

Decca stood looking down at Sadie, who was lying on one of the chaise lounges.

"The usual?" Decca asked.

"Oh yes," Sadie said, getting to her feet.

They grabbed two leftover bottles of champagne and went past the pool and out the gate in the hedge fence that separated the Ames house from the golf course. Picking a spot with no trees overhanging, they each popped the cork on their bottle.

They gave the toast they'd been giving since they were six with apple juice, saying "To friends like you" in unison. Then, sitting back-to-back for support, they looked up at the sky. It was dark enough that they could see thousands of stars.

"You should have let me start a fire," Decca said. "We could have been doing this hours ago."

Sadie took a gulp of champagne. "Right. I promise I'll listen to you next time."

"That would be confusing," Decca said, and they laughed.

They stayed like that, sipping from their bottles, watching the sky and talking only to point out a shooting star or comet.

"What's he like?" Decca asked after a while.

"Who?"

"Your guy. The one whose head you'll be in. What does he look like?"

"How do you know it's a guy?"

"Is it?" Decca asked.

"I'm not supposed to say anything," Sadie told her.

"Why? Is it like a wish, and if you share it won't come true?"

"Exactly." Sadie watched the bright light of a satellite moving slowly across the sky. "He's really cute," she said finally.

Decca hooted. "I knew it. What color hair?"

"Dark. And blue eyes."

"*Mmmm,* I love that type." Decca leaned her head back against Sadie's shoulder. "I know it's confidential and all that, but I have an incredibly important question that you will be uniquely qualified to answer."

"What is it?"

"What guys talk about while peeing at urinals."

Sadie laughed and pretended to flick her on the head. "I'm going to miss you," she said softly.

"I'm going to miss you more."

"*Two . . .*"

After Decca left, Sadie had curled herself into the window seat of her bedroom. Her parents were asleep, and silence had settled over the house.

When Sadie was younger, spending time alone in the echoey

house when her parents were out had scared her, so she'd made a list of different kinds of silences. Silence of anticipation, silence of grief, silence of tranquility, lonely silence, welcome silence, intimate silence, pregnant silence, silence of contempt. The silence surrounding her now was familiar, the silence of gates and guards and wide lawns and double-paned windows that kept you safe. Locked in. The silence of home.

She left the lights off, not needing to see the slate-gray walls of her room, the string of ribbons won over ten years of spelling bees hung above the six tennis trophies and three cups from the national debate championships. The pictures of her and the tennis team, her and Decca, her and Pete. Especially the ones of her and Pete.

Instead she stared out into the darkness that spread in front of her like an inky carpet, past her backyard with its perfect squares and rectangles, past the golf course to the shimmering glow on the horizon.

City Center.

She knew what she was seeing was just the halcyon lights on the highway that marked the outer perimeter of the City Center. And she knew the twinkling was an optical effect caused by humidity in the air. But to her it still looked like a mystical Valhalla, sparkling with passion, adventure, and—

"*One. Syncopy engaged.*"

—life.

She opened her eyes.

CHAPTER 5
WEEK 1

It was pitch black.

Sadie blinked to make sure her eyes were open. Syncopy between her and Subject 9 should have been established instantaneously. She should be seeing and hearing everything he did.

She was getting nothing. Something had gone wrong.

Where am I?

The pounding of her heart flooded her ears. Oh god, she was trapped somewhere, stuck between his mind and—

From far away, she heard a faint, eerie whistling, like wind blowing through a deserted graveyard at night. It was joined by a sound like bones rattling, and she felt a jolt and heard a voice say, "You bastard. You did it."

Light flooded in all at once, making Sadie reel. *A blindfold,* she thought. *We were blindfolded.*

He was blindfolded, she corrected, reminding herself she was supposed to remain objective. She blinked but was having trouble making out details.

"Now you see why they call him Frosty the Snowman," a male voice said. "Stays icy cool under pressure."

A hot wave of sensation crashed over Sadie, knocking her back, but in the time it took her eyes to adjust, it fizzed and became sticky and uncomfortable and then vanished. An emotion? A thought?

Things began to swim into focus. The first thing she noticed was that they were in a room filled with probably fifteen guys, all of them in their early twenties. Subject 9 had been standing, but he sat down now, joining three others at a table with a pile of poker chips in the middle. The others formed an attentive audience on the perimeter. One of the guys at the table was playing with the chips, shuffling them in one hand, which accounted for the rattling-of-bones sound.

Unlike the guys Sadie knew who wore tailored khakis and fitted collared shirts, the crowd here was nearly all dressed in overalls, a white V-neck or Henley shirt, and black work boots. *Chapsters*, she thought to herself.

She'd learned about the Chapster style in the "Film and Society" seminar she'd sat in on at the university, a look that was borrowed from Charlie Chaplin's assembly-line worker in the movie *Hard Times*. The professor had said it was popular among residents of urban communities. The Chapsters even named their boys after former presidents, to glorify an older and presumably better era. Compared with Pete and his friends, she thought the Chapsters looked a little bit menacing. *No*, she corrected herself after a second glance. *Masculine*.

The door to the room opened, and Sadie heard the sound of music, voices, and laughter from other parts of the building. *What is this place?* she wondered, recalling advice Catrina had given them at a lunch Q&A during orientation. "Think of yourself like an anthropologist dropped into an unfamiliar locale. To get your bearings, you'd note the terrain and the wildlife and make yourself acquainted with the important people in the village. You should go through the same exercise when you begin Syncopy. The more detail you can collect, the better your assessment of the internal mindscape will be."

Sadie took in what she could see of the room. It had a high curved ceiling and wide windows framed in stone with pointed arches at the top, like a Gothic university building, or the Detroit Union Club, where her Mind Corps interview had been. Only here the windows were missing most of their panes, the wood-paneled walls were covered with brightly colored graffiti rather than demure hunting landscapes, the wide-screen television was showing advertisements rather than market updates, and she was pretty sure these guys weren't leaders of industry and law. Leaders of lawlessness, more likely.

At least with so many people she'd be able to learn Subject 9's name, she thought.

"That was epic, Frosty," a guy with big ears standing behind Subject 9 said, reaching down to pump his hand.

The guy next to him nodded vigorously. "Seriously, Snow. You killed it."

Killed what? Sadie wanted to know. And was it really so hard to use a name?

While they spoke, the graveyard-like whistling Sadie had noticed at first rose and fell in pitch, and she realized she'd been wrong about it coming from far away. It was actually inside Subject 9's head, the sound of chemicals—thoughts and emotions—moving through his mind faster than the speed of sound. It oscillated, as though it was made up of several different threads superimposed on one another.

"They're like the electronic relays that make your computer work," Catrina had explained during the Q&A lunch. "At the beginning the impulses will probably sound like white noise, a low hum. To start with, focus on how and when they change. With practice you should be able to key them to the specific mental processes they represent."

Catrina had made it sound banal and basic, but the reality of it—*she was listening to his mind working!*—was amazing.

Sadie tried to focus on the behavior of the sounds, but the number of people speaking around them made it hard to process.

A guy on the left who seemed to have the sniffles said, "Got to say, thought you were going to end up more like a snow-flake than a snow*man* after that last one, if you get my drift," prompting a chorus of laughter around the table.

"So you going to tell us your secret, Ice Baby?" a little guy with red hair asked.

Ice Baby? Sadie repeated. This was getting ridiculous. And secret to what?

"I was just lucky," a voice very close to her said, and she realized it was the voice of Subject 9. It was low but not too low, and nice, she thought. It wouldn't be a bad voice to listen to for six weeks.

From his left a voice said, "Lucky that all of you are such

crap card players, that is." The speaker, a guy with dark skin and slicked-back hair, leaned forward to touch Subject 9 on the shoulder. "No offense, friend."

"None taken," Subject 9 assured him.

The guy directly across the table hefted himself out of his chair and pushed a pile of poker chips toward Subject 9. "Take your winnings, Little Ice."

There was a slight uptick in the volume of sound inside Subject 9's head, and Sadie saw a flickering out of the corner of her eye, but when she turned to look there was nothing there. "Thanks, Willy," Subject 9 said.

A name! Sadie thought. Even if it wasn't his, it was a start. An associate. Her first entry into her mental notebook.

"You earned them," the guy called Willy told him. Sadie concentrated on making mental notes of his characteristics the way they'd been taught in orientation. He was big, from muscle not fat, but with wide-spaced gray eyes, light brown hair, and a genuine, open smile, he looked too much like an overgrown schoolboy to be intimidating. He wore a chalk-striped denim cap far back on his head, with matching chalk-striped denim overalls. "I think it's pretty amazing, you sitting there blindfolded for three hands and predicting what we had just from hearing how we bet. Tell you the truth, felt like you were reading my mind."

Sadie agreed that was pretty amazing. If Subject 9 had actually done what Willy had described, it would mean he was either exceptionally good at both poker and reading people's voices, or exceptionally lucky.

Or cheating, she added, which, given Curtis's warnings about his criminal tendencies, was probably the most likely.

"Wouldn't take long to read your mind, Willy," the guy with the red hair said, and everyone, including Willy and Subject 9, laughed.

A voice directly to Subject 9's right cut in, saying, "Are we done with the circus performance yet? I want to play some cards."

Another momentary rise in volume followed his words, and Subject 9 asked, "You in a rush to lose more money, Linc?" His voice sounded lower to Sadie, and strained.

But she had a second name. Linc. *Short, no doubt, for Lincoln.*

Sadie expected Subject 9 to turn toward Linc, the way he had whenever anyone else addressed him, but he gave only a quick glance, just enough for Sadie to get the impression of a well-built guy with pale skin, chin-length black hair, and lips pressed together tightly in distaste. She didn't see his eyes, and she had the impression Subject 9 was deliberately avoiding them.

Clearly there was some history between them. For a second time Sadie thought she saw something flutter at the edge of her range of vision, but when she looked, she found nothing there.

The guy with the slicked-back hair said, "What's wrong, friend Linc? Tired of having money slip through your fingers?"

Linc was on his feet so fast his red leather club chair tipped backward and thudded to the ground. "What the hell is that supposed to mean, *friend*?" he hissed.

There was a collective intake of breath in the room, and everyone seemed to stiffen. Subject 9's eyes moved very slowly to stare at Linc, and everything inside him went silent. Sadie had been to a lot of debates, but she'd never seen an atmosphere go from jovial to explosive so quickly over words.

If there's a fight, I won't push the panic button, she resolved, steeling herself. *I told Curtis I could handle violence, and I won't let him down.*

The guy with the slicked-back hair seemed oblivious to the tension. His teasing smile stayed in place, and he was meeting Linc's eyes defiantly—but, Sadie saw, his hands were trembling. "Word gets around is all," he said. The Chapsters who had been standing near his chair shifted away as though wanting to disavow even a physical proximity. He added, too brightly, "And you lost on those last three pots. That had to sting."

Arms braced on the sides of the table and head lowered, Linc looked like a bull ready to charge.

Willy chuckled, jumping in. "Relax, Linc. Nobody meant anything by anything. Our old friend is just trying to get under your skin and win back some of his loot. You see how he's dressed. Could use it, I'd say."

Linc's eyes moved from the guy with the slicked-back hair, now an island in a sea of empty space, to Willy, who pushed a deck of cards toward him and said, "It's your deal."

Linc nodded and reached for the deck, and everyone started breathing again. The Chapster with the big ears and the one with the red hair rushed to right the chair Linc had kicked over and get it under him, as though Linc were some kind of aristocrat.

Or some kind of psychopath who had to be constantly appeased, Sadie thought. *At least I seem to have found the village elders.*

"Once you've got your bearings in the landscape, start charting your Subject's mindscape," Catrina had advised during orientation. "Each one is unique, but they are all built around three basic components: emotion, thought, and memory. Just as your computer takes the programs you see on your screen and translates them into zeros and ones for processing, the mind takes joy, ambivalence, your thoughts about what to have for dinner, and the quadratic equation you memorized in sixth grade and converts them into chemical impulses, each associated with a different sensory system. Your job is to create a key to translate them back."

Poker is actually a good place to start, Sadie thought. She'd played poker once with Pete and his friends, a strip game that had ended up with her minus one sock and everyone else naked, so she knew how the game worked, but she wasn't a pro. Was Subject 9?

Pete and his friends spent a lot of time staring one another in the eye and talking about one another's "tells," but Subject 9's eyes stayed mainly on the tabletop and on the other player's hands, as though he was uncomfortable looking up.

As Linc dealt the cards, several other guys took seats at the table. Willy said, "You've been a stranger here at the Castle too long, Little Ice."

His tone struck Sadie as kind, but Subject 9 stayed tense. His eyes moved to Willy's chips, arranged in four neat stacks, and the windy sound in his mind spiked. "It's been tough at home," was all Subect 9 said. "What have you been up to?" He took two chips off one of the tall stacks in front of him and tossed them into the middle of the table. Sadie noticed for the first time that his hands were crisscrossed with scars and cuts.

From fighting, she thought, and felt a twinge of nerves. The violence Curtis had suggested as a possibility seemed real in this setting, with these guys. The room felt like a tinderbox, a single wrong word enough to set it all off.

"I've been working at my uncle's appliance store the past four months," Willy told him.

"You? Selling fridges and washer-driers?" Subject 9 chuckled.

"Naw, mostly security. Making sure no one runs off with the washer-driers."

The guy with slicked-back hair said, "Raise, fifteen dollars."

Sadie had the impression that someone had momentarily dimmed the lights. Subject 9 said, "Call."

Are you nuts? Matching that bet? Sadie wanted to ask. Even with her rudimentary knowledge of poker she knew that he had nothing, while the way the other guy was betting indicated he must have a good hand. *Maybe dimming vision means dimming brains.*

But Subject 9 got lucky. The guy with the slick hair had been bluffing, and Subject 9 won the pot.

"How does appliance protection pay?" Subject 9 asked as Willy dealt the next hand.

"Not bad," Willy told him. "Got myself a car. *And* gas."

A quick cloudburst of noise filled Subject 9's head, and he looked up to meet Willy's eyes. "No way." Based on both the rise in sound and the elevation of his heart rate, Sadie thought he was genuinely impressed. It had never occurred to her that gas could be as much of a luxury as a car.

"And a girl," Linc said drily.

Willy's grin got even bigger. "Yep. She'll be along soon. You can meet her."

Subject 9 folded. His head got quieter as he watched the others finish the hand, but he seemed distracted, as though the game had lost interest for him. He kept checking his watch, which Sadie was surprised to see was an old Mickey Mouse one, the kind with hands that you probably had to wind. *That hardly seems in character for a bad guy*, she found herself thinking, before remembering that objectivity meant not prejudging.

He was so disengaged that he didn't even pick up the cards he'd been dealt on his next hand, but his vision dimmed when Linc bet, so Subject 9 matched it—and won again when Linc flipped over his cards to show he'd been bluffing.

Dimmed vision means he knows someone is lying, Sadie decided, setting it down in her mental notebook. It had to be something instinctive, because his pulse and the sounds in his head showed no change.

When it was his turn to deal the cards, Subject 9 said, "Any of you know how I can get in touch with James's girl? Was hoping to ask her a few questions."

The question was followed by silence, not a normal silence but the kind that made the hair on the back of his neck prick up and the lights seem to dim again.

Who is James? Sadie wondered. *And why was that question so loaded?*

Everyone at the table got very busy with their cards for a while. Willy broke the quiet, saying, "Which one? You know James. Loved the women, and the women loved him."

Another flicker along the edge of Subject 9's vision. "I'm not sure. A brunette, I think."

"Maybe it was Virginia," the Chapster with the sniffles volunteered. "The cashier at that casino."

The guy with big ears offered, "Or Ala, the girl at Sirios? With the angry father."

Willy puffed up his cheeks and made a comical face. "She was a dangerous one. Right up James's alley. Any of you remember—"

Linc tossed his cards on the table and looked directly at someone for the first time. "If you're just going to sit here wiki-wacking off about the past, you should find another game. I'm sick of talking about dead people."

Whoever James was, he was dead.

The windy sounds in Subject 9's head stopped as though someone had hit pause on the haunted-house soundtrack. "He was your best friend," he said to Linc.

"Operative word *was*." Linc's phone buzzed, and he unlocked his eyes from Subject 9's to glance at the screen, then frowned and stood. "I'm going to get some air," he said, striding out of the room.

As soon as Linc was out of sight the clutch of guys who had been around the table began to disperse as though they'd only been there to attend him. Watching them slip away, the sounds in Subject 9's head intensified, getting not louder but broader, as if new skeins had been added.

Are the sounds thoughts? Sadie asked herself. *And they get louder because he is wondering what is going on?* Sadie decided to set it down in her mental notebook provisionally and see if it held up.

Her Subject and Willy were alone at the card table now and nearly alone in the room. Sadie wondered how long the piles of pizza boxes and beer cans overflowing in the garbage cans had been accumulating; she imagined the Castle, as Willy had called it, didn't have a cleaning crew that came in at two A.M. like the Union Club did.

Acting like a fond parent trying to distract from the outburst of an infant, Willy said, "What have you been doing since we last saw you around the Castle, Little Ice? How's your love life?"

"Still with Cali. I'm a one-girl guy," Subject 9 answered, rearranging his stacks of chips into five uneven skyscrapers. "Too much trouble otherwise."

Oh, charming, Sadie thought.

"He says that, but really it's because he found the *one*." A girl in a pencil skirt and cardigan that managed to be anything but demure walked up to the table. She slid onto Willy's lap. "Isn't that it, Papa Bear?"

She was wearing a lot of makeup, so she looked older, but Sadie thought she probably wasn't even twenty. Which meant she and this girl were nearly the same age, but totally different species.

"You know it, kitten," Willy said, kissing her hand. "Let me introduce you to an old friend."

Finally, Sadie thought. A name. This was it.

Willy said, "Kansas, meet Little Ice."

I'm going to strangle someone.

Kansas said, "Pleasure to meet you, Mr. Ice."

Two someones.

Subject 9 cleared his throat. "Nice to meet you too, Kansas. But actually, my name is Ford," he said. "Ford Winter."

Thank you, Sadie thought, with a warm surge of gratitude. *Ford.* She wondered if he'd been named for the car or the president. *Nice to meet you, Ford Winter.*

Kansas frowned and leaned toward Ford, giving him a view straight down her sweater. "Why do they call you Ice if your name is Ford?"

Ford moved his attention from her cleavage to her face, and Sadie sensed him trying to tell if she was joking. "I think it's the way I play poker," he deadpanned.

She nodded earnestly. "Oh."

Nope. Not joking.

"He's James's brother," Willy explained.

Her face and Sadie's heart fell at the same time. James, the James who was dead, was Subj—Ford's—brother. And the fact that he'd been asking about James's girlfriend now meant it probably hadn't happened that long ago.

Sadie heard a phone buzz, and Willy pulled his out, glanced at the screen, and lifted Kansas to her feet with one arm as he stood. "Kitten, I've got to go check on something for the boss. Will you entertain my friend Ice while I'm gone?"

"Of course, Papa Bear," she cooed. She slipped into a chair next to Ford's and said, "Do you work for Mr. P too?"

A low, quick spike in sound. "Who?"

Kansas shook her head. "I guess not. What *do* you do?"

Ford said, "Demolition. You?"

Demolition. That's a job? Sadie was familiar with construction, but she didn't know destruction was its own profession. Given what Curtis had hinted about her subject's potential for violence, it sounded perfect for him.

"I'm an executive assistant," Kansas said, with a coy smile. "They call us work mistresses."

"Ah." Ford's eyes were moving like a tennis match, except the competition was between Kansas's neckline and the door

Willy and Linc had left though. The door was winning, and he was getting ready to stand up when Kansas blurted, "I was real sorry to hear about your brother. Dying and all that. James seemed like a great guy. And they looked like they were so happy together."

Ford's attention immediately focused. "They who?"

"Him and his girlfriend," Kansas said. "We all spent New Year's Eve together, me and Willy and Linc and James and . . . what *was* her name?"

The sounds in Ford's mind spiked like a powerful radio burst, and Sadie had that feeling again of catching a glimpse of—something—out of the corner of her eye. She turned to look for it, and again there was nothing to see. She turned back slowly, and—

My god, she gasped. Focusing her eyes not through Ford's but somewhere closer, she found herself watching as points of color, red and green and yellow and purple, hundreds, then thousands of them, materialized like a Georges Seurat painting into a shimmering image of a boy smiling blissfully while a girl, face hidden by a mass of dark hair, kissed the corner of his mouth.

It was dazzling, magical. As Sadie's eyes adjusted to this new focal length, she saw that this image wasn't the only one, it was happening all around her in his mind, millions of points of color, a massive, fluxing universe of shapes, images, and scenes forming and fading synthetically into one another. It seemed boundless, an endless stream, whipping by at the speed of thought and yet clearly visible to Sadie. A fall day at a lake, a crushed beer can, bunk beds, a hand reaching—

"Plum," Kansas announced triumphantly. "That's her name. Real pretty, right?"

The images—memories? Fantasies?—vanished. Sadie heard a low thump and realized the entire episode had taken place in the space of one of Ford's heartbeats.

Amazing. Syncopy was exhilarating. Both space and time seemed rubbery, capable of stretching into new dimensions, unconstrained by normal boundaries, and she felt similarly unconstrained. Similarly capable of stretching to anything.

"I don't have her number or anything," Kansas went on, "but ask the guys, they all know her."

Sadie caught a whiff of something that smelled like bleach and thought she must have underestimated the level of staff at the Castle since clearly they did have a cleaning crew.

Willy rejoined them then, trailed by a small clutch of Chapsters. "Papa Bear has to go to work," he told Kansas. "You understand, don't you, kitten?"

"Of course," Kansas said. "I'll wait for you at the car."

"She's great," Ford told Willy as they both watched her bottom slalom out the door.

"One in a billion," Willy said. He turned to Ford, and his eyes were sparkling. "Tell you a secret?"

"Sure."

"I'm gonna propose." He slapped himself on the leg. "Me, Willy. To a girl like that. What do you think?"

"I think you'll be really happy," Ford told him.

"Thanks, man," Willy said. His expression softened. "James was the one who got me to ask her out, you know that? Did it as a bet. Never would have had the guts to do it otherwise. Great guy, your brother."

Sadie felt Ford stiffen. "Yep."

Willy put his hands on Ford's shoulders. "And so are you."

Ford laughed. "Thanks."

"You've been a stranger at the Castle for too long. Guy could get his feelings hurt, his friends stop coming around. I was starting to think you'd pulled a Bucky and left without saying goodbye."

Ford's mind exploded with a fireworks display of images: a boy of about eleven with dark hair, huge intelligent eyes, and a tool belt slung around his skinny hips, staring earnestly at a hand-drawn map; the same boy a bit taller, wearing a helmet covered in aluminum foil and standing in front of a scraggly bush; taller still, now a gawky teenager, in the middle of a derelict factory building, grinning and holding up an old-fashioned beat box; finally, not taller but older, probably eighteen, with a beard and a backpack and a bandana tied around his head, his big eyes now wild and angry, jumping on a Greyhound bus just before its doors closed.

Ford said, "Bucky disappeared years ago. I've only been out of circulation four months."

"Lot happens in four months around here," Willy told him. "Practically a lifetime."

Another burst of sound in Ford's head. "Yeah, seems that way." Big daubs of blue, black, and white swept together into a blurry image of Linc leaving the room earlier, and Sadie had the sense that Ford wanted to say more, but Willy cut him off.

"We all miss James, same as you," he said, draping his massive arm over Ford's shoulders. "But we've got to come together when bad things happen, right? It's what we do. We're family"—Willy brought his grin close to Ford—"the kind you pick yourself, so it really counts."

A warm sensation washed through Ford, and he laughed. "Thanks, Willy."

Willy pulled him into a bear hug. "Course. Only don't stay away anymore, okay? You know I'm not the sharpest, and I don't want to forget that ugly mug of yours."

They separated, and Willy was about to go when Ford blurted, "Does Plum ever come by?"

Willy paused, meeting Ford's eyes with a frank, unblinking glance. "Who?"

"Plum. One of James's girlfriends?"

Willy shook his head back and forth slowly, eyes not leaving Ford's. "Name's not familiar. Course, as we were saying, your brother." He elbowed Ford. "Quite a Casanova."

Looking into Willy's wide, smiling face, Ford's vision dimmed and kept going, the darkness encroaching from around the edges and moving toward the center until Sadie couldn't see anything.

As his mind blacked out, it flooded with a roar of such force it seemed to have mass and density, some thick, heavy substance that filled every corner, every gap, taking all the available air. The space that had seemed infinite only heartbeats ago now shrank to nothing, trapping Sadie inside of it.

The air was crushed out of her lungs. She gasped for breath and felt herself choking as though she was drowning, flailing. *I have to get out of here,* she thought, panicked. *I have to escape.* The darkness was suffocating her, pulling her in like a constricting vacuum, twisting the breath, the life, out of her. What was happening, what was this sensation, what—

Anger, she thought, claiming her first emotion.

Everything went black.

CHAPTER 6

Sadie awoke to a guy's voice saying, "I was at work all day. I told you, babe."

"Sorry, I must have forgotten," a girl answered. "I figured since it was Sunday—

"Overtime," the guy interrupted. "Day shift, noon to eight P.M."

Sadie, waking fully, recognized the guy's voice as Ford's. She opened her eyes and saw a living room. And a girl. Or at least her nose, since the conversation was being whispered while they kissed.

All the signals Sadie was getting from Ford felt subdued, as though everything was covered in a layer of dust. It was more all-encompassing than the dimness before, making not just his vision but his voice seem muffled.

Was it because she'd passed out? Sadie recalled Catrina at lunch discussing how "Syncsleep"—moments when the Minder's consciousness got overloaded and temporarily withdrew from Syncopy—was common during the first few days of Syncopy. "It usually happens at times of intense emotion for your Subject, distracting you so much you forget to breathe."

Intense emotion, Sadie repeated and shuddered at the memory of the clawing, suffocating darkness of his anger.

If it was after eight now, she'd been in Syncsleep for at least four hours. During that time, Ford had been at work doing—

He hadn't been at work, she realized, at least not when she was awake. Which meant he was lying. To the person who was presumably his girlfriend—*Cali*, Sadie remembered, adding it to the list of his associates' names in her mental notebook.

So you're a liar, Ford Winter, she thought with a twinge of disgust, before reminding herself that she was supposed to be objective.

Maybe the lying accounted for the dusty quality of his thoughts, a sort of film between him and reality. Tying it in with the way things dimmed when someone was bluffing, she added *Lying interferes with vision* to her mental notebook.

Cali was sitting on the arm of the sofa, with Ford standing between her legs. He pulled her toward him and kissed her forehead. Her eyes closed, but his stayed open, giving Sadie a chance to look around.

The room they were in was small, with a single window in the same wall as the front door. The walls were light blue, the carpeting beige. An old wooden footlocker served as a coffee table, which, with the navy slipcovered sofa, gave the room a sort of a nautical feeling. Behind the couch was a short hallway that led, presumably, to the bedrooms and bathrooms. The wall facing the couch had a wide arch opening into the kitchen, and half of a bricked-up fireplace mantel. The other half, along with part of the plaster medallion in the ceiling, disappeared into the wall.

Between the arch and the fireplace hung a medium-sized television showing *Cookie Wars Deluxe*, the picture completely framed with Ad-Spaces. Like everyone in their neighborhood, Sadie's parents paid to outsource their ad watching to other people so their content was always ad-free. Intellectually she understood that gave other people the chance to watch extra ads in exchange for less expensive television, but she'd never considered what that really meant until now. The Winters' television screen was so crowded with Ad-Spaces that it took Sadie a moment to find the small rectangle showing Team Chocolate Chip going up against Team Snickerdoodle in the Cookie Wars Championship among the promos.

Sadie was fascinated and had to suppress a momentary feeling of frustration when Cali pulled away from the kiss and Ford shifted his attention to her.

Cali was blond and pretty, although Sadie thought she would have been prettier with less makeup, less TanTerrific, and less of the unnatural glossiness that straightening tubes imparted to hair. Especially since studies suggested they caused cancer. She wore a white button-down shirt that strained over a white lace-edged bra.

Ford's eyes focused on the bra as he curled a strand of the carefully straightened hair around his finger and said, "I'm sorry I kept you waiting." That, at least, seemed true, because his vision didn't get hazier. Sadie noticed there were cuts on his hand that hadn't been there before. What had happened after she passed out?

Cali reached up and took his hand, moving it from her hair. "That's okay. It gave me a chance to keep Lulu company."

"Thanks, babe." His hips rested between her legs, and his nose touched hers.

Cali started talking about plans for the rest of the week, and Ford's mind filled with dots. They arranged themselves into a flurry of images—leaving the poker table, walking out of the Castle, staring at a bank machine screen that read INSUF-FICIENT CREDIT. Bashing his hand against the wall next to it. *Explains the new cuts*, Sadie thought.

The dots got smaller as the memories went on, giving them a tense, brittle kind of clarity: him opening his wallet and painstakingly counting out bills—ones mostly, a few fives and tens, presumably his poker winnings—ending with only two singles left over. Dropping the wad of bills into a mailbox with a notice next to it that read, ALL RENT MUST BE PAID IN FULL BY 8 A.M. EVERY MONDAY OR TENANT WILL FACE IMMEDIATE EVICTION, with DON'T EVEN THINK OF ASKING FOR AN EXTENSION— THE LANDLORD, written in black pen along the bottom.

"So you're good with that?" Cali asked.

Sadie had been listening while she watched Ford's memories, but based on the way all the dots suddenly vanished and the sounds combined into a low hum, she realized he hadn't heard anything Cali was saying.

He nodded anyway. "Totally. Whatever works for you, works for me."

Why not just ask what she's talking about? Sadie wondered. *It would be so simple.*

"You're the best," Cali said, bringing her lips to his.

He's not, Sadie wanted to tell her. *Ask him what he just said yes to.*

"No, you're the best," he told Cali.

She rubbed his nose with hers. "No, you are."

Sadie groaned in frustration.

From the couch behind them a high-pitched voice said, "Agree to disagree. I'm the best. And now that we have that settled, can you please stop? I'm only eleven and whatever you're doing is far above my pay grade."

A golden Lab's head came over the top of the couch to nuzzle Ford's leg, and Sadie had the impossible thought that the dog had spoken. Then Cali shifted and Sadie saw that a little girl had come in and curled herself into the far corner of the sofa.

She was as blond as Ford was dark, but had the same firm chin, the same stubborn mouth. The same very blue, very serious eyes.

Ford laughed. "Sorry to disturb you, Princess Lulu." He glanced at his Mickey Mouse watch. "Weren't you supposed to be in bed half an hour ago?"

Lulu pulled herself up to her whole four-foot height and said, "I don't think I'm the one who needs to get a room."

"Is that really how you want to talk to your older brother?" Ford asked, a threat rumbling in his tone.

Lulu put her hands on her hips. "Yes."

"Your strong, ferocious older brother?" he went on, narrowing his eyes.

Lulu snorted. "Oh, right."

Sadie didn't detect the kind of anger she'd felt at the Castle, but Ford's tone was definitely menacing as he said, "You asked for it," and lunged for the little girl.

Stop him, Sadie wanted to yell at Cali. *Don't let him hurt—*

Ford snatched Lulu into his arms and started tickling her ribs. "Help!" Lulu cried through her giggles.

Sadie was fascinated. Ford's mindscape was radically changed from the windy place it had been at the Castle, the sounds in a completely different register and somehow slower, simpler. *As if his thoughts and feelings for his sister were uncomplicated,* Sadie noted.

The dustiness of his conversation with Cali vanished as well, and instead of images the points of color were moving around freely, like people at a station waiting for their train to be called. His mind seemed pliant, flexible. *Playful,* Sadie thought, although that didn't sound very scientific. She'd have to think of a better way to describe it when she was in front of the Committee.

He lifted Lulu up and swung her over his shoulder. Sadie found herself laughing as Lulu protested, "That's not fair, you're bigger than I am, so you shouldn't be able to use your arms, next time you can only use your feet, or maybe what if you just don't bend your elbows and—"

He paused to give Cali a kiss and said, "I'll be right back."

"No he won't," Lulu told her from behind Ford's back as he carried her to the hallway. "I'm going to get him for this, I'm going to—"

She went silent as they approached a partially open door on the left, and Ford's mind filled with static that didn't subside until they got to the door at the end of the hallway with a purple marker sign taped to it that said: PALACE OF PRINCESS LULU. NO ENTRY WITHOUT PERMISSION.

"Permission to enter," Ford asked on the threshold.

"Permission granted," Lulu told him. "But you have to read me a story."

"You can read yourself a story," Ford said, flipping her onto her bed.

Only the bedside light was on, but the room was small, so it was enough to take in the bunk bed with pink comforters, an unfinished dollhouse, and two stacks of milk crates, one side holding neatly folded clothes and the other side holding books. The room was meticulously tidy. Sadie felt at home.

Sadie hadn't seen the dog follow them, but he nosed the door open, lumbered up onto the bed beside the girl, and sat looking at her expectantly.

"See, Copernicus wants you to read to him," Ford pointed out.

Lulu rolled her eyes. "You just want to go make out with Cali."

"True," Ford said. He bent over and looked under the bunk bed. "Nothing lurking," he announced. "Good—"

"Mom didn't go to work again today." Lulu's voice was quiet and tense. "It's the third week in a row."

Another burst of static. Dots of color collected into the image of the ATM screen saying INSUFFICIENT CREDIT in Ford's mind. "I know. But I'm sure she'll be better soon."

"How do you know?"

"Because that's what always happens. Don't worry, okay?"

Lulu nodded, her little face somber. She leaned toward him to whisper, "Could you look again? Just to be sure?"

Ford put his finger to his lips. In one swift motion he dropped into a push-up position and peered under the bed.

"Still no monsters," he reported, standing back up. "No way they could have hidden that fast. You're safe."

Lulu held up two dolls that appeared to be from the doll-house and said, "Kiss Bless and Noshe good night."

Ford grabbed one of them and pretended to start making out with her, causing Lulu to squeal with laughter, then dropped the dolls and reached for her, and she squealed even more. Sadie tried to imagine what it would be like to have someone who made your mind relax the way Lulu made Ford's.

He gave his sister a soppy kiss on the forehead and was at the door when she spoke.

"How come when Cali says 'I love you' you don't say it back?"

He stopped on the threshold and turned to face her, his mind staying even and unaffected. "I do."

"No you don't," Lulu told him. "You say 'you too' or 'me too' or 'uh-huh.'"

Ford laughed and turned back toward the door. "Agree to disagree."

Lulu narrowed her eyes. "That's my line. You can't just take it."

He pantomimed catching something in his fist midair, grinned, said, "Too late," and shut the door.

Cali's bare legs over the top of the couch, one ankle crossed over the other, were the first thing he noticed walking down the hall toward the living room, and the reaction in his body was immediate. Sadie felt his lower abdomen tighten and heard something that sounded almost like music in his head.

"I hope you don't mind, I made myself comfortable," Cali said.

He slid onto the couch next to her, his arm coming around to rest conveniently on her breast, his crotch against her leg. "You look like you might still be a little uncomfortable. Maybe you should get out of your shorts."

Cali laughed. "I was thinking, on Friday you could wear the blue checked shirt. You know, the one you were wearing the first time we met."

"Mmmm?" His lips roamed over the smooth skin along the base of Cali's neck, and tiny clusters of sound and color broke loose in various parts of his mind, like dandelion seeds being blown free in a breeze, a momentary *poof* and then gone.

During training Sadie had resolved to use any intimate time her Subject had to review her findings and take down new data, but now she found herself unable to break away. She felt the tension building inside of him as though it were inside of her, each trill and riff adding another layer. It was like having butterfly wings tease over her skin, making it tingle and prickle in the most exquisite and exquisitely distracting way. She let herself slip into it, willingly, even gratefully, breathless to find out what happened next—

From very far away a voice said, "You know, the one you wore on our first date."

It had happened again, she realized—a world of experience in the space of a heartbeat. The music in his head stopped, the tickling evaporated, and Ford blinked his eyes open, saying, "Friday? What's happening Friday?"

Dinner with her friends, Sadie volunteered. *Remember when you were too stubborn to ask what she was talking about? I guess we know who is the best now.*

Cali laughed and shimmied up him, setting off a momentary tinkling of bells. "Silly. Going out with Georgia and Clinton. We have a reservation at Trattoria Olivio."

The tightness in Ford's lower abdomen shifted from pleasure to something more like pressure. "Sorry, babe, I have another commitment." Sadie didn't need the feeling of the lights suddenly dimming to know he was lying. *Why do that? Why not just say "I don't want to go"?*

Cali's perfectly arced brows came together in a frown. "You told me you were free all weekend. You just said Friday was just fine."

"To see you," Ford answered. "You didn't tell me about Trattoria Olivio. You know I don't like going to those frou-frou places." His mind filled with pointillist images of bread sticks, a carafe of wine wrapped in straw, salad—

"How would you know you don't like it if you've never been?" Cali asked.

Ford said, "It just seems stupid."

It didn't seem stupid when you were picturing it just now, Sadie observed. *Why would you say something so intentionally antagonistic?*

Cali pulled as far from him on the couch as she could. "Do you care about me? Love me? Because if you want to end this, you should do it now. It's not fair to drag it out."

Ford sat up, the noise in his head spiking with surprise. "Whoa, where is this coming from? Because I don't want to pay forty dollars for some crappy Italian food?"

Cali took a deep breath and, like someone jumping off the high dive, said, "I got a new job."

Ford sat up even straighter. "A new job? You mean a promotion?"

"No. A whole new job." Another deep breath for courage. "I started interviewing in April, and I found out I got it on Friday."

"April?" Ford repeated incredulously. "You kept this from me for two months?" Sadie caught a whiff of the same bleachy scent she'd noticed at the Castle. Only she'd been wrong; there hadn't been a cleaning crew, it was *inside* Ford's head.

"I was afraid of how you'd take it," Cali said.

"How should I take it?" Ford demanded. "I thought we were a couple. Now you tell me you've been looking for new jobs behind my back." The smell of bleach got stronger. "What else have you been lying about?"

"I didn't lie." Cali reached for him, but he pulled away from her hand, turning his back. From behind him she said, "The job is with CitCent Neighborhood Bank. I'll be an executive assistant to one of the bankers. It's a great opportunity, Ford. More money, more responsibility, chances for promotion. It's a career, the way I always said I wanted. We'll be able to get a place together, like Georgia and Clinton."

Say congratulations, Sadie urged. *Tell her that's great news and you're excited for her.*

Ford's mind flashed back to the imagined dinner scene with

Georgia and Clinton, the dots forming pictures of dessert, tiny cups of coffee, the final bill. His wallet with the two dollars in it. It brought with it a rush of the same sticky, dirty sensation Sadie had noticed at the Castle.

He turned to face Cali and said, "You know what they call executive assistants? Work mistresses. They'll screw you but they won't promote you."

Or you could say that.

Cali's lower lip was trembling. "Ford, don't act this way."

"I'm just telling you the truth. Would you rather I lied to you and said you were off to a great start, your future looks bright?" He shook his head. "I'm sorry, I'm not comfortable lying to the people I love."

Seriously, Mr. Ice? You're not comfortable lying? Careful you don't slip and lose your tenuous hold on the moral high ground.

"I'd hoped you could be happy for me and not need to lie." Cali sighed. "But I guess I already knew that's not how it would go."

Ford blinked, and dots of brown, yellow, magenta, blue, and beige formed a very faint elevator carrying Cali dressed like Kansas had been that day, surrounded by men in business suits with bulging wallets eyeing her cleavage. "I'm sorry I'm such a disappointment."

He's deliberately provoking her, Sadie realized. As if he wanted to fight, wanted to make it escalate.

"You're twisting everything around," Cali whimpered.

"I'm just listening to you. Isn't that what you want? And you know what, babe? You're right. You deserve better than me."

That's a neat magic trick, Sadie thought. *Turning from the person in the wrong into the person who was wronged. What's next? Pulling a rabbit out of a hat?*

"I don't want better, I want you," Cali said, falling for the trick. "I just want you to be happy. You used to be, but now—it seems like you never are."

"I'm sorry I'm not happy, Cali," he said. "It's just that my brother is dead and my girlfriend is a liar."

Cali's mouth made an O, and she froze like she'd been stabbed in the stomach. *Oh, I see. Your next trick is cutting the woman in half.*

The tears started down Cali's cheeks, streaking her mascara, and she didn't even lift a hand to smooth them away. "I'm gonna go."

Followed by making her disappear.

At the door, Cali faced him. "Is this—are we—?"

"I'll be in touch," he said, half closing his eyes. "Soon."

I'll be in touch. Sadie heard the echo of Pete's words the night before, and worked to push it away. The point of this fellowship was to experience someone else's life, not her own.

Besides, Pete had called and apologized that morning—god, was it only that morning?—saying he was sorry, it was just that he was going to miss her so much. Everything between them was fine now.

But everything was *not* fine between her and Ford. Sadie wanted to shake him and ask what kind of person acted the way he did. Couldn't he see how much Cali cared about him? Why would he try to tear her down rather than be happy for her? Keep their fight going instead of ending it? Worse, there was something cool and calculated about it, as though he was pushing Cali away so she'd have to work even harder to stay with him.

Humiliation, Sadie realized. *That was what the sticky sensation was.* He'd felt humiliated that he couldn't pay for dinner, but instead of admitting it, he'd tried to humiliate Cali by making her new job sound tawdry. Like something she should be ashamed of. *How immat—*

Stay objective, Sadie reminded herself. *Record, don't judge.* She added *humiliation—sticky, unpleasant, dirty—*after *anger—heavy, dark, suffocating, restless—*in her mental notebook, and then in a separate section wrote *bleach—?.*

So far, Ford Winter's mind was living up to the darkness she'd seen in his eyes.

Sadie expected he'd go to his bedroom now—she imagined something decorated in dirty gym socks—but instead he went to the trunk that acted as a coffee table, pulled out a pillow and a blanket that had been shoved in there, and tossed them on the couch. He did it without triggering any change in his mind, making Sadie think this was where he regularly spent the night.

So what's behind the other door off the hallway? As though he'd heard her question, he went to it, took a deep breath, and pushed it open.

The air in the room was so thick with smoke that the bedside light made a golden halo. It was Spartan, more like a cell than a room, with only a dresser, a mirror, a night table, a light, and a bed.

A frail woman lay on the bed, above the covers. She wore a faded red housecoat that looked garish against her pale skin. There was a word jumble book on the bedspread next to her, an overflowing ashtray on the night table beside the lamp, and a picture in a silver frame resting in the hollow of her chest. A beige uniform dress with a white collar and a nametag that said VERA WINTER—WELCOME TO WAFFLE CITY lay draped haphazardly along the foot of the bed.

His mother, Sadie thought.

Ford stood looking at her for a moment before approaching. His mind was full of a busy emptiness, as though all his thoughts, emotions, and memories had hidden themselves like animals sheltering from a predator in tall grass.

"James?" the woman whispered. Her arm hung off the bed, and a burnt-down cigarette dangled from between her first two fingers. They were red and blistered, and there were dark burn spots on the rug beneath her hand.

Ford took the cigarette from her and balanced it on top of the pile in the ashtray. "No, Mom. It's Ford."

"Where's James?"

Sadie expected a flood of heavy anger, but Ford's voice was calm. He lifted the photo off her chest and put it on the nightstand without glancing at it. "James isn't here."

"When will he be back?" the woman asked.

Ford said, "He won't. He's gone."

His mother's eyes came open. "I thought maybe that was a dream. That he was alive and you"—she paused—"were him."

The Ford Sadie had seen with Cali would have been ready with a scathing retort. Instead she had the sensation of someone leaning into a door, using their weight to keep it closed.

Sadie realized this had been going on in the background of Ford's mind all night, even when he was with Cali, the effort increasing incrementally until she only now became aware of it. As though whatever was behind the door was always hovering beneath the surface, trying to get out. Ford said evenly, "That would be nice."

His mother slid out of bed, went to the dresser, and began arranging the few objects on it—brush, comb, box, lipstick— moving them around one another nervously. "I tried to go to work today, but—" Her voice trailed off. Ford settled on the edge of her bed, but she remained standing, keeping her back to him as she said, "I was thinking tomorrow you could go see your father."

In Ford's mind very faint blue and green and gray dots sifted themselves into a dozen grainy pictures of a man, one superimposed upon another, creating a monstrous tableau. They were all different, but they were all sneering, and as Sadie watched, a fist punched through all of them, scattering the images into a red spray of blood.

Sadie felt the door in his mind jostle, and Ford leaning harder into it. "Why? Do you want me to end up in jail?"

His mother ignored that. "He hasn't sent a check in a few months, and with me missing work we need the money."

"I've been covering it," Ford told her. "You said you were going to talk to the Roaches about Dad."

"Don't call them that. It's disrespectful."

"Fine. You said you were going to tell the Roque Community Health Evaluator about Dad not paying."

She lined up the box with the brush and comb. "I didn't want to bother her."

Sadie felt the door starting to open and Ford struggling to push it back. "Mom, that's what she's for."

Mrs. Winter turned around, agitated eyes seeking his. "Don't you see we can't have them know? If they knew that we had no money, if they knew he was behind—"

"If I get in trouble, if we miss our RCHE appointments, if we do anything to draw attention to ourselves, including ask for help we deserve, or request to see the file on James's death, or ask why they've refused our requests to see the file, they could split the family apart," Ford finished, as though reciting the end of a familiar fairy tale. "We all have to behave like good little boys and girls and not upset Father."

His mother's hand whipped out, and she slapped him. "Stop it! This isn't a joke. This is our *family*."

Sadie caught a whiff of bleach, but the pain barely registered in Ford's mind. "You know James didn't die the way they say he did. Don't you want to learn the truth?"

"The case is closed," said Mrs. Winter, trembling. "It's *closed*." Her tone was a plea, and her eyes looked afraid, but whether she was afraid *for* Ford or afraid *of* him, Sadie couldn't tell.

They were less than a foot apart, mother and son, but loneliness yawned between them. Ford was completely still, as though all his energy was concentrated on keeping whatever was behind the door at bay. Only his eyes moved, sliding to the photo on the night table, allowing Sadie to see it.

It had been taken at Ford's high school graduation, him in a cap and gown, standing next to the same blond guy Sadie had seen before in his mind being kissed by the mysterious woman with the dark hair. *James.*

In the photo Mrs. Winter stood between Ford and James in a pantsuit, thin but robust, nothing like the wisp of a woman in front of him now. Lulu held her hand and part of James's sleeve and grinned adoringly up at her brothers. He and James were looking at one another, Ford making a goofy face, both laughing, as if they'd just shared a hilarious joke.

They were hardly recognizable as the same family. With a shock she noted the date stamp on the bottom corner of the photo. It had been taken only a year earlier.

"I miss him," his mother said, following Ford's eyes to the picture.

Sadie felt hot flares starting to slip through the cracks in Ford's mental door and realized the emotion it was holding back was anger. It was anger that hovered beneath everything in his mind, pressing forward, restless, eager. And his desire or ability to contain it was weakening.

"Everyone loved James. He was such a good boy. So full of life," Mrs. Winter went on.

"He sure was." Ford stood, his mind noisy with the effort of holding the door closed. "You fell asleep smoking again, Mom. If you keep it up you'll set the house on fire and kill us all."

"You worry too much," his mother answered.

They spoke the words like actors delivering well-worn lines, and Sadie imagined them having this same conversation a dozen, two dozen times before. For a moment they stood still in their poses, each waiting to see if the other wanted to finish the scene.

Then Ford pivoted and went back to the living room. He didn't say *good night* or *sleep well* or any of the things Sadie always said to her parents, and his mother didn't call them after him. It was as if they didn't know how to talk to one another if they weren't fighting. *Was that why he'd purposely goaded*

Cali too, because conflict was more comfortable to him than affection?

Unhooking his belt, he dropped his jeans and stepped out of them.

You're not really going to leave them on the floor like a pile of—

He took two steps to the couch, stretched out, and turned off the light.

You are, Sadie marveled. *Well, that makes sense. Because operating drawers is such a challenge.*

His eyes closed, and the anger settled in like a lapdog finding its accustomed bed. His mind went quiet except for a regular, low thrumming. *His heart*, Sadie realized, feeling an unexpected flash of intimacy.

I am still very displeased, she reminded herself.

Sadie was prepared to be wide awake even after he fell asleep—they'd been told at orientation that the advanced stimulation of their brains might make sleep elusive the first few days even if they were tired—and had intended to use the time to go over her observations from the day. But her thoughts kept returning to the photo from Ford's graduation of the Winter family, happy and full of hope. Losing James had shattered them in a way that seemed to go beyond mere grief.

How did James die? she wondered. *Who is Ford so angry at?*

As she drifted off to sleep, lulled by the sound of his heartbeat, she saw a faint image of a skein of golden rope curling slowly downward, and had the strangest idea that if she could just grab it she'd have her answer.

CHAPTER 7

"**D**ude, your breath is foul. Get off!"

Who said that?

Sadie came awake in an instant. Her eyes and Ford's snapped open simultaneously, giving them both a close-up view of Copernicus's big wet nose and lolling tongue.

Pushing it aside, Ford lurched to the bathroom, relieved himself, and started brushing his teeth without washing his hands in between.

Good morning, Sadie said to him politely.

He looked in the mirror and grunted. Still brushing his teeth, he turned left and right, inspecting his profile. Finally he smiled with a mouth full of toothpaste foam, and for a moment he resembled the guy in the graduation picture, goofy and carefree. He spit out the toothpaste, rinsed his mouth, wet his hair to slick it back, and stood up, and the boy with angry eyes was back.

From purely scientific motives she was glad when he removed the T-shirt he'd slept in, providing her first glimpse of any part of him unclothed. In the mirror Sadie observed that his shoulders, arms, and chest looked like something from the ancient Greek wing of the Detroit Institute of Art, while the scars and cuts crisscrossing his knuckles and forearms told of a more recent history. Together they gave him the appearance of a kind of epic hero fighting against long odds.

Which he'd adore, she thought, since as far as she had seen, Ford had done nothing but purposely create conflict with every person he came into contact with except his sister. The Me vs. Everyone Else paradigm apparently appealed to him, and she wondered if some of his more antisocial behaviors—

At least put the seat down, Sadie called as he left the bathroom without showering.

—could be attempts to deliberately antagonize people. That way he could always feel like others wronged him, and never have to take responsibility for his own actions.

Subject in above average physical condition but emotionally stunted, Sadie recorded in her mental notebook, because "looks like a hot guy, behaves like a five-year-old" didn't sound very scientific.

He got dressed in the clothes he'd been wearing the previous day, had "breakfast"—cold water poured over a packet of instant coffee, which he drank down with the unmixed globs of powder still floating on the surface—and headed down two flights of stairs and out of the apartment building, the anger from the previous night banking around the surfaces of his

mind like a trapped fly. Unlocking his bike from beside the DO
NOT LOCK BIKES HERE EVER!! sign he pedaled the wrong way
down his street toward the busy intersection at Bob's Burger
Boulevard.

As he rode, his mind unfolded into an old-fashioned map,
roads and buildings appearing like they'd been sketched out in
front of him. His imagined streetscape had some of the same
buildings as the one he was riding through but without most
of the graffiti, and often with different signs, so that Cha Cha's
Liquor-n-Things and Time 4 Pawn were merged together on his
mental map into one building marked SUPERMARKET. A church
with broken glass in the windows and a sign in front proclaim-
ing OUT OF SINESS appeared spruced up in Ford's mind with a
sign that said INDOOR SKATE PARK (LASER TAG TOURNAMENTS
MONTHLY). There were other buildings on his "map" too, older
looking, as though he was simultaneously picturing the streets
as they had once been and as they could be.

He rode like he was in a fantasy world of his own design,
treating stop signs as optional and the rules of the road as something best avoided. As he jumped his bike onto the sidewalk to
avoid the posted twelve-minute wait time at the intersection
of Calm Colon Avenue and H_3O Purified Water-Style Beverage
Way, his phone buzzed with a text. In violation of the hands-
free-only laws he pulled it from his pocket and read it without
slowing down or braking. It was from Cali, and it said, "I'M
SORRY. YOU WERE RIGHT. I SHOULD HAVE TOLD YOU. FORGIVE?"

Sure, babe, he thought. *Later.*

Why later? Sadie demanded. *What is this stupid game that
boys play? You know you're going to write back to her, why
don't you just—*

She interrupted herself. She'd *heard* "Sure, babe. Later." Heard the words. *In his head*. For the first time, she'd been able to hear what he was thinking.

Naturally, it had been something annoying. But she was still excited.

Now that she was aware of it, she began to hear other thoughts. It wasn't easy and primarily she got fragments, but it was clear that most of the sounds in his head weren't just noises, they were actual *words*. Some looped in and out, like *can't be late*, while others appeared only once. She heard him think something that sounded like *burger for lunch*, and then a series of blurred dots became his wallet with the two dollars in it and she caught a hint of the stickiness again before it was consumed in a flare of anger.

It was like watching the gears on a clock. A thought triggered a memory, which triggered an emotion, which triggered—

A dozen horns honked, brakes squealed, and a delivery van shuddered to a stop inches from Ford's back tire as he went speeding across Chef's Best Lasagna Avenue against traffic.

—action.

Idiots, he thought, as though the commotion were everyone's fault but his, and Sadie was torn between laughter and dismay.

At five minutes to eight he parked his bike in front of an enormous stone building with a sign that said, THE FORMER ST. CLAIRE APARTMENTS IS BECOMING CLAIRE FARMS! ANOTHER MASON BLIGH COMMUNITY ASSET. Distracted by the effort of holding back his anger, Ford didn't see the tall, red-headed guy standing on the front steps of the building until he'd plowed into him, nearly knocking him to the ground.

The guy regained his balance and turned to see what had happened. "Are you okay?" he asked Ford. He was skinny and gawky with pink cheeks, red hair, and big green eyes behind round tortoiseshell glasses. At least that was what Sadie noticed. What Ford saw was a guy with four inches on him in height but ten pounds lighter, built like a wimp, around twenty-three years old.

Ford said, "You should watch where you're standing." Like it was the guy's fault Ford had walked into him. Sadie realized he was itching for a fight.

The man, looking a little dazed, blinked. "You're right. Sorry." He held out his hand. "I'm—"

Ford walked right by it, into the black-and-white-checked marble hall. An older man wearing jeans and an ironed plaid shirt stood leaning against a fluted wood pillar with a clipboard in his hand.

"Winter, you're late," he barked when he saw Ford.

"According to my watch I'm exactly on time, Mr. Harding." Ford held up his right wrist, pointing to Mickey's two hands on the twelve and the eight.

The foreman shook his head. "You're all the way back, with Nix." He poked a thumb to his right. "And no need to saunter— I want this floor picked clean as a turkey carcass by lunch."

Ford spotted a sign in the far back corner of the once-grand lobby that read LAUNDRY ROOM, and Sadie heard him think, *Nice work, Nix.* But when they reached it, she couldn't see the appeal: There were long channels ripped through the baseboards and across the ceiling and strips of floral wallpaper rolled up from the middle of the walls like chocolate curls on a wedding cake.

A compact dark-skinned kid, younger than the Chapsters

Sadie had seen, leaned against one of the walls, two sledge-hammers next to him. Seeing him, Ford's mind struck a single, pleasant chord, and the feeling was apparently mutual, because when Ford walked up, the guy ground out the cigarette he'd been smoking and gave him a dazzling smile.

"Did I or did I not hook us up?" he asked. "With all the wiring and pipes in here to harvest, the scabbies've already done most of the work for us."

A soft, warm sensation Sadie hadn't felt before spread through Ford. Out of the corner of her eye she caught pinprick images of tomato soup and grilled cheese and soggy mittens as Ford started to laugh.

Amusement, she thought. Amusement felt like tomato soup after a snowball fight.

"Couldn't have picked better myself, Nix," Ford said, hoisting one of the sledgehammers. "Though the St. Claire was built as a hotel, so no way was this originally a laundry room. They wouldn't have put it on the first floor off the lobby."

"Are we betting? I say dining room."

"Too small," Ford said, shaking his head. "I say manager's office or bar."

"Loser buys lunch," Nix said. "On your marks, get set—"

For the next hour all sound and thought was blotted out of Ford's mind by the noise of the sledgehammer smashing through plaster and brick as they skinned the building's car-cass. The two of them worked opposite sides of the room, their hammers settling into a call and response, where one of them would do a set of strokes, and the other would match it and add one.

Ford working, Sadie discovered, was much calmer than

Ford doing anything else. She was making a mental note about the importance of jobs to self-esteem when he stopped and dropped the hammer.

"Did I win?" Nix asked over his shoulder.

"Maybe," Ford said. "It's a dumbwaiter. It would have gone from here to the kitchens. And it works!" As he spoke he tugged a faded cord, bringing up a dusty wooden box that arrived with a clatter of clinking plates and cutlery. They were filthy and stacked haphazardly, apparently forgotten decades earlier by the last person to use the room. *That is very cool*, Sadie thought, and Ford gave a *whooooop* of joy. He was nearly dancing with happiness, shifting from one foot to the other and pointing. "Do you see that?" he asked Nix. "Someone's last supper."

Ford carefully stacked the dishes on the floor, surreptitiously pocketing a tiny crystal saltshaker, and poked his head into the dumbwaiter's shaft. "One of the gears is stamped 1932," he called to Nix.

"And one of your time cards is going to be stamped FIRED," the foreman's voice said. Ford pulled himself out of the wall.

"Harding, you've got to look at this," Ford said, gesturing the foreman over. "It's the entire mechanism, intact, from 19—"

The foreman shook his head. "Yeah, I heard. Your job is to smash it."

"But it's perfect. If we take it out I bet some decorator—"

"Smash, smash, smash." The foreman pointed to the sledgehammer Ford had dropped to the floor. "Go on, show me you know how to use it."

"It will be easy to get it out," Ford kept on. "I swear to you if you tell whatever jackass we're working for about it, they'll thank you. It could be worth something."

"You're right," the foreman agreed. "Could be worth your job. Now smash—"

"I'm the jackass." The tall red-headed guy from the front steps walked into the room. He held out his hand to Ford again. "Mason Bligh."

This time Ford took it. "Ford Winter."

"What did you find?" Mason asked.

Ford, suddenly taciturn—*You're shy!* Sadie realized, feeling a tiny bit of kinship with him—just pointed his finger up into the shaft. "Dumbwaiter."

"For the dumb worker," the foreman said, laughing at his own joke.

Mason gave him a forced smile and looked at Ford. "How would you get it out?"

"Saw around it. Shouldn't take long, maybe an hour."

"I'd like to see that," Mason said. "Let's do it." He turned to the foreman. "Do I need to sign anything, Mr. Harding? Pay you more money? Why don't you draw up contracts for this spot project, and I'll pay you today."

"Whatever you like, Mr. Bligh," the foreman said pleasantly.

Phony, Ford thought, perching himself on the edge of the opening and leaning in. Sadie watched his mind tracing a map of the mechanics of the dumbwaiter the way it had produced the street map earlier. He turned to Mason and asked, "What are you going to do with it?"

"Nothing yet. But it's too neat to destroy. Have you got a use for it?"

Ford poked his head out of the hole to look at the guy Sadie heard him describe in his head as a twenty-three-year-old bajillionaire nerd. He couldn't figure Mason out. He said, "I might."

"Great, you take it. And you find anything else like that, tell me. You're right, I want to know." Mason was heading for the door when Ford's voice called him back.

"Excuse me, sir," Ford said, his voice sounding young and unsure.

Mason turned. "Yep?"

"I took this." Ford held out the crystal saltshaker. "I didn't think anyone would care, but obviously it's yours. I—I just wanted it for my sister."

Right, Sadie thought. *Because all eleven-year-olds really want a saltshaker.*

Mason shook his head. "All yours."

Ford worked with steady concentration after that, barely pausing to eat, but Sadie sensed an increasing jumpiness in him. *Anticipation? Anxiety?* By the time he scanned out at the end of the day she was certain he was about to do something illegal, and she was torn between excitement and wariness as he steered his bike in the opposite direction of his apartment.

He rode from the mostly deserted neighborhood around the job site through two traffic-gnarled intersections into an area of wide, silent streets lined with the crumbling hulks of commercial buildings. His bike bounced over a portion of downed chain-link fence and up a cracked asphalt driveway to the front entrance of a large brick factory. It had what looked like a chimney on one side and appeared to be about seven stories tall, but peering through the open door Sadie saw it was empty inside from the floor to the roof except for rusted machine parts, some decaying wood pallets, and broken bottles. The sign propped next to the door read DETROIT WIRE CO.

Ford left his bike and walked around the building to a set

of fire escape stairs along the far wall. He climbed them all the way to the top and stepped off onto the roof.

It seemed like they could see for miles all around. The river was a ribbon glittering between buildings in one direction, the traffic on the highway looked like the links in a metal watch-band in another, and beyond that the suburbs extended like a rolling green carpet. *That's where I live,* she thought to herself.

Suddenly she was flooded with panic. All at once she real-ized how high up they were, how close to the edge. Her throat got tight, making it hard to breathe, and her heart raced. *The edge is right there.* She squeezed her eyes shut, but she couldn't escape the voice in her head, her voice, cool, logical. *One step and you could be over, one step and it would all be over, so easy, just one—*

Ford tipped his head back, spread his arms, and gave a loud Tarzan-of-the-apes call. It echoed through the empty landscape back to him, reverberating through him, through her.

You're safe, she breathed. *Safe, here with Ford.*

And then he turned and headed across the roof directly toward the little shed with the DANGER DO NOT ENTER! sign.

CHAPTER 8

Sadie was relieved to see that whoever had put up the danger sign also had the foresight to attach a big padlock to the door. So unless Ford had a key or super-strength to wrench the door from the building—

Ford walked up to the door and pressed his palm gently against the side with the hinges. There was a click, like a latch being released, and it swung open from there. *Camouflage*, Sadie registered. The lock and the knob were fake, to fool casual visitors.

I'm impressed, Ford Winter.

Inside he had set up a little workshop with a desk, a chair, an old-fashioned beat box, and an odd assortment of objects she imagined he'd gathered from different construction sites. An easel with a map of Detroit, embellished with drawings and annotations that looked like the ones in Ford's head, stood on one side, but Sadie only caught a glance at it before he stepped to the wall and pushed a button. There was a grinding noise, and the entire space began to move down.

Maybe the DANGER sign *wasn't* a fake.

The "office" cleared the ceiling and stopped, leaving them suspended about sixty feet in the air over the floor of the abandoned factory.

His office was actually the top of the freight elevator, Sadie realized. Wide metal grids formed the four walls, but the view was still unobstructed and, Sadie had to admit, pretty cool. He hit PLAY on the beat box and sat down at the desk.

Sadie braced for some AltCor Trance or Heavy Trip, but it was Louis Armstrong, the jazz trumpeter, and she again found herself thinking, *I'm impressed*.

The music seemed to fill Ford in a way nothing else had, not just covering up his thoughts and emotions but weaving into them, so that they all harmonized, like his whole mind was, for once, working together. He pulled a multicolored round medallion about the size of his palm toward him, and Sadie saw that it was a small stained-glass window of a dog. His mind vibrated with pleasure when he looked at it, and a rainbow of dots came together into Lulu waking up and seeing it installed in her dollhouse, her dolls Bless and Noshe rendered speechless. There were a few pieces missing, and following the quick succession of images and drawings that were now tripping along Ford's mind in every direction, Sadie realized that he planned to use the curved bumpy exterior of the crystal saltshaker for the dog's belly.

Sadie felt confused and like she owed him an apology. Was this really the same guy who hung his clothes on the floor and worked to make people mad at him?

He pulled a brush from one carefully organized drawer and opened the other and froze. There was a manila envelope in it that Sadie could tell he'd never seen before.

His mind flipped back and forth like a just-caught fish, his thoughts saying *Bucky is the only one who knows about this place* while his memory repeated the image of the wild-eyed boy getting on a bus out of town.

Sadie wanted to shake him. *You're right, the best thing to do is sit here debating with yourself. Do not, under any circumstances, open the envelope and see if the answer is inside.*

Finally he tipped its contents onto the desk. It was the Serenity Services file on the death of James Winter. He sat and stared at it for a moment, and Sadie sensed his excitement, but also fear. *What is he afraid of seeing?* she wondered.

Hands shaking, he flipped it open.

```
FILE# 8874-9
VICTIM: JAMES WINTER
STATUS OF VICTIM: DEAD
STATUS OF CASE: CLOSED
SUMMARY:
```

The body of James Winter was found on February 17 at 6:23 A.M. in Playground K just off Happy Alley by two men (occupation unknown, address unknown) who relieved him of his coat, shoes, overalls, and watch but left his underwear.

The victim was shot twice in the head with a small-caliber gun, not found at the scene.

ACTION:

Due to crime's location in City Center drug corridor, the report from the coroner that "the victim had a very high level of the recreational drug R22 in his system," and a ballistics match to a gun used in at least two similar crimes, the incident has been classified as Drug Based Altercation.

Family claims no knowledge of drug use by deceased, but statements from close friends are more ambiguous.

Lincoln Liu: "James and I had a falling-out and had not been spending time together, but I did see him at a nightclub in January at a table well stocked with drugs."

Wilson Moore: "I was with him earlier in the day and he seemed just great. Normal. Probably went to Happy because his girl kept him supplied and she was out of town. But that's just speculativeness."

The girlfriend remains unidentified but wanted for questioning.

UPDATE, MARCH 1

CrimeMatch 2300X data analysis predicts 95.2% probability that victim JAMES WINTER was killed by Offender 00834, identity outstanding.

CASE CLOSED

So James had been a habitual drug user and was shot and killed in a drug deal gone bad. Sadie couldn't see anything for Ford to object to, except maybe that the killer had been identified by his profile but not yet named or arrested.

But that wasn't what bothered Ford. He turned to the coroner's report and waded through all of its technical jargon to the conclusion, which stated that James had been a regular drug user for some months before he died.

"Liar," Ford shouted aloud, startling them both.

He balled his hand into a fist and with three strokes smashed the window he'd been making for Lulu to pieces, *bam bam bam*. Grabbing his hammer, he went to work on the rest of the workshop, smashing the jars where he'd separated tiny pieces of lumber by size, crushing a box of marbles. His eyes weren't focused; he swung at random, holding on for the sound of the crack and the feel of something giving way under his strength.

Stop, Ford, Sadie cried. *You're destroying things you love. You're only hurting yourself.*

Smash smash smash. A pitcher. A jar of seashells. The crystal saltshaker.

He had his hammer up, ready to destroy the old beat box, when the storm of his anger ended. It dried up all at once, replaced by a cooler, more temperate mood. Dropping the hammer, he sank into the desk chair and put his head in his hands.

Hurting yourself, Sadie repeated and realized that was the point. He was mad at himself. But why?

He texted Cali on his way home, not the apology Sadie recommended but with "ALL FORGIVEN," which was better than his first draft, "WHATEVER."

For dinner that night he made something called Spaghetti-n-Meatballz that came in a can and made Sadie glad her taste buds weren't yet in sync with his. And after Lulu went to bed he pulled out a dusty box filled with maps of Detroit.

There were at least twenty, each labeled with a sticker in

handwriting that ranged from that of a ten- or eleven-year-old to that of an adult, but all of it, Sadie thought, Ford's. He flipped past the maps with intriguing names like TREASURE HUNT 3: UNDER DOG and TREASURE HUNT 5: MOTOR SKILLS until he found one labeled BUCKY.

The writing on that label wasn't quite adult, so Sadie guessed it was from when Ford was about fifteen. He shook it, and a card fell out with "Bucky's Rules" handwritten across the top, and below it:

1. Camouflage. Best is Open Secret Variety
2. Secret exit
3. Explosives
4. Safety rope
5. Back-up plans make you weak

I'm not sure I can endorse all of those, Sadie thought.

Ford replaced the card in the box with the other maps and returned it to its high shelf in the closet but put the BUCKY map in the bag he took to work. *If Bucky had left the file*, Sadie heard him decide, *then Bucky must know something and must be nearby.* He'd revisit their old hideouts and find him.

On Tuesday after work Ford went to an old boat that he entered from a secret tunnel beneath a picnic bench, and a fort made out of a decaying camper entirely engulfed by bushes. On Wednesday he rode to a completely deserted tree-lined residential block in the middle of the city, where he stopped at an abandoned house with a secret room through the fireplace. There was no sign of Bucky.

By Thursday he was a tinderbox ready to explode. He was on his way home from work when his phone buzzed with a text. It said, "I HEAR YOU'VE BEEN ASKING ABOUT ME. I'LL BE AT THE CANDY FACTORY TONIGHT AFTER 10:30. YOUR NAME IS WITH THE VIP HOST. PLUM."

Boom! thought Sadie.

CHAPTER 9

His mother was sitting at the kitchen table when Ford walked in the door that night. She was wearing a faded blue sweater, jeans, and a gold locket. Sadie hadn't seen her dressed and out of bed before, and although she still looked frail, she seemed more substantial. More real.

She marked her place in her word jumble with a pencil, folded her hands over it, and looked at him with a smile. "We had a visit from our Roque Community Health Evaluator today." Her tone made Sadie think of Jell-O, artificially bright and sweet. "It went very well."

"Oh, good," Ford said, matching her artificial cheer. He pulled the two cans of Spaghetti-n-Meatballz he'd bought on his way home from his bag.

"They offered to send someone over to help Lulu feel more

comfortable leaving the house again. We just need to set up a time."

"Can they also bring James back to life? Because I actually think that's what it would take." *Stop it*, Sadie wanted to tell him. *Why can't you just listen to your mother instead of having to remind her constantly that James is gone?*

Her brightness dimmed a little. "Why do you always have to be so negative?"

"I'm not."

"Yes you are," Lulu said stepping into the room. She was wearing a pair of purple corduroy pants that were three inches too short and a gray men's Henley shirt.

"That's my shirt," Ford said. "Who said you could borrow it?"

"The fairies that live on the floor of my room, where I found it."

"Copernicus must have put it there." Ford looked sternly at him and said, "Bad dog."

Lulu said, "It's not his fault you failed Drawers in school." She stood on her tiptoes to peer into the pot and made a face. "Spaghetti-n-Meatballz again?"

Ford said, "There's also nothing. We've got plenty of that."

Lulu rolled her eyes. "Why is it spelled with a *z*?"

"It stands for *zee good stuff*," Ford explained solemnly. "It's Italian."

For the first time since Sadie had been in Ford's head, the three of them had dinner together. That meant that Lulu and Ford ate like savages while Mrs. Winter pushed her food around on her plate. "I'd hoped you would be here when the Evaluator came," she said, arranging her Ballz into a pyramid.

"This new one is nice," Lulu put in. "She knows fun games."

"It's the fifth visit you've missed," his mother went on. "But she'll be back Tuesday."

Sadie felt the muscles in Ford's back tense. He kept his eyes on his plate, concentrating on holding back his rising anger. "I'm sure you kept the Roaches entertained."

His mother knocked over her pyramid. "Please don't call them that. They've been very helpful to our family."

"Have they?" Ford looked up, like he was interested, but Sadie knew it was only sarcasm. "As far as I can tell, they come and spy on us—"

"Check on us," Mrs. Winter corrected.

"—to make sure we're not doing drugs, just because one member of our family, who's not even here anymore, did drugs. I'm not sure how much I trust people who think drug addiction is a communicable disease."

Mrs. Winter sighed. "They come to see if we need support. If there's anything they can do to make our family life easier."

"There is," Ford said, and Sadie felt as though he wasn't just leaning into a door to keep the anger from coming through, he was bracing an entire wall. "They could leave us alone. Can you point to one thing they've actually done?"

His mother looked away. "They paid for James's funeral."

Dots of blues and yellows streaked with black coalesced into a churchyard with patches of snow on the ground, a man in a suit speaking, people, more than a hundred of them, crowding close to listen. Finally Lulu in a dress three sizes too big for her, dropping crystal stars on a coffin. Sadie felt whole new registers of anger blossom in Ford as the images faded.

"May I be excused?" Lulu said.

Ford glanced at her plate. "You hardy ate anything."

"Copernicus doesn't feel good," the girl said.

Ford looked at her hard for a moment then said, "Go on. I'll come in to say goodbye before I leave."

Lulu nodded and ran down the hall to her room, slamming the door.

His mother said, "You upset your sister."

"Yeah, it was all me." Ford got up from the table and began to clear the dishes. Sadie noticed the deliberateness of his movements and sensed how much he'd like to smash every plate against the floor.

His mother lit a cigarette, took a short drag, and said nervously, "You're going out?"

He leaned against the counter, drying his hands. "Yep."

Don't do it, Sadie said, sampling the anticipation he was feeling. It was impure, mixed with a little malice and a lot of pain, and it was designed to do only one job.

He said, "I'm going to meet James's girlfriend."

There was a long silence. And then, "You selfish boy."

His mother's words set up a relay in Ford's mind, pinging around his memories like a pinball. His father in a janitor uniform smelling of bleach, the man's face clear, teeth yellow, eyes furious. "You selfish shit, I work to put food on the table, a roof over your head, and you thank me by running away?" His face in Ford's face, the image slightly less clear, Ford's saying, "I wasn't running away, sir, I was at my friend Buck—" interrupted with a growled "Shut up." The man's voice yelling, "Do you know how upset your mother was? Do you know how much pain you caused her?" The dots bigger, images blurrier as though harder to see since the situation made less sense to the child, his mother's arms covered in bruises. "Look how much you hurt your mother when you don't obey. Tell him, Vera." Large dots combining into hypnotic smears making a woman with no face, just a voice that says, "Please, Ford, please, can't you just behave? Why can't you stop upsetting your father?"

Sadie was knocked backward by the memories. The scent of bleach was overpowering. *Betrayal*, Sadie realized. That's what bleach meant. The deepest, most fundamental form of betrayal.

Poor Ford, she thought. *No wonder he and his mother have so little to say to one another.* It was incredible to Sadie that they communicated at all, even in their stunted way.

Then the scent of bleach faded, and Ford demanded, "I'm selfish because I think we should know what really happened to James?"

"You don't care about James," she said, one arm crossed over her chest, the other balanced on it, smoking in small, nervous puffs. "You're doing this for yourself. And to hurt me."

Ford laughed bitterly. "Yeah, can't imagine why I might want to meet my dead brother's girlfriend. The person he spent the most time with before he died. The one he was so busy with we never saw him anymore."

His mother, looking genuinely confused, asked, "Why *would* you?"

He said, "To know. How did this happen? *What* happened?"

His mother stabbed out her cigarette. "I know what happened."

Ford's stomach dropped. Over the lingering scent of cigarette smoke Sadie thought she caught a whiff of cinnamon. It took her a moment to realize that he was surprised and something else . . . hopeful? Was that what the cinnamon meant? "You do? What?"

His mother nodded. "It was a terrible accident. And no amount of looking or asking questions will bring him back. We have to move on with our lives."

Sadie felt Ford's hope twist into an even tighter knot of anger. "Is that what you call this?" He made a wide gesture with his arm, taking in the apartment but clearly meaning more. "Moving on with your life? Our lives? Lulu is afraid to leave the house, I'm destroying beautiful buildings I'd rather be rescuing, and you sit in your room week after week doing these." He picked up her word jumble and fanned it open.

He put it down and then, as though just registering something he'd seen, picked it back up and flipped through it.

It was blank. Every page blank. Not a single puzzle had been done.

Ford frowned at his mother. She looked back, defiantly.

"What do you do all those hours if you're not doing this?" he asked, waving the book toward her.

"None of your business," she said firmly. Only her hand patting the top of the table indicated she wasn't completely calm.

Ford's voice softened. He sat down and reached toward her. "Mom, what is going on?"

She pulled a cigarette from the pack on the table, took one, lit it, and exhaled. Settling back in her seat she said to Ford, "I lost my glasses." She shrugged. "I can't see to do my jumble without them."

"How long?" Ford's voice was still calm. "How long ago did you lose your glasses, Mom?"

"A month." Her eyes went left. "Maybe two."

Ford nodded slowly, taking that in. "Why didn't you tell me?"

"You always seem so upset. I didn't want to give you more to worry about," she said, still not looking at him. "You already worry too much."

Ford's anger rose like a swollen river, blotting out reason. His vision blurred, and his ears rang. He stood with such force that his chair fell backward, sending Copernicus fleeing. "That's it. I can't do this anymore. I'm going out."

"No, Ford. Please don't," his mother said. "Not—not when you're in a mood like this."

"I assure you," he told her, picking up the chair, "it's when I'm in a mood like this that you want me out of the house."

"You'll call attention to yourself or do something stupid, and that could cost us everything."

There was no subtlety in Ford's fury. "How can I avoid doing something stupid? It's in my genes."

Mrs. Winter froze, half in and half out of her seat, staring at him. "You cannot speak to me that way."

"You're right," Ford said in a tired voice. "I owe you an apology. I'll give it to you later." He went to the door. "I'll be home late. Don't wait up. I promise I won't do anything stupid."

At ten forty he was standing in the parking lot of the defunct Surprise Party Outlet Store, opposite the art deco façade of the Candy Factory, watching the streams of people and cars lining up outside.

He'd spent the previous two hours walking through City Center. It was different than Sadie expected, the densely popu-lated parts alternating with abandoned, almost desolate blocks, making a patchwork of light and dark, noise and overgrown silence.

But for the last half hour Ford had been following the elevated train tracks, and there was no quiet there, just noise, from the train and the traffic and the sounds echoing off the partitions. Sadie wondered if that was what appealed to Ford about walking beneath the tracks: that with all that noise it was literally too loud for him to hear himself think.

Now, as he watched a limo disgorge a party of five girls, all wearing only candy, he felt hungry, thirsty, and spent.

You don't have to go in, Sadie told him. *You can skip this.*

He crossed the street, headed up the stairs, and gave his name to the first person he saw. A moment later a petite blonde wearing a Candy Factory apron and boy shorts approached him with a wide smile. "Welcome to the Candy Factory. I'm your VIP host, Morning. Please let me escort you to your party." She linked her pinkie with his and led him into the club.

"Is this your first visit?" Morning asked, looking up at him through her lashes.

Sadie figured Ford would be intrigued or flirt back, but he had almost no reaction at all. "It is."

He seemed more interested in the architecture of the club. It was built in an actual old candy factory, and they'd preserved many of the industrial elements, including one of the old sugar melting vats, which was now a DJ booth topped with an oversized candy thermometer.

"You party is in the Hard Candy section," Morning told him. "We provide a number of services for our VIP guests, should you be interested." She gave him another through-the-lashes glance.

"Thanks. I'll, um, see where tonight goes."

He was nervous, Sadie realized. That's why he'd suddenly become so subdued. It hadn't occurred to her that he might be uncomfortable around large groups of new people just like she was, or that meeting his older brother's girlfriend could be intimidating.

Without thinking, he stopped dead in the middle of a busy doorway as they entered the main part of the club, and Sadie could tell he was dazzled by what he was seeing. The space was cavernous, with thirty-foot-high ceilings. A gigantic chandelier was suspended over the dance floor, probably fifteen feet across, in the shape of a crystal candy bowl filled with enormous blown-glass candies. When his eyes landed on it, Ford laughed with pleasure, and Sadie did too.

Morning coaxed him forward, toward the Hard Candy booth. He followed her up a set of stairs that looked like large plastic-wrapped butterscotch candies. As he climbed them, Sadie heard Ford repeating *I'm Mr. Irresistible, I'm Mr. Irresistible, I'm Mr. Irresistible* in his head, like a mantra.

You have got to be kidding, Sadie thought.

Plum was on a couch but facing away from them, which meant they were seeing just her mass of hair, pretty much exactly the image he had in his mind, only without James.

She turned when he reached the top of the stairs. Beneath the mass of hair were wide-set brown eyes, high cheekbones, and a tiny rosebud mouth. Her olive skin glowed as though it had been polished, and Sadie wondered if that was natural or if she used something to get it to look that way. Their eyes met, and Plum moved her gaze from Ford's eyes to his lips and back again, causing a flurry of trumpets in Ford's mind followed by a tightening in his lower abdomen. Plum gave him a small, know-ing smile.

Was that a trick that worked on everyone, or was Ford just an easy mark? Sadie was asking herself when she realized the horns in his mind had abruptly stopped playing. In their place was the single thought: *Dangerous. Be careful.*

You surprise me, Mr. Winter, she told him, impressed.

Plum motioned Ford into the seat next to her, leaning in to kiss him on both cheeks before giving him her hand and saying, "I'm Plum."

"Ford," he answered, shaking her hand.

"You could have kissed it," Plum said.

His voice low, he said, "I don't kiss until the second date." Despite his caution, Sadie felt the warm wave of his pleasure when Plum laughed. *And presenting . . . Mr. Irresistible*, Sadie thought.

Plum sat back against gold satin pillows to study him, although what she was really doing, Sadie was certain, was giving Ford a chance to study her.

Ford looked from her face to her ankles to her hands to her breasts. His mind was noisy as he took Plum in, but Sadie had trouble gleaning the specifics of his thoughts, partially because the club was so loud and partially because much of it was hap-pening in registers she still hadn't completely deciphered.

She was intrigued to find that the rhythm of his thoughts had begun to mirror the rhythm of the music playing. Maybe that's why people like going to clubs. Because when their thoughts are aligned by the music, they get a sense of intense connection, of thinking alike.

That seemed potentially hazardous to Sadie, especially

when she noticed that the new rhythm made the voice in his head that labeled Plum "dangerous" hard to hear.

Plum leaned over to pour Ford a cocktail from a silver pitcher on the table beside her. She gave him his glass, took her own, and clicked them. "To long Winter nights," she said.

Sadie heard the words forming in his mind a second before he said them. *Seriously? You are better than—*

"And warm juicy Plums," Ford answered.

Sadie groaned. Plum froze, not looking completely nauseated by the terrible line the way she should have, but surprised. As though she'd seen a ghost. "James said the same thing," she told Ford. "The second time we met."

"I guess I rubbed off on him." Ford downed his entire cocktail in two gulps. Sadie couldn't taste it, but she felt its warmth crawling through his body, dulling the ache that the mention of James's name had evoked.

Plum refilled his glass, leaned toward him, and rested her hand on his knee. "Are you like him in other ways?"

"What do you mean?" Ford asked in his deep, Mr. Irresistible voice. His eyes strayed back to her ankles, and Sadie heard him thinking appreciatively that she was curvy in all the right places.

And dangerous, Sadie reminded Ford. *Curvy but dangerous.*

Plum said, "Well, you sound like him. You smell like him. You smile like him. Do you screw like him?"

As I was saying.

"I don't know. We never shared a girl." He downed his new drink in one gulp, and Sadie was aware of the same sticky sensation she'd experienced her first day in his mind.

Plum put her hands on her cheeks in a classic expression of surprise. "Then I may be your only chance to right that wrong."

Ford brought his glass to his mouth, apparently forgetting he'd finished his drink. Black, brown, blue, green dots whisked together into a surprisingly detailed image of Plum lying on a bed, clearly naked but half covered by a tousled blue spread with a pair of red and blue patterned shorts tangled in it. Sadie was sure it wasn't any bed at his house. She wondered if it was what he imagined Plum's bed would look like.

In the next image Plum's face was replaced by Cali's, and Ford said, "Unfortunately, I have a girlfriend."

Sadie would have preferred it without the "unfortunately," but it was nice that he remembered.

"The more the merrier," Plum offered, refilling his drink.

Ford took a gulp. "She wouldn't feel the same way."

Plum sighed. "There goes our bold experiment." She picked up a candy tray from the side table and held it toward him. "They make these special for me. They all have a bit of an extra kick, if you know what I mean."

Ford had been reaching for one, but he pulled his hands back. "Thanks, I'm—I don't use drugs." He took another gulp of his third drink, and Sadie could tell he was starting to get a little fuzzy.

Plum ran her tongue around the edge of a green lozenge and eyed him speculatively. "I was told I should steer clear of you, that you're a bad boy, but I see I was misinformed. Your mother must so proud."

The mention of his mother sent things clanging around Ford's mind. "I wouldn't say that."

Plum looked at him with wide, searching eyes. "Problems with your mother? You know, I'm studying to be an early child-hood psychologist."

You are? Sadie asked incredulously, a second before Ford said, "You are?"

"Yeah, when I have time for classes. Recently it's been tough."

"Because of your job?"

Plum laughed. "No, puppy, I don't have a job. I've just been busy."

"Oh," he said.

"But you can tell me about your mommy problems."

"I just feel like I always let her down," Ford told her.

No no no, Sadie urged. *This is a very bad idea. Someday, somehow, you are going to regret this. If you stop and laugh and pretend you were kidding, you might be able—*

Plum nodded sagely. "In general, when parents make you feel that way, it's a form of projection because they feel helpless. You should try telling her how much you value what she does. It might help turn things around."

Sadie was flabbergasted. That actually sounded like good advice.

Ford's thoughts said the same thing. "Thanks."

Plum gave him a wide, radiant, and very real-looking smile. "I'm not just a pretty face." She leaned close to him. "I also have nice jugs."

He laughed, and Sadie heard him think that she and James must have been really compatible.

Plum moved her shoulders to the music, swaying back and forth next to Ford, and Ford swayed with her. He was picturing her and James together, making up fictitious picnics and outings for them, imagining James telling her about fights they'd had at home over the remote control, about funny things Lulu had said, about their mom. In all of them Plum looked at James with adoration bordering on worship.

They were like his regular memories, suspended dots of color dancing into others, except the colors of these manufactured images were a little brighter, the edges a little more perfect. Ideals. *Fantasy untarnished by reality*, Sadie thought.

He imagined Plum asking James when she'd get to meet his family and James saying later, soon, next month. James wanting to keep her to himself because—

Why? *How had it all gone so wrong*, Sadie heard Ford ask himself. Talking loud, to be heard over the music, he said to Plum, "Why did you give my brother drugs?"

Sadie inhaled sharply. *I don't think not calling attention to yourself means what you think it means.*

Plum kept swaying next to him. "I didn't. He didn't want them. He wouldn't even try them."

It was like someone played every note of a pipe organ at once in Ford's mind. *James didn't do drugs*, he repeated to himself. James didn't do drugs, and he had proof! Plum said it as though there were no question, no dispute. "Why didn't you go to the police and tell them that?" he said loudly over the music.

Plum tilted her head to look at him. "What happened to your brother had nothing to do with me."

"But—"

She put a finger on his lips. "This is my club. I make the rules. And I say we've talked about James enough. No more. Okay?"

Nothing was making sense to Ford now. Sadie felt his mind

reeling around, grasping at random snippets as he tried to find something substantial he could count on for support. "If you don't have a job, how do you have a club?" he asked.

Plum laughed with real amusement, wafting it over the sound of the music. "I have rich friends."

"Like a sugar daddy?" Ford's mind got even more noisy, the technicalities of James dating a girl who was kept by another man boomeranging around.

Plum stopped him with a flick of her wrist. "I do not have a sugar daddy. I have a *patron*." She gave him a coquettish look over a one-shoulder shrug. "A very generous patron."

"What do you have to do for his *patronage*?" Ford asked.

She tapped him on the nose. "Nothing that would affect you, puppy."

Ford said, "He really doesn't care what you do?"

"There's a vast difference between caring about *me* and caring what I do." She walked her fingers up Ford's chest on the last three words playfully, but something hard had come into her eyes, and Sadie had the impression Ford had struck a nerve.

Be careful, Sadie warned. *Don't provoke her.*

"Why doesn't he want you all to himself? Doesn't he love you?"

Or you could provoke her.

Plum's gaze became steely. "You really are just like your brother. You don't do drugs, you get drunk on three drinks, and you think that the ultimate compliment for any girl is that a guy wants her to belong to him." Plum shifted, moving away from Ford. "Your brother was going to rescue me from this," she sneered, her hand making a wide gesture that took in the club, the chandelier, the beautifully groomed crowd, ending with the thick gold bangle on her wrist. "He was going to *let* me be his full-time girlfriend, pick me for his one and only, free me. As though he was doing me a favor."

Ford's mind was a windstorm of confused thoughts. He said, "When was the last time you saw James?"

"Before he died." Plum snapped her fingers, and two women in leather pants, tank tops, and shoulder holsters took up stations behind her. "Mr. Winter isn't feeling up to par tonight," she said. "Please show him out the back."

"I'm not done," Ford protested.

Plum patted his face. "But I am, puppy."

She slid down the couch toward her other guests and the two women flanked Ford. As they walked him down the stairs he stopped and turned back.

"Did you love him? At all?" he called, but Plum, busy nuzzling the neck of a girl with a purple pixie cut, didn't seem to hear.

The question was so raw, so sincere, it caught at Sadie and made her heart ache a little. *How do you keep doing that, Ford Winter?* she wanted to ask. *Have me swallowing back a lump in my throat one minute . . .*

CHAPTER 10

And rolling my eyes the next. "I don't have a sugar daddy, I have a *patron*," Ford repeated in a terrible approximation of Plum's voice as he relieved himself on the wall next to the "rear VIP entrance" of the Candy Factory.

There were no VIPs there that night, so Ford had the whole alley to himself, and he was running through all the things he wished he'd said to Plum, an alarming number of which seemed to begin with "Oh yeah, well," when Sadie felt his senses go on alert and his ears prick.

There were shuffling footsteps and whispers coming from the darkness farther down the alley. A voice rang out sharply, "Careful with that!"

A voice Ford recognized. Linc's voice.

He stood stock-still, listening.

"Put some pep in that step pronto, we don't have all night," another familiar voice said. *Willy.* "Hate to have to tell the Pharmacist we got us a bunch of slackers."

Willy's voice was good-natured, but there was definitely a threat beneath it. *You should go*, Sadie told him. *Whatever is going on down there is none of your business.*

As though he'd heard her, Ford buttoned his pants—
Excellent.

—and started down the alley thinking, *Good, it's time we all had a little chat.*

No, Sadie admonished. His motor skills seemed dulled by the drinks, and he wasn't entirely steady on his feet. *Not good. No chats. Chats in dark alleys fall squarely into the "don't do anything stupid" category your mother was talking about. You should go in the other—*

Something crashed. Linc's voice boomed, "Idiot," and the sound of a kick connecting with hard bone echoed off the walls.

Ford's mind flashed with images from childhood, a cookout with James and Linc and Willy, building a raft at the lake, playing cowboys and outlaws, telling ghost stories. Over it she heard his thoughts slurring, *Got to talk to them, find out what happened to James.*

"What are all of you looking at? Get back to work. Wouldn't want my friend to have to do any more damage," Willy said, still lighthearted, now even more threatening.

This is bad, Sadie pressed. *You need to go.*

Ford stumbled forward. *Why'd they lie about Plum?* his mind asked now. *Supposed to be James's friends, but they lied about every—*

The alley suddenly went quiet.

He kept going, taking another step, and another. His head was noisy, but the silence in the air was raw and unnerving. *As if something is waiting at the end of the alley*, Sadie thought. *Something you don't want any part of.* Unhappily she felt for the panic button, just to know it was there.

Ford stopped walking. Sadie let out a breath she hadn't realized she'd been holding.

And then he stepped into the middle of the alley and hollered, "Hey! Hey, guys."

Are you insane? she yelped. *This is idiocy. You're going to get—*

A bright light flashed in Ford's face, a hand grabbed him by the neck, and Linc's voice growled in his ear, "Tell me what the hell you're doing here and I might not slit your throat."

Ford's mind froze. Sadie pushed the panic button. From somewhere far away she heard a computer voice say, "Alert system on standby. Press to proceed to Ready."

Linc's arm was on Ford's windpipe, pressing him against the hard brick wall of the alley. Ford twisted toward him, to try to see his face, but Linc was wearing a headlamp like a miner, and the brightness was blinding.

Ford's eyes veered off, giving Sadie a glimpse farther into the alley. There was a panel truck with four guys standing motionless in front of it. They had computer boxes in their arms, clearly in the process of unloading them into the building opposite Plum's club.

"I was over there," he managed to choke out finally, gesturing across the alley with his chin. "Heard—your voice. Wondered why—"

Linc's arm pressed harder against Ford's windpipe, cutting off his air. "Don't wonder. Don't think. Don't ask any questions. Do you understand?" His eyes, below the light, bored into Ford's. They were calm and deadly.

Ford started to nod, but the pain of trying to move made him realize the question was rhetorical.

"I haven't beaten the crap out of you because you are James's brother," Linc went on. "But that ends now. You are going to turn and leave. If I see you around here, if I see you, period, I will beat you so you can't walk for a week."

A slideshow of images resumed in Ford's mind, the group of friends at a winter formal, a spring dance, hayrides, joyrides, prom. "Why are you doing this?" he croaked.

"I said no questions. Leave. Now. Before I change my mind." Linc stepped back and Ford staggered against the building.

He stayed there, rubbing his neck, trying to gauge what would happen if he lunged at Linc.

Walk away, Sadie shouted.

"Go," Linc said.

Ford started down the alley, bleach-scented betrayal washing over him. Stepping into the street, he was engulfed by the noise of cars and people arriving at the club. The voices roared in his head, and his eyes flicked from one dark building to another, like an animal seeking refuge.

He turned at the first major intersection and zigzagged back toward the noise of the elevated train tracks. Sadie realized he wasn't wandering idly, and after ten minutes she sensed there was something familiar about the street they were on.

They'd passed Huang's PawnIt and were in front of DollarDollarDollar when it clicked: This was where Ford had been in the video footage of him she'd seen at the Survaillab before entering Syncopy. He'd been standing with his back to the camera, a little farther along, looking through a fence into—

Ford stopped in front of Your Neighborhood Drug and stared straight ahead into the playground that filled the space between it and the corner. Even though the CCTV video had been shot during the day, the playground had been deserted, and she saw now that was because the gate, which opened off an alley behind it, was padlocked shut.

It was lit with one light that blasted the middle, creating a weird pastiche of peeling red and blue paint and stark shadows. There was a swing set with three swings, a tube slide, a set of monkey bars, and two large plastic animals, a rabbit and a turtle, on thick springs for kids to ride like horses. In the center was a merry-go-round, and when Ford's eyes reached it his mind started to vibrate.

Sadie couldn't figure out what was happening at first. The pressure in his head built quickly, but not in the contracting, suffocating way it did when he was angry; this was more expansive, like something on the verge of exploding. Dots and colors ricocheted around, starting to settle into an image one moment and knocked out of it the next, as though some force was deliberately interfering with what his mind wanted.

All at once the pressure gave way. The dots fell into place, forming an image of a man in his underwear propped up on the merry-go-round. His feet were bare, toes turned outward, his mouth made an O shape, and there were two dark holes in his head where gunshots had entered. His eyes, above the O, were wide open. They looked like Ford's eyes, the eyes she remembered from that first day in the video, only they weren't. This was James.

This was where James had died.

Ford gave a low, agonized groan and shut his eyes, turning to rest his head on the brick wall of the pharmacy for support. A tornado of sound rose inside of him, blotting out the image. Voices whipped by, faster and faster, and Sadie struggled to tease them apart. She caught Ford's mother, ". . . such a good boy . . ." Official-sounding men's voices, ". . . found this morning . . ." ". . . gunshot . . ." ". . . drugs . . ." ". . . sorry for your loss . . ." ". . . come around to see if there's anything you need . . ."

And then the dots pulled together into the interior of a wooden shack, white winter light, everyone wearing parkas and hats and mittens. Years ago, six or seven, Willy big even then, saying to Ford, "And what will you do with your part of the fortune?"

"Build a nice house for me and James and my mom and Lu."

The memory of everyone laughing, Linc the hardest. "You think you can get James to come live with you forever?"

Ford, confident, nodding. "The house is going to be sweet."

James smiling. "That's my brother. Me, I'd get a motorcycle, throw a huge going-away party for all my friends, and then take off and ride around the world. What about you, Willy?"

"Gun range and rabbits." Willy, needing no time to come up with an answer. "Never be lonely or hungry."

Linc set apart even in the memory, nervous, balking when they ask him about his plans for the fortune, saying, "If I tell, you'll laugh." Heads shaking, hands raised in solemn promises not to so much as giggle or fake cough. "I want to be a pastor. I'd use the money to go to divinity school and give the rest to my mom."

The dots dispersed, and Sadie saw a faint image of a golden rope spiraling downward, with a black glove reaching toward it.

Ford turned and slammed his fist into the wall of the drugstore.

The stinging seemed to clear his head, help him focus. He slid down the wall and lowered his head, his left hand clutching the prickling knuckles of his right. There were tiny beads of blood on it, but Ford didn't seem to notice. He was shaking, wracked with grief. "I'm so sorry, James," he said aloud. "I should have been there. I should have paid attention. I'm so sorry."

The pain in his hand was no match for the pain inside of him. It was huge but also somehow weightless, leaving him feeling hollow and vulnerable.

Light strafed his eyes. Sadie felt every muscle in his body tense, immediately on guard. It was just a Royal Pizza delivery van, he saw, and relaxed, but it brought him back to reality.

He pushed himself to his feet and began walking, navigating around knots of people trying to outbid one another to win the favor of the scarce taxis. Crossing the street under the tracks he headed up a block, where the absence of the train made it slightly quieter, if no less busy. While Ford waited to cross at an intersection he pulled out his phone and checked for messages. There were none from Cali.

Sadie expected him to get angry and decide to wait her out, but instead he surprised her by dialing Cali's number.

Between the noise on the street and the way his thoughts were still subdued, almost muffled, Sadie had no idea what he was going to say. Apparently he didn't either, because when Cali's voice mail picked up he hesitated so long he was disconnected. He dialed again, and this time he was ready.

"Cali, it's me. Ford. Your stupid boyfriend. God, I hope I'm still your boyfriend." He walked as he spoke, weaving between people. "Look, I know you're mad at me for . . . it doesn't matter for what. I was an ass, and I'm sorry. I—"

Watch out! Sadie yelled in his head as he stepped off a curb in front of a car, and Ford jumped back. The driver yelled, "Pay attention, idiot!" and Sadie braced for Ford to do something dumb, but he just waved and kept talking to Cali's voice mail.

"Did you know when my mom was younger she wanted to be a painter? She had an art scholarship and everything, to go study in Paris."

He came to another corner, but this time he stopped before stepping into oncoming traffic. "That's where she was heading when she got pregnant with James. Can you imagine? She wanted my dad to go with her, said they could be a family in France, but he said his prospects were better here so they stayed. *Prospects*," Ford snorted. "He was an accountant at a fertilizer factory, did I tell you that? When I was in kindergarten someone noticed he'd been giving himself an unauthorized weekly bonus. After that the only job he could get was as a janitor. And he always blamed it—"

Ford turned a corner and was standing on the edge of an eight-lane street with thick, fast-moving traffic.

"—on me," he finished his sentence.

The closest crosswalk was blocks away, so he decided to cross right where he was.

This is a very bad idea, Sadie said. Her hands tightened, looking for something to hold on to, and a distant a computer voice said, "Alert system ready. Press for immediate removal."

"No!" Sadie yelled, her heart rate skyrocketing. That had been a mistake; she'd completely forgotten about the panic button. She didn't want to leave. Not now, not at all. She wanted to stay, to hear everything.

Using her fingertips she thrust the panic button as far out of reach as she could, so there would be no chance of accidentally touching it, and took three deep breaths to slow her pulse.

"My mother gave up everything to have James," Ford said, experimentally stepping into the road and then jumping back as a motorcycle sped by. "And I don't think she regretted it. I was an afterthought, and Lulu came after my dad got out of jail, when they were 'trying' again. There's no way I can ever take James's place for her, I know, but I'm worried now that he's gone she regrets"—Ford crossed one lane, waited for a minivan to pass, then ran across the other three to the center divider—"having us."

He stood there watching for a break in the traffic. It was heavier in this direction, and harder to see because it came from around a bend. "It's probably why she feels like me trying to find out what happened to him is disrespectful. Because nothing matters except that he's gone. And maybe it's why I'm so desperate to figure it out. Because I feel like I'm responsible. Like I should have been able to prevent it. Should have given him a lifeline." He took a deep breath. "Who knows, maybe I feel like if I can give my mom the truth, she'll love me too."

He moved the phone from his ear to sprint across the next four lanes, sending up a chorus of horns.

"Are you there?" he panted when he was safely across. "Of course you are. Or aren't. I wonder if you'll even listen to this. You're the only good thing in my life, and I've been driving you away. When I look back, over my past, I feel like I've lost a lot of people I should have been able to count on. My dad. Bucky. Linc. Sometimes I feel so completely alone. I think—maybe— I'm pushing you away so I can't lose you too. Like I'll hurt me before you can hurt me. Does that make sense?"

He waited at another light, and Sadie saw they were almost at the end of his block. "But you've always fought for me— you're the only one who thinks I'm worth fighting for. Will you accept my apology? If you will, I'll be at your house to pick you up for dinner tomorrow night at seven P.M. In the blue-checked button-down." He turned the corner onto his street. "And if you—oh god, no. *No!*"

There was a fire engine, two Serenity Services cars, and a RCHE van parked in front of Ford's building. He looked up and saw Lulu being held between two green-shirted RCHE men.

Lulu saw him too. In a single, fleeting motion she slipped away from her guards and took off running toward him.

A car horn blared, brakes squealed, and Ford yelled, "*Sto—*" Silence.

Something was wrong.

Sadie couldn't see or hear anything. Her head spun and nausea swept through her. She felt like she'd been pushed out of a carnival ride, only there was no ground beneath her stumbling feet. She hung there like that for a moment, suspended.

Then all at once her body became incredibly heavy and she was plummeting, being dragged down into a freezing cold void.

Where was Ford's heartbeat?

Fear gripped her. She recalled him running, eyes only on Lulu. Heard the horn, the brakes—

She groped desperately around her mind, looking for any sign, any trace of him.

Why can't I hear your heartbeat?

He was gone.

Don't you dare be dead, Ford Winter, she thought desperately. She fumbled for the panic button. *Do not let go. You're not alone. I'll fight for you. Don't you dare give up, where the hell is your heartbeat, come on, Ford, come—*

White light flooded her eyelids and she heard the long, thin, solid beep of a monitor flatlining.

CHAPTER 11

"Minder Seventeen out of stasis."

Sadie opened her eyes and saw Catrina's face silhouetted against the dome of the Stasis Center.

"Thank god. We have to get help to—" Sadie tried to sit up, but her head was jerked back by the sensors attached to it.

Catrina put a hand on her chest, gently pushing her down. "Relax."

Sadie started ripping sensors off. "There was a terrible accident. Is Ford dead?"

Catrina's lips pursed slightly. "It's more correct to call him Subject Nine. For anonymity."

"Yes, fine, Subject Nine." Sadie struggled with the sensors on her arms. God, there were so many. "Did he die? What's beeping? How did I get here?"

Catrina frowned. "Calm down. Your Subject is fine. That was us pausing Syncopy to take you out of stasis."

Sadie realized the beep of the monitor had stopped. "What? Why?"

"Everyone gets reviewed after a week," Catrina said. "I'm sure Curtis went over that."

"It's two days early," Sadie objected, plucking off the wires she could reach. "Never mind, we need to help. I think Fo— Subject Nine was hit by a car."

Catrina pulled the computer attached to Sadie's Stas-Case toward her. "Your Subject's monitors are all reading normal."

"No," Sadie breathed, her hand going to her mouth. "Lulu."

Catrina tapped the keys. Across the side of the Stas-Case, Sadie was able to see a monitor with an overhead view of the area around Ford—Subject 9's—house. "There are no ambulances dispatched to your Subject's present location," Catrina reported.

Sadie closed her eyes and let out a long breath. *Thank you*, she said silently. *Thank you for being alive*. There were tears pricking her eyes, but she was sure they were just from coming out of stasis.

She opened her eyes and looked at the screen again. She was surprised by how neat and organized it appeared from above compared to how chaotic the neighborhood felt on the street. "How did you know where to find him?"

"Each neuronano relay has a serial number," Catrina explained, reaching over to pull the relays from Sadie's back. "It transmits the Subject's location coordinates to our systems as a safety measure so we can find them if we have to."

"You can find anyone by serial number?" Sadie asked, fascinated.

"Anyone with a neuronano relay," Catrina said. "There are legal limitations, of course. We're only allowed to track individuals who are Subjects in our studies, and only for scientific purposes. We can't just go looking up serial numbers randomly."

Sadie was still focused on the satellite image, but she felt Catrina watching her closely. "There were security cars all around his house. I only see one now. Is there any way to know why they were there?"

"5-29. Noise complaint from a neighbor about a dog barking," Catrina said. Then, speaking to someone over Sadie's shoulder, she said, "Sadie was concerned that something might have happened to her Subject."

"By all means put her mind to rest," Curtis answered, coming around to smile at Sadie.

In a slightly too bright voice Catrina said, "Apparently the dog wouldn't stop barking. It was because a cigarette had started a small fire in one of the bedrooms."

It has happened, Sadie thought, forgetting about everything else. *Ford's worst fear.* His mother had lit the house on fire, and Copernicus had saved them. Would Ford be angry or relieved?

Relieved first, Sadie concluded. After, he would slip back into anger and somehow turn it against himself, deciding that he should have been there, it was his fault.

Curtis gave her a hand to help her out of the Stas-Case, and Sadie wobbled against him. "Sorry."

"Totally normal," he assured Sadie.

Sadie felt Catrina's eyes boring into her. Her legs felt jittery, like someone had replaced her knees with uncalibrated gyroscopes. "What happens now?"

Catrina looked up quickly from the monitor at Curtis, then back down. Curtis said, "Now you rest. And later we'll do your debrief."

"How long does that last?" Sadie suddenly felt tense. What did the glance Catrina had given Curtis mean? Why were the lights so bright? Why was everyone looking at her?

Curtis gave her a bland, pleasant smile. "They'll ask you some questions and then make their recommendation. Strictly routine."

"You mean about whether I continue," Sadie said, remembering what he'd said about only half of the Minders making it past the first week. It had seemed hypothetical then, no big deal, but now—

She looked frantically from Catrina to Curtis. Catrina was busy on the computer, but Curtis said, "I'm on the Committee myself. Don't worry."

Was there something off about his smile? Sadie wondered. Was it . . . condescending? Nervous? As the adrenaline from her return faded, everything was becoming hard to read and opaque. Even when she didn't know what a sensation meant in Ford's mind, at least it was real, raw. From the outside people seemed so carefully processed and bland.

Catrina cupped her chin in her hand. "Interesting. This wasn't the first 5-29 at your Subject's residence. There was a similar fire before, the dog barked, and a complaint was filed. Under the Domestic Animal Security and Safety Code, if there is another incident the dog will be terminated."

Sadie had learned through Ford's collection of mental images that Copernicus had been James's dog—their last living connection to the golden boy. "It would be a real blow to the family if they lost him."

Catrina's eyes lit up. "You could get lucky then."

Sadie steadied herself against the edge of the Stas-Case. "What?"

"If termination is ordered. The removal of a pet from a family is a perfect catalyst for mild to low trauma."

Sadie's mind stumbled over that. "I'm not sure I would wish that on someone."

"This isn't *someone*, it's your Subject," Catrina reminded her coolly. "That's why we don't personalize them."

Sadie felt like she was at sea, floating somewhere out of her body.

"What Catrina is referring to is the tendency of trauma to work like a crucible." Curtis made a cup with his hand. "It concentrates underlying family dynamics, burning off the extraneous elements so you can blow them out of the way." He gave a puff and his pretend cup vanished.

Catrina looked at Sadie, critically. "Progress comes from being unafraid to make hard choices. Science is brutal."

Her words chimed within Sadie's memory, but it was only when she was walking to her assigned guest room that she realized what it was: They reminded her of her own words in her Mind Corps interview.

The debrief the next day was scheduled for eleven in the morning on the garden terrace of the manor house. Sadie rode alone in the elevator to the surface, still disoriented by her removal from stasis. It wasn't just the change in viewpoint without

Ford's additional four inches. Getting out of the shower she'd looked in the mirror and almost screamed at seeing a stranger in the bathroom before realizing she was looking at her own reflection.

A man in a dark suit escorted Sadie through a set of French doors onto a flagstone terrace bordered by a rolling lawn that sloped down to the lake. After the uniform, sterile atmosphere of stasis and subbasement fourteen, being outside was like waking up with new senses. She felt the air on her skin and experienced a touch of vertigo at so much empty space, so much green. It was amazing how quickly your perspective could shift. Sadie couldn't see City Center from where she stood, but she felt it.

It was a pleasant Saturday morning, little clouds whipping across the sky above the bend in the river where it met the lake. A table with a white cloth was set with a gilt-edged teapot and cups for five, but she was the first one there. She was hovering awkwardly near the table when a voice from the French doors said, "Sadie Ames," and she turned and saw Miranda Roque.

Miranda was dressed in a cream-colored pantsuit with a large gold necklace. She wore a mammoth sapphire on her second finger, easily an inch in diameter, but no other jewelry. Her face was tanned and lined and beautiful, Sadie thought, from years of actually using it, without relying on the fillers that Sadie's mother and her friends all used.

"Come chat," Miranda said, sitting down in one of the seats around the table. "If the others can't be on time, that's their problem."

"Hello, Ms. Roque." Sadie took a seat near her, catching the scent of roses and wood smoke.

"Miranda," she corrected, pouring tea. She pushed a cup toward Sadie. "So, are you enjoying it?"

There was no reason to ask what "it" was, but Sadie had to think a little before answering. "Yes, although I'm not sure if *enjoy* is the right word. Syncopy is amazing, though. I'm anxious to get back."

Miranda gave a little cackle. "Don't try to butter me up, Ames. Not good for my arteries."

Sadie felt herself blushing. "I didn't mean—"

"Oh, yes you did. Don't do it again." Miranda put a plate of butter cookies between her and Sadie. "Tell me about your Subject."

Sadie plunged in. "He's impulsive, which can be maddening. And—"

"Be specific, Ames," Miranda barked. "What do you mean by *impulsive*? He speaks without thinking? He's spontaneous? Those are not the same."

Sadie had never thought about that before. "I suppose both."

Miranda nodded. "Often go hand in hand, a continuum. It's the sign of a consciousness that's still growing. He must be passionate."

Sadie was sorry to see the others arrive then. Miranda was the only person she'd encountered since she'd been back she felt comfortable talking to.

The rest of the Committee came together in a single elevator load: Curtis, a woman with auburn hair and olive skin named Naomi from Neurotraction, and a guy with short curly dark hair and tawny skin named Johann from Paracartography. Miranda tapped the table impatiently while they were introduced and then jumped back into her questions.

"What was the first emotion you identified from your Subject?" she asked.

"Anger," Sadie answered without needing to think. "He's very angry."

Miranda stopped drumming her fingers, and her eyes sparked with interest. "Anger. So potent. I once funded a project about creating fuel out of anger. Never came to anything, but the premise was sound. Biggest untapped energy resource in the world."

Sadie tried to imagine that. "How would you harvest it?"

Miranda laughed. "Getting the anger was the easy part. You can do that on a street corner for free. No"—she leaned closer to Sadie—"the challenge was converting it once you had it. Anger is like oil, it bubbles up from the subconscious and is available to be collected at a fairly superficial level. It may feel like it's the basis of all your subject's actions now, but anger is just a sign of much richer and more complex veins below."

"Like what?" Sadie asked, riveted.

Miranda shrugged. "Most common is probably guilt. Very, very rich source because it's directed inward. A good vein of guilt will produce forever, providing no one messes with it." She rolled her eyes upward, thinking. "Thwarted wishes and hopes are good too, but those weaken over time." Her eyes came back to Sadie. "In general it's the damage we do to ourselves that lasts the longest. We love to take responsibility for things outside our control and then blame ourselves when they fail."

"Do you think people do that because it confirms some sense of inadequacy in them?" Sadie asked, thinking of Ford.

"Absolutely," Naomi said, and Sadie sensed she was more interested in impressing Miranda than doing any debriefing.

"That's a bit clichéd," Miranda countered. Naomi looked chastened. "I'd say it's because taking blame is more comfortable than admitting we might be powerless. That's our flaw: our fear of not knowing. As I get older, though, I find the unknown much more interesting. Nice to have surprises sometimes." She leaned back. "Of course, he could actually be guilty of something."

Sadie felt like her mind was bending in new directions. "If my Subject's anger is the result of a guilty conscience, should I help him get past it?"

"You can't," Johann said. "That's not what you are there to do, and you'd need to get into the subconscious. No one can do that."

"That's B.S., Johann," Naomi snapped. "It's rare, but it's been done."

"Only a handful of very gifted Minders have ever seen a subconscious, let alone gotten in," Curtis explained. "It's hard to find the door and even trickier to get past it. You need to thoroughly understand the Subject's defense mechanisms."

"What about dreams?" Sadie asked, wondering if she should admit that she hadn't yet been able to access Ford's. "Couldn't you get in that way?"

"It's not possible to enter dreams while in Syncopy," Johann said, and Sadie was flooded with relief. "The dreaming mind is the closest to stasis state, so it doesn't trigger the relay the same way."

Naomi rushed to add, "But every Minder who's gotten into the subconscious has done it when their Subject is asleep. Maybe minds are structured that way on purpose."

Sadie took that in. "Are there big differences between minds?"

That made everyone at the table laugh. "Vast differences," Miranda said. "I've been in minds that use sounds to generate holograms, minds like prisms, minds where there was only scent."

"I had one that was like rocks, heavy and hard to get through," Naomi said.

"That's what I always imagined my ex-husband's mind was like," Miranda said drily, giving Naomi a nod of approval.

Johann said, "Once I was in the mind of a boy who went blind when he was twelve. It was like a picnic on a huge green lawn. Groups of people all around in clusters, talking. Some of them were real people, and some of them represented projects he was working on. There was a band, and it played songs that went with his emotions. And there was a tent, because when he got upset or angry it rained."

"Wow," Sadie breathed. She looked at Curtis. "What about you?"

He shook his head. "My claustrophobia prevents me from entering Syncopy."

There was one of the threadbare silences around the table that you get when someone asks after the health of an aunt who died years earlier. "I'm sorry," Sadie said, "I had no idea."

"That's okay. Our technology is always changing, and I'm still hoping for a shot one day." He gave her a nice smile, then shifted back to the interview. "Let's get back to your Subject. Would you say his life is stable or unstable?"

Sadie thought about it. "Stable. For the most part it has just been going to work and going home."

"For the most part?" Curtis repeated, cocking his head.

"One afternoon he got a file anonymously. It was the Serenity Services file about his brother's murder."

Naomi said, "It came in the mail? We can trace that."

Sadie shook her head. "He has a makeshift workshop in an abandoned building, and one day it just appeared there, in his desk."

Naomi asked, "Did he know who it was from?"

"He suspected someone named Bucky, a friend who disappeared a few years ago, but he doesn't even know where Bucky is."

Curtis looked at Johann. "Check your Off Grid files for a Bucky when you get downstairs." He turned to Sadie. "How did he react to the file?"

"He was glad to get it." Sadie thought about the havoc he wreaked afterward. "But disappointed by its content."

Naomi started typing on a tablet. "His brother's name was James Winter?"

Sadie nodded, and within a minute Naomi had downloaded the file to her computer and circulated it to the others. Sadie was struck by how easy it was for her, and yet how hard for Ford, whose requests for the file had been repeatedly denied.

Everyone but Miranda scanned it. She sat looking into the distance like she was bored.

Naomi set her tablet back on the table. "There doesn't seem to be anything suggestive here. What was the issue?"

"He was struggling with the idea of his brother as a drug addict," Sadie explained.

"The coroner's report seems to be pretty definitive," Johann said.

Sadie said, "His brother's girlfriend made it sound like he didn't use drugs at all. I know there were drugs in his system, but what if they were forced on him? Or introduced after he was killed to make it look—"

Every pair of eyes at the table was wide, staring at her, and she realized she'd made a mistake. Trying to solve your Subject's brother's murder was probably a little more objectionable than objective. "Sorry, I think maybe spending so much time in my head has made my imagination . . ." She let that taper off as it dawned on her that "imagination" wasn't much better.

Miranda's fingers tapped the tabletop again. "So he is undertaking a private inquiry of his own." Her eyes made a circuit of the others. "I've heard enough. I think we can—"

Johann said apologetically, "I've got one more quick question. You mentioned a workshop in an abandoned building. Can you tell us where? We keep a register of alternative building uses. We're trying to see what creates communities versus what creates crime."

Sadie felt herself hesitate for a split second as though she was violating a friend's confidence. *What is wrong with you?* "It's the Detroit Wire Company," she said. "But I don't know where it is exactly. My sense of direction is—"

"Legendary," Curtis put in with a wry smile.

"I haven't heard of anyone using that before." Johann typed the name into his tablet. His expression changed. "It looks like the building was pulled down three years ago."

Sadie sat forward. "That's impossible."

"I should remind you, Sadie, that we expect full disclosure about the activities of your Subject," Curtis said, no smile now. "Our project can only proceed with complete trust and candor." He wore a polite, somewhat perplexed expression, and his voice was mild but his eyes had hardened.

The gazes of the others at the table became reptilian, cool and appraising, as though looking for a crack to explore.

"That's what the sign said," Sadie told them. "It might be what he and his friend Bucky call camouflage, hiding things like entrances in plain sight by disguising them. All I saw—"

Naomi pounced. "I thought 'Bucky' disappeared. When did you hear them discuss this?"

"I didn't. It was written on an old note For—Subject Nine had in a box." Sadie felt panicky, desperate for them to believe her. "And there was a map of other secret hangouts where he and Bucky spent time. He visited three of them."

Johann said, "Where were they?"

I can fix this, Sadie thought. "They—" She had no idea. "One of them is an old ferry boat in an empty lot. The lot has a high wall around it so you can't see it from the street. Another was an old camper, completely overgrown by bushes so it looks like a bush itself." She felt the clammy attention of predators waiting to strike. "And there was an abandoned house with a big tree in the yard, on a block of other abandoned houses, with a secret door through the fireplace."

Johann read from his tablet: "A ferry behind a tall fence, a camper concealed in a bush, and a vacant house with a tree. Is that right, Miss Ames?"

"I'm afraid so." What was she supposed to say? Her mouth filled with the bitter taste of coffee grounds. A bead of sweat rolled down her back. "There's one other place. It's where he was when I first entered Syncopy. They call it the Castle, and it seems to be a sort of social club for Chapsters. All of Ford's brother's friends go there." She added. "I think some of them might be gangsters."

"We already know about that place," Curtis said dismissively, with a glance at Johann. "The old University Club."

Johann put his tablet down. "Right."

"I think we have enough," Curtis said.

"Are you sure?" Sadie asked. "His brother's friends seem to be involved in something criminal. We saw them beating someone up because he didn't have money for—"

"*We?*" Miranda asked, cutting her off.

"That is, For—I mean, Subject Nine did," Sadie stuttered.

The table was a sea of hostile faces. Curtis gave her what she assumed was meant to be an encouraging smile and said, "You can go, Sadie. We'll be in touch."

CHAPTER 12

"*Subbasement fourteen, going up*," the pleasant female voice of the elevator said Sunday morning.

We'll be in touch. Even now, almost twenty-four hours later, the words echoed unpleasantly in Sadie's head. She gripped the rail against the back wall to keep from shaking.

"*Subbasement twelve, going up.*"

She'd spent the afternoon after her debriefing in her room in Mind Corps guest quarters, wallowing in self-recrimination and doubt. She'd gone to dinner, picked at a plate of meatballs she didn't remember asking for, and had been slinking back to her room when Catrina stopped her in the hall.

"I heard about this afternoon," Catrina said, aiming right for Sadie's most tender part. She crossed her arms over her chest and shook her head. "I feel partially responsible. I warned Curtis this would happen."

Sadie felt a flash of confusion mixed with anger. "You warned him? About what?"

Catrina's voice stayed flat and emotionless. "That you're too soft. Too gullible." Catrina's eyes were cool hard stones, appraising and unreadable. "You think you know your Subject. You believe what you see. But you have no idea of the deception he's capable of. You have to be ruthless if you want to do good, and you don't have that in you."

Sadie felt like her entire perspective, all her perceptions, were completely off. *Soft? My problem is that I'm too cold, too analytical,* her mind protested. "Wouldn't being ruthless yield just as compromised results as being too trusting?" she shot back.

Catrina gave her a tiny smile. "I've made you defensive. I'm sorry." Nothing in her tone backed that up. "When you're feeling rational again, you'll see that I'm right." Her eyes shifted and Curtis appeared then, walking in their direction. She gave him a brusque nod. "Curtis."

He was equally cool back. "Catrina. You two look like you're discussing weighty matters."

"Tradecraft," Catrina told him. "You don't have to worry your pretty little head about it." She said to Sadie, "It was a pleasure talking to you," and disappeared across the hall, through the door marked BRICOLAGE.

"Subbasement ten, going up."

"What do they do in there?" Sadie had asked Curtis, nodding toward Catrina's retreating back. She was desperate to do anything other than talk about the debriefing. "I've been wondering since the first day of orientation."

Curtis had raised an eyebrow at her evasion but played along, saying matter-of-factly, "They work on the targeted use of archetypes and myths to channel behavior. The idea of the boogeyman, for example, which begins as a tool of parental control to frighten children but assumes mythic powers as members of a community hide their misdeeds under his name. An old idea but an effective one that plays on the way minds link thought, memory, and emotion to create meaning."

"Fascinating," Sadie said, hoping he'd go on.

Curtis laughed. "Maybe, but that's all the deflection you get. Are you going to tell me what just happened with Catrina, or should I guess?"

Sadie hesitated for a moment then blurted, "She said I wasn't ruthless enough. That I'm too soft."

Curtis looked bemused. "Did she?" He shook his head and dug his hands into his pockets. "I wouldn't listen to Catrina. I think you're perfect."

Sadie's stomach fluttered. "I thought you and she were"— she swallowed, looking for an adult way to put it—"intimate." *And failing miserably*, she congratulated herself.

"How did you—?" Curtis started to ask but changed his mind, saying evasively, "We were." For the first time since she'd known him, Curtis seemed less than confident.

Which made Sadie feel bold. "What happened?"

His eyes settled on her face now in a way different than they had before. They moved lazily from her lips to her chin, and back to her eyes. "Let's say someone else got in the way."

Sadie's heart was racing. Was he really saying what he seemed to be? Despite her performance at the debriefing? Could that mean that maybe she hadn't destroyed her chances after all? He seemed to be drawing closer to her, his eyes on her lips now, close enough so that she could feel the warmth of his chest and smell the soft citrus scent of his cologne, about to lean in and kiss her with his delicious—

But she hadn't gotten to find out what delicious flavor his lips were because a guy had come out of the Bricolage office just then and said, "We're waiting for you to begin."

And also of course because she had a boyfriend.

"Subbasement six, going up."

She'd slept fitfully until the call from the Committee had woken her that morning. "We have decided not to extend your Syncopy. Thank you for your service." Two sentences, no explanation. Pack your bag. It was over. Done.

"Don't take it personally," Curtis advised as he walked her to the elevator. "We'll see each other soon."

"Subbasement five, going up."

And now here she was, heading home after less than a week. *At least you won't ever have to taste Meatballz*, she tried to console herself.

She choked on a sob.

For the first time in her life, Sadie was a failure. It had always been there, lurking in the corners of her mind, an alert, preening bird of prey waiting to sweep down and sink its claws into her at the slightest sign of vulnerability. She'd felt the beat of its wings on the back of her neck during debates, the caress of a feather against her cheek late at night when a thesis statement eluded her, heard its mocking call during exams, but so far she had always beaten it back. Knowing it was there, watching with unblinking eyes, kept her on her toes, kept her humble, alert. Now it was right on her, talons digging in, staring into her eyes. And it hurt.

Maybe Catrina had been right. Maybe she was too soft, too—
"Subbasement three, stopping."

The door slid open, and Miranda appeared, yelling, "Idiocy!" and trailed by a group of people in the different-colored lab coats of five floors and a security detail. "How hard is it for you to find one girl?" She turned to Sadie, said, "Hello, Ames, pardon me for a moment," turned back to the security personnel, said, "You're all fired," and jabbed furiously at the elevator intercom.

"Yes, ma'am?" the intercom prompted.

"Joe, take us back to fourteen, please." Miranda closed her eyes and pinched the bridge of her nose.

"Are you all right?" Sadie asked.

She opened her eyes and gave Sadie a melancholy smile. "I'm surrounded by nincompoops, Ames. How am I supposed to get anything done when I'm constantly running around fixing the messes they make?"

"I'm—I—"

"It was rhetorical," Miranda said, rubbing her temples. "I'm sorry about the mix-up this morning. The board tried to go over my head—or under it, crawling around on their yellow bellies—but it's all straightened out."

"What do you mean?"

"You didn't think I was going to let them send you home, did you? When I handpicked you for this myself? *Bah*." She made a gesture to push the suggestion away through the air. "You're doing an outstanding job. Keep it up. Stick by your instincts and beliefs. They'll lead you where you need to go."

"I wish I shared your confidence."

"You're an idiot if you don't. Haven't you figured life

out yet? There is no right answer. Convictions are as good as it gets, Ames. You're going to pay for yours at some point, so make sure you like them. Now stand back, I'm about to breathe some fire."

Three hours later Sadie lay in her Stas-Case. The automated voice said, "Syncopy in nine . . ."

Thank god, she thought, closing her eyes with relief.

CHAPTER 13
WEEK 2

Sadie opened her eyes and screamed. The ground was rushing toward her—

"*Whoooosh!*" Ford cried as they abruptly stopped falling and started to dangle eighteen inches above the pavement.

He started to laugh, and her terror instantly changed to pure, undiluted joy. *Welcome back*, she thought.

Ford hung there for a moment, catching his breath, watching a line of ants moving a piece of leaf along a crack in the asphalt. Sadie tasted the tart sweetness of cherries on his lips and felt his heartbeat knocking against hers like knees on a first date. She shivered with pleasure as a breeze blew gently across his forearm, and the last two days were forgotten. She was not going to think about failure, about how close she'd come to not being there, she was just—

Ford took a deep breath, filling her nose with a mix of nutmeg, warm honey, and musk that made her feel light-headed. *His skin*, she realized. *My god, that's how he smells.*

Deep stasis was extraordinary.

He put his fingertips down, careful not to interrupt the supply line, and got his feet under him in a squat. Sadie was astonished by his weight and power. He tilted his head backward and looked up along the trunk of an old oak tree to a wooden platform under construction among its branches. A tree house, Sadie thought—*knew*—as though his thoughts were running directly into hers now. A piece of the platform corner was dangling by a few splinters, and Sadie heard him think *Right again, Bucky,* as he unhooked from his belt the safety rope he'd been wearing when the wood gave.

Standing below the tree, he glanced over his shoulder through the yard at the dilapidated house. Sadie recognized it as one of the places Ford had visited while he was looking for Bucky. It was the old hideout with the turret and the hidden room through the fireplace. Sadie now watched his mind strip the place like a puzzle, assessing each piece of lumber and spare wood as a possible fix for the platform corner. It happened at blinding speed, with a soundtrack of words—"too big," "bumpy," "sawing," "maybe," "smell bad," "diagonally?"— that she heard intuitively now.

Find the address, Sadie told herself, determined not to repeat her failure of the day before. The house was on one of those abandoned blocks that existed like pockets of forgotten tranquility in the middle of City Center. There was no street sign visible but there was also no traffic, and between the quiet and the way that the uninhabited buildings and their plants had merged into one another, it felt a little otherworldly.

It was balmy, the air buzzing with the sound of the insects tucked into the overgrown yard. Ford spent the next three hours cannibalizing the surrounding houses and yards for parts and hauling them up and down with the dumbwaiter, which he'd installed on the side of the tree trunk. Sadie's mind was working feverishly to assess all the new physical sensations she had access to: the smell of warm pavement, sweat running down his back, a bug in his mouth. He worked constantly, pausing only to swig water from a gallon bottle he'd suspended so it could be easily accessible from the treetop or the bottom.

It was like watching a performance, Sadie thought, the sleek motion of his mind as he thoughtfully chose pieces from the other buildings to realize his vision. He had a specific idea, but what fascinated her was his flexibility, his willingness to change as the reality evolved, taking advantage of a whole window with a pane of glass he found hidden inside a ruined house, compensating for a door that had looked solid but was rotted through. He knew generally where his final destination lay and trusted he would get there.

By the time he was done there was a roof with a window as a hatched skylight, four walls, one of them hinged so it could open completely like an awning, a short table with two chairs, a rope ladder, and his favorite part, the head of a rocking horse he'd cut off and, mounted like a piece of taxidermy. *Now the place has some class*, she heard him think to himself, and she laughed.

Cali called as he was finishing the last of his water. The

sensation of strength and ease she got as he crushed the bottle with one hand gave Sadie a little rush.

It was clear from the warmth in his voice when he said, "Hey, babe," and a few gossamer images that Sadie caught that his dinner with Cali on Friday had gone well.

"Hi, lover," she said. "What are you up to?"

He glanced around the tree house. "Nothing. Working. You caught me on my break."

And yet, Sadie thought, he was lying to her.

Tiny perfect points of color filled in the rest of the tree house in his mind, adding candles, a picnic basket, plates, and Sadie realized that he was building it for Cali, to take her to dinner. As a surprise. That's why he was lying.

Wow.

He did all this for her, Sadie marveled, aware of a strange tight feeling in her chest. He built the entire thing, just for her. Of course, Cali loved him so she knew how special he was.

"I just wanted you to tell me again that I'm going to be great at my new job and everyone will like me," Cali said. "I'm nervous."

"You're going to be great at your new job and everyone is going to *love* you," he told her.

And you're getting a tree house, Sadie said. *Which shows that one person in particular loves you very much.*

"Thanks," Cali said tremulously. "I tried listening to your message from the other night again—are you sure you weren't drunk? It was really long, and you know how when you're drunk—"

Ford chuckled. "I wasn't drunk."

"Well, I tried, but it was too noisy to hear anything, so I gave up."

"Like I said, it was mostly just me telling you over and over how spectacular you are and how lucky I am."

Now you say, "And I'm lucky too," Sadie prompted her. But Cali went with "Which is exactly why I wanted to hear it. So you promise to tell me all those things on Wednesday?"

"Yep. I might even make up a few new ones. And to show you I've been listening, I found somewhere really special to take you. Somewhere new."

Sadie suddenly had a lump in her throat.

Cali said, "Sounds promising."

That's all? Sadie demanded. *What about "Thank you," or— and I can't believe I'm suggesting this—"You're the best"? You love saying that.*

But Cali just said, "Bye."

Sadie found herself feeling very dissatisfied with Cali. All her words about loving Ford seemed hollow in the face of her self-centered behavior on the phone. Ford had poured his heart into that message he'd left and all she could say was that it was hard to hear, and was he drunk? That didn't seem very loving at all. Sure, she was pretty and had nice boobs, but Sadie began to think Cali wasn't sensitive enough to be with Ford.

Ford didn't seem to be upset at all, though, and as he looked around the tree house it was impossible not to share the excitement spilling from him. She felt a shimmering current of sensation that started in his toes and radiated through his entire body and knew, with the new clarity of deep stasis, it was pride. The idea that he felt good about something he'd done began to fill her with her own sense of warmth. *He is not your friend, he is your Subject,* she reminded herself sternly. *Your job is to assess and consider but not empathize.*

As he gathered his tools together, Sadie thought that maybe Cali's self-centeredness was part of the appeal for Ford, because it allowed him to stay emotionally aloof. No matter what she said, she was too wrapped up in herself to ever require more than attention and praise, so Ford never had to actually open up.

But you deserve more than that, Sadie wanted to tell him. *You deserve someone who makes you stop fearing the unknown and instead want to jump into it.*

Jump into it. The phrase tinkled softly around her mind like a can being blown over a cobblestone street.

Ford patted the rocking horse on the nose, said, "See you soon, sport," grabbed his hammer, and started down the rope ladder. He was a foot from the ground when Sadie heard a shuffle of feet and felt something being pressed over his mouth and nose. There was a cloying sweet smell, his head foamed with black and white dots like bubbles, and he passed out.

CHAPTER 14

When Ford opened his eyes he was on a bed in a low-ceilinged room with powder-blue walls. He was lying on his side, staring at a radiator with something taped above it. He squinted, trying to see it, but couldn't make it out.

Are you sure you should be this calm? Sadie asked him. *You were just kidnapped and drugged. Don't you think maybe a little panic or—*

Ford sat up, making the horizon heave in front of his eyes, and Sadie experienced his nausea as hers.

Deep stasis might be a touch less fantastic in this context.

He took a breath to settle his stomach and leaned toward the radiator. Sadie saw a five-dollar bill hanging on the wall. Someone had doodled over Abe Lincoln's portrait to make him look like Bigfoot and written "#41 of 120" as though it were a limited-edition work of art.

When Ford saw it, his heart began to pound, and Sadie sensed an emotional composite made up of gooey warmth that felt like friendship, cinnamon hope, and a dash of anger. His mind filled with sounds, not the windy ones from shallow stasis but a whole school playground of noises. Semitranslucent circles organized themselves into a bubbly picture of a young James, wearing a striped sweater and sitting at a pink plastic picnic table. Hand flat on the surface, covering something, saying, "Are you sure you're ready to know the truth about Abe Lincoln?" and then triumphantly revealing Bigfoot.

The image fizzled now, the sounds bubbled away, and Ford, sitting on the edge of the bed, roared, "Where are you?"

Whatever Ford had been drugged with made everything in his head a little carbonated, and his voice sounded fizzy. Combined with the complex cocktail nature of the emotional experience in deep stasis, Sadie was having trouble getting a clear grasp of his state of mind.

A black kitten came and stood next to the door and stared up at Ford. "Go get someone," he said to it, but it didn't move.

"She's deaf but I'm not, so would you mind not shouting, Citizen Ford?" The guy who had spoken was about the same height as Ford, but skinny instead of muscular, with broad shoulders. He slouched into the room almost apologetically, like someone who didn't spend a lot of time around other people. His brown hair was carefully parted and trimmed. He wore a goldenrod cowboy shirt with pearl snaps and blue forget-me-nots embroidered over the pockets, a thin leather bolo tie with a gold buffalo-dollar clasp, khaki jeans, and brown cowboy boots that looked handmade. He carried a beige cowboy hat in his hand, since the ceiling was too low for him to wear it.

Hot anger, warm friendship, hard grief, and the bleachy scent of betrayal crowded each other for space in Ford's mind. "If my head wasn't aching I'd punch you, Bucky."

"Sweet as ever," Bucky said.

"What the hell?" Ford's head was a shooting gallery of emotions, a different one flipping up every half second. "I don't understand. You're here? How long? And what's with the enemy agent tactics?"

Bucky looked uncomfortable, his eyes staring beyond Ford. "Not much to say about that, Citizen F." Sadie caught a glimpse of the bearded, wild-eyed Bucky from Ford's memory, sitting across the table at a diner, picking invisible bugs from himself and looking over his shoulder. "I take my privacy very seriously. Why don't we just start from scratch?"

Ford's mind was going nuts: bleach, anger, grief, happiness, anger, but Sadie noticed the cinnamon scent she thought was hope surfacing more and more, as though Ford wanted to forgive Bucky but he just wasn't sure how. "James was here. He drew the Bigfoot for you."

"Incorrect," Bucky said. "James made the Bigfoot, that's true, and Bigfoot is here, but it doesn't follow that James was here. Bigfoot is a good-luck charm. For safe keeping."

"But—"

"Talk and walk," Bucky said, heading out the door. "Places to see, wonders to learn, Citizen."

Ford struggled to his feet and followed him into the next room, but he was almost knocked back again by what he saw.

It was a big space with light-colored walls, EvergreenLawn

Superturf covering the ground, and filled with at least fifty miniature-golf sculptures. Some were set up for putting while others waited along the edge like an army ready to be called up. A
couch, a coffee table, and a hot plate completed the furnishings.

Ford lost track of his anger as soon as he walked in. Sadie
watched him trying to match each sculpture to a miniature-golf
course he knew, eliciting cloudburst showers of memories of
games with James, Willy, Linc, and Bucky.

His eye zeroed in on a dinosaur near the back of the room.
"You got Daisy?" he said, skirting a castle and a UFO to reach it.

Bucky bit his finger and nodded.

Ford shook his head. "I went the next day to get her."

"I broke in the night they put the locks on." Bucky had
moved to the far end of the room where the couch and hot
plate were, and started pacing.

"I should have known it was you." Ford patted the dinosaur. "I'm glad she went to a good home."

Bucky paused in his pacing to take something white from a
bowl at the end of the room and put it in his pocket. "Did you
find the present I left for you at the old bottling plant? Nice
sign, by the way. Although no one with half a marble would
believe that had been a wire factory."

*Maybe people with more than half a marble have better
things to do than know how wire factories are supposed to
look*, Sadie pointed out.

"I thought it was you." Sadie felt the warm flush of Ford's
vindication, followed by a hint of anger. "Why, though? Sort of
out of the blue. I haven't heard from you in two years."

Bucky frowned. He picked up something red from a second

bowl and put it in his other pocket. "You'd been papering half
the desks in City Center trying to get your hands on that file. I
thought I'd help."

"How'd you get it?"

Bucky waved that away. "I also thought that once you saw
it, read it, and learned how James really died, you would stop
asking questions. You've been irritating a lot of people, Citizen Ford. I did it to shut you up. But that didn't work, so I've
resorted to an alternate plan."

"I thought you didn't believe in backup plans," Ford said.

"I said *alternate*. And generally I avoid interfering with
people as stubborn as you, so backup plans aren't necessary."

"I don't need any interference," Ford said, his anger rising,
"not after two years." There was something else mixed with the
anger, Sadie sensed. Something subtle and gritty.

Bucky took a breath. "You think I abandoned you. I didn't,
Citizen F. Believe me when I say if I could be friends with anyone, it would be with you. But I have work, projects, that make
that impossible." He was pacing around as he spoke, not in
straight lines but curvy eddies, as though his discomfort and
frustration kept pulling him back.

The sense of grittiness inside Ford grew more pronounced,
as though a wave of anger had churned old pebbles from the
bottom of his emotional ocean. Sadie felt them grinding together
while Ford took in the miniature-golf collection. "Yeah, I see
how crucial your work is."

"Everyone is entitled to company." Bucky stopped pacing.
His hands fell to his sides, and he stood looking forlorn but
also determined. "I want to help you, Citizen Ford, but I can't,

I *can't*, if you won't move on." His long fingers curved into fists of frustration.

Sadie saw images of Bucky flashing through Ford's mind: showing up at their house at three in the morning with a pillow and asking to spend the night, at the park all day watching men play chess and winning the state chess championship the next year, refusing to leave his jail cell after serving his two days for stripping off all his clothes and running raving through a restaurant screaming that aliens were burrowing into his skin.

Ford packed his anger away, but a hint of gravel stayed. "I'm guessing you wouldn't do this unless you thought I really needed your help."

Bucky nodded and resumed pacing and biting the edge of his thumb. He said, "Have you heard of the Pharmacist?"

Dots spun into the alley outside Plum's club. "I've heard the name, but I don't know anything about him. Who is he?"

Bucky made wispy gestures with his hands. "Vapor. Smoke. Nobody."

Ford sank onto the edge of the couch. "I heard Linc beat someone up, saying he was working for the Pharmacist. That doesn't sound like nobody to me."

"People do things they don't want to do when they lose their minds," Bucky said. "Fact of life."

"You think Linc is out of his mind? Like, crazy?"

"Oh, yes." Bucky nodded. "The Pharmacist does that to people—one look, and they lose their heads completely." He stopped to take another white object from the bowl.

"Who *is* the Pharmacist?"

Bucky shrugged, "All-seeing, all-knowing invisible entity

who governs hearts and minds, controls the power of good and evil, life and death, et cetera, et cetera."

It reminded Sadie of the boogeyman Curtis had talked about when she'd run into him after her debriefing. When he'd almost kiss—

Stay focused.

Ford asked, "You mean like a criminal mastermind? Why isn't Serenity Services after this guy?"

"By all means, go tell Serenity Services about a bad seed no one's ever seen who controls most of the population of City Center," Bucky admonished. "They'll listen politely and then explain the Pharmacist is simply a figment of the collective imagination. That no one like that could possibly exist. And then—"

Sadie heard the low buzzing of Ford's exasperation. "So the Pharmacist *isn't* real?"

"—and then a few days later your body will turn up in some scenic spot. The Pharmacist prefers not to be a topic of conversation." Bucky stopped and cocked his head to one side, listening, then resumed his pacing. "That's the perfection of it. An idea so far-fetched it can't be true. Only it is." Bucky's eyes had taken on a strange, excited sheen. "And I'll give you this for free. Whoever denies the Pharmacist's existence the most, you can bet they're part of the smoke screen."

Genius, Sadie thought. *Every denial is proof of existence.*

Ford said, "So since Serenity Services would deny his existence, they must be in on it."

Bucky tapped his head and nodded wisely.

Sadie saw a bunch of dots jump from one place to another in Ford's mind, from the memory of Linc and Willy in the alley backward to Kansas at the Castle. Ford said, "Does anyone call him Mr. P?"

Bucky looked surprised by Ford's question. "Yes, although it's a misnomer. Where'd you hear about Mr. P?"

"Willy's girlfriend. She asked me if I work for Mr. P too."

"Oh, dear, Citizen F. Not good. That 'too' is not good at all." Bucky resumed pacing and biting his thumb. "It's mainly the Pharmacist's inner circle that uses that name."

Sadie felt Ford watching Bucky, waiting for any of the clues his mind usually gave him that someone was lying, but all he got was white noise. None of his normal systems for assessing people were working. "So the Pharmacist controls Serenity Services. And all he has to do is look at someone and they go crazy? How does that work if no one's ever seen him?"

"No one *knows* they've seen him. That's why I prefer to stay where the Pharmacist can't see me."

"Is that what you're doing here? Hiding from the Pharmacist?"

"Hiding? Maybe. Needed somewhere quiet, somewhere I could be alone with my thoughts. Otherwise they have a tendency to—" He made a spinning gesture with his fingers. He put another white thing in his pocket. "I'm trying to keep you from losing your head too."

Ford pointed to the two bowls. "What are you counting?"

"These?" Bucky looked surprised. "The white beans are white vans. Suspicious, but not always troubling. The red beans are Royal Pizza delivery trucks, of course."

Oh boy, Sadie thought.

"Where? How can you tell when they go by?"

Bucky pointed to the back wall of the room, where Ford saw a long jumpy image of upside-down tires on the street running near the ceiling, like a moving wallpaper border. Ford used the same puzzle solving from the tree house to come up with an explanation. "Pinhole camera," he said. "You've got a few at street level, and you're projecting the images down here."

Unexpected, Sadie thought. *Clever.* But not reason for the surge of credibility she sensed Ford felt toward Bucky.

"Exactly. Lets me keep track of the enemy without being seen."

"Pizza vans are the enemy?"

Who do they battle? Sadie wondered. *Vietnamese delivery? Pizzilla vs. Pho-Fighter?* She knew that Ford was clutching the idea Bucky was mostly sane, but it seemed wise to preserve a healthy skepticism.

"*Royal* pizza vans." Bucky's eyes latched on to Ford, and he said, "When is a pizza not a pizza?"

"When it's a Royal," Ford answered, reciting what Sadie could tell must be a ubiquitous slogan for a well-known pizza chain, but one she'd never heard of in her neighborhood.

Bucky grinned happily. "Genius. Says it straight out, in plain sight."

"Says what?"

"When is a pizza not a pizza," Bucky repeated slowly. "You ever had a Royal Pizza delivered?"

Ford shook his head, and Sadie was caught off guard by a flame of anger. It was explained when he said, "Too expensive."

"Ever seen anyone get a Royal Pizza delivered?"

"I don't know. I've never thought about it."

"Start thinking about it." Bucky shook the red beans in his hand. "Can't tell if they're circling or there's just an action going on nearby." He puffed up his cheeks, then exhaled. "Come on, let me show you around. I don't get a lot of visitors."

Ford followed Bucky into a corridor. "You think those pizza trucks are fakes?" A layer of gooeyness had begun to creep over Ford's thoughts, and based on his tone Sadie decided it meant increasing doubt. *Good for you!*

"Of course they're fakes," Bucky declared.

Sadie sensed both Ford's frustration and concern for Bucky intensifying. "Why would someone want fake pizza trucks?"

"Your tone right there, Citizen Winter. That 'Come on, be real, man' tone." Bucky put his hands up and waggled his fingers like he was performing a Broadway dance routine. "That's how they get away with it. A plan so convoluted and unlikely that anyone who believes in it must be insane."

Because something seems too crazy to be true, it must be true, Sadie paraphrased. What would it be like to be in a mind like Bucky's? What did conspiracy theories look like when they were taking shape?

Sadie noticed the lines of Bucky's face thicken slightly in Ford's vision and his features become more pronounced. Like a caricature, she thought, and wondered if it was because Ford could no longer take him seriously. "Who are *they*, Bucky?" he asked, following Bucky through a hidden door and up a set of stairs. Sadie sensed the air was cooler now, and she smelled a combination of mustiness and bushes. "Who controls the pizza trucks?"

"Take your pick. *Eenie meenie minie moe,*" Bucky recited

as they stepped into a high-ceilinged space painted black. He kept going, and Ford realized they were on a stage.

Bucky moved to the center of it and waved Ford over. "Come see the view." When Ford joined him Bucky draped an arm over his shoulder and said, "Nice to have company. It's been a while."

Sadie felt Ford stiffen, but she also heard a tiny chime inside of him that seemed to be the response to the call of Bucky's loneliness. The two of them stood in the middle of the stage, gazing out in silence.

What had once been the theater was now rows of green velvet chairs overgrown with bushes. The roof was gone, and the tops of the walls were uneven, some sprouting green grass, giving the space the feeling of a pastoral dreamscape. For a moment Ford's mind was wholly absorbed with its strange beauty, and Sadie was treated to the double magic of the space and Ford's appreciation for it. A mass of green dots, hundreds of shades, blanketed the theater in his mind, clustering like fireflies around a bush at dusk, becoming a shimmering record of the theater. He was archiving the image, Sadie realized. She was watching him actively commit it to his memory.

Beautiful, she breathed.

"Beautiful," Ford said. Her arms prickled, and she realized he was so moved he had goose bumps. That had never happened in shallow stasis. "Where are we?"

"My playhouse," Bucky said. "Don't tell me you don't recognize it. You, Ford Winter, who knows every building worth knowing in Detroit from the past hundred years?" He chuckled to himself.

Sadie heard a drumbeat in Ford's mind like a summons into battle. He studied the seats, the stage, the few patches of plaster you could still see on the walls. "I give up," he said.

Bucky said, "You'll figure it out when you need to." Then he let out a long exhale and put his face directly in Ford's. His breath smelled like jelly beans. "Listen to me close, because this is important. 'Get the tiger by the toe, when he hollers let him go.' Going head to head with a tiger, you're always going to get mauled."

Sadie felt the gravelly sensation in Ford's mind again now, like someone pan-sifting rocks for gold. *Sadness.* Ford blinked. "What are you talking about, Bucky?"

Bucky stepped away, his eyes looking everywhere except at Ford: the sky, the ceiling, the theater. He jammed his hands in his pockets and rattled the beans around while he talked. "Your damn brother who always had to be a damn knight slaying the damn monster, of course. Swashbuckling into the tiger's den, stealing his treasures, planning to ambush him. No matter what I said, he didn't listen." He walked to the edge of the stage then back to the center, counting the steps under his breath as he spoke. "I put that file in your office so that you'd read it and be content—*six, no, seven, damn, start over.*" He was getting increasingly agitated, pacing faster, losing count. "Stop rattling cages. Stop asking questions. Stop—*three, no, five, START OVER.*" He paused in the middle of the stage and faced Ford. "That's what your brother would have wanted. Tried to do at least that." He shrugged. "Guess I owe you an apology."

Ford was like someone who keeps coughing to clear his throat but can't quite get it, groping for knowledge just out of reach. "For what?

"I was trying to trick you into giving up." Bucky put up a hand. "The Serenity Services file is legit. Real deal. Case closed. Only it's also wrong. James didn't use drugs. James was murdered. And they'll kill you too if you don't stop asking questions. James did what he did, however idiotic, to save you. There's no way he'd want you following in his footsteps, Citizen Ford."

"James was murdered," Ford repeated. *James was murdered*. His mind became still and flat, and for a moment that thought was the only thing inside of it.

Then Sadie watched as an avalanche of questions and furies and memories swept in chaotically. He didn't know how to feel, she sensed, what to think, what to ask. He should be glad, he told himself, he hadn't been wrong about his brother, everything he believed wasn't a lie. Plum had said it too, but Plum could say anything. Bucky—*who is at least 50 percent crazy*, Sadie put in—seemed sure.

"Who did it?" Ford managed to stammer.

Bucky leaned back on the heels of his boots. "Short answer is, he killed himself by needing to play the action hero. Longer answer is, the Pharmacist did, because James more or less dared him to." He put his hands on Ford's shoulders and shook him, fading in and out from normal to caricature in Ford's eyes. "Do you understand now?"

"Why did he dare the Pharmacist?"

"Going to set everyone free." Bucky laughed, a strange high laugh. "I tried to warn him, but he wouldn't listen. I tried and tried. Now I'm warning you. If you don't stop what you're doing and start asking all the wrong questions, you're going to end up with an overdose of lead like your brother. So cut it out."

The inside of Ford's mind felt like it was doing cartwheels, as though it was performing distracting tricks to keep him from having to acknowledge that the crazy but trustworthy Bucky of the past might simply be crazy. "All the *wrong* questions? Which are those?"

"Any but the ones you're thinking of asking. Who-what-where-why-when, kiss those goodbye. They'll get you nowhere or get you killed."

"What's left?" Ford asked, hands clenching and unclenching at his sides.

Bucky smiled happily. "That will be part of your adventure! Although you only need one. The right wrong question, asked enough times, could shake things up and make something fall out."

Ford's thoughts became all about wanting to punch something, as if that would quell the confusion he was feeling.

You're better than that, Sadie heard herself telling him. *And I'm going to find a way to make you understand that.*

While being ruthless, she reminded herself.

Breathing hard, Ford said, "The right wrong question. And that would be?"

"The one that makes people wrongly give the right answer. The one they don't mean to give you." Bucky snapped as though he'd just remembered something. "Also, you need to stop avoiding the Roaches' visits. In fact, you should embrace them."

Ford's mind transmitted the faintest scent of bleach, and Sadie felt him tense. "How did you know I've been avoiding their visits?"

Bucky ignored that, pacing the stage with his hands in his pockets. "Dress up for the Roaches, Citizen Ford. Entertain them, smile your biggest smile. Welcome them into your home.

They're your allies. It's when they stop coming around you should be worried. It means they don't need to watch—"

He broke off abruptly, pulling both hands from his pockets. There were nine white beans in one and five red in the other. He looked from them to Ford and whispered, "You're four years younger than James, right? Eighteen?"

"No, nineteen," Ford whispered back.

"Show me your ID," Bucky said. When it took Ford a moment to get his wallet out of his pants, Bucky tapped his foot impatiently. "Come on, come on."

Bucky jammed the beans into his pockets and took the ID. A few seconds later he was shoving it back at Ford like it was scalding him.

"Bucky, what are you—"

He grabbed Ford by the shoulders. "Forget all about me. I mean it. Never think of me again. Do *not* keep me in mind. Everything I've said sounds nuts because it is nuts." He put his arms in the air, opened his eyes wide, and let his tongue loll out. "Invisible overlords! Tiger toes! Coming for you, *ooga booga.*"

Ford took a step backward. "Are you okay?"

"Scary pizza," Bucky said, flicking his fingers.

"Um, Buck—" Ford said, taking another step backward.

Bucky stomped once, and the floor beneath Ford dropped away.

The fall was short and went straight into a large black canvas bag.

Ford's mind registered *Damn*, and then, *How long is this going to take?*

You seem very calm, Sadie said to him. *Does this kind of thing happen to you a lot?*

Bucky's voice came from outside the bag. "Comfy in there, Ford?"

Ford, more frustrated and confused than angry, said, "Trapdoor?"

"Yep. Rigged for large animals in magic acts."

"Hence the fur in my mouth." Ford cleared his throat. "Why, Bucky? We're on the same side."

"No such thing as sides where the Pharmacist is concerned," Bucky said. "Don't trust anyone, Citizen Ford, not even me."

"If you let me out I'll leave here and never come back, I promise," Ford said. *Although I might strangle you first,* he added to himself.

Bucky laughed. "Cheers, Citizen F, very thoughtful. The problem is, I need to get you out of here, but I don't want you to know where *here* is. So this is my offer: If you are a pain in the ass I will drop you on your head until you pass out. Otherwise, we can be pals. Which way do you want to do it?"

What charming friends you have, Mr. Winter, Sadie thought.

"Pals." Ford coughed, and Sadie was surprised to feel a suppressed but unmistakable ripple of laughter from him.

CHAPTER 15

On Tuesday Ford came straight home from work, brushed his hair, put on the blue checked button-down shirt from his date with Cali, and joined his mother on the couch five minutes before the Roque Community Health Evaluator arrived. Lulu was out on a four-hour session with a special counselor, so it was just the two of them, mother and son, no buffer.

Sadie had been worried about what the mother-son relationship might be like in the wake of the cigarette fire and Ford's cruel words, but it felt exactly, heartbreakingly, the same. They could each be kind to Lulu, shower her with open warmth, but they were frozen toward each other. Sitting side by side on the couch the distance seemed even greater, as if their physical proximity magnified rather than reduced their emotional rift.

Ford was still unsure how much to believe of what Bucky

had said, but he'd decided to take his words about the RCHE seriously and make a good impression. Sadie hoped that would also ease tensions with his mother.

Five minutes after six, Rondy Torch arrived in her green RCHE polo shirt and khakis. She was in her mid-thirties with shoulder-length dark hair that flipped on the ends, big brown eyes, dark brown skin, and a bright, warm smile.

His mother greeted her by her first name, as though they were friends, and, taking her arm, led her toward the couch. "Rondy, this is my son Ford."

"It's very nice to meet you, Ford," Rondy said. Sadie felt Ford looking into every cranny to find a hint of reproach or scolding in her voice, but he found none. But she could tell from the slate of hovering silver dots in his mind, lined up like an army battalion awaiting orders, that he was still on the defensive.

Rondy leaned forward and said, "I heard about the incident this weekend. Are you okay, Vera?"

Ford's mother wrapped her hand around the gold oval locket she was wearing. "I am. You know, I'm just so tired."

Sadie felt Ford's jaw, hands, and chest tighten with emotion he couldn't parse. He avoided looking at his mother and looked instead at Rondy, whose expression was understanding but not condescending.

Sadie sensed Ford's surprise and felt him relax his guard slightly.

Rondy smiled at Ford. "Since we don't know each other that well yet, I thought we could begin with a word-association exercise. It may seem a little hokey, but it helps to build rapport. Are you comfortable with that?"

"Sure." Sadie didn't recognize the mood Ford's mind was settling into, slightly immature but eager to please. She was filled with the insane hope that maybe, *maybe* Rondy could get Ford and his mother to hear one another.

Plus this would provide good, objective data, she told herself.

Rondy: Let's start with the word "sun."
Sadie: *Moon.*
Ford: Day.
Rondy: Dark.
Sadie: *Light.*
Ford: Beer.
Rondy: Happy.
Sadie: *Sa—*

Sadie was knocked sideways by a draft of anger from Ford. His contempt for *happy* was so potent that she wondered if part of his constant anger was simply a way to avoid the far greater discomfort *happy* apparently represented. If the very idea that he had to find a word to go with it enraged him.

Sadie heard him settle on *Ending—happy ending*, thinking that would show them for picking such a stupid word. Adding: *Here's what I think of your little—*

Ford: Ever after.
Rondy: Nude.
Sadie: *Dressed.*
Ford: Thigh highs.
Rondy: (Laughing) I've never heard that one before.
Ford: Does that mean I pass or fail?

Rondy. You're doing great. Feel.

Sadie: *Think.*

Ford: Free.

Rondy: Father.

Sadie: *Mother.*

Ford: Nothing.

Rondy: Sister.

Sadie: *Brother.*

Ford: Safe.

Rondy: Angry.

Sadie: *Calm.*

Ford: Door.

Rondy: Drugs.

Sadie: *Drinks.*

Ford: No.

Rondy: Snow.

Sadie: *Rain.*

Ford: Man.

Rondy: Winter.

Sadie: *Summer.*

Ford: Cold.

Rondy: Mother.

Sadie: *Father.*

Ford: Artist.

Rondy: Ice.

Sadie: *Water.*

Ford: Fear. Sorry, I meant to say "beer."

Rondy: Friend.

Sadie: *Foe.*

Ford: Jame—Bucky.

Rondy: Old.

Sadie: *New.*

Ford: Unexpected.

Rondy: New.

Sadie: *Old.*

Ford: Dull.

Rondy: Home.

Sadie: *Alone.*

Ford: Alone.

Rondy: Love.

Sadie: *Tennis.*

Ford: -ly lady.

Rondy smiled. "Excellent. Let's stop there. What did you think, Ford?"

"Fun," he said, and Sadie sensed bright candor and bouncy surprise. But he was also apprehensive, worried he hadn't impressed this lady, worried he hadn't done well enough. "What does it mean? Am I, um, normal?"

Not just this lady, Sadie thought. He was so nervous about what his mother thought that he couldn't even turn to look at her, and there was a constant low buzz as though someone was running a lawnmower around his mind. He was afraid to hear what they said, afraid he'd disappointed them both.

Sadie knew Ford felt his mother tense when he paired *thigh highs* with *nude*, but after that his word choices were almost all unconscious, sliding out without thought like a sled ending a smooth, easy run. She wasn't even sure he knew what he'd said for any besides *ice*, when he'd changed *fear* to *beer*, or *friend*, when his mind had gone blank and she'd glimpsed for the first time how James had been not just his brother but his best friend for his entire life.

Rondy laughed. "You're quite normal, and anything but average, Mr. Winter," she said, which acted like magic to reduce the volume of the lawn mower. "Your answers were all associations," she went on, glancing down at her notepad, "which means either phrase completions like 'sun–day' or 'snow–man,' which you favored more at the beginning, or words that had a personal connection to you. People with patterns like yours tend to be what we call integrated, suggesting you are at ease with others and adept at making connections."

Slightly milky opalescent dots hung as though suspended from filaments in his mind, turning from one side to the other in a swaying, pleasant rhythm as he listened to the woman. The feeling was a good one, but not associated with any powerful memories since there were no images, no voices to go with it. It resembled the shimmering current of pride he'd felt when he built the tree house, but quieter, like a private smile.

"What are other ways to do it?" he asked, and Sadie made a mental note about how a sense of personal achievement led to broader curiosity about the world and others.

"Some people use only antonyms, words that mean the opposite of the associative word," Rondy said.

The milky circles stopped swaying. "Why would they do that?"

Because it is sensible and orderly, Sadie told him. *It is the cleanest, most efficient approach to word association.*

Rondy's answer was similar: "It's their natural tendency to see things in opposition. It feels tidy and comfortable. These tend to be orderly, rational individuals."

"So everything to them is black or white," Ford said with a tiny bit of the mind-curling contempt he'd lavished on *happy*. "That sounds repressed."

Like you couldn't teach me a thing or two about repression, Mr. I-associate-"angry"-with-"door," Sadie pointed out.

Rondy shook her head. "We don't judge. Everyone's mind works in different ways."

And by the way, Sadie wanted to tell him, *my mind is flexible. Not all of my answers were antonyms. For example*, love *wasn't*.

Somewhere in the back of her own mind Sadie heard a shimmering laugh and a voice say, *You* picked *tennis. Are you sure that's the point you want to make?*

This isn't about me, Sadie snapped at herself. *Focus.*

Ford had shifted, nearly facing his mother, and now said, "Mom, what do you do?" Sadie could tell he genuinely wanted to know and that he was nervous about asking.

"Your mother has a brilliantly associative mind," Rondy said. "She pulls things together I wouldn't have imagined." Her smile became a look of concern. "Vera, are you all right?"

Ford's mother's lips pressed together, and she gave a tight little nod. "Thank you," she said and reached for Ford's hand.

Sadie felt Ford's pulse grow stronger and hers slipped into sync with it. The power of Ford's heartbeat overwhelmed her, as if he had been waiting to unleash it for a long time. The milky opalescent rounds began to turn and sway again, darkening in color to a silvery purple.

Rondy looked at the two of them. "That's about the end of our time today. Do either of you have any questions or concerns for me?"

Ford's mother shook her head, but Ford said, "I have a question." Giving his mother's hand a squeeze, he pulled his wallet out of his pocket and flipped out his ID. After Bucky's reaction to it, Ford had compared it with the IDs of the guys at work and discovered the only difference between them were the symbols in the bottom right-hand corner. He pointed there now, at a roman numeral three with a line through it: III. "Do you know what this is? I was talking to some friends at work, and we all have different ones."

Next to him his mother gasped and began to cough very hard.

The purply silver dots stopped twisting and began to vibrate in nervous unison. "Mom, are you okay?"

She shook her head and gasped, "Water, please."

He brought her a glass, and she sipped it. "I think—I need to lie down," she told Ford, then thanked Rondy and went to her room.

"I'm afraid I don't know," Rondy said, handing Ford's ID back. "Let me ask around the office. It was a pleasure getting to meet you, Ford. I hope you'll be able to get off work early again in the next few weeks."

"I'll try. This was"—he looked at his mother's door—"it was good. Thank you."

Sadie felt Ford's confusion but also the happy swaying of the milky circles. They seemed to glow from within, taking on the faint image of Rondy holding her notepad with his mother beside him on the couch, the image becoming more distinct and refined, as though being imprinted as a memory. He knocked on his mother's door and opened it.

"Mom? Are you—"

"Why did you do that?" Her voice trembled, with anger, Ford assumed, letting the force of it shatter the memory he'd just been etching. "Why did you need to ask about that mark on your ID?"

Sadie wasn't sure it had been anger, but once Ford unleashed his it no longer mattered. "Because I want to know what it means."

"You—" his mother started to say, but Ford put up a hand to silence her.

"No. Stop. I don't want another one of your lectures about behaving for the Roaches. I mean, RCHE." His voice was trembling and his entire mental landscape had become dark, hot, and viscous. There were no real images, just skeletal bits of memories devoured by anger. *It was an amazing equalizer*, Sadie thought, *capable of reducing the best and the worst memories to the same slop.*

"I did what you asked me to do," he told her. "I did my best." Sadie felt his voice catch as his vocal cords tightened and knew that was the real cause of his pain. He'd thought it had gone well. He'd let himself enjoy it, and then—"I did a damn good job. I thought you would be happy. But all you can think of, the very first thing out of your mouth, is to find fault."

"Because I care," his mother said, her voice low and tense.

"Care what RCHE thinks. Not about me." Sadie was torn between wanting to hug him and shake him.

The sound of a key in the front-door lock was followed by Lulu calling out, "I went to the park!"

"I don't want her to see me this way," Mrs. Winter whispered.

"Of course," Ford agreed, stepping out of her room and closing the door.

Lulu was standing in the middle of the living room twirling back and forth, wearing a khaki flight suit. "I went to the park," she repeated.

Sadie felt Ford working to keep his relief from Lulu's view, thinking that he didn't want her to know how much it meant that she'd done it so she wouldn't feel bad if she couldn't manage it again. He kept his hands in his pockets, *to hide their shaking*, Sadie thought. She didn't know if she agreed with his not telling Lulu how brave she was, but she was impressed by how thoughtful he was about it.

"How was it?

"Dirty. But I went. Can I tell Mom?"

Ford shook his head. "In a little while. She's sleeping."

"She's okay, isn't she?" Lulu's eyes filled with worry, and Ford's heart squeezed. *Misdirect*, his mind ordered. *Distract.*

"Mom's okay, but I don't know about you." He picked Lulu up and tipped her over. "You seem to have flipped your lid."

Lulu shrieked with laughter, and Sadie felt her heart expanding. She loved these moments with Lulu, loved the bouncy, supple feeling when his mind went in unexpected directions—even unexpected by him. *Spontaneity*.

"Let me go!" Lulu giggled. "That's not fair."

"Oh, yes, Copernicus, get in there," Ford said as the dog came to lick Lulu's upside-down face.

"No," Lulu squealed, wriggling. Soon she and Ford and Copernicus were collapsed on the couch, hiccupping with laughter.

When the hiccups subsided, Lulu laid her head on Copernicus's middle, said, "What did you and James fight about before he died?"

Ford's mind became a smooth glimmering surface, which Sadie knew marked the first steps in a self-protection sequence. Was this what he felt guilty about? That he and James had fought? "What do you mean?" he asked, and Sadie felt his deliberate effort to keep his tone light.

Lulu stayed sprawled against Copernicus, her eyes skewed downward, fingers fanning back and forth through the dog's gold fur. "The month before he died, you two hardly talked to each other at all."

"That wasn't a fight," he said, too quickly. "We were just annoyed with each other. Like how you get with me if—oh, wait, I can't think of anything. Since I'm perfect."

Lulu puffed out her cheeks. "Agree to disagree."

"Time for dinner," Ford announced. *Cop-out*, Sadie called. "Do you want mac and cheese or mac and cheese?"

"Let's flip a coin," Lulu said. "Copernicus, your call: heads or tails?"

CHAPTER 16

Ford was still asleep when Sadie woke the next morning. During shallow stasis Sadie hadn't had much trouble sleeping when Ford slept, but since she'd been back she'd found herself waking at odd intervals.

Or maybe, she admitted, it was intentional. When she woke like this his mind was quiet and still, exactly the conditions Naomi had suggested were perfect for accessing the subconscious. Any information she could bring back about the subconscious would improve her standing with the Committee.

The last time she'd had a chance to explore while he slept she'd thought she'd seen something flickering at a point along the perimeter of his mind, but he'd woken before she could explore. She saw it again now, and went closer.

It appeared to be coming from a door that opened and

closed rhythmically, like the portcullis on a miniature-golf castle, alternatingly revealing and concealing a landscape beyond. She approached but the door closed before she reached it, and stayed closed until she backed away, when it opened again. She tried again, once going slower, another time dashing toward it, but no matter what she did she couldn't get the timing right, and it shut before she could get past it.

A *defense mechanism*, she thought. How would Ford camouflage something he wanted to hide?

The answer came almost immediately. He'd reverse it. Like the hinges on the wrong side of his workshop door, the passage would be open when it appeared closed and closed when it looked open.

The next time she didn't stop when the door closed but kept moving toward it, then through it. And found herself in an entirely new universe.

She was standing in a vast hall with ornate moldings, elaborate chandeliers, and walls lined with gilt-framed mirrors, sumptuous but all slightly careworn—like a well-used Versailles, built of shimmering dots of color. There was music coming from somewhere, but it was too diffuse for Sadie to make out a tune.

The space, which seemed to stretch forever, was filled with thousands of figures made of twinkling dots. Some of them were static and faded, as though over time parts of the subconscious became ossified; others swayed and danced in front of the mirrors.

As Sadie moved through them she realized the music was actually snippets of repeated phrases, a girl's voice saying "your brother," a guy muttering "Liars! They are all liars!," someone humming "Frosty the Snowman," a man shouting

"Know what you deserve?" and, in Ford's mother's voice, "James?" They all sounded familiar to Sadie, and she thought this must be where the windy voices from his consciousness came from.

She saw Plum, clearer and brighter than many others, and Sadie wondered if it was because her introduction had been more recent. She was reclining on a couch with the tiered candy plate, her hand extended the way she'd held it out to Ford at their meeting. She was chanting, "Show momma you love her, just like your brother, show momma you love her, just like your brother." The tone was grating but tenacious, the phrase "just like your brother" echoing after Sadie as she moved away, like a song lyric that sticks in the mind.

Sadie had sensed that Plum's words had left an impression on Ford, but it was incredible to actually *see* the impact materialized.

The hall of mirrors ended at a lake, on a beach fringed with pine trees and bordered by a series of boulders that formed caves. This wasn't a fantasy creation, it was a real place that Sadie knew. It was called Pirates' Cove and was popular because it was a little hard to get to and secluded from passersby.

An image of James, literally a shimmering golden boy, was sitting on the edge of a lake, skipping rocks. He smiled at her when she walked over. "I haven't seen you before," he said.

Sadie sat down next to him. He looked a lot like he had in the photo from Ford's graduation, but taller and slightly less handsome. As though in Ford's psyche he was both larger than life and clearly flawed. "I'm just visiting."

"That's what you think. There's not much leaving once

you're inside. Maybe some dream work, but other than that we're pretty much on lockdown these days."

"What do you mean?"

"Things have been static around here for a while." James eyed her. "Although today's been strange. What's going on out there? This afternoon there was more traffic shuttling in and out of here than there's been in months, and now you show up."

The session with Rondy, the social worker, Sadie thought. "Maybe things are changing."

"What do you say you take me out with you? When you go?"

Sadie shook her head. "I'm not sure I can do that."

"I know where a lot of Ford's secrets are buried," James offered. "Juicy ones."

Since he was actually a piece of Ford's mind, Sadie figured that was true. "Like what?"

He cocked his head to one side. "I haven't decided if I'm going to tell you." Then a smile. "Maybe you'll make it worth my while."

Was part of Ford's subconscious flirting with her? "Do you always hit on Ford's friends?"

"Every one," James affirmed. "Had to sample all his girl-friends to make sure they were worthy."

Sadie frowned. "Does he know?"

"I'm here telling you, aren't I?" he answered. "I know everything he knows. Of course, what happens between here and there"—he pointed up, presumably toward Ford's conscious mind—"that's a different story."

Sadie thought back to the night Ford met Plum. Ford had said he and James hadn't shared any girls, but his claim had been followed by that strange sticky sensation that Sadie knew meant humiliation. He *had* known. He'd just chosen to deny it. Lock it away in his subconscious.

Fascinating.

James said, "He never wants to see me anymore. Never even calls me up for a dream, nothing. Sometimes he'll pull out some memories, but those aren't really me, just representations of me he's cleaned up." He got quiet before adding, "I suppose he's angry at me."

Sadie hesitated. James was the one person Ford's anger was never directed toward, even in his mind.

Unless Miranda was right, Sadie thought excitedly. What if Ford had a guilty conscience about something involving his brother, so he was repressing all but the most superficial memories. "Why would he be angry at you?"

"Leaving. Dying." He shook his head. "It's not fair, you know. I did it for him as much as anyone." His eyes looked around restlessly. "Let's take a walk," he said, getting to his feet.

"Did what?" Sadie prompted.

"I promised I was going to change our lives, you know." He gave a little laugh. "Sure did, didn't I? My life, his life. But not the way I meant. He knows I didn't mean for this, it's just sometimes . . ." His voice trailed off.

"What did you two fight about before you died?" Sadie asked.

"That I wasn't home enough. Where was I, why was I always out, why wouldn't I introduce him to her, was I embarrassed. He felt left out and jealous about Plum. I told him to drop it, that he didn't know what I was doing." Sadie saw that he'd picked up a length of rope and was now coiling it over one arm. It reminded her of the rope she'd caught glimpses of in Ford's mind.

"What *were* you doing?"

"Getting myself freaking killed," James said with a weird high-pitched laugh. "Making up some stupid plan and getting my ass handed to me on a platter."

The anger was real, and it reminded Sadie that this wasn't James, this was the James that lived in this part of Ford's mind. James as Ford really felt about him. A James Ford *was* angry at.

"Why did you do that?"

"I don't have to tell you," he snapped. "Stop asking."

Of course, Sadie thought. This James couldn't explain what he had done or how he was killed, because Ford didn't know. It was the limitation of the projection Ford kept in his subconscious. But that was the question Ford wanted answered more than anything. *What had James done, and why?*

James pointed into the distance, where she saw a two-story house with a porch. "That's where we lived when Ford was born. Mom used to make the best cinnamon raisin cookies."

Was that why the scent of cinnamon stood for hope? Sadie wondered. Next to the house was a squat gray factory with a smokestack. "What's that?" she asked.

James seemed to be ignoring her, so her eyes moved to a white clapboard house built on a layer of ice that sat improbably on the surface of the otherwise clear lake. It reminded her of the memory Ford had near the playground where James had been killed, when the boys had all been talking about what they'd do with their "fortune."

"Tell me about the icehouse," she said to James. "What happened there?"

He whooped and ran over toward it. "Only one of the best days ever. Guy I knew told me about a wreck in the lake right here, boat from Prohibition that went down with a ton of gold heading to Canada. We didn't want anyone to know what we were doing, so we decided we'd dive for it in the winter, use the icehouse for cover." He rubbed his hands together happily. "Didn't find the treasure, but man, did we have a great time."

There was a pile of beer cans near the door, each crushed in exactly the same way, and he was winding up to kick one when a voice yelled, "Get away from there."

James pulled back and made a face. "See? Won't let me near anything." He loped off, childishly angry, and Sadie jogged to catch up with him.

Why wouldn't Ford want his memory of James near the icehouse? she wondered. What had happened there? Was it related to the hand with the glove reaching for—

The rope. She'd seen James coiling it earlier, but he wasn't holding it when they were standing at the icehouse.

"What did you do with the rope?" she asked when she caught up with him.

"Dropped it," he said with a shrug. He was staring intently into the distance. Sadie followed his gaze and somehow without moving they were standing back at the edge of the hall of mirrors.

"Shift change," James announced. "End of a dream." As he said it they watched the crowd part hastily, and an ambulance with the word HARMACY stenciled on it came barreling through, driven by a tiger in a cowboy hat. The doors opened, and twin versions of Cali wearing ER scrubs climbed out.

James said, "It's time. He's ready for the message. You have to get it to him."

"What message?" Sadie asked.

"Something's wrong with the rooster," he said, like he was talking to himself.

Sadie looked for a rooster but didn't see one. She turned back to ask James where it was, but he'd vanished. Instead, she found she was standing near Plum again, still on the couch with her candies, hand out, chanting the same refrain, "Show Momma you love her just like your brother."

Sadie had been so focused on the "like your brother" part of the chant that she hadn't really paid attention to the first half. But looking at Plum with her hand out, as though waiting to be kissed, Sadie had an idea. What if the advice Plum had given Ford about his mother, to tell her that she was valuable to him, was actually just what Plum wanted? Maybe all it would take to get her to tell Serenity Services that James never did drugs was to play her game. Kiss her hand.

She had to take Plum with her into Ford's conscious mind and make him realize this. Ford wanted James's case reopened, and Plum—the girlfriend wanted for questioning—was the best hope. If he was sweet to Plum, she'd be sweet to him.

Sadie said to her, "Can you come with me?"

Before she could get an answer, there was a rumble like an earthquake. Ford's subconscious bucked once and vanished as he opened his eyes. Sadie found herself in a slightly hazy version of Ford's mind, staring up through his lashes at the living room ceiling.

Had she caused that? Did something in her conversation with Plum wake him?

His mind came into clearer focus. He grunted and stretched to reach his phone. The screen said six A.M., half an hour before his alarm.

Dropping his phone on his chest, he closed his eyes and sank back into the cushions.

And then sat up abruptly. *Sugar momma*, Sadie heard him think. *If I'm sweet to Plum, she'll be sweet to me. Serenity Services will have to listen to her.*

Sadie's head whirled with astonishment and excitement. Had her conversation with Plum moved from his subconscious to conscious mind? Or had she just been channeling a conclusion he had already reached? She felt like every part of her was tingling.

Apparently the discovery excited him too because his hand strayed down his stomach and slid beneath the waistband of his boxers. Sadie's breath caught as with a clash of cymbals, a jazz band reached for its instruments and began grinding to life in his head. They started off separate, each instrument playing its own wave of sensation, tickling Sadie in different, unfamiliar places, then picking up speed as they began to knit together into a powerful, pulsing sound.

Ribbons of color streaked across his mind, shimmering and dissolving as others took their place. *This is nothing like shallow stasis*, Sadie thought, her pulse quickening faster than his, her mind trilling with the vibrations of a French horn leading the other instruments as it twisted its joyful throaty sound upward through a virtuoso series of chords. This was—*oh god!*—not like anything—*open your eyes, Ford*—she'd ever—*please, I want to see, I want*—experienced or even—

She moaned aloud and over the noise of the band heard his stifled grunt in her ear as his body pitched and hers convulsed, sending golden shock waves of sensation bouncing from her to him then back again—

—dreamed.

Ford lay on his back breathing hard, and now he did look down, but all Sadie saw was the wet place on the front of his shorts. She was dizzy from the spinning in his head and the thoughts in hers, wanting it never to end, wanting to do it again, wondering how long he'd have to wait until he was ready—

Absolutely not, she told herself. *There would be no repeat. Are you out of your mind?*

Yes, in fact, I am, she answered, stifling a laugh at her own bad joke.

There was nothing funny about it, she knew. Her behavior had been unscientific, unobjective, inappropriate. Given what she'd just done, the Committee had been right to doubt her suitability as a Minder. What had she been thinking, letting herself go that way? Acting so—

Passionate, she thought. *I, Sadie Ames, was passionate.*

"Wow," Ford said aloud.

Sadie tried, but she couldn't contain the bubble of laughter that burst from her then. It rubbed against her self-reproach, taking the edge off, making her recognize that she'd made a mistake, but it wasn't the worst thing in the world. Her objectivity had only been momentarily compromised.

Still, she felt shy facing him in the mirror that morning as he brushed his teeth.

It won't happen again, she resolved. She could control herself. Would control herself.

But now she knew what everyone else felt. And she'd felt it too.

Thank you, Ford, she whispered, completely forgetting to be annoyed when he left the toilet seat up.

CHAPTER 17

Tiny prickles of impatience teased Ford all day at work.

He'd texted Plum that morning—"I CAN'T GET YOU OFF MY MIND. I'M SORRY I WAS A DISAPPOINTMENT. WILL YOU GIVE ME ANOTHER CHANCE?"—and had been checking his phone all day for a reply that didn't materialize, but Sadie knew his anticipation was really due to his excitement about his date with Cali that night.

He stopped at the tree house on his way home from work, and as he put out candles and set the table he hummed to himself, his mind almost as playful as it was when he was with Lulu. He hung a mirror he'd found at a job site on one wall, and grinned when he unwrapped a bottle of Bailey's Irish Cream he'd skipped lunch for three days to afford because it was Cali's favorite.

Watching him go through the preparations, Sadie was envious of Cali. Not because of Ford, of course. Because of the hours he'd spent planning to make the night a success. He'd built a whole tree house just for her.

He rushed home to get dressed, and he'd been tucking in a surprisingly unwrinkled dress shirt when his mother came out of her room and said, "We need to talk, Ford."

"No we don't," he told her, his mind filling with matte dots, as though ready to repel anything that might try to penetrate it.

"We do."

"Well, I can't right now."

"Soon," she insisted.

He shrugged, already pushing the conversation to the farthest corner of his mind, determined not to let anything spoil the night. "Fine, tomorrow after work."

"Okay," she said, nodding to herself. "Okay." Disappearing back into the gloom of her bedroom.

He rode his bike the two miles to Cali's house, a yellow one-story with its own yard and a front porch. Leaving the picnic basket on the porch, he rang the bell then walked through the unlocked screen door.

A man in a tank top and work pants sat on the couch, his face lit by the television.

"Hello, Mr. Moss," Ford said.

"Hello, Ford," Cali's father answered without taking his eyes from the television. "Have a seat."

Ford sat and watched a show about making fondue for ten minutes while his mind buzzed impatiently with different imagined versions of Cali saying, "Ford, no way!" for each surprise she discovered in the tree house. Cali came out wearing a tight dress and high heels with her hair pinned up.

Ford's mind played a drum flourish. Sadie thought she looked pretty, and there was no denying that she had boobs.

"You look—" Ford began, searching for words. "Better than dinner."

"Must not be much of a place you've picked out then." Cali smiled at him.

"Oh, it is. It is." Their fingers twined together, and Sadie felt his heartbeat pick up.

Cali said goodbye to her dad, and they stepped out onto the porch into the warm night. Ford bent to grab the picnic basket, and Cali tugged her hand from his. "No," she said emphatically. "No, no, *no*."

What was going on? Sadie wondered as Ford's mind filled with even lines of dark circles hovering in protective formation. "Cali?" he asked.

She shook her head, her cheeks flushed, arms crossed over her chest. "Not again," she told him. "You said we were going somewhere new. Somewhere special."

"We are," Ford assured her.

You totally are, Sadie agreed.

"Then what is that?" She pointed a long, harlequin-painted nail at the picnic basket.

"Dinner?" Ford said.

"I am not spending another one of those nights climbing over people's discarded crap to one of your 'special' places in some old building with no working bathroom."

Sadie hadn't thought about the bathroom part.

"Look at me," Cali said, running her hand down herself

like a TV presenter. "I'm the kind of woman who should be taken out and shown off. Not the kind who should be sitting on the floor eating off paper plates in some moldy house no one else wants to be in either."

Sadie was shocked. She'd expected Cali to be so excited, thrilled. Because Ford had expected her to be excited, she realized.

And because I would be.

Now Ford's mind hummed with anxiety. He set the basket down. "I thought you liked that. You said you liked it when I found secret spots to take you. They're way more special than that place we went for dinner on Friday."

"Really?" Cali said, raising an eyebrow. "Because I think toilets are special."

Sadie started to feel annoyed with Cali. *If she's going to be that way, she doesn't deserve to see the tree house*, she told Ford.

But he didn't agree. *Fix this, fix this, fix this*, his mind chanted. "Please, Cali? Please will you come? I think you'll really like it."

Cali teetered back on her heels. "No. I can't. If I go you'll be funny and we'll have sex and nothing will ever change." She let out a long ragged breath. "I think it's time for this to be over."

Her words caught Ford completely off guard. For a moment his mind froze, every sound gone, every dot stuck, suspended in place. "Over?" he repeated, and Sadie felt how tight his vocal cords were. "You and me? Because of a picnic?" He kicked the basket. "Forget the picnic. Fine, let's go to a restaurant."

"It's not the picnic. It's everything."

Points of color flared agonizingly and Ford's head filled

with noise, as if Cali saying "it's time for this to be over" were a magnet for other voices—"piece of crap," "puppy," "I miss him," "drop it," "let go," "get out of here"—lashing him, causing real, physical pain.

Sadie felt the stickiness of humiliation, the heat of his anger, scented the bleach of betrayal, the raw hurt of having worked so hard and been rejected. He did the only thing he knew how to do, the thing he always did. In a harsh, cold voice he said, "Are you sleeping with your boss already?"

"You asshole." Cali turned to go back into the house.

"Cali, wait, I'm sorry." He reached for her arm. Sadie was impressed with him, impressed with his accepting responsibility and being willing to admit he was wrong. "That was a terrible thing to say. I didn't mean it. It's just—you said everything was wrong. But I thought we were fine. We went out with your friends the other night, and it was great. I loved George and Cotton." Ford's vision dimmed, and Sadie felt him recoil from the lie but sensed his hopelessness, his desperation. "I always just assumed it was you and me together forever. That's what we said. And now we have some little disagreement and you say everything is over."

Cali looked at his hand on her arm. "It's Georgia and Clinton. And you didn't like them. You hated them. You pretended to, but you were bluffing."

Ford blinked, and Sadie felt a rising sense of vertigo, as though he had no idea where he was or which way was up. "That's not—"

Cali stopped his protest. "You were so busy this weekend, I had a lot of time to think. And the more I did, the more it became clear."

Something in her tone made Ford let go of her arm. The feeling of vertigo stayed with him. "What?"

"You—you're all about the past. Old houses, old friends. City Center. Things staying how they are. But I'm not. I want to move forward. I'm tired of picnics, and crawling through rafters to see some great view of the city, which is just the same dirty city no matter how you look at it. I like eating off plates with silverware at a table with chairs. I adore restaurants and new homes in new developments with new furniture and new carpets. I want to live somewhere with a bathtub no one has ever used and a refrigerator that makes ice. Like Georgia and Clinton's town house."

Sadie watched Ford rooting around his mind, hunting for patches, anything he could use to fix this like he fixed the tree house, only the materials were much more sparse. He considered a memory of an old porch swing they'd sat in on an abandoned porch and watched the sunset, but settled instead on "We agreed that place was hideous. All that fake plastic molding and wallpaper that looked like tile."

Wrong choice, Sadie thought.

Cali shook her head. "*You* said it was hideous. I—I liked it." She looked down, knitting her fingers together. "Actually, I loved it."

"But the windows were aluminum. They'll be freezing all winter. And the front door wasn't even real wood. Everything was fake. A lie." *Stop!* Sadie called out to him. *You're completely missing the point.*

Cali sighed. "That's not what I saw. I saw something clean and pretty. For happy people with a bank account and plans for the future."

Sadie watched miserably as Ford flailed around, finding all the wrong handholds. "It's not going to look pretty for long. That stucco was already starting to—"

"Stop it!" Cali said. "This isn't about the damn house. It's about us. About us being over."

Ford's mind heaved and rolled from anger to desperation and back again. "Why now?" he said. "What changed?"

"Nothing's changed, Ford. That's the problem." Cali's expression was almost pitying. "I've been waiting for you to change for months. You say you want to grow up, have a construction company of your own. You talk about all those old buildings, restoring them to the status they deserve, like they are members of your family. But it's all talk. In the end, you're still a scrapper."

Ford's mind continued to rise and fall in stormy confusion. "That's not true. I salvage."

"That's just a fancy name. Like when alcoholics call themselves wine connoisseurs. You go into old buildings and take stuff no one else wants. All you do is get distracted by one thing or another. I waited for you. I was patient. I believed you— believed in you. But you never meant it, did you?"

Sadie felt Ford looking for a horizon line, for anything stable. "Of course I did."

"Have you looked into getting a contractor's license? Or asked the foreman if you can be the head of your crew? Have you done anything?"

He saw a lifeline and reached for it. "Well, with James dying—"

"No," she said, stomping her foot. "You've been hiding behind that for too long. James is dead. He's not coming back.

You should be as loyal to those of us who are still alive as you are to him." She shook her head. "God knows he wasn't as loyal to you."

Hundreds of images of Cali spun through Ford's mind, too fast to be clear, as if he was running through their entire history trying to make sense of what was happening. Finally they slowed without giving him any answer, and he said, "All those times you said you loved me, did you ever mean it?" There was raw pain in his voice, and also fear.

"Of course I did." Cali's eyes looked sad. "I'm just tired of waiting for you to become the person you said you wanted to be."

He nodded, letting that sink in. After a long minute of silence he said, "I guess I should go."

Cali nodded. "Yeah."

He picked up the picnic basket. "Just so you know. The place tonight has chairs and a table. I built them for you. Because I thought it would make you happy." Sadie's chest felt tight, and she was having trouble breathing.

At the bottom of the stairs he turned around to look at Cali standing above him. His mind was still stormy but he strove not to show it. "You look really beautiful," he said. "Good luck with the new job. And thank you for everything, California. I—I really enjoyed our three years together. Or three years minus a week."

Red, white, and blue dots in Ford's head became fireworks during a party, a younger Cali setting a roasted marshmallow between two graham crackers, saying, "I've never met anyone else who likes s'mores without chocolate before," and then kissing, more fireworks, a number in a phone.

The Fourth of July was their anniversary.

Cali's shoulders sagged. "Me too. Next week is going to be weird."

"Yeah," he agreed.

Tears hovered at the corners of Cali's eyes, and her lower lip began to tremble. "Ford," she said, reaching toward him.

Remarkable, Sadie thought. That one simple gesture, that show of ambivalence, had calmed the turbulence inside of Ford. "Don't," he told her, on solid ground at last. "It's better this way."

As he went, Sadie thought she smelled pine needles.

Like a man on autopilot Ford continued on his preprogrammed route, riding his bike from Cali's to the tree house. His mind was beyond quiet, it was absent. Frozen. *Numb*, Sadie thought. Nature's antidote to the pain of being alive.

He hauled the picnic basket up into the tree house but didn't unpack it, just left it on the table, his phone next to it, and collapsed into one of the chairs he'd built specially for Cali.

Goddamn chair, Sadie heard him think, and she laughed, feeling the prickle of tears in her eyes at the same time.

That's not objective, she chided herself.

Goddamn objectivity, she answered back.

His numbness started to chafe at Sadie, making her feel isolated and out of sorts. Ford closed his eyes and drifted into a penumbra state between sleeping and being awake. His mind was filled with milky white light, and now, set against it, she saw dots dancing into an image of James's face. It wasn't the James of the graduation photo, it was five or six years younger, and Sadie noticed the image seemed sort of stylized, as though James had been polished like a trophy.

The dots shifted, showing James with a young Ford, probably around twelve, the golden rope Sadie recognized from his other memories now stretched between them. James lifting one end and saying to Ford, "Got it?"

Ford answering, "Got it," and holding up the other end.

James checking, "You're sure you're ready?"

"Ready." Ford nodding, but nervous.

James putting out a white winter glove and Ford putting out a black one and the two of them shaking. James, serious, saying, "I'm counting on you. Don't let me down."

Twelve-year-old Ford solemnly promising, "Never."

James, his handsome face lighting up, saying, "Okay. Let's go get rich!"

Sadie's heart began to pound with excitement as she watched. *This was what had happened in the icehouse.*

The next moment, Ford opened his eyes and reached for his phone, and the memory vanished. Sadie had no idea who he was calling when he dialed, until an automated voice answered, saying, "You have one saved message. Message saved for one hundred twenty-four days. Press one to play, two to delete."

One hundred twenty-four days was a little more than four months, Sadie calculated, which meant this message must be from around the time of James's murder. Was this the message Ford's subconscious had wanted him to hear?

Ford took a deep breath and pushed one.

"Thursday, six thirty-nine P.M., from: private number," the computer voice said. There was a pause, the sound of a throat being cleared, and then a guy saying, "What's up, Ford? It's me, James. Listen, my meeting is running a little long, so

I was wondering if you could do dinner. Lulu wants lasagna. You know how to make that. If it's too hard just do mac and cheese."

The message was slow, each sentence punctuated by a long silent pause as though James were distracted. *Or on something*, Sadie thought. But she felt her heartbeat slowing to keep time with its rhythm. "Sometimes I add those tiny meatballs if you can find them at the store. Mostly the key is the sauce, that's the part she likes. Really pretty much any noodles will do."

Finally the speed picked up, and the words began to come out in a rush.

"Probably this is way too much detail, I promise if you help me out you'll be glad—more than glad because I'm doing this for you as much as anyone. Everything is going to change after this, it's going to be you and me, brother, the way it used to be. What the . . . oh god, I've . . . shot . . . *hel*—"

The message ended.

Sadie's heart dropped, and she gasped in disbelief. *She had just heard James's murder.* He'd been leaving Ford a message when he was killed. *Oh, Ford*, she thought, *oh, you poor boy.* No wonder he felt guilty.

There wasn't anything he could have done, but to have to listen to that cry for help over and over had to be excruciating.

The numbness deepened then, his mind becoming a solid monolith. She wanted to wrap her arms around him, hold him, make him know that he wasn't alone. She wished she could sit with him and tell him that it wasn't his fault until he believed it. Do anything to shatter the stone-like silence that had settled over his mind.

But there was nothing she could do, no way to touch him. This was the powerlessness Curtis had talked about, and it was terrible.

The tree house was filled with dark shadows when his mind began to whir with sounds again. They began low, indecipherable, but one of them came into focus, James's voice from the memory in the icehouse saying, "I'm counting on you. Don't let me down." Initially it repeated every few seconds, but it sped up, cycling faster and faster until it was overlapping, as though there were two Jameses, then four, then ten, all saying it at just slightly different times, like an echo chamber. As it reverberated, the phrase eroded, becoming "you don't let me down," "don't let me down," "let me down," "down," "drow—"

Ford's phone buzzed with a message, loud and startling in the silence, yanking him from his thoughts. Sadie heard him think *Cali*, and for a split second she glimpsed a crack in the numbness.

But it wasn't from Cali, it was from Plum. It said: "COME TO MY PLACE. BOSUN BUILDING, PENTHOUSE A. TELL THE DOORMAN YOUR NAME IS ROMEO. DON'T KEEP ME WAITING."

Just what the doctor ordered, Sadie heard Ford think.

Only if it was Dr. Frankenstein, she said. *Or Dr. Bad Idea. After everything that's happened tonight, do you really think—*

"ON MY WAY," he texted.

CHAPTER 18

I still think this is a very bad idea, Sadie whispered to Ford an hour later as he watched Plum slide down next to him on the brown wool sofa.

Plum wore a white linen caftan that was see-through when the light hit it directly, as it was doing now. "You were incredibly dull the last time I saw you," she said, shifting in a way that made it clear she wasn't wearing anything underneath. "What makes you think you won't bore me this time?"

"I'll try my best," Ford told her, pitching his voice low. During the ride over Ford's numbness had taken on a hard, sardonic edge, lack of feeling turning to reckless boldness.

Plum laughed and leaned toward him, giving him a glimpse down the front of her caftan. *No need to trouble yourself,* Sadie assured her. *We could already see just fine.* "Say 'hardest' and you might have a shot."

"My absolute hardest," Ford pledged.

They were sitting in her wide-open living room. The furniture was clean and modern, a low sofa, leather shag rug, a massive television. In front of them, a wall of floor-to-ceiling windows showed a terrace that seemed to wrap around the whole apartment, with the city twinkling sixty-three floors below it.

Plum's penthouse in the Bosun Building was less than an hour's bike ride from where Ford lived, but as he'd chained his bike, Sadie had heard him thinking it might as well have been another planet. He was struck by how quiet it was, with no foot traffic, just the low purr of well-maintained car engines and the regular whirring of helicopters landing and taking off from the tops of the sleek towers.

It was quieter inside the cocoon of her apartment, and she was amused to hear Ford think that even the silence was nicer in this part of town. Plum handed him a glass and a cocktail napkin monogrammed with a double *P*, and said, "Your text said you couldn't get me off your mind. What, exactly, were you imagining?" She took a sip.

Ford's new recklessness seemed to eliminate nerves. It was like he was a different person, a shallower, more confident—

"The reality is much better than the fantasy," he told Plum.

—more cheesy one.

Plum laughed. They were both barefoot, and her toes skimmed his as she shifted, somehow making her caftan even less opaque. "You can't fool me. You came here to ask about your brother."

Watching the light dim in Ford's range of vision, Sadie realized he thought Plum was testing him. If he agreed that he'd come to talk about James, he'd be thrown out. If he denied it, said that he'd come because Plum fascinated him, he'd be allowed to stay. It was a devious but clever way of engineering the outcome Plum wanted, essentially telling Ford how to behave.

"I could have done that on the phone," Ford said, skirting the trap. "Or I could have suggested we meet somewhere in public." He looked at her, and Sadie felt him setting a trap of his own. "I'm sure we could think of more interesting things to talk about than James. God knows he wasn't that interesting when he was alive."

Plum took the bait. "That's not a very nice thing to say about your brother."

"Didn't you say he bored you? Never wanted to have any fun?"

"No." She leaned forward and straightened the cocktail napkin beneath her glass. "We had fun."

"I'm having trouble picturing James up here." That was a lie, Sadie knew. During the ride up to the penthouse in the Bosun Building's glass-and-chrome elevator, Ford had thought of how perfect it was for James, no wonder he'd stopped coming home. "Did James give the doorman his own name, or did he call himself Romeo too?"

"He had all different aliases. He'd come to the door and do a different voice for each one: Professor Barmy, Officer Lockup, Mr. Mopeson." She shook her head. "He was such a ham."

A crack appeared in the frozen surface of Ford's mind at her words. He hadn't expected anything genuine, Sadie thought, and the *realness* of it, this glimpse into a whole life James had lived without him, was a shock.

"He was," Ford said quietly. "He used to be able to make Lulu and me laugh for hours."

"Lulu?" Plum asked.

"Our sister." When Plum still looked puzzled Ford added, "Didn't James tell you about her?"

Plum shook her head. "He didn't really talk about his family much. It didn't come up."

A flare of anger shot out, threatening Ford's entire cool demeanor. He swallowed hard and said, "What did you talk about then?" His chest was tight, his voice was strained, but Plum didn't seem to notice. Sadie wondered if she had any idea of the pain she was causing.

"My club. What we were going to do that night. What to have for dinner."

"Your patron?" Ford tossed out.

Plum ignored it. "My movies."

Ford frowned. "You make movies? I thought you were going to be a child psychologist."

"I can do both," Plum said, but her tone was a little snappish, as though, Sadie thought, the question bothered her.

Pieces of ideas floated through Ford's mind, and he grabbed at them haphazardly. "Did you and James make any movies together?"

"Of course," Plum said, eyes gleaming with amusement. "James was a very good"—she paused to lick her lips—"performer."

Ford's thoughts skittered from her suggestion. He shifted to put a little more distance between them, and Sadie sensed him groping for a safe question. "How did you two meet?"

Plum leaned toward the coffee table and slid open a drawer beneath it. "At a party." She pulled a tablet computer from the drawer and started flipping through it as she spoke. "The handsome one with the dangerous eyes . . . Linc?" She glanced up at Ford, who nodded. "He introduced us."

Ford's mind filled with a grainy gray, blue, and black image of Linc's silence when he'd asked about James's girlfriend, the dots getting darker and darker until they fizzled into black. "How do you know Linc?" he asked Plum.

She shrugged and said, "Friend of a friend." She was distracted, tapping through the screen in front of her like she was looking for something specific. "Can you explain how you know all your friends?"

Ford's mind was running through a pointillist slideshow of Willy swearing he didn't know Plum, which expanded to all his brother's friends. "Yep." *All liars*, Sadie heard him think.

"You're not very popular then," Plum told him, finally looking up. She smiled and held the tablet toward him. "This is some video of James I shot the day before he—you know."

"That's okay," Ford said, making no move to take it.

Plum laughed. "It's not *that* kind of video, at least not the first four minutes and twenty-two seconds. He's fully clothed that whole time. I promise it won't offend your sensibilities."

Ford left every other thought behind as he took the tablet. "Thanks," he said, a tiny breeze of loneliness caressing his cheek. Sadie felt his hands trembling and his heartbeat pushing against his ribs. He sat back, nestling into the couch cushions to keep his arms steady, and pushed PLAY.

The screen filled with a picture of James watching TV. Sadie felt the effort it took Ford not to reach out and touch his face. Winter sunshine streamed in through the large plate-glass windows of the same room they were sitting in now, basking James in a golden glow. Eyes not leaving the television, James said, "Hey, sugarplum, come over here, look what I found. It's you, in a school play or something, a hundred years ago. You were quite the performer even then."

Sadie had seen photos of James, experienced him in both Ford's subconscious and his memories, and she'd heard his voice on Ford's voice mail message, but this was her first view of him as a fully realized person. He was handsome, but the word that came immediately to Sadie's mind was *fun*. He had a mischievous, ready smile and looked like the guy who would be the life of any party.

The camera stayed on James's face, looking with concentration at the TV. There was the sound of a little boy saying, "If you prick me, I will blee—*ouch*, you cut me. You weren't supposed to use a real dagger. You stabbed me. There's blood."

A girl's voice answered flippantly, "Something to remember me by when I'm gone."

The boy, sounding desperate now, "Don't say that. You can't leave me. I promise I'll get you everything you want. Just say you'll never leave."

A ripple of laughter from the girl. "Define *everything*."

Watching this, James guffawed, and Sadie felt Ford's chest tighten. Hearing James's laugh set up a tug-of-war inside of Ford, pulling between wanting to savor the joy of that sound and wanting to howl with missing him.

James looked away from the television, right into the camera, and asked, "What is this, sugarbear? Wait, that kid is your *brother*."

"When we were little," Plum's voice affirmed from off screen.

James leaned forward to stare at the TV. "He's so small. No wonder."

"We were young," Plum's voice said, a little curt. Her hand appeared in the movie, outstretched for the remote. "Turn it off."

Grinning, James took the remote and shoved it down his pants. "Come and get it."

The camera moved closer to James. It stopped right in front of his face, recording up close as his expression went from amusement to surprise to desire, and he said in a husky voice, "Damn, woman, that's not the remote."

"Funny," Plum said, "I could have sworn—"

Ford pushed PAUSE. "I don't think I need the rest." His mind became quiet and empty, a single thought drifting around it like a leaf being blown in a spring breeze: *He looked so happy. He looked so happy with her.*

He moved his gaze to Plum, and Sadie felt him probing for some sign that she'd felt the same way about James as James had felt about her.

Plum cleared her throat. "That was the last time I saw him," she said. "I left for Paris that next day, and when I came back . . ." Her lip quivered. She got up. "Let's have a little drinkie." When Ford hesitated she said, "You wouldn't make a girl drink by herself, would you?"

He followed her toward the kitchen, his thoughts saying that he had to stay focused, he was there to get her to talk to the police. But beneath that, Sadie sensed the deep pit of loneliness, now lit with a tiny spark of cinnamony hope that here was someone he could miss James with.

She's going to hurt you, Sadie wanted to tell to him, though she realized she had no real basis for saying that. For a split second she wondered if she was jealous of Plum, but that would have been ridiculous. Ford was a subject of study to her. It was far more likely that she was reacting to the fact that Plum had shown herself to be nothing but self-serving. Even in the video with her brother they'd just heard, she'd treated his feelings cavalierly.

Jealous. Absurd.

He watched Plum mix vodka with lime juice, listening to the clear chime of the silver spoon against the chrome shaker. He said, "Why didn't you come to the funeral?

She sprinkled the top with powdered sugar. "Funerals aren't really my thing. I didn't go to my parents' funeral. I'm not going to start now." She took a sip from the shaker, made a face, and added more vodka. "Besides, like I said, I was on my way to Paris when it happened. I didn't even know James was dead until I got back."

Good, Sadie thought. *So Plum has nothing more to tell us, and we can go.*

But Ford's mind began the process Sadie now identified as problem solving, picking up pieces and trying them in different places.

"You didn't want to come to the funeral," he said. "And you said you didn't want to talk to Serenity Services, even to tell them about James not using drugs."

"Because it has nothing to do with me," Plum snapped. "Because I believe in minding my own business. And because James is dead, so it can't make any difference to him. Don't start on that again."

Ford put up a hand. "I'm not. I'm just wondering, since

you've seemed to put James completely behind you"—he looked at her hard—"why did you want to meet me?"

She cracked ice into two tall glasses and filled them from the shaker, apparently unconcerned. "I told you. I heard you were asking about me."

"From who? How did you get my number?"

She pushed one of the glasses across the counter toward him. "It's not that hard to come by, is it? Why won't you let this drop?"

Ford shook his head. "I'm just trying to figure out what happened to my brother."

Plum took a sip of her drink and came and stood very close to him, looking at him over the top of her glass. "You want to know what happened to James?"

Her leg brushed his thigh. Ford's pulse leapt forward, and Sadie heard the shimmer of a tambourine. "I do," he said. "I want to know—"

"A *lot* happened to James," Plum answered. She gulped her drink and set it on the counter with an elegant *chink* of ice. "A lot of it right here." She pushed Ford against the counter. "I told you I went to Paris, right? Did you know the real French kiss has nothing at all to do with two mouths?" She slid her hand to his crotch and moved her eyes to his lips.

A xylophone clanged in Ford's head and drums sounded like they'd been knocked over. *She's trying to distract you*, Sadie warned him. *Which means they were good questions. Stay focused. Don't fall for it.*

Ford said, "No. I, uh, studied Spanish."

Plum tugged the end of his belt out of the buckle and had her finger on the top button of his waistband. She brought her face close enough so their mouths were almost touching. She smelled of vodka, lime, and perfume.

Sadie felt Ford's pulse jump, and his arousal tickled like tiny butterfly wings all over her body. Plum whispered, "Let me show you how it's really done," and slid her body down until she was on her knees in front of him.

The sound of every instrument playing hard at once in Ford's mind was almost deafening. *You don't want to do this*, Sadie told him despite substantial evidence to the contrary.

Plum lowered his zipper and ran a finger down the front of his boxers. All the instruments went on playing their loudest but now with the first hints of some kind of structure. *You're just feeling vulnerable*, Sadie told him. *You broke up with your girlfriend, and you like the attention, but—*

A thousand bombs of sensation exploded over Sadie's body and the keyboards pounded as Plum slipped her hand into the slit in Ford's boxers. "Oh, *my*," she breathed. "You're definitely not the little bro—"

The sentence died on her lips, and she withdrew her hand. Casting a panicked look at the front door, she said, "You've got to go."

The band in Ford's head stopped playing chaotically, each instrument cutting off mid-phrase. Ford's thoughts felt dizzy and slow. "Why? What's happening?"

Sadie hadn't heard anything over the clamor in Ford's head, but the sound of knocking on the front door was clearly audible now.

Plum pushed him toward her bedroom, detouring by the couch to grab his shoes. "You have to get out of here. Now."

He took the shoes and looked around, wondering if he'd left anything else. "How?"

"Hide in the closet. I'll create a distraction in the office. Wait thirty seconds from when you last hear voices and make for the back door in the kitchen. It goes to the service stairs, and you can take those all the way down to the garage. Then you can avoid being seen by the doormen."

It sounded like a good idea to Sadie. But Ford's vision dimmed as he listened to Plum, and his voice was harsh as he demanded, "Hide in the closet? Sneak out? You've got to be kidding."

"I'm not doing this for me, I'm doing it for you," Plum told him seriously.

Sadie thought that was okay too, but Ford's mind screamed, *Liar!*

There was another knock on the front door. "Go," Plum insisted, pointing to the closet. "Now."

He caught her wrist as she turned to leave, stopping her. "How did you get my number?"

She tried to shake his hand off. "Not now."

He didn't budge. "Just tell me. Where did you get it?"

Her eyes slewed away from him, toward the bed. "I don't remember, okay? Now get in there," she urged and left, shutting the bedroom door with a click.

Ford cocked his ears, listening for sounds from the other room. He heard Plum's footsteps padding across the floor, the front door opening.

Plum's voice, perhaps slightly too loud, saying, "I wasn't expecting you." The sound of a kiss, the front door closing.

Sadie watched Ford running through different possibilities in his head. Saunter out of the room and say "thanks" and leave. Saunter out and make the other guy leave. Hide in the closet.

"Sorry it took me so long to get to the door. You woke me," he heard Plum going on.

Sadie tried to imagine what it would be like to be beholden to someone that way. To have to pretend to be happy to see them even if you weren't, put whatever else you were doing aside just because they told you to.

The sound of glasses shifting, murmurs, then Plum again, not as loud: "Oh, yes, I had company earlier, but they're long gone."

Ford went and stood by the closet. It was big, bigger than his mother's room, and full. There were plenty of things to hide behind, but if someone actually came in and looked, it wouldn't take them long to find him.

The voices from the other room receded until Plum's voice pierced the quiet, saying, "You're checking up on me." Points of white and black pulled together in Ford's mind to form a picture of Plum, her expression petulant, her arms crossed beneath her boobs. "I don't care what you said, I can do what I want."

The sound of footsteps quickly approaching filtered through the door of the bedroom.

"Where are you going?" Plum demanded, her feet pitter-patting behind the other set. "What are you doing?"

Sadie heard Ford teasing out the threads of Plum's tone, part concern, part expectation.

The bedroom door flew open. The footsteps didn't stop but made straight for the closet, and Sadie heard Ford wondering how many times these two had played out this drama before.

He was curious about what the man looked like, but seeing him wasn't worth the risk of getting caught, Ford decided. As soon as he heard the sound of the closet door being thrown open, he slipped out from behind the bedroom door where he'd hidden. He caught a momentary glimpse of Plum hovering outside the closet, looking as though she was about to get a treat.

Ford had been right, Sadie realized as he took off. Plum had been setting him up. This was a game for her.

Bedroom to kitchen to back service stairs took him less than thirty seconds. He ran down two flights, then pushed through to the main hallway and took the elevator the rest of the way. By the time he reached the garage his pants were buttoned, his belt was done, and his shirt was tucked.

An older couple driving by gave him a strange look, and he realized he was still barefoot and carrying his shoes.

This is why it's a good policy to stay dressed while at strangers' houses, Sadie told him.

Night had fallen over the city, clear and sweet, with a deep blueberry sky that made the stars look like diamonds. Or maybe the stars always looked expensive around here, Ford thought. He glanced up at the icicle-shaped skyscraper he'd just left and began to laugh.

His mind replayed the last hour in dots of color: Plum on her knees; Plum reciting bad movie dialogue; Plum shoving his shoes into his arms. Sadie heard him wondering what usually happened to the guy in the closet: Was he horsewhipped and sent down in the elevator tied up, or did they give him a drink and dinner? Was this how they got their thrills?

Then he flipped to a much older memory of tomato soup and grilled cheese and a snowball fight, rolling a huge snowball off the edge of the roof onto James's startled head. His brother's eyes huge with surprise like Plum's had been, James saying, "You got me good," and then the two of them cracking up for hours.

God, James was going to laugh when Ford told him about what had just—

Ford stopped walking, stopped breathing. Sadie felt pain jolt him like a hard punch to the chest, racking his body, making every muscle, every sinew tense. Jagged shards of ice pierced him, his head rushed with noise, and he bent double right in the middle of the street in pure agony.

This wasn't ordinary grief, Sadie knew instinctively, it was far worse than that. Because he'd forgotten. For a moment, for a second, he forgot James was dead. And when he remembered, the force of it was too much. This was grief so profound it was like being turned inside out by it, left with the most vulnerable parts exposed to the air. There was no escape from this pain. Every gesture, every motion made his body scream with it.

He didn't want to go on, she heard him think, didn't want to go anywhere. He wanted to stay in that place forever until something happened to take the pain away.

A car roared up, its horn blaring, and he stumbled forward blindly, barely making it to the curb before it passed. He sank back against the wall and closed his eyes, breathing unevenly. Sadie felt the agony inside him change, not subsiding but becoming less jagged, less piercing. Its sharp edges receded; its ache deepened and became more like a smooth round rock, still hard but now more the constant throbbing of everyday grief than the sting of a fresh gash. She thought she smelled pine again.

After a few minutes he pulled himself to his feet. Sadie felt the effort it cost him, but his breathing was normal and his head was clear. As he unlocked his bike his thoughts replayed Plum's reaction when he'd asked how she knew his phone number. It should have been an easy question. She could have answered honestly, or picked one of a hundred simple lies. Instead she'd been evasive.

Looks like I found the right wrong question, he thought. If only he had any idea what it meant.

CHAPTER 19

Storm clouds massed all Thursday afternoon, mirroring the dark mood inside Ford's head. His crew was demoing a library built in the 1920s, full of gorgeous details that Ford was devastated about destroying. He'd called and left three messages for Mason "Just Pretending to Care" Bligh, telling him about all the great stuff there, but the guy hadn't called back once. No surprise, Ford figured. People who lived in those fancy spaceship buildings were selfish liars.

Oh, good. At least you're keeping this all in appropriate perspective, Sadie said.

As he worked, crashing his hammer through a stained-glass window, smashing a water fountain shaped like a shell, he was haunted by his mother's voice saying, "We need to talk."

Ford disagreed. In fact, Sadie heard him thinking, he was

sure that he didn't need another lecture about how unlike his brother he was, how much he'd let her down, how disappointed she was . . .

"Storm coming. Unsafe conditions. All work to cease," the foreman's voice rang out from two rooms away. At nearly the same moment a silver thread of lightning split the sky, followed four seconds later by thunder that shook the twelve-foot ladder Ford was standing on top of, but he made no move to get down.

He was up there struggling to pry a hand-carved wooden medallion of an owl from the doorframe he was supposed to be smashing. Sadie loved these stolen moments at work with him when he went from destroying to rescuing things. He talked to them, flattering, cajoling, teasing. Sadie didn't even think he knew he did it.

"Come on, boy," Ford coaxed the owl now, leaning into the chisel he was using. "You've waited up here long—"

The medallion came flying off, hitting Ford in the shoulder and making him rock dangerously back on the ladder.

Sadie gasped with fear as it tipped backward. For a moment it hung suspended in midair at a forty-five-degree angle with Ford clinging to its underbelly. Then it tottered and rushed toward the floor. At the last possible moment before being smashed beneath it, Ford whipped his body to the side and rolled. He hit the ground a second before the ladder.

"*Whoooooooooooooooooooop!*" he hollered, a victory cry, and both he and Sadie started laughing. "That was close," he said aloud.

It was, she agreed, wondering what he looked like when he laughed like that. *Close, but fun.*

He tucked the owl under the tarp with the three other similar medallions he'd rescued and went to clock out. On his way to his bike he checked his messages and experienced a moment of surprise not to see one from Cali before he remembered the breakup. The same thing that had happened that morning when he checked and saw that Cali's normal seven thirty A.M. "HAVE A GOOD DAY :)" text wasn't there, and at lunch. Sadie had caught a pang of nostalgia but not sadness, and she had the sense that it was the rituals of the relationship he was missing more than Cali herself.

A wishbone of lightning flashed across the sky, followed by a crackle of thunder. The storm hadn't come yet, but the wind was picking up. The Advert Alert Board over the intersection across the street advised all commuters to return home as soon as possible to avoid being caught outside.

Sadie heard his mind racing, trying to think of anywhere he could go besides home. He was considering all his old hideouts with Bucky, mentally cataloging them by proximity, when a Royal Pizza delivery van stopped in traffic directly in front of him.

I have to follow it, Sadie heard him think. *It's a sign.*

A sign of what? she wanted to ask. *That you are so afraid of having a conversation with your mom that you'd rather follow a crazy hint from an insane person and risk being stuck in a storm on a bike?*

Apparently yes. Letting two cars go in front of him the way he'd seen in movies, Ford pulled his bike into traffic and started following the delivery van.

Now that you're such a believer in signs, maybe you should consider paying attention to those that say STOP like the one right in front—

He sped through the intersection heedlessly, and Sadie wanted to shake him with frustration. How could he be so brave in some ways and so cowardly in others?

Ford followed the delivery van onto a residential street, where it slowed like it was looking for an address. Sadie smelled cinnamon and wondered if he was hoping to find that the pizzas were real or that they were fake.

The delivery van stopped in front of an apartment building in the middle of the block and honked twice. An upstairs window opened, a guy yelled, "Be right there," and a moment later came stumbling down, hair smashed to his head, pulling on a shirt like he'd just woken up. He leaned in, paid the driver, and came out with three pizza boxes.

That looked real, Sadie said. *Can we go now?*

But Ford wasn't done. The van's next stop was a two-story house. The driver honked twice again and a girl came out clutching a dog in one arm, a thick wallet in the other, and her phone cradled against her ear. Without pausing in her conversation she paid the driver and took her pizza, almost tipping it over before he called, "Watch how you carry that," as she went up the stairs.

The rain still hadn't come, but the air was heavy and the wind was wrestling him for control of his bike. As the girl disappeared into her house without a single suspicious gesture or sign, his body suddenly felt heavy and tired.

His mind teemed with doubts. What was he doing? Following a pizza delivery van as though it could lead him to—what? Answers about James's death? It was completely moronic. Despite the slogan, Royal Pizza was just pizza, and the delivery vans were just delivery vans. *Bucky must have been wrong,* he decided. He might as well go home and let his mother yell at him.

Lightning made a Z in the sky. He started to pedal faster, determined to get home before the rain started, and was about to pass the delivery van when it signaled a right turn onto Love Your Feet Road. Almost unconsciously Ford jerked hard on the handlebars of his bike and swerved to follow it.

As soon as he turned, his mind wove glowing colored points into a rich tapestry of images. Using that fire hydrant as third base for baseball, the large oak tree as a goal for soccer, Bucky rigging up a lighting scheme for night games, a go-kart race. Some of these were less clear, and Sadie realized that was because those were multiple images superimposed on one another: dozens of games of baseball, a decade's worth of soccer, a hundred different go-kart races.

The pizza van passed a house that Ford registered as Bucky's old house, before stopping in front of 116 Love Your Feet Road. Linc's place, Ford's mind told Sadie, with a stack of other Royal Pizza boxes already on the porch.

Ford pulled his bike into the shadow of a tree to watch, and caught a fat drop on his forehead. *Just let the storm hold off a little longer*, he thought.

The delivery guy went up to the door—different than at the other houses, where he'd just honked—and was met by a girl in a bright pink dress. Against the white porch and gray sky she looked like she'd fallen from the tail end of a rainbow.

Maya, Linc's sister, Sadie gleaned, watching Ford's memory of her blossom into a multicolor array of dots. A little girl, his age but always younger seeming. People telling him that "Maya is simple" or "different" when he asked why she spent all day making necklaces with beads instead of going to school with him and why when she talked it sounded like birds instead of words. Now she stood grinning at the pizza guy before turning and chirruping something into the dark interior of the house.

Linc came out, shirtless, one strap of a pair of denim overalls on, the other dangling, a chicken drumstick in his hand. "I didn't order pizza," he said, loud enough for Ford to hear. He sounded bored.

The pizza guy shook his head. "I got a rush order for two larges, both with anchovies. For 345 EvergreenLawn Supplies Way."

"Don't know what to tell you," Linc said, boredom replaced now with annoyance. "You got the wrong address, buddy."

"Sure?"

"Positive. EvergreenLawn is on the other side of town."

"Nuts." The guy looked at the pizza, then at Linc. "Won't be good by the time I get there. Why don't you take it?"

"Okay. Here," Linc said, fishing a tip out of his pocket and handing it to the guy.

Ford's vision had dimmed as soon as the pizza guy spoke and became slightly blurry, as though the edges of the scene didn't match up.

Sadie sensed it too, but she couldn't pinpoint it until red and white and black dots in Ford's mind arranged themselves into a pizza box and she heard Ford think, *There's a pizza missing*. The delivery man had said the order was for two pizzas, but he'd only had one in his hands.

Could still be in the car, Ford thought. But instead of

continuing to follow the delivery van, he decided to stay where he was, and five minutes later Linc came down the front stairs of his house with a briefcase, dressed like a guy going to an office job. He bypassed the car in the driveway and the bike on the porch and headed for the bus stop.

Ford trailed the bus, the sky tossing out occasional big drops but nothing serious, and forty minutes later he was propping his bike next to a fence around the corner from 345 EvergreenLawn Supplies Way. He'd gotten tangled in traffic and lost Linc's bus, but he'd taken a chance on the destination and was just in time to see Linc leaving the house. Whatever his errand, it hadn't taken long. Now he was strolling down the street toward Ford but on the opposite side, briefcase swinging.

Lightning tore across the sky, followed by a jolting crash of thunder. Linc bent to pat a tiny terrier on the head, offered to carry the groceries of a woman in a purple shirt, and had just turned the corner onto Hump Burgers Highway when a scream pierced the air. The woman in purple ran out of 345 EvergreenLawn shrieking, "Call Serenity! They've been shot! Someone shot my boys!"

Ford's mind convulsed and his ears rang, as though refusing to let that in, refusing to hear, to believe—

"Dead! My boys are dead!"

Impossible, impossible, impossible, Ford's mind repeated, but he took off running after Linc, every step echoing with another denial in his head. *No way, not Linc, impossible, not him.*

The storm opened up as Ford rounded the corner. Ford had to struggle to keep Linc in sight, weaving through patches of umbrellas that had sprung up like stalky mushrooms on the crowded street. He saw Linc stop walking, and at the same moment a black Range Rover pulled up alongside him. The door opened from the inside. As he stepped toward it, Linc turned to glance behind him, and his expression chilled Ford. It was serene. He could almost have been smiling.

Ford was halfway home when it hit him. *The Pharmacist*, Sadie heard him think. That had to be the explanation. Bucky had been right about Royal Pizza and he was right about this. Somehow the Pharmacist had changed Linc from the guy he'd grown up with to this . . . monster.

Which meant the Pharmacist was real.

And dangerous, Sadie added.

CHAPTER 20

The apartment was quiet and dark except for the flickering of the muted television when Ford got home.

The ride had been harrowing. For the first fifteen minutes the rain had sluiced down in sheets, making it nearly impossible to see. When it had slowed to a drizzle, the gutters lining the streets were so flooded that there were waves and currents dragging on the tires of his bike.

He left his soaked shoes and jacket in the hall outside the apartment door and was stripping off his sodden pants when a strained voice from the darkness said, "It's time for our talk," and the light next to the armchair clicked on. His mother was there in a faded oatmeal-color sweater and jeans. She looked frail like always, but also determined.

"Not now, Mom," Ford told her, shivering uncontrollably, only partially from being wet. "I really—"

"Sit down."

The shaking had started when he'd started thinking about the Pharmacist, and he didn't seem able to stop it. It was as though there was some internal battle between how he'd believed the world worked and what he now had to acknowledge was true. "I really need a shower," he said, teeth chattering. "My clothes are soaked. Can this wait until later? Tomorrow? Does it have to be now?"

"Yes. Now. Put on dry clothes and sit down."

Sadie was astonished at the steel in her voice. She'd never seen Mrs. Winter like that, and she wondered what it meant. But Ford was too cold, too shell-shocked to give it more than a cursory thought.

He put on a sweatshirt and dry boxers from his closet, leaving his jeans and T-shirt in a wet pile on the floor, and sank into the couch. "Mom, look, I just saw the most horrifying, unbelievable—"

He stopped because she had set a folder on the trunk and was pushing it toward him. There was a handprint along the edge from where she'd clearly been clutching it, waiting for him, for a long time. On its cover it had the ⊞ symbol that was on his ID, printed large, with the words HEALTH HARVEST BY ROQUE, A GLOBAL FORCE FOR PEACE OF MIND written beneath it.

"I've been trying to protect you," his mother said, shielding her eyes from the light and avoiding his gaze. "All this time. All I ever wanted was to protect you."

Ford stared at the folder, hearing "All I ever wanted was to protect you," over and over. His mind filled with dark dots, black, green, yellow, a little boy saying, "Why did you let him stay?" the female figure with a blank face answering, "He's your father. He didn't mean to hurt you." It vanished as quickly as it had appeared, just a flash. Ford said to his mother, "What is this?"

"Read it," she said nervously.

Sadie wasn't sure what to expect, but both she and Ford were slightly disappointed when all it contained was a contract.

She started reading it, and her heart caught in her throat.

Contract between Vera Winter, hereafter PARENT, and HEALTH HARVEST (hereafter HH), a division of Roque Community Health Evaluators (hereafter RCHE) concerning health insurance and care for Ford Winter (newborn), hereafter CHILD 1, one of 3 members of the Winter family (include all relatives who live at same address), hereafter FAMILY.

RCHE agrees to provide comprehensive medical and dental care including regular checkups and all immunizations to CHILD 1 from the date of the contract until his twenty-first birthday. In exchange PARENT agrees to periodic scheduled visits from RCHE to interview FAMILY (not more than once per quarter except in special cases SEE BELOW) and one unscheduled visit per year (except in special cases SEE BELOW).

FAMILY has opted IN to inclusion in periodic opportunities to assist with high-level scientific research; all such opportunities are voluntary.

FAMILY has opted IN to Interperception.

Interperception is a risk-free procedure that allows members of your community between the ages of 19 and 25 to shape its future. If selected to participate in Interperception, your CHILD will serve as a HOST for a researcher GUEST who will chart his or her movements and thoughts for six to twelve weeks, using the collected data to improve social service and lifestyle programs in your community. GUESTS will undergo a rigorous selection and training process and may range from top scholars in their fields to artists, journalists, designers, intellectuals, and students.

Data is gathered passively by means of a neuronano relay chip (hereafter CHIP) implanted in the child's bloodstream between four weeks and fourteen years of age. It is painless and undetectable to the body or the eye.

HH, RCHE, and all programs now or in the future involved in Interperception guarantee that you will never be approached or identified by former GUESTS. Punishment for GUEST-HOST interaction outside of Interperception is severe (see pamphlet WHO'S ON YOUR MIND for greater detail). Because of the profound influence of data gathered, HOSTS are never told of their selection but serve in complete anonymity.

Parents must agree not to inform their children of their status as potential HOSTS until after the date of their 25th birthday, when that status is revoked. Should a parent violate this provision, the case becomes a matter for Serenity Services, subject to the full spectrum of punishments available under the law, including but not limited to fines, permanent suspension of parental rights, and jail time. Your signature on this contract signals your acceptance of all conditions for yourself and your FAMILY.

Sadie finished reading before Ford did, but she kept staring at the contract. She was fascinated by the differences between the materials she'd been given and these. There was no nuance, none of the excitement that bubbled from the Mind Corps

Fellowship application materials. The translation of Subjects into Hosts and Minders into Guests made the enterprise feel less scientific and more accessible. And there was no mention of Syncopy—because, she realized, it hadn't existed nineteen years earlier when the contract was written, and neither had Mind Corps.

The entire mission had been nebulous because they hadn't known what their technology could do, just that in time it could do something extraordinary. Sadie admired the audacity of that, the ability to look beyond the factual and plan for a potential but not yet *conceivable* future. She felt a rush of pride to be part of something that visionary.

Ford's reaction was completely different. As he read, the words started to vibrate, and she felt him shift to keep the door of his anger closed. His mind got noisier, voices muttering furiously, some full sentences, some no more than growls. At one point he barked with uncomfortable laughter, and that seemed like the worst of all.

"Hosts. Guests. Like we're having a damn party," he said. "The condescending assholes, to think we'd fall for something like that."

His mother said quietly, "When you brought up the symbol on your ID the other day, I knew I had to tell you. No matter what."

He stared at her blankly. "You mortgaged my brain to Roque Industries." His tone was acrid.

His mother flinched at his bitterness. "That's not how it was. Your father was in jail, we had no money, and then you came early." She leaned forward, urging him to understand. "They wouldn't let me stay in the hospital without insurance.

And you were so small, if we didn't stay you would have been in danger. It was the only way I could take care of you."

His mind was curling in on itself, filled with the stinging, noxious scent of bleach, of betrayal. "You gave complete strangers permission to rifle through my memories, entertain themselves with my secrets, spy on my life, with no notice, whenever they wanted. To do whatever they wanted inside my head secretly, no questions asked. You turned me into a lab rat, something to run experiments on."

That's not fair, Sadie said. *I'm not a stranger, and I'm not experimenting on you. Everything I do is for your own good.*

Mrs. Winter's eyes were defiant, but she was trembling. "I did what I had to do as a parent to protect my child."

"Protect me?" He gave a mirthless laugh. "No. Let's not be like these"—he pushed the contract aside—"hypocrites, and play with language to hide the truth. Let's be very clear." He leaned forward, his eyes burning into hers. "You sold my most private parts to Roque, for them to use as they please. *You whored me out*, Mother. How is that fulfilling your duty as a parent? How is that *protecting* me?"

Mrs. Winter's face was a mask of horror. *Stop*, Sadie said, half yelling, half begging. *That's not how it is.*

It was too much for his mother. She collapsed, elbows on her knees, face in her hands. "I'm sorry," she said. "I'm so sorry." She was sobbing, shaking. "I did what I had to do. I wanted you so badly, I wanted you to live. I didn't know what else to do." Her body rocked back and forth, as though it couldn't contain all its pain. She gazed at him, her eyes red, her cheeks tear-stained. "Look at you. You're healthy. You're strong. Why do you resent me so much? Why?"

Inside of Ford the slick contempt, the furious screaming, the bazaar of disgust and self-loathing, the bitter incense of bleach all vanished, replaced by the velvety pain of self-recrimination. "I don't, Mom." He knelt beside her and put his arms around her. "I'm sorry. I don't. I understand why you did it. I'm sorry."

Instead of getting softer her sobs got louder, as though only now, in the comforting circle of his embrace, could she finally let go.

Sadie heard him think how small she was in his arms, how fragile. He saw the roots of her hair, darker than the ends, and the tight, dry, sallow skin on her hands. His mind formed an earlier memory of her wearing a long strapless dress, a two-year-old Lulu holding one hand, both of them smiling. She looked beautiful, a real knockout, soft and round and glowing.

"I don't resent you," he said, smoothing her hair. "I resent our life. I'm tired of being poor and not seeing any hope in sight. I'm tired of eating what's on sale, wearing what's on sale, having to endure visits from counselors who think they have a right to judge how we live and invade our privacy, just because we're poor. They can't even leave me my secrets and dreams. Rich kids don't have to live this way. That's what I resent."

Sadie wished she could curl up in a ball and hide. *That's not how it is*, she wanted to protest. Only it was. It was exactly like that.

"Maybe you could put it out of your mind," his mother suggested. "Maybe just not think about it." She watched him hopefully, but Ford wasn't seeing her.

Put it out of your mind rolled and echoed around his, picking up speed, becoming "People do things they don't want to do when they lose their minds" and "The Pharmacist does that to people, one look and they lose their heads" and "I'm trying to keep you from losing your head too." Bucky's words from the other day.

It was as if an explosion went off in Ford's head, making everything sharp and clear. *This* was what Bucky had been talking about, Sadie heard Ford thinking, losing your mind, not metaphorically but *actually*. This was how the Pharmacist manipulated Linc and everyone else. The Pharmacist didn't have superpowers that bent people to his will; he had a chip implanted in their brains that allowed him to control their minds.

But that's not how it works, Sadie objected. *No one is using interperception or Syncopy to mind-control anyone—I can't even get you to put the toilet seat down. Even if someone wanted to, they couldn't, it only goes one way, only from you to me.*

Ford's mind slowed, drawing together into dots of color to show Bucky saying, "As long as the Roaches come around, you're safe," and the cool, musty scent of relief filled Sadie's nose. If the Roaches were still checking up on him, she heard Ford think, there must not be anyone in his head. Which meant he still had time.

Except there is someone, Sadie thought with exasperation. *Me. Proving that Bucky has no idea what the chips actually are.*

Ford's attention refocused on his mother. "When did you tell James?"

She looked at him, puzzled. "Tell him what?"

"About the chip in his brain."

Mrs. Winter's head went back and forth. "James didn't have it. When James was born we were living in the other house, your father still had a job. There was no need . . ."

Sadie heard Ford thinking that if James didn't have the

chip, the Pharmacist couldn't have had any hold over him. So why would James have gone up against him?

Maybe he didn't, Sadie countered. *You only have Bucky's word for any of this. And if he did, doesn't that just prove the Pharmacist has nothing to do with chips or Interperception?*

He needed to find the Pharmacist and make him pay for what he'd done to James, Sadie heard Ford decide.

Sadie wished she could shake him. *Great idea. Find a criminal mastermind no one has ever lived to tell about. What could go wrong?*

Ford kissed his mother on the forehead, pleasantly surprising both of them. "Thank you. Thank you, Mom."

As he got up and headed to the kitchen to make dinner (*Note to Ford: If I could mind-control you, we would not be eating Chicken N Biscuits from a can*) he cursed himself for having been so distracted he'd missed the license number of the black Range Rover that picked Linc up.

I got it, Sadie said. *It was 145T90. Of course, I can't tell you because I can't mind-control you.*

Luckily, he had another plan for finding the Pharmacist.

But if I could, you would not use the word luckily *that way.*

And you would not text Plum anymore. Twice today is more than enough.

CHAPTER 21

Ford got fired from his job Friday afternoon. The foreman called him into his office and accused him of stealing. "Found those gewgaws you set aside. Birds and such."

"I wasn't stealing those," Ford said. "I was preserving them."

"Not the gewgaws. You're stealing from my time, boy," he said, leaning in. "I put up with your Frosty Jones and the Temple of Scrapping for a long time, you working slower than everyone else because you find a door handle or a dumb blonde or a piece of a piece of a painting you think is pretty to look at, but I've had enough."

Ford was still having trouble believing it. "Dumbwaiter," he murmured to himself before saying, "Please don't fire me. My family needs the money, sir."

"Kept you on as long as I did in memory of your brother, rest his soul. Great kid. Swing first and ask questions later, that was his way. Fine demolition man." He looked away. "You're a good worker, but you just don't have the spirit to destroy."

As though to prove the man wrong Ford went outside and bashed his hand into the wall so hard his mind flashed red, yellow, and blue.

If I were mind-controlling you, Sadie told him as he painfully flexed and straightened his knuckles, *there would be a lot less punching of walls.*

Saturday evening Ford sat on the couch with TREASURE HUNT 4: CURTAINS CALL in front of him. Finding Bucky was part one of his plan to find the Pharmacist, Sadie had learned, so he was ransacking his memory for details of Bucky's theater to match to one of the six probable locations he'd marked on the map. Copernicus, his head in Ford's lap, had the other half of the couch.

It was slightly past the time when he should have turned on a light but he hadn't, so the room was filled with shadows, which, Sadie saw, helped him bring out the details of his memories. She was amazed by how much he recalled about the theaters, tiny things like the design on a molding, or the exact width of a door—nothing she'd paid attention to. It made her a little melancholy to realize that you could get all of someone's brain input and still only know him partially.

"Maryelise's boyfriend is back. He must really like her, he was here this morning," Lulu announced from her perch at the window. Ford had insisted on keeping the television off, so in revenge she was narrating everything she saw. "Hamilton got a new bike, piece of paper flipping over, three leaves, another leaf, Vitacrisp package doing somersault, Vitacrisp package doing another somersault, fancy gray car going down the street, fancy gray car stopping at the curb, fancy gray car door opening, fa—"

Ford covered her mouth with his hand. *Thank you*, Sadie breathed.

He stood next to her, looking down at the street. Ford didn't recognize the fancy car, but both he and Sadie recognized the tall, red-headed guy who got out, walked up the path to the front door of their building, and buzzed their apartment.

Mason Bligh was so tall he'd had to duck slightly to step into their apartment. Then he'd been forced to stand just inside while Lulu and Copernicus gaped at him with instant infatuation. Sadie suspected that didn't happen to Mason Bligh often, but the girl and the dog were unquestionably smitten.

When Ford asked Lulu to step aside she'd turned and run toward their mother's room, yelling, "Mom! Come see the beautiful man!" Copernicus had stayed to stare at his new idol.

Surprise, concern, and wariness all flashed through Ford's mind. Before Ford could say anything antagonizing, Mason said, "I'm sorry to bother you at home."

"It's no bother, it's not like I have a job," Ford answered, but not in a menacing tone. Sadie had the impression that he was keeping his aggression in check so he could hear himself think. *As if he's too curious to be angry.*

He gestured Mason toward the couch and sat opposite him, tense and expectant. "I'm sorry I didn't return your calls," Mason said. "I was out of range until last night, but first thing this morning I went to the job site, and you're right, there were—are—some treasures."

Ford stared at him while he spoke, and Sadie knew he was genuinely baffled. *What's this guy doing at my house, being nice to me?* was the first question pinging around his brain. Almost instantly it became *What does he want from me?* and finally ended as *He's going to try to rip me off.* It was like a tragic opera, Sadie thought, the way Ford could interpret the most benign gesture as something harmful.

Not knowing he'd just been cast as a villain in the Life of Ford Winter, Year 19, Mason said, "I came because of these," setting on the trunk one of the medallions with the carved birds that Ford had salvaged. "And this." He pulled out a large city plan and laid it over the map Ford had been using to search for Bucky.

Without waiting for Ford to say anything, he went on. "I have a vision of what this area could be. Farmers' market, skate park, fish hatchery, plus housing, an arts center. Three new schools." His hands moved over the dark blue plan, which covered a light blue rendering of the existing area. "I need someone like you to help me bring it to life. What do you think?"

Sadie realized she was holding her breath. Mason was offering Ford a chance to work on the kind of thing he dreamed of, what he fantasized about when he should have been concentrating on the laws of the road. Would he run with the opportunity, or would he find a way to destroy it?

Ford turned on the light and glanced at the map. "I think it's a nicely updated version of a plan someone proposed five years ago that never got finished."

Copernicus, who had been making a circuit of the room, put his head in Mason's lap. "You don't think it's feasible?"

"People lose interest," Ford said, looking away into the shadows, and it was clear to Sadie he was talking more about himself than City Center. "This may be a game to you, but it's not a game to the people who live here."

Mason rubbed his hands through his hair as if trying to come to a decision. "Ten years ago yesterday my whole family was killed in a car crash. I was twelve and inherited a lot of money, but I was angry and miserable and only thought about myself. Basically, for a long time I was a spoiled brat. I feel like it's time for me to reverse that. Give something back, do something meaningful." Mason scratched Copernicus behind the ear. "Something that will be meaningful to other people too. It's not a game to me."

Ford studied him. "Why City Center? You're not from here."

Mason blushed. "There's, ah, also this girl."

Sadie felt a pop of surprise from Ford, but he kept it out of his voice. "From Detroit?"

Mason blushed even more. "She lives here now. She's beautiful and smart and wants to change the world. I want to impress her."

Ford frowned. "By rebuilding City Center?"

"She's hard to impress." Mason blinked earnestly at Ford from behind the lenses of his glasses. "Will you help me?"

Ford leaned toward the map. "If you're serious about doing something meaningful, you're going to have to scrap all that"—he waved a hand casually over three-quarters of the plan—"and put in things people really want." He grabbed a pen. "May I?"

Mason nodded.

"Keep your farmers' market, why not, but what we need are supermarkets. All we have are convenience stores and liquor stores." Ford drew the store where he'd envisioned it on that first morning Sadie went to work with him, and another at the intersection of five major roads, where, Sadie saw from his memory, a vacant record store stood as though auditioning for a makeover.

He kept drawing as he spoke, the images coming into his mind a moment before communicating with his hand, turning themselves or adjusting slightly as he put pen to paper but clearly working from the ideas he'd been forming for years. "Put in bike paths, since most people around here can't afford gas even if they have cars. A skate park. An indoor pool. Playgrounds that aren't asphalt. Make this mixed use, roller skating in summer, ice skating in winter, maybe concerts. Get some food vendors too, but good ones, not the ones that make the air smell bad." This, Sadie thought, from the guy she'd seen eat Bits O'Beef straight out of the can. "Take these old tracks and turn them into a park. That would change everything, give people a place to walk that's not the street."

Mason had been rubbing his hand over his head, and now his hair stuck up even more assertively. "You have a lot of ideas."

"Sure." Ford dropped the pen and leaned back into the cushions, and Sadie felt the warm, excited sensation fizzle into the sticky gumminess of humiliation. As though he'd shown too much of himself, revealed how deeply it mattered. The stickiness drew a plume of anger toward it. He pushed the map away and Sadie heard Ford think, *Don't pretend like you care. You're just another rich kid coming down here to play games with us puppies before running back up to your penthouse condo.*

Mason looked at the plan, took a deep breath, and said, "Okay, how about three?"

Ford was still lost in a part of his brain where three meant half the number of texts Plum had not responded to. "Three what?" he asked.

"Three thousand a month."

Sadie heard bells ring and a kettledrum start harrumphing and over them Ford thinking, *Be cool. He's bluffing. Be cool.* But another part of his mind was already imagining what that money could do, the images spinning around: Lulu on a tire swing behind a newly painted house, his mother on the front porch painting at an easel, coming home with bags of groceries, Lulu poking her head into the kitchen and wrinkling up her nose and saying, "Steak *again*."

Warmth filled Sadie at the last image, and she wasn't sure if it was hers alone or also Ford's. She heard him repeating *stay cool* to himself then heard him say in a voice that sounded almost right, "Three thousand dollars? To do what exactly?"

"Be my consultant. Scout properties, look over plans." Mason sounded a little like he was making it up as he went along. He scratched behind Copernicus's other ear, buying some time. "Find owls hidden under the drop ceiling at the library, dumbwaiters from the 1930s. You're good at it, better than anyone, Frank says."

"Frank?" Ford asked, his mind still on the money, now imagining taking Lulu and his mother to the mall and being able to say, "Pick what you want." The thought of it made his chest feel too small, unable to accommodate the way his heart was swelling.

"Frank, your ex-boss," Mason said. "He tells me you've got the eye. Something about you being passionate and outspoken. Although the way he put it was more like stubborn and not knowing when to shut up."

Ford surprised Sadie by laughing. "Sounds like Frank." He eyed Mason. "Will you do what I say?"

Mason shook his head. "No way, not all the time. I'm passionate and outspoken too. But I'll listen to your suggestions seriously." He took a deep breath. "I should tell you that I'm not always easy to work with. I want someone I can argue with. Someone who has different opinions. Someone I can yell at, and get yelled at by during the day, but still get a burger with at night because we respect each other."

If someone had purposely composed a script with all the right words to say to Ford—*respect, passion, argue, burger*—it could not have been more effective than Mason's speech, Sadie thought. Even she couldn't have done better, and she knew him . . . well.

Mason had managed to touch Ford not only in his thoughts and his emotions but also, she sensed, at some deeper level. A guy who was around the same age as James offering him not just a job but a friendship. It made Sadie happy for Ford, but also a little nervous. It seemed like a lot for Mason to live up to.

Ford looked not at Mason's face but at his hands, which were loose over the knees of his pants. "Five."

It's like he's playing poker, Sadie realized, watching Mason's hands. The way he'd watched the hands of the other players that day at the Castle.

Mason's hair seemed to stand up a little more on its own. "Five thousand a month?"

"You'd go to seven, but I'm taking it easy on you," Ford told him.

Mason said, "You play poker. Fine, five."

Ford nodded. "Let me think about it."

Mason laughed so hard his face turned bright red, and Sadie felt a tiny glimmer of the happy, warm-tomato-soup-after-a-snowball-fight feeling in Ford's chest. "You think about it," Mason said, getting up, but he didn't escape until after he'd petted Copernicus one last time and given Lulu his phone number so she could sleep with it under her pillow, "like a real princess."

Sunday was gusty, the clouds skidding across the sky. It was James's birthday, and at Lulu's request they'd gone to the planetarium to look for the star she was certain James had turned into when he died, but they weren't able to find it. "I knew it was a long shot," she told Ford, as though she needed to console him. "Four months is not very long for someone to become a star."

"No, it's not," Ford agreed.

There was clearly something on Lulu's mind during the bus ride home, and Sadie was fascinated watching Ford's internal landscape expand and contract, as though calibrated by a very precise machine that constantly measured the exact right arm's length to keep Lulu feeling safe but not smothered. *Concern* was the best name Sadie could come up with for it, although she thought it might be mostly love.

Sadie felt lucky to witness it, and a little jealous. She loved being an only child, but a part of her couldn't help wondering how different her life would have been if she'd had a little sister like Lulu.

They were four stops from home when Lulu turned to Ford and blurted, "Do you miss him? Every day?"

A hundred jagged shards of grief sliced ribbons in him, and he fell into an abyss of pure pain. He wanted to cry out, crawl from his skin, and beg for mercy until the pain was gone.

Why didn't it get any easier? she heard him think, aching for him, with him. This grief was as potent as the grief after he left Plum's, only now there was Lulu watching him. Needing him.

His eyes locked on her, and Sadie heard him say to himself, *You must not let her see this.* By sheer force of will he yanked all the threads and shards and sinews together, gathering them up into an untidy ball and pushing them deep into his mind to be sorted later. He was left with the smooth everyday grief.

"I do," he said.

"How come we don't talk about him?"

"It's hard to know what to say."

"You could say, 'Remember the time we went bowling?' or 'Remember the time we made cookies?' See? It's easy. You do one."

Sadie saw Ford's effort, but his mind was a frozen block of stone, unyielding. "Um, remember—"

"Forget it!" Lulu stomped her foot against the rubber floor of the bus. "I knew it. I *knew* it!" Her voice rose, and people began to turn and stare. Sadie felt mortified for Ford, felt his own mortification, and saw him ignore it to listen to Lulu. "You're trying to erase him. You want to make it like he was never there. You wear his clothes. You've even tried to steal his girlfriend—yes, I heard you talking to Mom, saying you were going to see her. But you can never be him. *Never.*"

"I know, and I don't want to be." Sadie knew that might not always have been true, but it was true now. And it felt good to Ford. "I don't want to be," he repeated.

Lulu glared at him defiantly then burst into tears, burrowing into his chest, crumpling handfuls of his shirt against her face. "I'm sorry. I'm so sorry. I didn't mean it."

Ford held her. "It's okay even if you did."

"It just hurts so much sometimes."

"I know."

Her cheek was against his chest. "He wasn't supposed to die," she said, her lip trembling, and Ford hugged her even tighter. "We were going to have adventures and be rich." She started to cry again, but softer, not hysterical.

"We still can be," Ford said, and Sadie felt how heavy the lie sat on his chest.

They were quiet as they got off the bus and walked home, but by the time their building was in sight Lulu was back to her regular self, declaring, "We'll be rich when I marry Mason. In ten years."

"Does he know about that?" Ford asked.

Lulu stood in the middle of their front walk in her khaki flight suit and spun around, fluffing up her hair. "Really, darling, who's going to say no to me?"

"Who indeed," Linc said, stepping out of the shadows around the door and catching Lulu in his arms. Lulu shrieked and giggled, but the gaze Linc leveled on Ford was steely cold.

"Linc. Please put my sister down," Ford said. His mind was focused on Linc with such intensity that it was like being pulled by centripetal force.

Linc put Lulu down. "You messed up my hair, you big lug," she told him, and he gave her a smile, letting it dissolve slowly as his eyes held Ford's.

"Lulu, go upstairs and wait for me, please," Ford said.

Lulu frowned. "Isn't Uncle Linc coming up?"

"No," Ford said, speaking to her but watching Linc, as if daring him to disagree. "Not tonight."

When she was gone Linc said, "I hear you've been trying to get my attention."

Ford's mind hummed with nervous anticipation. "Not that I know—" The words stopped in Ford's throat as Linc held up a photo of Ford standing just down the block from 345 Ever-greenLawn, then another of him taking off after Linc.

"Talk. How did you end up here?" Linc rattled the paper.

"I followed you."

"Not possible." Linc's hand snapped out, and he grabbed Ford around the neck. "Tell me how you found me."

"I didn't mean to," Ford squeezed out. Sadie's vision went spotty as he gasped for air. "I followed a pizza delivery truck, and it went to your house."

"Why weren't you at work?"

"We got out early . . . storm."

Linc's eyes flickered with something that looked like sur-prise, and he let go of Ford's throat. "You have either the worst luck or the best of anyone I've ever met."

Somehow those words, coming from Linc, weren't hearten-ing, Sadie thought.

Ford massaged his neck. "What does that mean?"

"It means I'm going to tell you one last time to stay away

from me and anything concerning me and beat you senseless to make sure you get the message."

"Is that the good luck or the bad luck?"

Linc said, "That depends on your perspective. I came here today to kill you."

It would have been funny in its baldness, Sadie thought, if Linc hadn't been so very cold and serious.

"Did you kill James?" Ford asked.

Linc's eyes hardened. "You need to stop asking questions like that. Soon I won't have any control over my actions. Don't do it again."

"Or else?"

"You've used up your *or else*s," Linc said. "How many choices do you think you have right now? Your choices are: one, do what I say and stay away from me, or two, pay with your life." He held up two fingers. "And when you're gone, who's going to take care of your mother?" He folded the two fingers down into a fist. "Your sister?"

Ford's astonishment made his mind buck like a room in an earthquake, overriding his anger. "Did you just—are you threatening my *little sister*?"

"I'm educating you about your choices." Linc's eyes burned into Ford's with the intensity of the insane. "What would you do for Little Lu's well-being? What kind of choices do you have with that in the balance?"

Plants were falling off shelves in Ford's mind, pictures skewed, the floor still rolling, and he was speechless. "At least tell me who ordered you to do this. Was it the Pharmacist?"

Linc looked angry. "If I tell you the Pharmacist is responsible will you listen and take it seriously? Then yes. The Pharmacist sent me."

"Who is it? The Pharmacist?"

"The Pharmacist has many forms, almost all of them too good to be true, at least at the beginning."

"That's not an answer. Why won't you just tell me?"

"You know why no one answers that question?" Linc asked. "Because the only people who know wind up dead."

"You're not dead."

Linc's face twisted into a sardonic smile. "Something to think about." He pointed a finger at Ford's chest. "I tried to keep you out of this. I figured I owed James that. But no matter how clear I make myself, you still keep turning up. So this is your last warning. Take it. I won't enjoy killing you."

Sadie watched Ford prepare to fight in his mind, but he said, "It doesn't have to be this way, Linc,"

Linc's eyes flashed over Ford's shoulder. Slowly, like he was thinking something through, his hand came up to rub his chin, and he said, "You're right, maybe I should kill you now—"

Ford's fist plunged into Linc's unprotected abdomen. *Are you kidding?* Sadie said. *There's no way you can—*

Linc staggered backward and fell to the ground.

From behind Ford came the low clack of Kevlar boots. Swinging around he was confronted by two Serenity Services Counselors in full matte black body armor and helmets. A computer-modulated voice said, "Citizen Ford Winter, you are in violation of Part 445-W of the Good Neighbor Initiative. Place your hands out and state your intention to accompany us, or risk serious injury."

Thank god, Sadie thought, seeing the Serenity Services

uniforms. *Tell them that he was going to kill you*, Sadie urged Ford. *Tell them you were just defending yourself.*

"He was going to—"

"Citizen Ford Winter, comply with our order or we will fire on three," the same voice said, and both Counselors leveled their tasers.

Ford put out his wrists. "I agree to accompany you."

Ford's processing at the Serenity Services Compliance Center happened in a kind of fog. They asked him almost no questions, and when he tried to explain that Linc had been about to beat him up, the Counselor gave him a weak smile and said, "That guy had, what, ninety pounds on you? If he'd been trying to beat you up, you would have been beaten. As it is, you're lucky we came around when we did. He wouldn't have stayed down for long."

After forty minutes, another Serenity Services Counselor came in and announced, "Your brother posted your bail. You're free to go."

If only, Ford thought. His last thought before punching Linc, Sadie knew, had been how disappointed his mother would be.

Ford braced himself, but when he walked into the waiting room the only person there was Mason.

"You?" Ford looked behind him. "For me? Why?" Then, getting it, "That's why they said *brother*."

"I told them we had a family emergency, Mom was sick, that's why you'd flown off the handle, contrition all around, and they sped things up." *That was slick*, Sadie thought, and was conscious of a twinge of unease. *Too slick? Too easy?*

Ford was impressed. "Nice work." Mason pried himself out

of a chair made for someone half his size, and they headed for the exit. "You're taller than my brother."

Mason chuckled. "I'm taller than everyone's brother."

"Why'd you do it?" Ford asked, looking up at him.

Mason jammed his hands in his pockets. "Wedding present for Lulu."

Ford laughed outright, and so did Sadie, momentarily shelving her apprehensions to share Ford's openness toward Mason.

"No, I figured this way you'd owe me, I could knock your salary down."

Ford shook his head. "You must be a really bad poker player. This way I know what I'm worth to you and can ask for a raise."

"Don't push your luck," Mason cautioned.

Sadie felt Ford reaching into a part of him he didn't share with everyone, a rich, warm place. Gratitude, she thought. And also friendship. "Thanks," he said, offering both. "Was it expensive?"

"No. Couple hundred. He's not pressing charges." Mason seemed impressed. "Pretty bold, though. He's a big guy. I don't think I could have knocked him out."

"You just have to know where to punch," Ford said, but he was distracted inside, thinking, *That was too easy.* As if Linc had somehow orchestrated the whole thing on purpose.

Sadie had the same idea, but it didn't make sense.

"So, you'll take the job?" Mason prodded.

Ford's insides still felt warm like melted caramel. "I guess. But it has to be a real job. No charity. I want to work hard. I'm useless otherwise."

Mason said seriously, "I'm counting on it," and Sadie felt

Ford's warm contentment increase. He trusted Mason, she realized, trusted that Mason's professions of respect were real.

Don't let him down, Sadie cautioned Mason in her mind.

Mason dropped Ford off. When Ford got upstairs Lulu was standing in the open door. She put a finger to her lips and whispered, "I thought you'd never get home. I'm starving."

Ford glanced behind her and saw their mother's door was closed. "Did you call Mason?" he whispered.

"You mean Mr. Lulu? No, he called me. Really he called you to ask about his offer, but I had your phone so I answered. I told him I'd seen those people from Serenity Services take you away, and he said he'd take care of it. Isn't he just lovely to look at?"

"Sure," Ford said. "And Mom . . ." He let it trail off.

"I didn't think it necessary to advise her majesty," Lulu told him.

"Thanks." Ford smiled, a real, genuine, from-his-toes smile that lit Sadie up too.

Lulu curtseyed. "At your service." Then she looked at him with narrowed eyes. "But you owe me. Which means you're making dinner."

As he brushed his teeth later, Ford's mind kept replaying Linc's description of the Pharmacist: "Many forms, almost all of them too good to be true."

Ford fell asleep thinking of Plum. Sadie fell asleep thinking of Mason.

CHAPTER 22
WEEK 3

The invitation was printed on washcloths.

Wee Willy Productions proudly presents:
The Fourth of July
A Midweek Drunktacular
At: The Old Baths
Dress: To Impress While Wet
Bring: Cheer, Beer, No Fear

Ford had never been to the Old Turkish Baths before, and he was impressed by the entrance. Thick pillars of rose marble topped with griffins flanked a set of brass doors, nine feet tall with spikes poking outward.

"They took off the doorknobs when the rulers came in so

they could bathe in peace," Willy explained when Ford was
inside. "Impossible to get the door open without slicing your
arm off. Neat, huh?"

Willy was wearing a white boater hat, a white linen shirt
open over a white tank top, white shorts, and white loafers. He
looked ridiculous, Sadie heard Ford think, but she also picked
up a twinge of jealousy at how new everything was.

"Yeah, neat," Ford agreed.

The baths weren't as fancy inside as they were outside,
although Ford's eye directed Sadie to a half-hidden mural on
the ceiling that suggested they once had been.

Mason would like that, she heard him think, and he reached
for his phone.

Sadie gritted her teeth. *This is a party. On a holiday. You're
not supposed to spend it texting your boss.*

Of course, Mason had quickly become more like a friend
than a boss. Very quickly. Objectively Sadie thought it was fine,
but there was still something about their relationship that made
her . . . uneasy.

She was glad for Ford to have a friend, or she was neutral
since her job was to observe, not judge, but she wished Ford
would be more careful. More reserved. He was so thirsty for
affection, so hungry to be appreciated that she feared he might
trust the wrong person or make bad decisions that would haunt
him.

He and Mason talked the entire time they looked at places,
and that was another thing that annoyed Sadie. The constant
conversation made it harder for her to hear Ford's thoughts, and
those she could hear mostly consisted of things like *Mason's so
great* and *I need to show this to Mason.*

Maybe you should get matching outfits, she suggested. *Or a Mason's #1 Fan foam hand.*

Like two days earlier when they'd been on the third floor of the former Petite Trianon Theater, checking out a gilded frieze that ran along the balcony. Mason had said, "So this is really your hobby? I'm not sure your job can be your hobby."

Ford had shrugged off Mason's comment, cantilevering himself off the side with a rope secured to the balcony railing. "I like finding things that have been lost and rescuing them."

Mason handed him a pink tab to mark the part of the frieze they wanted to take. "Sounds like you have a guilty conscience."

How could Mason know that? Sadie wondered uneasily. Miranda had said the same thing, and she'd been right, but Miranda was . . . Miranda.

For a moment Ford's hearing got muffled and the sound of his breathing was louder in her ears. Then everything was back to normal, and Ford said, "Why would you say that?"

"It's been my experience that people who feel the need to rescue others generally have some guilt they're working through."

Bright splashes of yellow, blue, and brown made a blurry image of James and Ford and Cali grinning at a motel pool. The dots became smaller, the image more distinct, and Sadie caught the sticky feeling of humiliation, saw a bed with a pair of red and blue flowered swim trunks on the end of it. Cali, tangled in its blue comforter and obviously naked, turning to look at the door and saying in a voice a little too loud, "Ford, I thought you'd left?" Ford backing out of their motel room, not even realizing he'd dropped the milkshake he was bringing her—strawberry, her favorite—until it was dried and tacky on his hand, still staring at it when James came bounding out in his red and blue floral swim trunks and did a cannonball into the pool, the three of them laughing together like nothing ever happened.

Abruptly the image vanished into blankness and Ford was saying to Mason, "My brother wanted to rescue everyone, be a hero, and he never felt guilty about anything in his life."

Sadie was thunderstruck. James had slept with Cali, and Ford had known about it. Knew about it.

But not consciously. He'd repressed it, using mental alchemy to sublimate it into a single sensation: the sweet-tacky feeling of dried milkshake on his hand. The memory acted as the source text for the emotion, the sensation persisting even though— or maybe precisely because—Ford refused to acknowledge the event that caused it.

It was a thrilling discovery about how his mind worked, but also puzzling. *Why won't you admit that James wasn't always the great guy everyone says?* she wanted to ask him. *He's dead. Who are you protecting from the truth?*

Mason looked apologetic. "I could be wrong. Would it take some of the sting out if I said I have a lot of experience with guilt myself? Nothing like being the only survivor of a car crash on the first day of your family's vacation to give you a pretty good dose of the GCs."

"Guilty consciences." Ford nodded. "That must have been—"

"Yeah." Mason cut him off.

Ford steered back to safer topics. "Does that mean you think you're rescuing me?" It was designed to change the subject, but it wasn't an idle question. He tried to lighten it by adding, "Because you're not really what I picture in my rescue fantasies."

What do *you picture?* Sadie asked, genuinely curious. After all the time she'd spent in his mind, she actually didn't know the answer.

"Let's make a deal," Mason suggested. "I won't try to rescue you, you don't try to rescue me."

"Sure," Ford said, shaking on it. "Deal."

Mason handed Ford another pink marking tab. "You used the past tense about your brother."

"He's dead. Murdered. A little more than four months ago." Ford hoisted himself back over the railing. The blankness that followed the memory of Cali and James spread in his mind, taking on mass, becoming milky.

"That's tough. Grieving is hard, and four months is recent. Was he a good brother?"

Without thinking, Ford said, "Everyone loved James." Through the milky whiteness Sadie saw dots forming the image of a rope, taut now, held in a black-gloved hand. "He was perfect." He picked up one of the toolboxes and started for the stairs.

Mason grabbed the other toolbox. "Perfect. Wow." He said it with admiration, not contempt. "What was that like?"

The image in Ford's mind evolved. The fingers of the black-gloved hand opened and the rope slipped away, swallowed up by the whiteness. "Great," Ford answered. The whiteness vanished, his mind cleared, and his gaze raked the interior of the theater. "It was great."

Sadie felt Mason's eyes on him, but all he said was "Looks like we've tagged the whole building to take with us. I should probably just buy the place."

Show-off, Sadie thought.

"Right," Ford snickered, stopping when he saw Mason had his phone out. "Are you serious? You can buy a building on your phone?"

Mason laughed. "No, but I can find out who owns it, what else they have, get a feeling for what they'd take for it."

Sadie could tell Ford was impressed. He was thinking about it, about what it would be like to have that kind of money, when Mason loped toward him, holding out his phone. "Place is owned by MRP. Know anything about them?"

Mr. P, Ford said to himself, rephrasing it slightly, and Sadie felt his pulse pick up. "I might know something. Do they own anything else?"

You're jumping to conclusions, Sadie cautioned him. *MRP could be someone's initials. A development company. A real estate trust.*

"They own about twenty buildings, all in City Center," Mason reported. "Mostly derelict theaters and factories. I'm surprised I've never heard of MRP with holdings like that. They must keep a very low profile. I'll forward you the list."

The phrase "very low profile" echoed from Ford's mind to Sadie's. Or MRP could be the Pharmacist, she admitted. But why would an invisible criminal mastermind want a bunch of abandoned buildings?

The Old Turkish Baths were number fourteen on the list. Willy's party was in full swing now, and several hundred people filled the main floor. Sadie heard Ford wondering if the Pharmacist might be one of them, when his eyes stopped on a beige cowboy hat in the middle of the dance floor.

Bucky? their minds asked in unison.

Sadie felt Ford's heart rate pick up as he navigated across the dance floor toward the hat. The crowd got denser as he got closer, and when the DJ started a new song everyone threw their hands in the air, blocking his view.

His eyes flicked back and forth over the heads of the dancers, and out of his peripheral vision Sadie caught sight of the hat alongside them. *To the left*, she shouted, and Ford turned and spotted it, almost as though he'd heard. He dove through the crowd, grabbing for it.

"Hey, what do you think—" The frosted blonde who was wearing it swung toward Ford, indignant. Her outraged expression softened when she saw who it was. "Mr. Ice!" Kansas squealed, leaning close to give him a kiss on the lips that turned a little sloppy.

You're getting lipstick on you, Sadie warned him. *Kind of a lot, and not really your color.*

When he finally pulled himself free he said, "Hi, Kansas. Nice hat."

"Thanks." She giggled. "Willy gave it to me. It's a little big, but that just means I have to make my hair bigger."

"Can I see it?"

"Sure." She winked at him. "But don't ask me to take anything else off. Willy'll get jealous." She flipped the hat off in one neat move and handed it to Ford.

Sadie wondered if she'd practiced that.

He peered inside, and Sadie held her breath. After less than four seconds Sadie heard him think that it definitely wasn't Bucky's, but she had no idea why and could tell he didn't either.

It was just a gut instinct. Disappointed, he handed the hat back to Kansas and ducked away before she could kiss him again.

You could be wrong, Sadie pointed out. The gut is not the most reliable organ for thinking.

Grabbing a handful of napkins, he made a beeline for the first mirror he spotted to wipe Kansas's lipstick off his face. Four napkins and five minutes later he was checking to make sure he'd gotten it all when Sadie heard him ask himself why. There was no girl whose feelings he had to worry about. If he came home with lipstick all over him it wouldn't matter.

His eyes shifted to the reflection of the crowd behind him, everyone laughing and dancing. Maybe he should just go. If he left now he'd be home in time to watch the fireworks on the roof with Lulu. *If* he could convince her to go up there. With Copernicus.

You are not going to spend the fourth of July with your dog, Sadie heard him reprimand himself. *Have some self-respect. You are going to stay at this party and have a good time.*

You forgot to say "or else," Sadie told him.

He stared hard at his reflection in the mirror, turned slightly to one side, and said aloud, "You are Mr. Irresistible," so sarcastically that Sadie almost choked laughing. He did it again on the other side, sounding more bored than sarcastic. The third time he started with his chin lowered to his chest and raised his face slowly to meet his own eyes, saying in a cheesy television announcer voice, "You are Mr. Irresistib—"

The words died. Sadie's breath caught. All of a sudden she wasn't watching him look at himself, she was looking at him. *Really* looking at him, their eyes meeting, hers and his.

It shouldn't have been possible, but it happened. She felt it, felt him. Felt his gaze holding hers. Felt him look at her, into her. Felt him see her the way she'd longed to be seen without knowing it, with intensity and interest and surprise, as if he'd found something he'd been seeking for a long time. He smiled at her and she smiled back, and her body lit up with the thrill of their connection.

Not bad, she heard him think. Before she could agree his hand came up to rub the shadow of stubble he'd let grow on his chin and he said aloud, serious now, "Pretty irresistible."

Sadie's cheeks burned with mortification. He hadn't been looking at her or through her or for her. He'd been looking at himself. Smiling at himself. *Of course.* She shook herself. How could she have been so stupid? God, she was embarrassing. At least he would never find out, since they would never meet.

There was some comfort in that. In knowing they would never see each other across a crowded room, at a party, at the mall. Never bump into one another and have a moment of recognition, never have a casual conversation, share a coffee, accidentally let their knees brush. She would never turn at a movie and see him laughing in the seat next to hers, never watch his lids lower so his lashes touched his cheek in the moment just before a kiss. Never be seen by him at all.

She swallowed back a knot in her throat. *Yes, that's a real relief.* He ate Meatballz for dinner and liked to punch walls and cheated at poker—at least she assumed he cheated, because she still couldn't figure out how he'd guessed all those hands her first day with him. She wouldn't even know what to say to him if they met.

"Hey, Ice," Willy's voice bellowed, and turning from the

mirror—*finally*—Ford saw him beckoning from a bar set up at the edge of the dance floor. "Get over here. You look thirsty."

When Ford joined him Willy gestured with a bottle of beer over the heads of his guests. "Isn't this something?"

"It sure is," Ford agreed. "How did you find this place?"

"Linc put me onto it," Willy said. He signaled the bartender for two beers, then leaned against the bar and faced Ford, his expression serious. "Heard about your dustup the other night. Don't worry, he's not coming, parties aren't really his thing anymore." The bartender set the beers in front of Willy, and he pushed one toward Ford. "But you might want to keep out of his way. Don't know what you did, but he's a little loony about it."

"I just—"

Willy put up his hands. "Don't know and don't *want* to know."

"Got it," Ford said, taking a sip of beer. It was cold and tasted good to Sadie. "What happened to him? He used to want to be a priest."

Willy took a swig of beer. "Way I see it, there's two parts to being a priest. Part where you save souls. And part where you give out punishment." His eyebrows went up suggestively. "Who's to say which part appeals most to Linc?"

Sadie watched Ford's mind flip through images of Linc from childhood. Linc breaking up a fight between strangers at a dance, Linc persuading James not to steal the principal's car. Sadie heard him thinking that none of it went with what Willy was saying, but neither did the angry guy who'd sworn to kill him. Ford shook his head. "I don't understand why you all do it."

"Do what?" Willy was looking out at his guests.

"Work for him. For the Pharmacist."

Everything about Willy changed. He pulled himself up to his full height and turned to face Ford. He would have looked terrifying if his eyes hadn't seemed so afraid. "Don't say that name," he whispered, his gaze darting left and right.

"Why don't you and Linc go against him? The two of you, with all your friends, could overthrow him."

"Takes a lot of trust, what you're saying, Little Ice. The right incentive can make a man do strange things."

"But you've been friends forever. You must trust Linc."

"Your brother did," Willy said with a sad smile. "James trusted Linc. Told him what he was planning. Trusted Bucky too."

Sadie felt Ford's heart skip a beat. "What are you saying?"

Willy looked at him hard. "Only that old friends are one thing, survival is another. You do what you got to in order to take care of what you love."

Ford said, "I think the Pharmacist killed James."

Willy cleared his throat. "This is no kind of talk for a party, Little Ice."

"You're right," Ford agreed, and Sadie heard him thinking that if Willy knew more he'd tell him. "Did you propose to Kansas yet?" he asked.

Willy grinned. "This weekend."

"She's a catch," Ford congratulated him.

"How's your girl?" Willy asked.

"We broke up."

Willy made a wide gesture with his beer bottle over the dance floor. "Lots of good fishing here," he said.

Ford took a sip of beer, and Sadie heard a regular, flat countdown like a launch sequence so she knew it was coming when Ford said, "Speaking of girls, which of you do I have to thank for putting Plum in touch with me?"

Willy put up his hands. "Not me. Doubt it was Lincoln either."

Ford frowned into his beer bottle. "Why do you say that?"

Willy picked up a cocktail napkin, held it in front of him, and recited as if reading from a paper, "I swear no matter what happens I will not put Plum in touch with Ford." He dropped the napkin and looked at Ford. "Your brother made us all sign it."

"You're kidding, right?" Sadie saw Ford trying to fit this in with other puzzle pieces and having trouble.

"Nope, that's the for-real deal," Willy said. "Paper with a solemn oath on it. I got it somewhere. Never know what might be valuable one day."

"Why would James do that?" Ford asked.

"There are rumors that you're very well, you know"—Willy paused—"*endowed*. Maybe he was jealous."

Kansas came over and wrapped her arms around Willy's neck as he said that. She planted an enormous lipstick mark on his cheek, gave them both a mischievous look, and said, "I knew you two were talking dirty."

Sadie felt a sharp prickle of impatience course through Ford at the interruption. "Jealousy wasn't really James's style," he said.

"Could be he still felt guilty about that day on the ice," Willy offered. "Trying to protect you."

Sadie's ears perked up.

"The day with the beer can?" Kansas asked, smiling. To Ford she said, "Willy told me all about it."

Sadie's breath caught in her throat, and she thought about the shack on the lake, the pile of beer cans. The voice telling James to stay away. Normally that would have triggered a river of images in Ford's mind, but now there was nothing.

Willy nodded. "I still tear up laughing when I think about the hand with the glove coming out of the ice—"

"And Linc screaming like a little girl," Kansas said. "That's the part I can't believe."

Sadie thought, *Not nothing*. Whiteness again. Still, placid. Boundless. Endless.

Inescapable. Sadie felt Ford's heart rate tick up. His breathing grew shallow, panicked, and his thoughts got choppy, *There's no way out, I'm trapped, hel—*

A bright strobe flashed in his mind, and the memory vanished.

Ford said, "What did he have to feel guilty about? I was the one who messed up."

Willy gave him a perplexed look. "I wouldn't say that."

Ask him why not, Sadie urged. Ask him to tell you what he remembers. Better yet, you tell the story. Everyone tell it. With lots of details. She felt like she had the first day of Syncopy, when she'd been desperate for them to say Ford's name.

As if the bright light were an eraser, Ford's mind bounced back to the moment just before Willy mentioned the cabin. He said, "There aren't really rumors about me being well endowed."

Also like that first day, Sadie wanted to strangle someone.

Fingernails teased the back of Ford's neck, giving Sadie

goose bumps, and a familiar voice at his ear said warmly, "I'm afraid there are."

Ford turned and looked at Cali. Sadie was hit with a wave of desire, followed almost immediately by anger, settling into a wary mix of the two. "Hey," he said.

"I thought I'd find you here," Cali told him, giving him a kiss on the cheek.

That tipped the scale slightly toward anger. "That's me. Predictable," he said sarcastically. "Stuck in the past. Not moving forward."

"Maybe," Cali said, her hand coming to rest on his chest. "Maybe that makes you reliable."

Sadie couldn't tell if it was Cali's words or his reactions that were confusing him, but his mind felt like it was being sloshed around.

Cali was wearing a new perfume, which he registered negatively as cheap daisies, but she was also wearing a skimpy bikini top, which he registered positively as small.

"You look good," he said, wondering when Willy and Kansas had disappeared.

About a minute ago, Sadie told him. *Between "hey" and when you got lost looking at her boobs.*

"You too," Cali said. She touched a finger to the stubble on his cheek. "I leave you for a few days and you grow a beard?"

"I've been busy."

"Too busy to shave? Intriguing," she said.

Sadie heard Ford think *She's jealous* and felt his moderate surge of pleasure. Of which, since she was supposed to be objective, she could neither approve nor think was immature. "How's it going?" Ford asked Cali.

She let her finger rest in the indentation at the base of his neck. "It's only been a week since we've talked."

Given the way Ford's pulse picked up and his body tightened, Sadie thought there should be rules about how close people could stand a week after a breakup. Finger-on-the-collarbone seemed a bit too close. "Feels longer," he said.

"Yeah."

Her gaze moved from her finger, up over his chin to his lips, and then met his eyes.

Sadie heard a clarinet give an experimental blast. Ford's eyes held hard to Cali's. "What's going on here?" he asked, taking the words right out of Sadie's mouth.

Cali exhaled deeply, and Sadie saw her chest rise and fall in Ford's peripheral vision. "We've spent every Fourth of July together since we were sixteen," she said. "It doesn't seem right to stop now." She took a step forward so her thigh was between his. "Does it?"

Ford's body thrummed like a taut vessel, sending reverberations through Sadie. "When you say 'spend Fourth of July together,' you mean—"

"I want you." Cali pressed her cleavage against his chest. "No strings."

Ford's mind was spinning and his throat felt tight. "No strings," he repeated hoarsely.

I know the no-strings thing sounds good, Sadie told him, *but statistically it's very hard to put into practice. People who get back together with their exes in less than a year generally find themselves in the same—*

"None." Cali ran her fingers down his arms, setting off a

jingle of bells. "Just two people looking for . . ." Her voice trailed off.

Trouble, Sadie finished for her. *Heartache. Arguing.*

Ford still hadn't touched her, hadn't grabbed her, pulled her in to him, the way Sadie knew his mind was begging him to. The restraint seemed to be twisting the sinews tighter, eking out a slightly higher note from the saxophone, a more discordant shimmer from the drums.

His mouth came within a hairbreadth of hers, but still he didn't touch her. "Looking for what?"

Sadie felt the heat of Cali's body, the warmth of her breath on his cheek. "Kiss me," Cali begged. *"Please."*

I know that seems tempting, Sadie acknowledged objectively, *but the best thing for you to do right now would be to just turn and walk—*

He bent and brushed his lips gently against her, and a steaming wave of passion tore through Sadie, knocking her backward.

CHAPTER 23

"Where should we go?" Ford breathed. His voice was raspy, the tension in his muscles heightening every sensation, like notes played on a tightly strung guitar. "I'm sure there are rooms—"

"Let's get away from here." Cali's eyes were wild, daring. Sadie wondered what it would be like to let someone see you that way and not care, not worry about getting it wrong. To feel—so much. So free. "What about that special place you were going to take me?"

"Really?" Ford asked, and his happiness at the prospect made Sadie ache for him. He was so hungry for validation, for someone to pay attention.

She felt a sharp pinch of envy. *Cali doesn't deserve to go there. Not her, not the first time. Take me. I love the tree house. I love—*

"I—it would be great to take you there," Ford said, gazing at Cali with heat and longing.

Sadie wished she could look away.

Ford drove Cali's car the half mile to the tree house. Tension sizzled between them as they left the bustle of the blocks around the baths and turned onto the quiet street. He made her wait while he went ahead to open the place up and get it ready. Working quickly he lit three tall tapers inside, and five hanging lanterns he'd arranged in the branches of the tree.

He didn't stop to glance at it, so Sadie's first time seeing it alight was also Cali's. Sadie felt his surge of pleasure at Cali's reaction, which made Sadie ache in a different, confusing way.

The tree house was beautiful, glowing golden and suspended in space. He helped Cali up the ladder and she smiled when she saw the table and chairs. "You weren't kidding."

He shook his head. "I wanted to give you everything."

She grabed his hand, leading him to the rug off to one side, but he shook his head again.

He patted the table. "We might as well get some use out of it."

The purr in his voice thrilled Sadie. Cali stood at the edge of the table, facing the mirror, and he moved to stand behind her. His hands roamed over her body, and Sadie reveled in the double thrill of feeling him touching her skin and the instinctive responses triggered by watching it.

Sadie's gaze followed his hands, tracing shoots of molten sensation around her limbs, across her hips, down the back of her thighs. Cali's eyes closed, her head tipped back, and Sadie's eyes moved to his face.

This time there could be no mistake. Their eyes met with a jolt, locking together, swelling the intensity of every sensation.

He looked down, and she saw his hands cupping breasts that were paler, more delicate. *Mine,* Sadie thought, *those are mine.* She looked in the mirror and he looked back, not at Cali but at her.

Being seen by him was everything she'd imagined and more. She reached up a hand to touch his face and he kissed her fingers, then turned her toward him gently and, cradling her face in both his hands, brought his lips to hers.

Fire ignited between them and what started as a soft gentle kiss seared through them both, destroying reason and thought. She could feel his hands all over her body, strong, confident, and her hands on his, tentative but eager.

Her ache for him felt never-ending. It stretched and twisted, being pulled taut until there was no further for it to go, until she surrendered to it completely. Her arms wrapped around his shoulders, and he crushed himself against her. Pleasure crashed over them, leaving them unsure if the firecrackers exploding were inside or outside their bodies.

A moan that wasn't either of theirs jolted them both, and Sadie realized Ford's eyes had been closed. He opened them now and looked in the mirror. The room was the same, everything was the same, but the back he was cradling had a tattoo, and he had a feeling of disorientation, like he'd woken up in the wrong dream.

A sharp wave of dislike hit Sadie, and she saw that he was looking at Cali. Cali gazed up at him with amazement. "How come we never did it like that when we were dating?" she asked. "I felt like you were in some whole other zone."

"I was," Ford said, confused, searching the mirror for clues.

A phone buzzed. "That's me," Cali said, diving for her

purse. She missed the call but got the message. "I probably need to get back."

He sent Cali back to the party, then stood on the curb looking at the tree house and wondering what kind of magic spell he'd just been under. *Amazing*, he thought, turning to go.

"Hey, Winter," a voice called from behind him, piercing the silence. Ford turned and saw the guy in the ski mask just as the brass knuckles connected with his chin.

Ford's head whipped back, and he staggered sideways, across the sidewalk, toward a vacant lot covered with gravel and rotting lumber. A sharp kick on the side of his kneecap sent him tumbling to the ground, barely missing a row of rusty nails sticking out of an old doorjamb.

He took two breaths and pulled himself to his feet. There were no street lights, so it was pitch dark. A cut in his forehead was bleeding into his eye. "What's this about?" he asked, turning his head in every direction, trying to make out his assailants.

At the curb a white van was idling. *See if you can get a license number*, Sadie thought. *Anything identifiab—*

A shiny black boot flashed out, kicking both Ford's legs out from under him, sending him sprawling on the ground.

Painstakingly he turned onto his side, facing the van. There was no license plate, but he thought he made out a figure inside. Was someone watching?

"Stay away from Plum," a voice near Ford's ear hissed.

Plum? Sadie thought.

"Plum?" Ford said. The voice that had spoken was different from the one that had called his name, which meant there had to be at least two of them.

"Yeah," the same guy elaborated. "She doesn't want to see any more of you. Understand?" To underscore his point, he kicked Ford in the ribs once, then again. There was a sickening cracking sound and pain so profound that Ford was beyond screaming.

Sadie wished she could wrap herself around him to protect him, especially when the other guy said, "Do. You. Under. Stand?" punctuating each syllable with a kick to Ford's ribcage.

The torture shattered Ford. He curled in a ball, completely defenseless, rendered powerless by the pain. The two assailants, shiny black boots barely soiled, stood above him breathing noisily and watched for some sign of life.

Sadie held her breath as Ford lay unmoving. His mind was showing rolling images with crackles and jumps in them, like an old-time television broadcast. Nothing was clear, dots of color jumbling together, sounds garbled.

Please, she thought, *please let him be okay.*

"He's faking," one of the guys said and aimed a hard kick right at Ford's groin.

Ford howled and writhed in pain. His mouth filled with the metallic taste of blood, his head exploded with shrieks and lights, and unending agony swept over him. He sank into oblivion.

His eyes were still closed when Sadie regained consciousness.

Ford, she whispered in his head. *Can you move?* She felt all the different nerve impulses running through him, but she knew she was only getting a fraction of his pain. It was enough.

The wind was picking up and she could smell rain on the way. She wished she could reach across the boundaries that separated them and cradle his head. She wanted to sit him on the toilet in his bathroom and carefully clean every one of his wounds. She'd try to make him laugh as she did it, think of any stupid thing she could to distract him from the pain. She wanted to brush the hair from his forehead and gently kiss him on the lips.

Come on, Ford, she said, putting every ounce of her mind and her will into reaching him. *You can do this. You have to do this.*

Can't . . . move, she heard him think.

He was conscious, and she could hear him. Sadie gulped back a sob of relief.

He was lying on his back in the scrappy grass of the empty lot, pieces of broken glass and debris littered around.

Ford, you have to move. Sadie didn't think she'd ever concentrated so hard in her life. *If we stay here you'll pass out again, and you'll be picked up by Serenity Services. Think how upset your mother would be. And Lulu.*

"Don't upset Lulu," he murmured. He pushed himself up to a sitting position on his elbow. His head swam, and his stomach heaved. He was about to lie back down when he repeated, "Lulu," and dragged himself onto all fours.

You're doing great, Sadie told him, not sure if he was hearing her and not caring. A section of fence still lingered along the property line, and laboriously he hauled himself up it until he was standing. Pain shot through his ankle. "Got to keep moving," he said through clenched teeth, wavering unsteadily on his feet. "Keep mov—"

His eyes fluttered, and his legs began to buckle at the knees.

Ford! Sadie shouted sharply.

His eyes snapped open and he called "Present!" like a student waking up in class.

It had worked. *It had worked.* Sadie laughed, and he started to laugh too and mutter, "Present!"

How had that happened? Was that even possible?

Later, she told herself. *Later you can think about that. Now you need to get him home.*

Somewhere to the south of them more fireworks began to pop. Clutching a decaying fence plank, he leaned out to get a view of them.

"Pretty," he said to no one. His eyes started to close.

Ford! she shouted.

"Present," he answered again.

Sadie remembered seeing a bus stop just beyond the next corner, but the lot between them and it was empty, and without anything to hold on to she had no idea how they'd get that far.

Ford let go of the splintery board, took two steps unsupported, and fell down.

Poor boy. Right on your caboose, Sadie commiserated.

"Choo choo," he said, amazing Sadie again. He had heard her. He had to have heard her.

Later.

Crawling on all fours, he pulled himself to the abandoned house in front of his tree house and dropped down to rest on its short stack of concrete stairs. The first drops of rain started to fall as he sat there. Propping himself on the handrail of the stairs, he stood and pushed off.

He staggered forward and was about to go sprawling when he caught a crooked NO PARKING sign. He stood, eyes closed, hugging it, the rain stinging as it hit the cuts on his face and arms. When he opened his eyes, the corner was in sight, and the bus stop beyond it.

Ford, you have to keep going, Sadie told him. *You can do it. You can't stop now.*

"Present," he said, but it was more like a yawn than a word.

I mean it, Sadie told him. *You're in a no-parking zone. Look at the sign.*

He laughed, then grimaced as a bolt of pain shot from his ribs. But he unwrapped his arms from the sign and with a supreme show of effort pushed off and made it the rest of the way to the bus stop.

The bus came, finally, and he dragged himself on, apparently not looking much worse than the other drenched commuters because no one paid any attention. Sadie talked and told every joke she could remember to keep him alert enough to notice when they reached his stop.

Together they counted the steps between the bus stop and his apartment, him out loud, her in his head. The two flights of stairs required the most effort, but finally, sweaty and bloody and dirty, Ford mounted the top one, scraped his key into the front-door lock, and fell face-first onto the couch. He muttered "Present" one last time before passing out.

Sadie didn't want to think back over the night. She lay very still, listening to his heartbeat and his breathing, letting the familiar rhythms of his body enfold her. She closed her eyes and whispered very quietly, "I love you, Ford Winter."

She began to sob.

CHAPTER 24
WEEK 5

Ford had been out for almost six days, when Sadie went into his subconscious in search of James. If anything could help rouse Ford it would be roiling him from inside, she thought, and there was clearly something to roil with his brother.

The great hall was quiet when she went through, all the images moving slowly and everyone talking in low voices, if at all. She felt like they were in suspended animation, lacking the will or force to spur them to action. She elicited a tiny bit of curiosity from a handful looking for news, but most were absorbed in themselves. She said hello to Plum as she went by but only got an "Oh, brother" in response.

James was by the shore of the pine-fringed lake, looking out at the icehouse, when she found him.

"You again," he said. "I'm not sure I should talk to you."

"Why?"

"It's been strange down here since you came last time. Look around. Things are dying."

Sadie shivered. "Since when? Because of me?"

"You can't just come in and poke at things and go. It's an ecosystem. You kill what you touch." His tone was reproachful.

"That's not true. You're just saying that to make me feel bad. You want me to go away."

He looked away from her, his mouth petulant. "Maybe."

She stayed quiet for a moment, listening to him sigh. Finally she said, "What happened that day on the lake? At the icehouse?"

He rolled his eyes, tossing his blond hair back. "God, you ask the worst questions."

"What was it?" she pushed.

"Ask *him*," he sneered, pointing upward.

"I can't. He's sick."

He nodded to himself. "That explains the Geronimo."

"What's that?"

"It's a piece of the mind that drops off when there's been trauma. Like a flyer bailing out of a bomber. Takes the important documents with him and parachutes out before the crash. We had one the other day."

Sadie looked around. "Where is he?"

"Think I saw him hanging around the weighting room on the plain. Most things start there before getting settled in. Lucky for you he didn't land in the lake. Lots of times that's where Geronimos end up. Sink deep, don't see some of them again for years."

"Ah."

"Weighting room's over there," he said, pointing behind him.

"Okay."

He looked angry. "Why aren't you going?"

"Tell me about the icehouse."

"You have to ask him, I *told* you that," he whined. "But I'll give you this: He knows what he did and what he didn't do, he's just lying about it."

"Why?"

"Talk to the boss," he said, pointing up.

"Could you at least tell me about the beer cans? They look like they're all identical."

"Multiples," he corrected. "This place is lousy with them. Repeated patterns, same object showing up in different places, sometimes as a distraction, sometimes to stand in for something else. Like say you have—"

"Pine trees." Sadie pointed toward the lakeshore.

"Sure. Could be a reminder of a great day you spent at the lake with your brother when you learned to skip rocks, or a symbol of winter, or the feeling of pining for someone. Keeps it efficient, one thing, lots of associations. Shortcut for the imagination." He yawned. "Never touch them myself."

"Multiples?"

"No, the beer cans."

She'd bent to look at them closer, and when she stood up, James had disappeared. She walked toward the plain he'd indicated, where there was a structure with a wide arch entrance and clusters of wood benches inside. It looked like photos she'd seen of the waiting room at Central Station before it was abandoned. A couple of figures she didn't recognize huddled together like refugees on one bench.

She spotted Ford on the other side of the space. He sat alone, shoulders curled in, repeating, "Howdy?" His eyes were wide and looked panicked.

"Howdy," Sadie answered.

He looked at her like she was nuts. "Howdy fine?"

"Howdy, I'm fine too," Sadie answered.

He turned his face away from her, holding the toes of his bare feet and murmuring to himself. Sadie bent closer to hear but just kept getting, "Howdy fine," "Howdy fine."

"What are you trying to say?" she asked, desperate to know the important piece of information his brain sent to safekeeping before losing consciousness. "Say it again," she implored. *Howdy fine, how define, how—*

CHAPTER 25

"How'd they find me?"

Ford woke with those words like a swimmer breaking the surface of a lake, wide-eyed, gasping, and thirsty. He'd been unconscious for five and a half days.

It was two thirty in the morning, although time had ceased to have any meaning in the Winter house. One day slipped into the next, someone always sitting in the chair next to the couch in case something—anything—happened.

"Who?" Lulu asked. She was the one on watch when his eyes opened. When he showed a sign of actual consciousness, not another false alarm, she called over her shoulder, "Mom, he's awake," and turned back to him to say, "Don't look in the mirror when you go to the bathroom, you'll be scared."

Ford took a deep breath, and Sadie felt him wince at the

pain it triggered in almost every part of his body. "Good to know," he said. He looked down at his arms and hands, which were criss-crossed with cuts and abrasions. There were bandages with smiling suns on both forearms, and one with Snoopy taped over his right knuckles.

Sadie had never been as grateful for anything in her life as she was for Ford waking up. She was overwhelmed by her love for him, by her relief, and by the vacuum left by worry and fear, but she pushed all of that aside to concentrate on Ford. *Whatever you feel doesn't matter*, she told herself. *You're here to be with him.*

To observe him, she corrected.

The first thing she observed was that the pain, which had registered as a fairly unobtrusive set of noises while he was passed out, was now like a noisy cityscape. Every time he moved, some kind of discomfort zigzagged through him, setting off different noises depending on its type and calibrated in volume to its intensity. Sharp pain sounded like a truck horn, throbbing pain resembled an extended bleating, stinging was the piercing jangle of bells.

Lulu gave him a tour of his primary injuries. "You have a bruise on your stomach that according to the Internet means at least two of your ribs are broken. The only thing to do is put ice on it, which we have been, and take aspirin, which you did about three hours ago, although you were a baby about it."

Ford smiled, setting off shrill bells. He reached up to touch his cheek and discovered another bandage. "Thank you for taking such good care of me," he said.

His mother came in then, looking even more exhausted

than usual. She was carrying a bowl, which she set on the trunk in front of him.

"Good, you're up." Her tone was completely flat, her face expressionless. "You should eat this. You'll need something in your stomach."

Ford's heart started to pound fast, and Sadie knew he was nervous. He was desperate for his mother to understand this hadn't been his fault, he hadn't picked this fight. "Thank you," he said, trying to catch her eye, but she wouldn't look at him. "Mom, I want you to know how—"

"Eat your soup." Her flat gaze moved to Lulu. "I'm going to lie down. Make sure your brother finishes that. And no gabbing, he needs to sleep."

His head turned to watch his mother leave the room, and a sharp thrust of pain overwhelmed him, filling his mind with blaring truck horns. Sadie saw his vision go misty and wished she could steady him.

His eyes refocused a moment later, on Lulu, who was watching him with unconcealed worry. *Show her everything's fine*, Sadie heard him think and wanted to kiss him. He licked his dry, craggy lips and said, "What day is it?"

"Tuesday." Lulu scooched her chair toward him and whispered conspiratorially, "Mom found you on the couch Thursday morning and you've barely moved since then. And neither has she. She sat right next to you the whole time. I think she might have prayed. She even started to *draw* again."

Ford moved his eyes to the bowl of soup, and Sadie felt a lump in his throat and tears prick at his eyes.

"Are you crying?" Lulu said.

"Yeah, no, it's just—" He swallowed back the lump. "The

pain." But it wasn't, Sadie knew. He reached for the soup and made a show of eating it. Holding the spoon caused a bus-sized horn blast, so he raised the bowl to his mouth and slurped.

"I need to ask you something, and I need you to tell me the truth," Lulu said, very serious. "Did James's monster do this?"

"What monster?" Sadie and Ford asked in unison. Hands shaking, he set the bowl down.

Lulu took a big breath. "He said I couldn't tell you. Not"— she rushed to assure him—"because he didn't love you as much as me. Or almost as much. It was because there were *circumstances*. But now this has happened, and I wonder if I had told—" She glanced away but not before Sadie saw the pain in her eyes.

She thinks she's responsible, Sadie realized, her heart aching.

"Tell me about this monster of James's," Ford prompted.

Lulu frowned, trying to figure out where to begin. "He said there was a monster in our city, taking control of people and making them zombies. They looked okay on the outside, but they were dead inside, and they fed off sadness. James said Serenity Services was powerless to stop it from happening, and you couldn't trust anyone except little kids like me, but he was going to fix it." She picked up speed as she talked, the story bubbling out of her. "He had a magic power that made him invisible, and he was going to find the monster and slay it, and then everyone would be free."

"How was he going to find the monster?" Ford asked, his mind spinning over the words *magic power*.

"The monster had a treasure hidden in a stone fortress. James was going to use his invisibility power to hide there, and when the monster went to count the treasure, he'd slay it. And then everyone, you and me and Mom and Copernicus, would all live happily ever after. But he was worried if he failed you'd go hunt the monster even though you don't have his magic power. I asked him why he couldn't just give it to you, but he said it didn't work that way, you either had it or you didn't."

Ford was having trouble keeping his eyes open. *Tell her she's not responsible for what happened to you*, Sadie urged. *You can pass out after, just tell her that.*

"But you went looking for the monster anyway," Lulu pressed on. "Because you're a hero, like James."

"No." Ford shook his head. Her face was an indistinct series of shadows, and his voice sounded like it was coming from far away. "I'm not like James. And what happened to me had nothing to do with the monster."

"You're sure?" Lulu asked. "Swear?"

"Swear," he said and plunged back into unconsciousness.

The next time he woke, thirty-six hours later, Mason was in the chair next to the couch.

Ford frowned. "What are you doing here?"

Mason glanced at his watch. "My shift. I have another hour. So don't think of doing anything rash until three thirty. That's when Mrs. Entwistle comes on, and your mom can't yell at me."

"Mrs. Entwistle?"

"Neighbor across the hall."

"I'm sorry they made you do this," Ford said.

"I volunteered," Mason told him. "What else am I going to do while my overpriced scout is out of commission?"

Ford sat up and frowned at the yellow envelope on the coffee table. "What's that?"

"I found it outside the door when I came this morning." Mason said. "It was hand delivered. Mysterious."

Ford's fingers weren't entirely steady as he ripped it open, and Sadie knew it was because he was excited. He'd recognized the writing on the envelope.

The card inside was a birthday card. It was unsigned, but "SAFE KEEPING" was written in big letters on one side, and the $5 Bigfoot bill was secured on the other.

Ford clutched the envelope and said, "Come on."

Mason looked up from his word jumble. "Where are we going?"

"To see Bucky," Ford told him, making to stand up.

He fell on his face.

"I don't think we're going anywhere," Mason said gently.

Ford glared at him. "We are." Pushing Mason's hand aside, he gritted his teeth and stood. He stayed leaning on the couch for a minute until his nausea and dizziness cleared, gave Mason a triumphant glance, and staggered to the shower.

At first the water stung on the cuts and abrasions, but once that passed he closed his eyes and let himself enjoy the hot water pouring over him, and so did Sadie.

She reveled in the way soap smelled on him, the way his fingertips felt on his scalp. She lost herself in the prickly sensation of face wash being rubbed through his beard, of his work-worn hands soaping his chest, his fingers cleaning his ears.

And she loved it when he smiled in the mirror.

On the way out of the bathroom, he stopped to put the toilet seat down. *You're going to break my heart, Ford Winter,* she thought.

• • •

Four hours after waking up, he was sitting in the passenger seat of Mason's car across the street from a low-slung cinder-block building. It had a sign that read U DRINK EM PACKAGE–LIQUOR–LUCKY LOTTO on the front and a thick chain and foreclosure notice on the door. It was still light, the evening sun turning the windshields of the used cars on the lot next door gold.

"The nurse told you to stay in bed for two weeks," Mason said casually.

"And I told you if you were going to be bossy I didn't want a ride. Guess we both suck at listening," Ford answered.

Mason grinned. He watched Ford compare the address on the yellow envelope to the one on the building for the fourth time. "I doubt it's changed."

"This just isn't what it's supposed to look like," Ford said. He was trying to reconcile the short, squat liquor store with the room big enough to hold fifty miniature-golf holes, not to mention an entire outdoor theater. Next door to the liquor store in one direction was the used car place, and the other side was an empty lot.

"You didn't see the exterior."

"True." Ford nodded and kept nodding as he said, "I don't think you should come in."

"That doesn't work for me," Mason said, nodding with him.

Ford stopped nodding. "I'm serious."

He's serious, Sadie seconded.

"We said no rescuing." Ford sounded almost desperate now. "This might be a trap."

Mason twisted behind the wheel to face him. "Let's put it this way. I'm not letting you out of the car without me. And if anything happens to me, up to or including death, I won't hold you responsible."

"That's not comforting."

Mason looked surprised. "Funny, it is to me. Come on." They got out of the car and approached the liquor store. "Don't forget, this is an MRP address."

"I'm not likely to forget that."

Sadie didn't know which one of them was more excited, her or Ford, and she couldn't tell whose heart was the one racing. Being out of commission for six days had left Ford both restless and weak, but the card from Bucky had been like a shot of adrenaline.

The front door was locked, for real, but the one on the side gave easily. It looked like a standard solid metal aluminum door on the outside, nothing camouflaged about it. It opened into . . .

. . . an abandoned liquor store. Just like the sign said. Sadie looked through Ford's eyes, watching the play of images fly by as he catalogued and filed what he was seeing. There were three doors—the front door, the door they'd come through, and the door to the bathroom. The linoleum floor showed the outline of shelves, but they were long gone. What was left: the counter— too big to move and not valuable; a three-year-old poster of a Korean pop sensation eating a lollipop; a toilet, ripped out of the wall and turned into a mini-shrine with candles and some plastic flowers in the middle of the floor.

Ford rubbed a hand through his hair, accidentally scraping a cut on his scalp, and winced. *If this was the right place then one of these things had to mark the entrance to Bucky's lair,*

Sadie heard him think. He and Mason spent an hour knocking on walls listening for hollow sounds, testing the door, verifying every set of hinges.

As they prodded the counter a second time, Mason announced, "Toilets and radiators. That's going to be the name of my community theater company."

Ford looked up. "Because you never want anyone to come see your shows? I thought you said you were trying to impress some girl, not *de*press her."

Sadie laughed.

Mason made a broad gesture. "They're everywhere. Every demo and salvage site we go to. They are the icons of this moment."

I noticed that too, Sadie said.

"Or the toilets have no resale value, and the radiators are too heavy to move," Ford pointed out.

"Still like the name."

"Good thing you can afford to lose some—" Sadie watched the points of color in Ford's mind do acrobatics, picturing where the toilet should have been. He crossed to the bathroom, pushed the door open all the way so the knob came to rest against the rubber stopper, and leaned into it until he heard a click. Then he stepped into the bathroom and closed the door behind him. The false wall came with it, revealing the passage-way concealed behind it.

The passage led to a descending flight of stairs that went to another passage that ended in a flight of stairs going up. As Ford and Mason climbed the second staircase something skittered across the ceiling. Sadie felt the hairs on the back of Ford's neck bristle. "What was that?"

"Best case? Rats," Mason answered.

Ford had been mentally compiling a map as they went, so when they reached the top of the stairs he knew they were in the big room where the miniature-golf statues had been, but it was unrecognizable. The fake grass had been ripped up, and piles of smashed fiberglass formed eerie colored mounds, an eye winking out here, a claw there.

The bed was gone from the light blue bedroom, and the partition that had separated it from the other room was flattened. The only thing that hadn't moved was the radiator.

"Case in point," Mason said, leaning against it.

The skittering noise came again.

The stairs up to the stage had been stripped to metal slats, but the stage was still there, and the outdoor theater. *Bucky, you sneaky rat*, Sadie heard Ford think, as he now realized that the theater he'd been searching for was actually a hanging garden, a completely fabricated outdoor space. Even the perfectly ruined walls had been constructed. *Sneaky rat genius.*

"It's even more beautiful when you realize Bucky built the whole damn thing," Ford said, echoing Sadie's thoughts.

"But why do that?" Mason asked. "Why not just move into an old theater like the one he took the seats from?"

"Camoufla—"

A shower of bullets strafed the front of the stage. Ford flattened himself to the ground, groaning as his ribs hit, and tried to make out where the shots were coming from. He spotted one ski-masked gunman in the audience—

Another round of bullets.

—and two more on top of the exterior walls.

Ford popped up and ran toward the back of the stage, shouting at Mason, "Come with me."

"Divide and conquer," Mason yelled back, giving a loud war cry and running the other way.

The men in ski masks all turned to look at him, and while they were distracted, Ford jumped on the lever Bucky had used to activate the trapdoor, opened it, and leapt through.

There was no bag this time, and he landed hard on his hurt ankle. It twisted out from under him, and as he staggered to right himself in the darkness under the stage he tripped over something, making it clang. He stopped moving and held his breath. Had they heard? Were they coming after him?

His heart was racing against his ribs, and his lungs contracted. *Don't panic*, she whispered to him, keeping her breaths long and regular. *Breathe and think.*

It worked. She sensed his attention sharpen as he took in his surroundings: light from the left, a sink across the way, tall shelf full of umbrellas.

Why would Bucky need a dozen umbrellas? Ford wondered.

There was a—*moan?*

Sadie held her breath, and so did Ford. *Was there someone there?*

Another moan.

"Do you need help?" Ford whispered.

The sound stopped. But it was close by, he thought, stepping around a pile of chairs, just—

"Oh, Bucky, no," Ford whispered, collapsing on the floor next to him. The hair on Bucky's forehead was matted with blood, his left leg was at an unhealthy angle, one eye was swollen shut, and his lips were caked with blood.

"Who did this?" Ford demanded. Sadie felt his rage

sweltering like a foundry in the summer, a hairbreadth away from complete combustion.

He needs water, she urged Ford, to focus him. *And a blanket. He's in shock.*

"Water," Ford's mind echoed, and he twisted around, assessing. Getting to the sink without making noise was going to be challenging.

There's a blanket to your left, Sadie told him. He looked to his left and was pleased to see a blanket. He put it on Bucky and started for the sink.

"Gotcha!" a voice—male, jovial—said, and a volley of bullets from above flew through the stage within inches of Ford's position.

He leapt back toward Bucky and stood stock-still.

"Lost him. Anyone got a chirp?"

Another guy, this one slightly nasal sounding. "No chirp."

Chirp? Sadie repeated. What did that mean? How had they known exactly where Ford was standing?

"He's still down there." This voice sounded older, and familiar.

The boards of the stage creaked with the weight of the gunmen as they moved over it in slow, concentric circles, searching for Ford.

The one with the sniffles said, "Stupid chippy thinks he can hide from us." *Chippy*. Sadie and Ford both repeated the word in their mind.

"Come out, come out, wherever you are, chippy."

Sadie's mind wouldn't let go. Chippy. Chip. Could they be referring to—

No, she protested against the thoughts pushing their way into her head. Her conscious mind dug its claws in, trying desperately to deny it, but she couldn't. *They were tracking Ford with his Sycnopy chip.*

With a shock, Sadie realized she'd known. Known subconsciously, and repressed it, like Ford repressing his memory of walking in on James and Cali. She'd kept her mind busy with misdirected suspicions about other people's influence on Ford, resenting Plum and Mason, how open he was with them, worrying they might hurt him when—god, the irony—*she* was the danger to him. She was the one leaving him completely vulnerable and unprotected. It was because of her they could hunt him this way.

James's "magic power" hadn't been that he was invisible, she realized. It was that he couldn't be tracked because he didn't have a chip. He was free. Safe.

Her presence stole that security from Ford.

The same chip that makes me care for him makes me betray him, she realized, horrified by the irony. By her powerlessness to stop it.

Anger filled her now, not Ford's but her own. Against her will she had become Ford's implacable, inescapable enemy. Somehow she'd been tricked, turned into an unwitting pawn in the Pharmacist's sick game.

"Yoo hoo, chippy," a voice coaxed from upstairs. "We're bound to get you. You might as well come out."

An unwitting executioner.

Ford took a step forward and said, "I want to talk to the Pharmacist."

I want to punch the Pharmacist, Sadie thought.

There was a deep, swaggering laugh. "Sure thing, chippy. Just come a little more to the center of the—*gotcha*."

The bullets started to fly again, nearly on target. Ford took two steps back toward Bucky, and the guns stopped.

Was it a trick?

From upstairs the older voice said, "That dead chippy down there's interfering with the relay. We need to pull him out."

Bucky's chip was blocking their ability to see Ford's when they were close together, Sadie and Ford realized simultaneously.

But then Ford took a step forward, away from Bucky. *What are you doing?* Sadie yelled as a hailstorm of bullets flew around him. He jumped back to Bucky and the bullets stopped.

Yep, looks like that's how it works, he thought.

That was not a hypothesis that needed to be tested, Sadie seethed at him.

"Go get that dead chippy," the older voice ordered.

"Could be an ambush," the one with the sniffles said. "They could be waiting with weapons down there."

Good idea, Sadie heard Ford think. He could make them think he had weapons even though he didn't. His eyes roamed the room for anything within hand's reach.

On the floor near his feet, Bucky groaned. "You weren't supposed to come," he said. "Card only for emergency purposes. All went wrong. So sorry."

"What happened?" Ford asked, leaning in close. "Do you know who the Pharmacist is?"

Bucky shook his head. "These are just thugs. Paid guns." He made a gun with his fingers. "Bang."

"Why are they here?"

Bucky grabbed Ford's arm and pulled him closer. "I'm sorry.

I saw—Fourth of July. They made me watch. That. This—" He rolled his eyes. "My punishment for not telling. Never tell. But hated seeing what they did to you."

Ford smiled at him. "You don't look so hot yourself."

Oh god, Ford, I love you, Sadie thought.

Bucky tried a chuckle, then gulped air. "Hurts too much." His hand squeezed Ford's hard, eyes closed against the pain. "I didn't tell. All still there for you."

"All what?"

Bucky opened his eyes. "The treasure."

"We'll have some fun with it when this is over."

Yes, Sadie vowed. *You will. I promise.*

"No, Citizen F. This is the end for me."

"Don't you dare say that, Bucky," Ford threatened, as if the force of his will could keep him alive. "Don't give up. I'm not going to let you go. We'll get out of this." *I'm not going to lose anyone else*, Sadie heard him think.

But something had changed in Bucky. His eyes were clear and alert, and he seemed calmer. He said, "Was always jealous of James. Not because of him." Bucky's hand clutched Ford's, and his eyes closed as a fresh surge of pain rolled through him. "Because of you. Always wanted a brother like you."

Sadie tasted tears and didn't know if they were hers or Ford's. "Bucky—" Ford said, part plea, part gasp.

Bucky's eyes opened and he smiled at Ford. "It's okay. Don't worry about me. Bet they have better treasure hunts where I'm going." He looked peaceful, but there was a hint of fear in his eyes.

It ripped Ford in half. "The best," Ford told him, struggling to breathe around the lump in his throat. "The very best." Sadie heard him praying: *Please don't let him die, please.*

Boots sounded on the stairs behind them. Bucky gave Ford's hand a feeble squeeze. "Hide."

Grief welled up in Ford as he flattened himself against the armoire. His heart was racing with fear, but over it Sadie heard him repeating that it wasn't fair, Bucky couldn't die too, it wasn't fair.

I'm so sorry, Ford, she cried, guilt making her feel like she'd been stabbed. This was her fault. Not consciously or intentionally, but she was still responsible. Without her, he wouldn't have been in this situation.

The heavy footsteps—two sets? More?—had almost reached the bottom of the stairs. Ford's heartbeat jumped with fear, and he thought, *I'm really sorry, Mom.*

Oh, Ford, Sadie gasped.

There were three gunmen, large guys wearing ski masks and body armor with weapons cocked at waist level. Two of them advanced toward Bucky to pick him up while one of them stayed by the stairs.

"Let's make it fast," the one nearest to Ford said. "All this dust is hell on my allergies."

"We should take a second to look around for Sub Nine. If we find him, we—"

"Stop talking and do this," the gunman at the stairs barked.

From above Sadie and Ford heard a baritone that hadn't spoken yet announce, "I got one!" and the sound of booted footsteps marching across the stage.

So there are four gunmen, Ford thought.

Sadie added, *At least*.

"He's not on our list," another voice they hadn't heard before said.

Five.

"He's not a chippy, but he was nosing around," the baritone explained.

"Not nosing." It was Mason's voice. The strain in it made Ford feel like someone was pulling on his guts and increased the crushing burden of Sadie's guilt. "I'm a developer. I'm just looking at the property."

"Put him in the transport," the newest voice said.

No! Sadie heard Ford think, and she caught quick flashed images of white, of rope, of the black glove, the icehouse.

What does that memory mean? she wanted to ask him. *Why are you thinking of it now?*

The two gunmen lifted Bucky's body from the floor. Ford's mind was raging. *You can't have him*, Sadie heard him think. *Not without a fight*. Sadie saw him putting together a plan, grab one of the umbrellas, use it to hook—

"Got a chirp on your chippy!" the baritone from upstairs called. "He's down there with you, I'm locked on—"

Get back! Sadie screamed, and Ford skidded away from the umbrellas, knocking the gunman carrying Bucky's legs to the ground as his colleague began shooting through the floor at the place where Ford had been standing.

"You hit me, you bastard!" the one with the allergies shouted.

Sadie felt Ford's grim pleasure, but it was short-lived. The other gunman kept moving and had dragged Bucky nearly halfway up the stairs, which meant he was getting away and Ford's chirp would be visible in five . . . four . . . three.

Duck, Sadie called to him as the gunman by the stairs opened fire, sending a barrage of bullets into the debris where Ford had been the moment before.

Shell casings clinked on the ground. The air stank, thick and smoky. Bucky was out of view.

They must be reloading, Sadie thought. *We're completely exposed now. Trapped.* She was shaking all over.

"Did we get him?"

Above them the guy with the baritone said, "I can't find Subject Nine. He's off screen."

What? Sadie asked. *How?*

"I've lost Subject Nine."

"Me too."

A knot began twisting in Sadie's stomach. She could see everything Ford saw, which meant his chip was active. And Bucky was gone. So how was Ford staying shielded? Unless there was someone—

Linc's big head filled Ford's field of vision. "I really didn't want it to come to this," he said, pressing the point of a knife against Ford's neck.

CHAPTER 26

"You say a word, I'll slit your throat," Linc growled. "But I'm going to get you out of here if I can. Do you understand?"

"Why should I believe you?" Ford demanded.

For a second it almost looked like Linc was going to laugh. "Because if I *wanted* to kill you, you idiot, I would have done it already. I can't believe James always said you were the smart one."

"Relatively speaking," Ford told him. The knife was still against his throat. "You keep that nice and sharp."

Linc got the same this-is-what-I'd-look-like-if-I-ever-laughed expression again. "Don't make me regret this." He sheathed the knife, said, "Come on," and started navigating across the debris-covered floor toward the back of the theater.

"Where are we going?" Ford asked, trying to fill in the

empty parts of his mental map of the building as they walked. Having a knife to his throat had stilled Ford's internal land-scape, making his mind lucid and supple. Sadie made a mental note to look up the effects of adrenaline before meeting with the Committee.

"They've staked out the back and main stairs," Linc said. "If we climb over the stage, we can get to the old coal chute. It's unguarded."

"Up and over the stage?" Ford whispered. "In plain view? That's nuts."

"I just did it. They're not looking for you, they're looking for your chirp. They keep their eyes down on the readers. But if anyone looks up, fight like you're fighting for your life. I will be."

You can do this, Sadie told Ford. *This could work.*

"Where's Bucky?" Ford asked.

"In the back of the Range Rover. With your friend."

"We have to get him."

"Impossible," Linc growled, and there was no question it was final. "If you make it out of here, call the highway patrol and report the car stolen. Black Ranger Rover."

"What make? What year?"

"You want me to wipe your ass for you too? You make a big enough fuss, they'll find it. Tell them it's your wife's car and you don't know all that information. They'll pull it over, should be time. Highway Patrol, not Serenity Services. Got it?"

"Got it."

"Stay within three feet of me. Farther, and you're blown."

The map he'd been compiling unfolded in Ford's mind, the path Linc had laid out most clear but the rest still visible. Sadie could see spots of color, images, hovering around the edges, but he was keeping the center clear of distractions. His heart rate was remarkably even, his breathing a little shallow but not fast, and Sadie concentrated on matching hers with his.

They got to the scaffolding that went to the catwalk and were halfway up when Linc stopped moving to take a phone call. There were three guys in ski masks on the stage, each holding a palm-sized monitor in one hand and an automatic rifle in the other, not more than twenty feet from them. Sadie felt Ford's heart beat *babum, babum* as he hung there, completely exposed, listening to Linc whisper, "I understand. Yes. I'll take care of it," before continuing on. His forehead was sweating and his mouth was dry, and his knuckles ached from holding on.

They made it up to the top and started across. Sadie willed Ford not to look down, but she was having trouble controlling her breathing, and her hands were shaking.

Linc dropped over the side abruptly to begin his descent. Ford hadn't realized the edge was coming, and it took him a second to catch up.

Too long. His relay chirped. Three pairs of eyes all swiveled toward him. Bullets started to fly.

Down, Sadie urged, but instead of descending the side of the scaffold near them, he ran back the way he'd come. She heard him assessing the outer wall of the building and thought, *No, oh, no*. The gap between it and the scaffolding was easily five feet across, and the wall was two feet higher than they were. *It's the only chance*, she heard him think at the same moment she thought, *There's no way—*

He made a mad flying leap for the wall. Sadie screamed and closed her eyes and didn't stop until his fingers had caught—just barely—the top of the stone. He hauled himself up, a bullet nicking his shoe, and slid down the wall on the other side.

He'd forgotten that the theater was elevated so he dropped five stories, more than the two he'd been expecting, and landed with a thud that made his recovering knee feel like it had been kicked all over again. He had to blink twice to clear his head, then blinked again in disbelief.

Wait, was that—?

He was standing across the street from the Candy Factory, Plum's club.

He turned to look behind him and started to laugh. The building he'd left, the one housing the theater, was the Surprise Party Outlet Store. *Surprise Outlet*. Sadie heard him repeat to himself. As in surprise exit. Bucky had written it right on the sign.

He started limping toward the Candy Factory, his mind plotting a map of the connection between the two buildings—a mile and a half on the streets but only about a quarter mile if you put tunnels that looked like hallways through the empty lots behind the buildings. Distracted, he walked in front of a limo pulling up in front of the club. It blasted its horn, which prodded Ford's memory.

The Range Rover. Jogging up the front steps of the club, he pulled out his phone and dialed the Highway Patrol.

"My car has just been stolen," he told the operator. *Sound more hysterical*, Sadie urged. "It's a black Range Rover. Recent. No, I don't remember what year. The license?" Sadie felt Ford's mind contract.

It's 145T90, Sadie said.

"It's my wife's car," he explained. "I'm not sure if she has it written down anywhere."

It's 145T90, Sadie repeated.

"Is there any way you can locate the car without the exact—

145T90! 145T90! 145T90! Sadie shouted.

"It's 145T90," Ford said.

There was absolute silence.

"Hello? Sir?" the operator on the other end of Ford's phone asked. "Sir, are you there?"

"Yes," Ford said. "I have to go."

He ended the call but didn't move. "Who are you?" he said aloud.

Sadie was petrified.

"Who the hell are you?" he growled, causing a group of women to turn and stare at him.

Anger rushed to fill his mind. He walked into the club, grabbed the first person in a Candy Factory apron he saw, and asked for the nearest bathroom. When he got there he announced it was closed for cleaning, kicked everyone out, and locked the door.

A seven-foot-tall gilt-framed mirror leaned against one wall. He went and stood in front of it, staring at his eyes.

"Are you in there?" he asked.

Sadie ducked, lowering her eyes. This wasn't a good idea. Nothing about this was—

"Goddamn it, I know you're there, look at me."

Fine, Sadie thought. She raised her eyes and met his.

A thrill reverberated through her but was almost immediately skewed and made jagged and painful by the force of his hate.

"I feel you in there," he said, grabbing his head between his hands. "I can feel you, and I want you out." He banged his head against the glass mirror, hard, making a long, V-shaped crack.

"Ford, no!" Sadie shouted.

He was staring wildly in the mirror again, and she realized he'd heard her. "I'll keep doing it. I'll keep doing this until you're gone." He banged his head twice.

Stop, please, she sobbed. *I'm sorry. I didn't mean to hurt you. I love you. Ford, I—*

"Shut up!" he screamed. Stepping back he ran at the mirror and smashed the crown of his head into it. The entire surface of the glass shattered, sliding like a silver avalanche over him, onto the floor.

He turned to the row of five small mirrors over the sinks. "I'm not done," he said, shattering the first one with the side of his head.

No! Sadie shrieked. She felt like she was trapped, being flung side to side with his rage. *Please stop.*

"What did you say? More?" His eyes were wild, glowing, pouring his hate into her. "This is for you, since you like watching people get hurt," he said and drove his head crown first into the second mirror. A crack appeared but it didn't completely shatter so he shook his head. "Not good enough, no, not good enough" and banged his forehead against it over and over, four, five, six times, until it shattered into powder and glass. "Look what you've done. Look at all the pain you've caused," he said in an eerie echo of his memories of his father.

Ford, please don't do this, she begged, crying.

"Are you happy now? Is this what you like? Driving someone out of their mind?"

No, she sobbed. *I love you. I want you to be happy. I never meant any harm. I never . . .* There was no room for the hugeness of her grief. Sadie felt like she'd swallowed all the glass he'd broken, all the fire, all the poison, and it was burning her from the inside.

I never wanted to cause you pain, she wept. *I'm so sorry.*

"SORRY? YOU'RE SORRY? GET THE HELL OUT OF MY MIND," he roared, bashing his head into the third, fourth, and fifth mirrors, backward and forward, over and over until they were nothing more than frames with the occasional piece of glass still clinging in the corner.

He picked up one of those now and held it in front of his eyes. "I will keep doing this until you leave. I will destroy myself every way possible unless you get out."

The door to the bathroom crashed to the ground, and two muscular women with guns, one a brunette with a crew cut, one bald, burst in. They stared at Ford, and Sadie pictured what they were seeing, wild eyes, blood, broken glass everywhere, a shard of mirror gripped in his hand. They both took aim.

"Drop the mirror and put your hands behind your head," the bald woman said.

Sadie couldn't cry anymore, couldn't do anything. She was numb beyond numb, sore beyond sore, hurt and angry and rejected. And now two amazons were pointing automatic weapons at the man she loved, and it was all her fault.

She watched Ford's mind hiccup into awareness of how everything must look, saw his fury that he was in this situation directed at her, at Syncopy, at the world.

He put the mirror down and his hands over his head. He tried a smile, which, judging by the reaction of the two women, did not work. "You caught me at a bad time. I was just in here yelling at myself. It—helps to motivate me. I'm meeting a girl? And I got a little carried away."

Wow, that's bad. And there's no way I am responsible for that, Sadie thought. She was careful not to make a sound since he only seemed to hear her when she actually spoke, but she had no idea how their connection worked, so she was relieved when he didn't react.

The woman with the crew cut pulled a set of cuffs off her belt and said, "Please put your hands out."

Ford kept his hands on his head. "Is that really necessary? I was arrested by Serenity Services a week ago, and they didn't even cuff me."

The argument that you don't need cuffs because you were arrested without them a week ago is a winner, Sadie thought.

"We're a bit more professional here than Serenity Services," the brunette said, gesturing to his hands. "We take the safety of our guests very seriously."

He held out his wrists. "You know, if you want I can save you all the trouble and just leave," Ford offered as she snapped the cuffs on. "Obviously I'll pay for the mirrors, but there's no need for paperwork or anything."

Could this really be the same person who guessed the poker hands of an entire table blindfolded? It seemed as if he had gone tone deaf.

The bald woman gave him a very pretty smile and said, "We appreciate your concern, but for your safety as well as the safety of our guests, we want to make sure you get looked at before you go. You may have lacerations or other underlying conditions that should be treated."

Please do not tell them that you already have lacerations from getting beaten up last week, Sadie thought.

"Do you have identification, Mr.—"

At least be bright enough to use an—

"Winter," he said.

—easy-to-remember name, Sadie finished the thought. *I hope you were smarter when I fell in love with you. Otherwise I have no excuse.*

The bald one radioed that in. "First name?"

"Mason." Sadie wondered if that was wish fulfillment, denial, or some strange act of friendship.

"Come on." The woman with the crew cut prodded him with her gun.

"Where am I going?"

"To our facility first," the bald woman told him. "And then, I'd imagine, to jail."

Sadie saw Ford looking at the exits, thinking of making a run for it, when a voice said, "Oh, my. It looks like someone has been a very naughty puppy."

CHAPTER 27

Plum stepped past the officers and looked around the bathroom. She shook her head sadly and said to Ford, "Another one of your little fits, Benji?"

"He said his name was Mason," the officer with the crew cut told her.

"That's a new one. Usually uses deodorant names. Come on, dear." Speaking loudly, as if to someone who was a bit slow, she presented Ford's wrists to the bald officer, who reluctantly removed the cuffs.

Plum smiled. "He's a cousin of mine. The more challenged side of the family." She looked at the bathroom and said, "Get a cleaner in."

"We should really make a report, ma'am."

"Of course." Plum nodded. "Silly of me. It's only that it's very embarrassing for the family. We try to keep it as quiet as possible. If you make a report, one of those gossip reporters will be on it instantly, and then Benji will never be able to get the help he needs."

The woman with the crew cut wasn't fooled, but she was a good employee. "Of course, ma'am."

Plum kept her arm tightly through Ford's as they walked. She glanced at him sideways and with an affectionate smile said, "So much work just to get my attention."

"That's not—" Ford tried to pull away.

Plum had dialed her phone as she spoke and now said, "Maribelle, it's me. Could you have someone drop my jacket and those folders by my place? I had to leave abruptly, and I don't want to go all the way back to the office."

She hung up and smiled at him. "Well, you wanted me, now you got me."

"I didn't come here for you," Ford growled.

"When a woman saves you from jail, doesn't insist you replace her thirty-thousand-dollar Venetian mirror, and is going to make you dinner, you could try a little flattery."

"I came here by accident." The interior of his mind was bleak, a landscape twisted by anger then denuded by despair. He wanted to be somewhere, anywhere other than this conversation. Anywhere other than inside himself.

Sadie ached for the part she'd played in making him feel that way.

"You can't seriously expect me to believe that you marched in here and destroyed *my* club for no reason."

Ford's eyes focused past her on the run-down building across the alley from the club where Linc had threatened him weeks earlier. There was a thick braid of cables running to it now, Sadie saw, but Ford didn't seem to notice. "There's a reason, just not one involving you," he snapped.

Plum gave him a look that was part amusement, part warning. "If you prick her she *will* bleed."

"Yeah, I'm the same way." Ford's mind flipped from Linc to the guy with the shiny black boots telling him to stay away from Plum. "Which reminds me, goodbye."

Plum was truly shocked. "You can't just leave, puppy."

A grenade of anger flashed through Ford. He grabbed her and turned her toward him, his eyes blazing. "I'm not your puppy, and I can do whatever I damn well please."

Plum's eyes blazed too, but with a different catalyst. Her gaze caressed his lips, her palm moved down his chest. "I like this. You're much more fun to fight with than James."

Sadie felt his pulse quicken, his jaw tense so the words were bitten out. "I am so tired of being compared with my brother."

Plum wasn't put off. "Okay, no talking about brothers tonight, how does that sound?" Her gaze followed her palm across his chest. "No talking about anything."

"That suits me, because I'm leaving." Ford stepped away from her. "I don't want another visit from your thugs."

"What are you talking about?"

Ford shed enough self-absorption to notice she was genuinely confused. "The guys with the shiny boots? Who beat me up on the Fourth of July and told me to stay away from you? I've been unconscious for the last week."

Plum's expression assumed a new seriousness. "Tell me what they said, exactly."

"'Stay away from Plum. Don't go near Plum.' Along those lines. There were two of them."

Plum's eyes narrowed, and Sadie thought she was truly angry, although she suspected it wasn't entirely on Ford's behalf. "Excuse me," she said, turning away and pulling out her phone. After a moment she started talking in clipped staccato tones, clearly leaving a message. "It's me, and I'm furious with you. This isn't high school, you can't just beat people up to get them to stay away from me. If you have a problem with my behavior, take it up with me, don't be a pussy and pick on my friends. And don't bother coming by tomorrow. I won't see you."

She hung up and stared at her phone for the space of three of Ford's heartbeats. "I'm sorry. That shouldn't have happened," she said, reaching for his arm again. "Let me make you dinner to apologize." When he didn't answer she said, "It won't happen again, I promise." There was a layer of steel beneath her words that gave Sadie goose bumps.

Ford, locked in his own echo chamber of anger, didn't register it. He registered hunger, not wanting to go home looking like this, and wanting to get out of the damn parking lot. "Fine," he agreed, possibly the least gracious acceptance of an invitation to dinner ever. It was the last thing he said until they had nearly reached Plum's, when he announced abruptly, "I'm not saying my name is Romeo."

Plum laughed. "That's okay. We're going in through the garage, so the doormen won't even see you."

That did nothing to diminish Ford's self-loathing or his sense that he was just a plaything to her. Sadie watched its destructive force as they rode up in the elevator and entered Plum's apartment, watched it crashing through Ford's memories as he stood in the kitchen, half listening to Plum rattling on about her day, watched it sharpening phrases—"piece of crap," "protect you," "move on," "guilty conscience," "like your brother"—into blades that sliced his interior landscape to ribbons.

Sadie felt like her heart was breaking. *Stop, please stop hurting yourself*, she called without meaning to and instantly regretted it.

Ford's mind stilled and became hypersensitive, like a security probe suddenly wheeling around in search of an intruder. It was the first time she'd actually spoken since the blowup in the bathroom, Sadie realized.

He was standing across the kitchen island from Plum and she stopped, a bottle of chilled white wine hovering over a glass, to look at him. "What just spooked you?"

"What are you talking about?" he barked.

"It happens to animals. They just freeze. You did that now. You're spooked."

"I've just had a long . . ." *What?* Sadie heard him wonder. *A long day? Month? Life?* "Week," he settled on.

"Why don't you take a shower?" Plum suggested. "You look like you broke six mirrors with your head. The towels in the bathroom are clean."

"That's a great idea," Ford answered, his mind still prodding for foreign bodies. He went into the bathroom, locked the door, stripped off his clothes, and turned on the water. Then he looked in the mirror.

The bruises on his legs were shades of yellow with purple on them, but his ribs still looked painfully purple, blue, and green. Even with them, his body was magnificent. She'd never seen Ford completely naked before. At his house the bathroom mirror really only gave a shoulder-high view.

"Look at me," he ordered, a low, primitive rumble that demanded obedience.

Her heart raced, and her mouth was dry. She felt vulnerable and naked and terrified of his contempt. His hate. She took a deep breath, poured as much love as she could into her gaze, and met his eyes.

The connection sparked, sending firecrackers of sensation through Sadie's whole body. His reaction was as strong as hers, making his body rock backward and his hands grip the counter in front of him.

His knuckles were white, and he practically spit the words out. "I don't want to hear you. I don't want to feel you. I don't want anything that reminds me you are there at all. I hate the thought of it. I hate you for doing it. I hate what you did to my friends. The less I have to think about it, the better. Got that?"

Sadie was trembling. She swallowed hard and tasted tears.

"You're pathetic," he sneered. "Watching someone else live their life instead of living your own."

It would have been easier to shrug off his withering contempt if there hadn't been some truth to it.

"Enjoy your perverted little show," he sneered over his shoulder as he got into the shower.

Sadie spent the rest of the evening curled up in a corner of Ford's mind, watching and registering his thoughts and experiences but doing her best not to interfere. As long as she kept her thoughts to herself, he didn't seem able to hear them.

This was better, she told herself. It would force her to be

objective, behave like a regular Guest. Minder. Whatever she was. The phrase was "I think, therefore I am," not "I feel," she reminded herself. Some distance between his voice and hers, between his thoughts and hers, was healthy.

It felt anything but right.

While he was in the shower, Plum had set the table at the counter with blue and yellow and aquamarine majolica china that a really good friend had sent her from Sicily. Dinner was butternut squash tortellini with pesto and a salad with blue cheese, hazelnuts, and orange and ruby beets. Sadie heard Ford wishing that Lulu could try food like this. See this place. Her eyes would be huge.

He called and texted Mason before dinner, then in the middle, then as they finished. Nothing. *He's probably asleep*, Sadie heard him tell himself. *Or at a fund-raiser. Or dead.*

Not dead, his mind shouted. *I am not letting go again.*

"Are you done texting your girlfriend?" Plum asked, coming around the island. She reached for his phone like she was going to read what he'd written, and he snatched it away.

"It's not my girlfriend," he snapped. "It's—"

She stood in front of him, running her pointer finger down the side of his neck. "I don't really care." Her eyes met his. "Take your shirt off."

I don't really care hung in the air in Ford's mind. For a few seconds Sadie saw his pure desire warring with his loneliness, aware that satisfying one side of that thirst meant leaving the other parched.

But his greatest desire right then, Sadie could tell, was not to think. And for that, Plum was ideal. Even if Sadie didn't like the hungry way Plum ran her eyes over him when he'd pulled his shirt off and breathed, "My god, Ford, you're a treasure," Ford did.

"I'm glad you approve." Ford's tone was smug, yet beneath the words Sadie felt the stickiness of humiliation.

You don't have to do this, she wanted to say. *I'm sorry, I'm so sorry. Please, just leave.* But she knew that would just make it worse.

Plum exhaled, then took his hand and led him through the apartment to her bedroom. It had tall windows, but she pushed a button on the wall and dark blackout blinds slid down over them.

Cupping the back of Plum's neck, Ford pulled her mouth to his and brushed her lips softly. Plum's mouth opened beneath his and she caught his lower lip between her teeth and nibbled it, setting off an explosion of sparks in his body.

Stop! That's not fair! a voice whispered from a far corner of Sadie's mind.

She hushed it, to keep him from hearing, and because it was a voice she was embarrassed about. The voice of a little girl in a flannel nightgown with tiny blue flowers and lace smocking being left alone in a house on Christmas Eve, scared out of her mind but instead of admitting that, saying, "It's not fair. How come you get to go out and have fun and I have to be here alone?"

Her mother holding a big pearl earring in one hand and a big square-cut diamond in the other, trying to decide which went better with her mustard-yellow gown. "Because Alma has the night off. It's Christmas Eve, Sadie. Don't be spoiled."

"Not the housekeeper. You. Why can't you stay?"

Her mother gave her a pitying look. "Now you're being silly. You know we have supper with the senator and her husband."

"Other people's parents stay home on Christmas Eve."

"Other people's parents don't get invited to the parties we do, darling," her mother explained.

"Why can't I come too?"

"Because it's for grown-ups. Now stop acting like a child or Santa won't deliver your presents."

"You can't accuse me of being a child and then talk to me about Santa as though he exists. Either I'm a child and can believe in Santa, or I'm an adult and can go to the party."

Her father said, "God, kid, you're giving me a headache." He looked over at her mother. "No wonder we have to go out."

No wonder.

"One day it will be your turn to have fun," her mother said on their way out the door, her cheek soft, just the faintest hint of perfume.

"When?" Sadie had asked, and the front door had closed on the sound of their laughter.

When will it be my turn? Sadie wanted to know now, suddenly afraid that she may have missed it.

You signed up for this, she told herself. *You agreed to the terms. You knew you could never have him.*

I didn't know what it was going to be like! she wanted to yell. *What he was going to be like. How could I have guessed—*

"Oh, *yes,*" Plum moaned.

—that I would fall in love with him?

Or that he would hate me so completely.

Sadie closed her eyes and wept.

A little while later Plum stroked his head and whispered, "Sleepy time for my big boy" into his ear as though he were a baby or a dog, which seemed demeaning to Sadie.

Ford didn't mind anything now. He relaxed and repeated "Sleepy time," like a macaw. "Can you set an alarm for an hour?"

"Sure," Plum said, unnecessarily giving him a kiss on the lips.

Ford's arms came around her. He held her to him and kissed her back, deeply and passionately. Sadie ached with envy and desire.

"Sleep," Plum whispered in a soothing voice.

He turned onto his side and she lay in the curve of his body, her head pillowed on his shoulder, and Sadie had to bite her lip from crying out. Ford kissed her hair and said drowsily, "Why are you being so nice to me?"

"Because it amuses me," Plum told him.

Ford chuckled as he dozed off, but Sadie didn't think Plum was joking.

CHAPTER 28

They slept until the *cock-a-doodle-do!* of an alarm woke him. He groped for it, knocking things off the night table, turned it off, and opened his eyes.

He was only partially alert, and Sadie sensed deep disorientation, not just because it was pitch black in an unfamiliar room but because he'd expected something entirely different. *Bunk beds?* she thought she registered. *Brown plaid comforters? The old room he shared with James*, she realized. But the air was wrong, and aside from the familiar alarm, the sounds were wrong too—

The next instant he was completely awake, aware that he was in Plum's apartment, his mind vibrating with the thought *It's too quiet.*

There, in the dark, it hit them both simultaneously. *It was *too quiet.* Not here, now, but in the message James left for Ford right before he was killed.

There were no trains, no buses, no horns on the message. Cali hadn't been able to hear a word of the message Ford left for her from the same place at nearly the same time, but Ford could hear every word of James's message perfectly. Because there was no background noise at all.

Which meant James didn't leave the message from the playground at Happy Alley, Ford thought. And that he wasn't killed there.

Then where? Sadie asked before remembering she should stay quiet. Why had he ended up at the playground? On the merry-go-round?

Ford was too distracted to notice her voice among the different sounds in his mind, too busy rooting around the destruction of the day before, trying to make sense of the confusion. He remembered the events of the previous night and saw he was alone in bed but shouldn't be. He glanced at the clock and saw it was seven. Hadn't they gone to bed at ten? How was that—

Ford scrambled to his feet, pulling aside one of the blinds and getting a face full of daylight. It was seven in the morning. *Crap.* Lulu was going to be terrified, his mother—he couldn't even imagine. He crossed to the wall and pushed buttons until the blinds went up, thinking, *Crap crap crap.*

The bedroom door opened with a click, and Plum peeked in, wearing nothing but a transparent robe and a smile. "What are you doing up, puppy?" she asked, grabbing the end of the black boxer briefs he was about to put on. "Go back to bed.

I just ordered breakfast, it should be here in ten." She sighed. "God, your body is great."

Ford, naked, towered over her, shaking with rage. "What the hell is wrong with you? I told you to set the alarm for an hour."

She looked at him innocently. "But you didn't say *which* hour, so I picked one. I hate having breakfast alone."

He stared at her. "Do you ever think about anyone but yourself?"

Plum let go of his briefs and took a step back. "You're joking, right?

"How would I be joking?" He stepped into his underwear. "I asked you to do one simple thing—"

"I don't understand what's so important." Plum retreated around the bed and bent to pick up the book and bear wind-up toy he'd knocked off the nightstand.

Ford yanked his pants from under the bed. "I was such an idiot. I knew you'd toyed with James. Why should I think you'd take anything seriously, even a simple request to set an alarm?"

"You don't know anything about my feelings for your brother," Plum said, her voice tight with emotion.

Ford was too busy looking for his socks—*by the wall*, Sadie whispered—to notice the intensity in Plum's tone, but Sadie heard it.

"I think you should go," Plum said. She was clutching the toy, almost desperately, and with her mass of hair she looked small, like a young girl.

"We're in complete agreement there." He turned around, looking for his shirt.

Kitchen, Sadie whispered, wanting to get him out of there.

He stormed into the kitchen and threw on his shirt, not bothering to button it.

Plum followed him and got busy straightening things, opening and closing drawers. "If it was so important, you could have set your own alarm. All phones have them."

"Everything is so simple for you," Ford said and headed to the front door. "How nice that must—"

He stopped. His mind settled. A beautiful, crisp image in glittering dots of brown, gray, and orange flashed together, his room with James, bunk beds, plaid comforters, early morning, his own voice saying, "Man, there's a reason we don't have real roosters—"

"Cock-a-doodle-do" had been the alarm on James's phone, Sadie realized. *It could have just been a coincidence*, she heard him think, but the next moment he'd whipped out his own phone and started dialing. The song "Frosty the Snowman" started to play from the bedroom.

It was James's alarm that woke him. James's phone was here.

"That's my brother's phone," Ford said, holding his up, now getting James's voice mail message, "James. Message. Bye." Sadie felt a stab of grief and caught a flash image of Ford dialing James's phone over and over after his brother's death just to hear the voice. Sadie hated the raw pain inside of him, hated being powerless to ease any part of its sting.

Plum's chest was heaving. "I'm calling security."

Information and connections began flooding Ford's mind, making Sadie dizzy. Image after image layered one on top of another like a huge glittering machine.

"It was here," Ford said, tugging together the silence from the message and the presence of the phone. "He must have been killed here."

"That's ridiculous," Plum told him, and Ford's vision didn't dim. It wasn't a lie, but she did look nervous. "Besides, I told you, I was in Paris."

"He called me from that phone right before he was killed." Ford's eyes bored into hers.

"So?"

"That means either James was killed here or someone brought you his phone after he was dead. You must know something."

Her hand came out from behind her, and it had a kitchen knife in it. Apparently she hadn't just been opening and closing drawers. "I know I want you to leave. Now. Or I'm going to call security."

Ford laughed. He grabbed her wrist and twisted it until the knife fell into his other hand. "Tell me what happened to my brother." He held the knife by the side of his leg, not outright threatening, but there.

"I don't know," Plum said, her eyes going from the knife to his face. "The day after I got back from my trip I heard something ringing in the couch and found the phone. It was you calling, actually."

Raw pain struck Ford, and hazy images formed of him alone on a street corner, in the shadows of the living room, in the morning at work, by the lake, dialing James's phone just to hear his voice. "James. Message. Bye," playing an endless loop in his mind.

"That's how you got my number," he said, shaking off the memory. *So it had been the right wrong question*, Sadie thought.

Plum nodded.

"Why did you keep the phone? And keep it charged? I stopped calling because I figured it would be disconnected."

Plum's eyes went behind him. "Sometimes I like to make calls I don't want anyone to know about."

Ford nodded sagely. "Must be hard having to sneak around. Your sugar daddy is a resourceful guy. His thugs found me in the middle of—"

"I told you, there is no *daddy* about it," Plum interrupted him, but Ford wasn't listening. He was thinking about his question when he regained consciousness, how the thugs who told him to stay away from Plum had found him at the tree house.

The chip, Sadie breathed, her thoughts keeping time with his. Of course. Just like the gunmen at the theater. The Pharmacist's men. Which meant—

"Your patron is the Pharmacist," Ford said.

Plum twisted her hair to one side. "You're boring me. I'd like you to leave now."

Ford toyed with the handle of the knife in his hand. "Can I meet him?"

"I'm going to call security."

We should go, Sadie urged silently.

"He murdered James," Ford said.

Plum picked up her phone and dialed. "Please send a security officer up to my apartment. I have an unwanted guest."

"Don't you care? Even a little?" Ford demanded.

"He has a knife," Plum said into the phone. "Yes, right away." She hung up and her mouth twisted into a bitter smile.

"You think you're the only one who cared about James? You didn't even know him. He loved me more than he loved you."

"Right," Ford grunted.

Plum's eyes flashed triumphantly. "He was going to run away with me to Paris. Did you know that?"

"Sure he was," Ford said. Thinking, *Not likely since James didn't even have a passport.*

"That's why I was in Paris when he died. James was supposed to meet me there two days later." Plum bit her lip. "He was going to set me free. And we were going to have breakfast together every morning for the rest of our lives."

Sadie heard Ford thinking that the setting-free part sounded like Lulu's story about James slaying the monster. Only her version didn't end with James leaving them and moving to France with the monster's mistress.

Security is on the way up. You should go, Sadie thought.

Plum held Ford's eyes as if daring him to look away or disbelieve her. Ford stared back at her levelly, but his mind was churning. Could it be true? Had James been ready to abandon them?

Ford said, "If you loved James so much, why are you protecting his murderer?"

Plum's eyes hardened, becoming two glittering dark stones. "You don't know anything about love."

There was a heavy knock on the door. "This is Security Officer Milan. We had a call from this apartment. Are you all right, ma'am?"

Go, Sadie urged.

Ford ignored the knocking. "I'm going to get him," he told Plum. "I'll make sure he pays for what he did."

Plum gave a high, brittle laugh. "Not if he gets you first." Beneath the hardness in her eyes, Sadie saw a glimmer of something else: fear.

Another knock. "Ma'am? I'm coming in." They heard the sound of a keycard sliding into the front door lock, and Sadie yelled, *What are you waiting for?*

Ford growled at the sound of her voice, but he listened. He crossed to the back door, ran down four flights, and called the elevator from the fifty-ninth floor. He rode all the way to the garage and was already on the street when the two security guys with their walkie-talkies burst out of the stairwell.

He had no idea how he was going to get home, but he started walking, and Sadie heard him thinking he wanted to get as far as possible from that nutcase.

You mean the one you had sex with, she thought, but did not say out loud. A white van passed him and he stiffened, like muscle memory, until it drove by.

"Ice!" a voice shouted from behind him.

Ford's head swung around, suspicion and anger flaring to life. It dispersed when he saw that it was Willy calling him from the driver's seat of an old yellow Camaro.

"Get in, man," Willy said, throwing open the door. "You're in trouble. Big trouble. They've been looking for you all night."

"Who?" Sadie felt Ford's mind scanning Willy for signs of deception. Out of the corner of his eye Sadie saw another white van turn onto the street. "Why?"

"Get in the car. If you're with me they won't be able to track you and you'll be safe, at least for a little while. It's the only chance you have." Willy looked over his shoulder. Another white van went by. "They ordered a large with anchovies for you."

"A what?"

"Large means the recipient is an adult male. Anchovies means he should swim with the fishes. Which means—"

"I know what that means," Ford said, getting into the car.

CHAPTER 29

"Where are we going?" Ford asked as Willy careened through the streets.

"I have a little bolt-hole. Nothing fancy, but should be comfortable enough. That okay with you, Citizen?"

Sadie counted a fifth white van.

"Yes, absolutely," Ford said, as Willy floored it through an intersection. "You sounded like Bucky just then."

Willy laughed. "Guess I did. Funny how things come bubbling up." He stepped on the gas, taking a corner on two wheels.

Ford gripped the armrest. "When you said *they* ordered a large with anchovies you meant—"

"From the top." Willy pointed at the ceiling. "Rush too. But don't worry, if we stick close together, you'll be okay." He reached out and patted Ford's leg. "Granted, it's only a short-term fix."

"Why are you helping me?"

Willy swerved across four lanes of traffic. "You're smarter than those other guys, but you never hold it over people." Horns blared. "Always liked that about you."

Sadie felt a lick of the warm, golden caramel feeling that was Ford's friendship. It made him think of Mason. *Was he all right?*

"I did that demo work with James for a while," Willy went on. Traffic had thinned, and he was weaving in and out smoothly. "Couldn't stomach it. Wanted to build something, not destroy it. Seems like you understand that."

Sadie heard Ford wonder how he hadn't really known Willy before, and think that James had been in front of him, in front of everyone, the whole time. He needed his own friends now.

Bright, new images popped up in his mind, tiny dots forming precise outlines of houses restored, parks built, a girl—

Willy made a sharp turn and slammed on his brakes.

"Here we are. Home sweet home." He'd pulled up alongside a gray stone building, parking next to a blue Porsche. "Former home of Woodland Baptist. Now home to yours truly." Willy tapped his chest proudly.

"The Porsche yours too?" Ford asked.

Willy grinned. "Just holding it for a friend."

They went around the back to the door of the chancellery. It had been beautifully refinished and buffed to a high gloss. "Did you do this?" Ford asked, running his palm lovingly over the wood.

Willy nodded. "Did all the woodwork myself. Left the front shabby so no one gets ideas." He punched a number into a keypad and the door clicked open.

They stepped into the cool, silent interior of the nave of the church. The pews had been removed, and the place was stacked with boxes of coffeemakers, salad spinners, curlers, Tupperware, and an inflatable pool. The boxes formed a corridor seven feet high that wound through the nave around other stacks of phone chargers, the complete Shakespeare collection, and a bulk of toilet paper.

Sadie felt nervous, and she was glad when the hair on the back of Ford's neck began to prickle. *Willy may be a friend, but he's clearly a troubled friend.*

"I've never seen anything like this," Ford said, and it was true.

"I like to know I have everything under control," Willy explained. "If anything happens, I got what I need to handle it."

What is the inside of his mind like? Sadie wondered.

Sadie heard Ford wanting to ask what situation called for six popcorn poppers, but he didn't.

The trail ran past Chia Pets, YourLastMop, and a ship-in-a-bottle kit, toward a room at the back, separated from the nave by a partition.

"This must have taken a ton of work," Ford said.

Willy looked genuinely pleased. "Yeah. Not many people see all this. Sort of a private hobby, I guess you could say."

Sparkplugs, rubber bands, grow-your-own tomatoes—Ford looked up and realized Willy was halfway to the door in the back wall. He rushed forward to catch up to him. "Don't we have to stay within three feet of each other?"

Willy turned around, frowning blankly, then his face cleared. "Oh, because of the chips. Nah, that doesn't matter here."

"Why not?" Ford asked.

"I have a surprise for you."

The hair prickled on the back of Ford's neck more. "Why doesn't it matter?" He followed Willy through the door into a big office, only partially filled with boxes. A large maple desk sat in the middle with a television behind it and a Crock-Pot beside it. The Crock-Pot was on, and the dried-out smell of three-day-old chili filled the air.

"You hungry?" Willy asked.

Ford shook his head, looking for a place to sit between the Accu-Lawn garden sprinklers, childproof knife set, beige cowboy hat, Miracle Ear hearing aid, drill—

The hat. Ford grabbed it and looked inside.

It was lined with tinfoil and had magnets taped around the edge. *Unquestionably Bucky's,* Ford thought.

"Where did you get this?" he asked Willy.

"Right off Bucky's head, would you believe. Was wearing it when they brought him in to chat." He winked at Ford. "I have you to thank for that. Never would have found him if he hadn't been so gung ho about talking to you."

Willy is the Pharmacist, Sadie said aloud, before she caught herself.

Ford flinched, then said, "You're the Pharmacist." His mind entered a state of suspended animation, as though disbelief had wrapped all his thoughts in cotton.

Willy smiled and took a little bow. "That I am."

It makes perfect sense, Sadie thought to herself. Willy was always the butt of everyone's jokes, but really the joke had been on them.

Ford, still struggling to grasp everything, stuck with monosyllables. "How?"

"I'm the brains behind the operation. Or, I suppose I should say, the brains behind the brains," Willy chuckled. "They all answer to me. Have a seat."

"I'm fine standing," Ford said.

"Sit the hell down," Willy thundered, towering over him. The whites of his eyes showed, and his teeth were bared.

Ford sat. Instantly, Willy was back to his old self, retreating behind his desk. "That's better. You wanted to see the Pharmacist. The Pharmacist is in." He spread his hands. "What can I do for you?"

Ford's thoughts were jumbled, and he had no idea where to begin. He stared at Willy's familiar face, trying to make any of it make sense. "Why call yourself the Pharmacist?"

"MRP," Willy said. He had a blue aluminum baseball bat propped on his thigh, resting his chin on the end. "Mr. Pharmacist. Keeping the civil body healthy and in good working order."

"Through violence."

"Most natural thing in the world," Willy told him. "Violence is the way of animals from birth on. Can't have order without violence. Everything worth having has violence in it."

"But people only do what you say because you're using mind control," Ford said.

"Not at all," Willy objected, sounding almost hurt. "It's an incentive-based system. People do what we want, and we give them what they secretly desire. Or they don't, and we give them what they most fear. It's up to them."

Ask how they know what desires and fears to use, Sadie said.

Shut up, Ford ordered. But he said, "How do you know what incentives will work?"

"From the chips," Willy answered vaguely. "It's a complicated process."

He's hedging, Sadie said. *Push him for specifics.*

Ford ignored her. "What about why you killed James? Is that complicated?"

Willy frowned, his eyes drifting around the room. "Who says I killed him? Lots of people wanted him dead. You, for one. He slept with your girlfriend. Don't look surprised, you knew that." The eyes now honed in on Ford. "Hell, he practically let you *drown*. He thought he was so great, but he wasn't anything."

Ford's mind tightened, like an old-fashioned toy being wound by a key. "So why bother with him?"

Willy sat back in his chair and put his feet up on the desk, slapping the bat against his palm. "He stole something of great value. Can't let stealers go unpunished."

"You mean Plum."

"You think that's why James was killed? Out of jealousy for that little tart?" Willy whooped with laughter. "Wrong."

Sadie heard Ford wondering what kind of patron Willy was. It was hard to picture them together. "What did he take?"

"Money," Willy said, like it was obvious. "James comes to me with this plan. Says he's going to free City Center, free *me*, from the tyranny of the Pharmacist. Great guy, your brother. Way it works, that ungrateful girl told him where all the cash is kept—right here, in fact"—he gestured around the room—"and how to get into the safe. She's only interested in the dough, but James aims higher." Willie tapped his head. "He's going to hide out here and ambush the Pharmacist when he comes in to count the money in his safe. The key being since James doesn't have a chip, he won't show up on the scanners in here. Just like he's the invisible man, he says." Willie grinned. "Only, he was plenty visible to me."

"He trusted you," Ford said.

"Beautiful sentiment. I didn't let him down, either. My job was to stick close, take care of any muscle the Pharmacist might have brought, keep the peace." He nodded boyishly. "And James sure was peaceful at the end. Hit him with a big shot of R22, and it mellowed him right out." Willy's expression got grave. "I hope that is of comfort to you and your family."

The key in Ford's mind tightened again, and Sadie caught a split-second image of Ford beating Willy's face with his fist. "Yeah, thanks."

"Too bad Bucky's dead." Willie stroked the bat fondly. "Would love to know how he got the money out under our noses. And where it went too. Don't suppose you know where it is?"

Sadie's chest tightened, and Ford's imagined fist connected with Willy's nose. "Bucky's dead?"

Willy shrugged. "More or less. His body'll be found in a car wreck tomorrow." He leaned forward, taking his feet off the desk. "But let's talk about you."

Ford was seeing a slideshow of images—James—Bucky—Mason—each one interspersed with a punch to Willy's face. "What about me? I thought I was going to swim with the fishes."

Willy waved the comment aside. "That day at the Castle, when you guessed our poker hands. How'd you do that? Fake blindfold?"

Ford shook his head. "No." The slideshow stopped, and his mind filled with darkness, except a slim margin where the blindfold was held off his face by his nose. Dots formed into the fingers of the other players, shifting their chips, tapping restlessly, moving around.

He knew people were bluffing not by their faces but by their hands, Sadie reminded herself. And it was easy enough to see the hands blindfolded if you were standing up.

"I just got lucky," he told Willy.

Willy guffawed. "Keep your friends close and your secrets closer." He stood up from his desk. "Tell you what I'll do. Let's make it a game. I'll put the bat on the desk between us and count to three, and whoever gets it wins. Test how good you are picking out bluffs under pressure."

Wins what? Sadie asked. *What does "winning" mean in this game?*

She'd spoken aloud, but Ford ignored her, his mind full of the feel of the bat in his hands—

"Sure," he said. "I'll play."

What are you playing? Are you seriously telling yourself that you're going to beat Willy up with that bat? Ford Winter, you are better than that.

—full of the *thwack* the bat would make hitting the desk. Hitting bone. Hitting—

"On three," Willy said, putting the bat on the desk.

This is insane. I know you hate me, but trust me, this is a mistake.

Viscous self-loathing flooded Ford's mind. Sadie heard him think, *Maybe this will get rid of you*, and realized the loathing was for her. She'd driven him to this, driven him out of his mind.

"On three," Ford agreed.

"One," Willy said.

A flash of blue metal, a thud, dots of color splattering every-where, Willy chuckling, saying, "I win."

Darkness.

She woke up feeling dizzy and had trouble making her eyes focus.

Her ears were ringing, and there was a metallic taste in her mouth.

Where was she? What had happened?

Sadie glanced around the room, the uneven stacks of boxes looming like cliffs in the inadequate light from the high win-dows. The sounds of someone clipping their nails and watching a nature program came from inside the office up ahead, the announcer saying, ". . . but the natural habitat of these majestic creatures is succumbing to the drumbeat of civilization."

Ford must have regained consciousness before she did, because he was on his feet moving toward the office. As he walked Sadie felt his right hand tighten and realized he was holding something, something she couldn't identify. His grip felt strange, less sensitive than usual.

Gloves, she realized as he brought his hands up and she saw them. He lifted the edge of the right one just past the scar on his wrist to glance at the Mickey Mouse watch, which showed nine thirty exactly. *Why would he be wearing glo—*

She saw it then. The object in his hand.

He was holding a gun.

Her mind reeled. *No*, she thought, then yelled, *No! What-ever you are planning, stop. Don't do this. It won't get you what you want.* But he'd perfected his ability to ignore her now.

She felt as if he'd built a wall between them, impervious and reflective, so everything she said just reverberated back.

He took a step forward, then another. Dread filled her. She wanted to close her eyes, look away, but that wouldn't change anything. He raised the gun, and as he stepped into the office she heard him think, *Watch this, Sadie.*

As if she had a choice.

Willy spoke without looking up from his nails. "I'm almost done," he said, nodding toward the nail clippers. "Tough on the mani—" He glanced up with a warm smile. It faded when he saw the gun pointed at his head.

"Hey, wait a sec—" he said, dropping his hands.

"Keep them up," Ford whispered. "Stand up and come around the desk. No more talking." His voice sounded strained to Sadie, and the windy noises she was used to were nearly silent and unreadable.

She was terrified. Everything felt wrong, as though the force of Ford's hate for her had changed his entire mindscape. It was disorienting, like being in the head of a stranger.

Where are you, Ford? she demanded. *I know you're in there.*

An image of James with Plum's head on his shoulder, looking up at him for a kiss, formed in Ford's head, not out of points of color but like a photograph developing. It went from indistinct to clear then began to bubble and curl, the image melting away like old movie film catching fire in the projector, until there was only blankness.

He steadied his arm and aimed at Willy, standing next to the Crock-Pot now, and the sensation inside of him was nothing like his regular anger, nothing Sadie recognized.

What are you doing? Sadie cried. *This won't solve anything.*

Another photographic memory forced its way forward, faint outlines becoming Plum holding her iPad, filming, a boy's voice saying "I promise. Anything you want. Just say you'll never to leave me." Sadie felt Ford struggling to hold the memory at that moment, freeze it, but it didn't stop, overexposure singeing its edges, eating through until it completely corroded and dissolved into ashes.

The interior of his mind was still then, and cold, so cold. Desolate. *Loneliness*, Sadie thought.

But you're not alone, Ford, she called. *I'm here for you. I—*

Ford's finger tightened on the trigger. Eyes locked on Willy, he punctuated each word with a shot. "She"—*bang*—"is"—*bang*—"not"—*bang*—"a"—*bang*—"tart."

Four hits, all to the chest.

Sadie was frozen. Time stood still. For an instant Willy's body hung in the air, and his face became James's against the same backdrop, eyes glazing over, an expression of pure disbelief as he mouthed the word "You?" Then the body fell to the ground with a thud.

Sadie opened her mouth to scream her horror, but it was too big, nothing could come out.

She had just seen Ford kill Willy.

She gulped, terrified, shaking. Could she have been in his head all this time and never really known the truth about who he was? What he was capable of?

A loud shrieking filled her head, and she realized it was her own screams echoing back at her as she plummeted into a bottomless hole of pure, terrifying darkness.

CHAPTER 30

"She's coming to."

"Is she lucid?"

"I have good brain scans."

"Her heart rate is spiking."

Curtis's voice said, "Sadie, it's all right, you're fine, you're safe. Can you look at me?"

Sadie opened her eyes, expecting to see the oval ceiling of the Stasis Center, but instead she was in what appeared to be a hospital room. There were no sensors; she was in a nightgown. Curtis was next to the bed. "Where am I?"

"You're in the medical wing at Mind Corps," Curtis told her. "You've been under sedation, but you're out of it now."

"Sedation? What happened to stasis? What's going on?" The heart monitor reacted with a loud beeping that felt like it was piercing her head. And then it came back to her: Willy, the church, Ford, the gun, gloves—

Horror. "I don't understand," she said. "Why am I here? Shouldn't I still be in Syncopy?"

Catrina said, "There was a glitch." Sadie thought she was avoiding Curtis's gaze.

Curtis interrupted, "You gave us quite a scare. Your mind disengaged itself from Syncopy. We've never seen that before. Did something happen?"

Sadie had no idea how to answer. Rationally, she knew it should have been simple. She was the eyewitness to a murder. She saw it. She had to report it. Had to turn Ford in.

I can't, she protested instinctively, recoiling from the thought. *He hadn't been in his right mind.*

Because of you, she went on, torturing herself. *You are responsible. You did this to him.*

Unless—

Immediately she saw an alternative that was worse. What if the Ford she thought she knew wasn't him at all? What if he'd really been hiding a monster inside of him the entire time? What if he was a psychopath so cunning, so cool, that he'd had her fooled?

It wasn't possible. Was it?

She had to get out of here. She had to see him. Hear his version of the story. Watch him while he talked. Then she would know. *Wouldn't she?*

It would mean betraying Mind Corps, the contract she'd signed, the rules. Betraying Curtis.

"Sadie?" Curtis said gently. "Is everything okay?" He sounded concerned, as if there could be something really wrong with her, and she felt a pang of guilt. He trusted her, and she was repaying him by lying and running away. Trying to run away, she corrected.

A faint memory from orientation, someone saying that if you're pulled out of Sycnopy too early it could cause—

"I'm sorry," she said, her voice almost hysterical in her ears. *That could work*, she decided. "I—I can't seem to remember anything past dinner last night. Tortellini. Butternut squash. There was a beet salad." *Too many details*, she told herself. "Then he went to bed, and—it's a blank."

"After that?"

"Nothing." She felt like the lie must be so obvious, the way Curtis and Catrina were studying her, but she didn't detect anything on either of their faces. They just looked like they were worried and trying not to show it. She felt another jab of guilt.

"What time is it?" she asked.

"It's a little after ten," Catrina told her. "You've been under sedation nearly twenty-four hours to make sure your brain scans were clear."

Sadie's heart dropped and she forgot about feeling guilty. *Twenty-four hours? He could already have been arrested.* She looked from Catrina to Curtis. Did one of them know more than they were saying? *Could someone else know what she'd seen?*

"Is there any way to read a Subject's mind without Minders?" she asked.

"Not yet," Curtis said, looking at her curiously.

"So all information from the chi—relays has to come from Minders," Sadie clarified.

Curtis nodded. "Yes. Why?"

At least Ford was safe from her.

"I—" Sadie fumbled with how to go on. "I was just thinking that it means—it's important that I remember. What happened. Because you won't know any other way." *Stop talking,* she ordered herself.

She felt Curtis studying her, but she avoided looking at him, hoping she seemed confused rather than evasive. Now, as though reading her mind, he said, "Given the minor amnesia, I think we should send Miss Ames home and schedule her debriefing in two days."

Catrina said, "I humbly disagree." The word *humbly* sounded laughable in her mouth, and there was clearly tension between her and Curtis. "I think it would be best if she began debriefing immediately. You and I should be sufficient."

"She doesn't remember anything," Curtis pointed out.

Catrina stared at him. "Or maybe she does and she doesn't want to tell."

"I don't," Sadie said to no one.

Curtis's voice had an edge. "Whatever the case, the best place for her to rest and remember is at home. She would go nuts wandering the halls here, bumping into people."

Catrina had seemed ready to object again, but his last words changed her mind. "I suppose that's true," she said. "Home is probably better."

"Excellent." Curtis gave her a faint nod. "Please give Miss Ames whatever assistance she needs. I'll bring in her parents. And then, when her memory returns in a few days, we'll do the debriefing." He smiled reassuringly at Sadie.

"Thank you," she said.

Sadie was clumsy in her body. It felt strange to move around, and she was struck even more forcefully by how different her perspective was from Ford's.

What she noticed most, though, was the silence. It was so quiet in her mind. So . . . even. After the constant buffeting of Ford's emotions, she was acutely aware of how little she normally felt.

God, she missed him.

Sadie showered and dressed and was escorted to a smaller elevator that whisked her quickly up the fourteen stories to the ground floor. A man in a dark suit was waiting to take her to a sitting room she'd never been in. It had French doors that opened out onto the terrace where she'd had her debriefing. Four weeks, four lifetimes ago.

She paused on the threshold, taking in the scene. Her father was standing by the windows, talking on the phone. Pete was near him, staring out and tapping on one of the panes. Her mother was on the sofa facing the door, in a posture of anticipation. Sadie put on a smile and stepped into the room.

The smile felt odd, as though her face wasn't used to it, which was nuts because she'd smiled plenty, laughed plenty, with Ford. But this was a different smile, she realized. A smile that was more considered and careful than the smile of the past five weeks.

Her mother rose as soon as she saw Sadie. She had tears in her eyes as though she'd just been told bad news. "Darling," she said, giving Sadie an awkward hug. "It's wonderful to see you. And a week early. We are delighted."

Sadie looked at her mother and felt like she was seeing her

for the first time. She was thinner than she remembered, with tiny lines around her eyes. But she also looked more formidable, somehow. "How do you feel?" she asked Sadie.

"Funny," Sadie told her. "It's odd being back in my body."

"You don't look odd at all," Pete said, coming toward her. "You look good enough to eat."

He hugged her, and she had to stop herself from pushing him away. He smelled like cologne, exactly like he always did, but for some reason the scent of it now made her want to gag.

Instead she pulled back and said, "Let me just look at you."

When she did, she felt nothing except a slight tremor of uneasiness. Looking into his eyes, seeing the flatness there beneath the big smile, she knew for certain he didn't love her.

And she had to admit what she'd known all along—she didn't love him either.

Yet they'd been together for nearly a year. A year of lying to each other and, worse, lying to themselves. Why would they do that?

Because you were afraid, the answer came to her as her father finished his call and joined them. Not afraid of being alone. Afraid of being unwanted. Uninteresting.

"Hello, kiddo," her father said, stepping forward to give her a kiss. His phone beeped, and he winced. "Sorry, have to take this, back in a sec."

Unworthy of attention.

Her mother watched her father go with an expression of annoyance, but when she looked in Sadie's direction again it shifted to one of triumph. *We may compete for his affections, but I will always win*, it said. Sadie realized she'd seen that expression over and over again growing up. Every day. She had mistaken it for love.

And in a way it was, Sadie understood. Because she allowed her mother to feel victorious, and for that her mother was grateful. Without Sadie, there would have been no competition for her father's attention, no affirmation of supremacy. Possibly no interest.

Instead of being upset, Sadie felt sorry for her mother. There was so much more to aspire to. Sadie felt like she could see everything so clearly, all the complex dynamics and pallid emotions that were the warp and weft of her life. It wasn't that she felt muffled *right now*. This was how her life had always been. Controlled. Safe. Buffered.

Numb.

"What's wrong, darling?" her mother asked, and Sadie wondered what would happen if she told her. If she said she didn't want to substitute words for feelings anymore, conversation for intimacy. Attention for affection. That she wanted to feel things, even if they were bad or confusing. That she was tired of smiles you had to remind yourself to put on. Would she understand?

Her father ended his second call and rejoined them. "How about lunch at the yacht club? I don't know about anyone else, but I could sure use a mimosa."

"That sounds great," Sadie heard herself agreeing.

Pete drove Sadie's car, following her parents but keeping up a steady stream of conversation. He kept glancing over at her and grinning.

"Did you miss me at all?" he asked.

"Of course," she told him.

"Do you still love me?"

"Of course," she answered, but the words felt like eraser bits in her mouth.

Lunch was filled with people coming by the table to talk to her father or mother. Pete kept leaning toward her to kiss her neck, and every time he did her muscles tensed.

She felt like she was a hollow shell and everything anyone said to her just echoed back to them. And no one noticed, or cared.

Halfway through lunch Decca showed up, dragging by the hand the bartender from the party her parents had given. She threw herself on Sadie and gave her a giant hug, and Sadie didn't want to pull away. "Thank god you're back," Decca said. "Bosko almost convinced me to take up marathon running, I've been so bored and lonely without you."

It was a lie, Sadie was sure, since Decca had hundreds of friends, but it didn't come off as a lie. As they waited for the server to set more places at the table, Decca took Sadie's hand and said, "We're going to the bathroom. And if you boys think we're going to talk about you, you're right."

Instead of heading to the bathroom, Decca led Sadie around the side of the club to the area outside the kitchen where the staff smoked. Club members never went there, so it was relatively discreet.

"We don't have a lot of time so I'll cut to it. What's the problem, sweetie?"

"Nothing," Sadie said. When Decca kept looking at her Sadie felt herself cracking. "I don't know. Everything is wrong. Nothing has changed, but everything feels completely wrong."

Decca bit her lip. "When my parents were still married, every time my father would come back from a business trip, whether it was for a night or a week, they would fight. Every time. It was like coming back made it hard to get the rhythm right again. I called it the reentry period. You were gone for almost six weeks and you took a trip somewhere very different. I'm sure it's normal to feel out of sorts."

Sadie nodded. That sounded right. True.

Except for the part where you were the eyewitness to a murder committed by the guy you love, and were helping to cover it up by not telling anyone. And the part where you couldn't stand to be touched by your boyfriend. And your parents looked like painted marionettes, and your life looked like a hollow baroque opera.

"What did your mom and dad do during the reentry periods?" Sadie asked.

"They found liquor helped."

"Then it sounds like we should be getting back to lunch." She hugged Decca tightly. "Thank you for being such an amazing friend."

Decca looked at her steadily. "You've changed."

Sadie had to take a deep breath. "Maybe. I—I felt alive for the first time."

Decca's eyes got huge, but all she said was "Come on. We may need to stop at the bar for shots."

After lunch Pete drove Sadie home. He bent over to kiss her at every light and held her hand the whole drive. The thought of doing anything with him made her skin crawl, but she wasn't sure how to say no without provoking a fight.

So, she asked herself, *why not provoke a fight?* The thought surprised her, stunning in its simplicity, so obvious and yet so foreign. Could she do it? Would she?

He pulled up at the end of her street a block from her driveway. "What are you doing?" she asked.

"I was hoping we could spend some time, just the two of us, before we got to your house. You know how your mom goes all puritan." He turned toward her. "I missed you so much, babe. I've been saving up all this stuff to tell you, but right now all I can think about is how much I want to kiss you."

He lowered his head and closed his eyes. She put her hand on his chest. "Pete, I can't do this."

He sat back and blinked, surprised. "Do what? Make out with me? I know the car isn't that comfortable. Should we risk going to your house?"

"No, it's not the car. It's—" Sadie ran through a dozen excuses. She was tired, she still felt strange from Syncopy, she shouldn't have done that Bailey's shot with Decca. They were all comfortable. Easy. What she would have done in the past.

She said, "I don't think we should be together anymore."

He stared at her. "I don't think I understand. Do you mean anymore today? Or anymore ever?"

"Ever." She said it quietly, looking at her hands.

"Did I do something wrong?"

He sounded so plaintive, she felt a twinge of remorse. "No. You were perfect. Great. I just—I've realized I need to make some changes in my life. Learn new patterns. Start fresh."

"Start fresh." He repeated the phrase as though he were new to the language. "That's what you call dumping someone you said you loved?"

"I did—do love you," Sadie said, feeling the situation get out of her control. "But not the way you deserve."

He stared at his lap, shaking his head.

"I'm really sorry, Pete," she told him honestly. "I didn't mean to hurt you."

"Well, that makes it all better then, your not meaning to." He kept his eyes on his lap a few more moments, and Sadie had the impression of someone pulling on a mask. When he faced her he looked confused and hurt, but there was something winking behind his eyes. "I waited for you for a year. A year of letting you tease me, pretend one day I'd be good enough for you, one day I'd be worthy, just 'not tonight.'" Putting the words in air quotes. "I can't believe what a fool you made of me."

"I never meant to. I never meant to tease you."

He ignored that, but his tone softened and became almost plaintive. "Are you sure about this, Sadie? Really sure? Because once you tell me to go, I'll go and not come back."

It was an invitation more than a challenge, Sadie knew, a subtle bump to steer her in the right direction. Pull out a nice ribbon of excuses—I'm tired, I have my period, I feel sick—and keep the game alive.

"I'm sure," she said.

The petty spite that had been concealed behind his mild exterior blazed out now. "A year. A year for *this*. Everyone told me you were cold, but I thought there had to be fire, a spark, something inside of you. News flash: There's not. You're just a manipulative bitch who likes attention and thinks she's too good for everyone."

After Ford's anger, after everything she'd seen, Pete's tantrum was more sad than scary. "Agree to disagree," she said.

He stared at her. When he didn't seem to be making a move to leave, she said, "Do you want a ride somewhere?"

He shook his head. "I mean it. When I leave today, I never want to hear from you again. Ever. Not even a big apology."

"Okay, bye," she said, willing him out of the car.

It still seemed to take forever for him to get his seat belt off and get out. When he finally did, his big exit line was "Have a nice life."

"I think I just might," she told him.

She should be sad, she thought. But instead, as she walked around to the driver's side of the car, she felt a soaring sense of relief.

She put on the radio and was about to turn into her driveway when a news bulletin said, "A spokeswoman from Central Hospital has issued a statement saying that millionaire Mason Bligh, who inherited the Bligh chemical fortune when he was twelve, has been transferred out of intensive care and is currently in critical condition. Bligh was found unconscious near the former France Stone quarry late Wednesday evening after the Range Rover he was driving exploded. The identity of the second victim in the wreck has not been released."

Sadie dialed her mother's cell phone. "I'm going for a drive to clear my head," she said, the lie coming without any compunction at all.

"Of course, dear," her mother answered.

Sadie was surprised by how little time it took to get to City Center.

CHAPTER 31

She had never seen him in person before. It hit Sadie as she was approaching Mason's room at Central Hospital. She was going to see Ford, on the outside, for the first time, and she felt giddy and terrified at once.

Mason was asleep on the bed and Ford was dozing when she walked in. It took all her self-control not to touch him. Even in the dim light filtering through the hospital room blinds he was spectacularly handsome: dark hair, slight stubble, wide shoulders, his hands broad and strong and—

For a split second she saw that last moment after he'd shot Willy, when Willy's face became James's, saying "You?" and she felt a shiver of fear. What if he really wasn't what she thought? What if—

There was an explanation. There had to be. It was an old memory that got looped in at the wrong time, an accident of the light, *something*.

He woke up and caught her standing there, staring at him. His eyes opened halfway at first, then all the way. He stared at her with what looked like alarm and said something she couldn't catch.

"I'm sorry, I didn't mean to startle you," she said.

He shook his head, a frown replacing his alarm. "Who are you?"

His voice sounded different than when she was inside his head, but still nice. Still familiar.

"I'm a friend," she answered quickly. "He's going to live, isn't he? Mason? What happened to B— to the other passenger?"

His eyes were taking her in carefully, and she wondered what he was thinking. Had his vision dimmed when she said she was Mason's friend? Did she merit even a flutter from the drums? It was so strange not to know what was going on inside his head.

He narrowed his eyes. "Are you a reporter?"

She'd planned her approach in the car, but seeing him had already made her go completely off track. "Actually," she said, giving up on the script, "I'm here to see you."

That made him alert, but not in a good way. "Why? Who sent you?"

"No one. I sent myself." She doubted the hospital was bugged, but it seemed wise to be circumspect. "I—I saw what happened when you went to church on Thursday."

"What are you talking about?" He was on guard, cagy.

She almost laughed, thinking, *Seriously, now is when you're going to start exercising restraint? Today is the day you start thinking before you speak?* But they didn't have time for that. "I know what you did. I understand. I wanted to ask you some questions."

Ford put up his hands. "Lady, miss, whoever, thank you for coming, but it's time for you to go."

"Where did you get the gloves and—the other thing?"

He looked truly baffled. "Do you need a nurse?"

"Are they somewhere safe?"

"I think you might be on the wrong floor."

"Where is *he*?" she whispered urgently. "Did you leave him there, or did you take him somewhere?"

"I bet someone in the psych ward is missing you. Why don't we find a nurse and—" He stood.

Sadie wanted to scream with frustration. "I want to help you, but you have to let me. We don't have much time. I have to tell them everything in two days."

"Okay," he said, nodding like he was trying to keep a crazy person calm. "Go ahead. Good luck."

He didn't seem to be pretending, Sadie thought. Maybe he really had no idea what she was talking about. Maybe he'd completely blotted it out. His mind had been strange, and it was definitely traumatic. Maybe if she asked him about something that happened before he snapped, some detail . . .

"You can tell when people are bluffing at poker by how they move their fingers. That's how you were able to play blindfolded and win at the Castle."

That got his attention. He took a step toward her. "What are you—"

She gave up on caution. "Willy asked you how you did the trick. You lied to him."

He took another step toward her. "How can you know that?"

"I told you, I was *there*."

He took another step and stopped, two feet from her. He looked into her eyes. Their gazes met, locked.

It was there, the connection, more powerful, a shocking surge through both of them. Sadie reached toward him.

He jerked back, away from her. His eyes weren't tired now, they were angry. Angry like they had been when he smashed the mirrors. "In my head. It was *you*?"

She swallowed hard and tried to get past the anger, make him hear. "I want to help you, Ford. But I need to know some details."

"It knows my name," he said, rocking backward with an agonized sound somewhere between a moan and a laugh. "Of course. Of course it knows everything."

"Please, if you would just—"

"Get away from me." His tone was a knife slicing at her.

Sadie crossed her arms over her chest to keep from shaking, from crying. "The gun and the gloves. Where did you get them? Do you still have them?"

"Leave," he said. His eyes seared her. "Turn around and leave here right now and do not come back or, I swear, I will kill you."

"Ford, you have to listen to me. I'm—"

"Security!" he yelled.

"Don't do this."

"Get away from me." His face was a mask of twisted pain. "Never come back."

"Okay," she said, turning to go. "Okay." She started walking, then running, then sobbing. *This is what a heart breaking feels like*, she thought. *This is it.*

She stayed sitting in her car outside the hospital, staring into space, for the next hour. She was empty, completely spent. She had no idea where to go or what to do. She felt like she had burned every crucial bridge in her life that day. Mind Corps, *poof!* Pete, *poof!* Self-respect, *poof! Poof poof poof!* All up in smoke.

God, she was a fool. What had she expected him to do? To think?

Hi, you hate me, you put your head through five mirrors to make that point, so I was thinking . . .

She noticed a white van pull up in front of the hospital, but she didn't really think about it until ten minutes later when visiting hours were over and Ford came out. Before Sadie could even get her door open, two guys in blue jumpsuits and ski masks had grabbed Ford, pitched him into the van, and taken off with him.

She veered into traffic after them, wishing that her red convertible was slightly less conspicuous on the streets of City Center. She almost lost them at an intersection when two other white vans turned between them, but she managed to pick her van out by a dent on the bumper—the plates were covered with mud. They followed a circuitous route, finally pulling up in front of the old downtown post office.

The façade looked like a neoclassical temple, and despite obvious signs of decay, its high arched ceiling still conveyed a regal air. There were towers of discarded cars inside and out, as though taking the place of the customary statues of gods and goddesses.

When the men in the blue jumpsuits dragged Ford out of the van he looked lifeless, but they didn't carry him like a corpse, so Sadie assumed they'd beaten or drugged him, possibly both.

She slipped inside the building, behind a truck with no wheelbase, to watch. They left Ford slumped against a pile of tires and went back to the van, returning with another body. Willy's.

It took all three men to drag him toward a green Chevelle and maneuver his bulk into the backseat. Once he was set, they started trying out different positions with Ford.

They weren't wearing ski masks anymore, and she recognized all of them from her first day in Syncopy when Ford had played poker at the castle: the short guy with the red hair, the guy with the big ears, and the one with the slicked-back hair who had upset Linc. He seemed to be the leader, standing at a distance and studying the tableau they'd set up.

"Can you make him lean against the side of the car, Red?" he asked.

These were guys who knew Ford. Who seemed to like him at the Castle. Yet they thought nothing of beating him or—whatever they were now doing. How was that possible?

"Orders are to make it look like an accident, not a photo shoot," Red protested, moving Ford around like a rag doll.

If the Pharmacist was dead, right there in the backseat, who were they taking orders from?

The one with the big ears said, "Maybe we leave him bending in at the window, like he was giving Willy here one last—"

"That's enough, Friend," the guy with the slicked-back hair interrupted. "What about putting him on his face?"

"That's good," Red agreed. "Then if we start the fire in the backseat, and sort of sweep it out and around, as if he accidentally poured fluid over here—"

Like a play, Sadie thought, feeling chilled. Making it look like Ford killed Willy and then died in the fire he lit to eliminate the body. A little elaborate, but guaranteed to make the papers.

When they'd set the scene, two of them left, and the one with the slicked-back hair lit a match and dropped it in the back with Willy. He crossed himself, kicked Ford in the ribs, and jogged after the others.

Sadie didn't wait for the van to pull out before she sprinted to the old Chevelle.

There was lighter fluid everywhere, so once the fire caught it would move fast. The backseat was halfway on fire, and she caught a whiff of something that smelled like meat on the barbecue. *Willy*, she thought, and gagged.

You don't have time for that, she told herself. She flipped Ford onto his back and tried to pull him by the legs as the first offshoot of the fire began to spread, following a vein of lighter fluid.

He was really heavy, and not moving. There was no way she was going to be able to carry him, and there was no way to drag him across the debris-covered floor.

He let out low moaning noises, and his eyes were partly open, but only the whites showed. *Definitely drugged.*

"Ford, can you hear me?" she whispered, getting her face next to his.

No response.

"Ford, we have to get you out of here."

Nothing.

Her head was resting against his chest, and through his shirt she made out his heartbeat, faint but regular. It was so different hearing it here on the outside than in his head. There it was organic, a familiar part of life. Here it seemed like something that went on its own, something impersonal. Everything was so different on the outside. He was so different. So much more opaque.

"Ford," she whispered to him. "I promise I'll leave you alone, never see you again. Just please, help me get you home."

Still nothing.

"Ford!" She sat up, her hands gripping his shoulders, putting everything she had into it, all her anger and fear and longing and hope and love. "Ford Winter!"

So softly she almost missed it, he whispered, "Present."

She laughed through her tears and hugged him. "Good boy," she said. He was the same. The exact same guy she'd lost her heart to.

He was still only half conscious, but with his help she managed to get him to his feet. He leaned heavily on her as they stumbled forward, their progress slow and awkward. He seemed limbless and nerveless and—

The room contracted and they were thrown forward when the Chevelle exploded in a hot white ball of flames.

Chunks of burning metal showered them, one of them hitting him on the shoulder, but he barely noticed as they struggled back to their feet.

The fire was higher now, the air thick with smoke, and two of the columns had caught, sending flames licking at the roof.

"Almost there," she told him.

"Hoooooerr," he answered.

"What?"

"Hot in here," he said and started pulling at his shirt.

"Not now," she said. "Let's get outside and—"

The light turned blinding white as another car exploded. The shock wave sent them sprawling forward. He braced himself against the carcass of a jeep but pulled his hand away fast and stared at the palm. "Burning," he said, holding it out to her.

Was that a siren?

"We need to go faster," Sadie urged.

They were five feet from the door when a loud rumble shook the walls and floor. With a crash the ceiling began to collapse, folding in on itself like a flaming origami crane.

Using strength she didn't know she had, Sadie hauled Ford those last five feet and pushed him onto the ground, throwing her body over him. The entire roof caved in, sending burning chunks of wood and metal and glass and billowing clouds of smoke rolling toward them.

Now there were definitely sirens.

Half dragging, half pushing, she got him to her car and into the passenger seat. She stumbled around to the driver's seat and floored it. A minute later she saw the fire trucks in her rearview mirror, heading to the blaze.

Her phone rang, he mother calling to say that she'd forgotten to leave a note but her father was insisting they keep their dinner plans with the Hamongs. "We made them before we knew you'd be back, but of course if you want we can cancel—"

Sadie laughed. "That's fine."

"Have you eaten?" Her mother's voice solicitous on speakerphone.

"Don't worry, I'll figure something out."

When she hung up Ford muttered, "Should have . . . said . . . having BBQ."

Sadie stared at him for a moment, shocked, and then began to laugh. Once she started she had a hard time stopping, as though the only other alternative was crying. She glanced over at Ford, and he had his eyes closed, but he was smiling.

"Tinkly bells," he said. "I've heard . . . before."

"What?" she asked.

"Your laugh." He tapped his head. "In here."

Sadie felt like her body was an ice-cold rushing stream. "You heard me laugh?"

But he was asleep again.

Without consciously knowing how, she drove to his house. He was still unsteady, so she helped him up the stairs and piloted him onto the couch. That part, at least, was much easier than it had been the last time.

The pockets of his jacket hung heavily, and reaching into them she pulled out a gun and a pair of gloves. She felt alternating currents of hot and cold through her body. Were they his? Or had they been planted by the guys trying to stage his fiery death?

It didn't matter, she decided. She would take them with her. If he needed to be charged with murder, all she had to do was testify. *But why was someone working so hard to tie him to Willy's death. And who?*

It was strange, being in the apartment like this. She knew

where everything was, what drawer had silverware, where the scissors were kept, as though it were her house. It was completely familiar but it also looked different than it had when she was in Ford's head. It was a little bigger, and maybe even a little nicer. As though his shame even colored what he saw.

That had to be true for everything, she realized. There was no real way to be objective because emotions always tinted perspective. She was in the kitchen as she thought this, and the force of it made her sit down.

For the first time she saw exactly how far she'd come from the girl who believed "I think, therefore I am." There was no thinking without emotion, she knew now. And the more you tried to keep emotion at bay, the greater and more widespread the impact. It bled into every aspect of the mind in unpredictable ways.

Scribbling her name and number on a piece of paper, she shut off the kitchen light and went back into the living room. Ford's breathing was even and less labored now. She could make out his profile against the cushion, and her heart ached. She'd never seen him asleep before, from the outside, and it surprised her how young he looked. All the tension and anger was gone from his face, and he seemed just like a little boy.

She couldn't help it. She reached down and kissed his forehead.

His arms came around her, dragging her toward him, and for a moment she thought he was going to yell at her again. But he was sleeping and he just held her next to him, brushing her hair from under his nose and feathering his lips against her temple.

"*Mmm*," he said, holding her tighter, and Sadie melted against him. She knew he had no idea what he was doing, who he was holding. She was fairly sure if he'd realized it was her he would have let go. But she (almost) didn't care. Because being in his arms felt more extraordinary than she had imagined.

"Relax," he whispered sleepily. "Heart racing."

Don't let him open his eyes, Sadie thought. *Let me be whoever he's dreaming about just a little longer.*

Closing her eyes to concentrate on slowing down her heart, she nestled against him, her cheek resting on his chest, her legs twined with his, toes touching. It was the most perfect feeling in the world, and when he whispered, "Amazing," she thought her heart was going to shatter.

Thin early sunlight was filtering through the curtains when she opened her eyes. She didn't know how long she'd been asleep, but it was too long.

Tucking the paper with her name and number on it in the pocket of his jeans, she untangled herself from his arms and slid away. She wanted to turn and give him another kiss, but she couldn't risk it. She tiptoed to the door and let herself out.

On the landing she looked at her phone. Six fifteen. She could just make it home before her parents woke up, if she didn't get lost.

She ran down the two sets of stairs, onto the street, and was unlocking the door of her car when the hair on the back of her neck prickled, like she was being watched. She swung around quickly, but the street was deserted.

A movement in the window of the Winters' house caught her eye. She looked up, and her gaze met Lulu's.

The next moment the curtain had fallen back, and the girl was gone. *She won't tell*, Sadie thought. Hoped. *Please let her not tell anyone.*

Sadie just had time to pull the covers up over her clothes, the scent of smoke and Ford still on her skin, when her mother peeked in to check on her.

CHAPTER 32

Sadie was at the tail end of dreaming that she was at a dance where everyone was wearing BIGFOOT SAVES T-shirts and yelling for the DJ to turn up the heat when her phone rang. *Of course*, she thought, still in the dream as she reached for it. *The answer is safekeeping.*

"I think you saved my life last night," Ford's voice said.

Sadie was immediately wide awake. *Breathe*, she told herself. Swallow.

"Hello?" he said.

Talk. "I guess I did. Yes."

He exhaled. "I dream about you. You probably know that."

Sadie was gripping the phone so hard her fingers ached. "No. I could never see your dreams. Daydreams, yes, but not dream dreams." Did she say too much? Did that sound stupid? *Oh, god, what if it—*

"That's why I was so shocked when you walked into Mason's room," he said. "It was like having—"

"Your dream girl?" Sadie supplied.

"I was going to say 'ghost,' but yeah, something from your imagination walk into your life."

Ghost. Of course. "I imagine it's weird."

"That's one word. But—can I see you? I'd like to see you." He suddenly sounded as nervous as she felt. "I have some questions."

Sadie remembered her own dream. Figuring that whoever had tried to burn Ford to a crisp the night before would assume they'd been successful, at least for a little while, she said, "Meet me at Bucky's in an hour. Where the bedroom used to be. And bring the Bigfoot bill."

"How do you—right, never mind. Bucky's in the bedroom with Bigfoot in an hour."

Sadie couldn't recall ever feeling this anxious before. Being back in her body made her acutely aware of how much she had dreaded situations outside her control, hated the vulnerability of not knowing how something would go, the risk that she'd mess up. That's why she studied so much, worked so hard at debate—to afford herself as much control as possible.

But there was nothing to practice here. No way to prepare.

She went straight to the room with the radiator and found Ford already there, holding the little black kitten.

"Look who I found," he said. He was wearing his blue

checked shirt. "She looks a little hungry, but all I can find is hot chocolate mix and beef jerky."

Already every single thing Sadie had thought of to say was wrong. "Bucky was pretty amazing" was what came out.

"Yep."

She had the feeling that they were both avoiding each other's eyes. There was so much she wanted to tell him, a lifetime of things, but there wasn't time. Willy's murder was the important thing, the whole point. *You need to figure out what happened. What he did. Who he is. Ask about Willy.*

Instead she said, "That day at the icehouse, you must have been terrified." *You wouldn't be procrastinating because you're afraid of what you might find out, would you?* she chided herself.

His eyes came slowly to hers. "How do you know about that day?"

"You think about it all the time. About the icehouse and what you were all going to do with your fortunes. About the rope."

Ford frowned.

"Tell me what happened," she coaxed.

His eyes focused on something far off. "My memory is sort of hazy. James had heard about this old-time schooner with a bunch of gold on it that sank around there. He was convinced that if we waited for the thaw, someone else would get our treasure. So we pooled our money and rented an ice-diving rig. James did the dive, and I let go of the rope. But it was fine in the end."

"That's not what happened," Sadie said.

Now his gaze came to her. "Are you calling me a liar?"

"No. It's just not what happened." She paused, putting it

together. "You're the one who made the dive, and James is the one who let go of the rope. Without it you couldn't find the hole you dove through, and you were trapped under the ice. You had no idea which way was up or down, which direction to look for an exit. I know how it feels to be trapped like that."

Ford shook his head. "I have no idea what you're talking about."

"The beer can saved you."

"Look, that's not—"

"'Never touch them myself,'" Sadie said. "That's what James told me in your subconscious. Like saying that he wasn't the one who found the beer can under water, that he'd never touched it. Because he wasn't the one who was trapped. You were lost under the ice, unable to find the way out, until you saw the beer can float down from the surface. You grabbed it and swam back up. And when your hand in the black diving glove came out of the ice and set it next to him, you made Linc scream like a little girl."

Ford looked uncomfortable. "Why would I say it was James if it wasn't? Why would I pretend?"

"Because you feel guilty about being angry at James. So you reversed it in your mind and punished yourself for the thing he did. Punished yourself for being angry. Reversal is one of your primary defense mechanisms. You use it a lot."

"It's so weird you know that." He shook it away. "James was a great guy. Everyone said so."

"And you think so too. But you can still be upset with him."

Ford stared into space for almost two minutes. When he spoke his voice was plaintive, and young. "He didn't even notice," he said. "He didn't even realize he'd dropped the rope."

His tone changed again, becoming James's voice: "'Why do you look so serious, Ford?' I told him, 'I could have died.' And he laughed. 'I'm here,' he said. 'I'd never let that happen.' He meant it too. He just couldn't always deliver."

Sadie said, "But you didn't need him. You rescued yourself."

Ford looked away. "Maybe. You said you know what that feels like to be trapped under the ice. Did it happen to you too?"

"Something similar. I've been lost and numb. I know what it's like to feel yourself turning to ice, inch by inch with no hope of escape." She thought about the Barrington Building, about how close she'd come to jumping. "To be so frozen you can't feel enough to trust your instincts." She paused, suddenly self-conscious. "When you're lost, every direction looks the same."

She was aware of Ford watching her, could feel his blue eyes on her skin. She certainly wasn't numb anymore. For a moment she let her mind play tricks about the future: them at the movies, them making dinner together, them lying on a couch being quiet, a hundred lifetimes of normal things she longed to do with him.

She'd decided in the car she wouldn't tell him any of that, wouldn't burden him with her feelings. There was no way he could share them—he'd known her less than twenty-four hours—and even if he did, there was no way to act on them. Better to pretend she had no feelings at all.

And there was still Willy's death to answer for. She said, "I took the gun and the gloves from your pocket last night and hid them, so you should be safe."

"You keep talking about that." He frowned. "Safe from who?"

She watched him. "What do you remember from the day with Willy?"

"I remember him taking me to the church and telling me he was the Pharmacist and knocking me out. And then when I came to I was in a shack about thirty miles outside of town and it took me most of the day to get home."

"Do you know how you got to the shack?"

"No, but it might have been Linc who took me, his place. There were all these little carved lions there, and he's always liked lions. Tell me about the gloves and gun."

"You wore the gloves while you used the gun to shoot Willy. You shot him four times."

Ford shook his head back and forth. "Never happened."

"I saw it."

"I'm telling you, no way."

She hadn't expected him to flat-out deny it. "You weren't in your right mind. You probably forgot or repressed it. Just like with the ice that day. You don't remember anything?"

"Nothing. Except that I'm positive I didn't do it." He was serious, concentrating. "What time did it happen?"

"Nine thirty."

"That's pretty precise," he commented.

"You looked at your watch."

He sat up. "That's weird. Someone stole my watch."

"It must have slipped off," Sadie said, but she had the sense that she was getting further from the truth rather than closer. She felt like she was overlooking a crucial question, and if she could just ask it, everything would fall into place.

"You think I killed him," Ford said.

"I *saw* you kill him. I felt you kill him. I pulled the trigger with you. That's not thinking, that's knowing."

"But I *know* I didn't." His voice was urgent. "You've been

inside my mind. You know me better than I know myself. Do you believe I could have done it? I want to know the truth."

She looked at him, into his eyes. And she was positive. Unquestionably, unhesitatingly, she knew she was not wrong about him. She knew him, and she knew he was not a murderer. She might not yet have an explanation for what she'd seen, but she was as certain that there was one as she was certain he didn't kill Willy. She couldn't articulate how or why, she just . . . knew. And it was enough.

"No," she answered him confidently. "I don't believe you could have done it. I don't know how it was done, but I know you didn't do it."

He gave her a crooked smile, and it took all her willpower not to reach out and trace her fingers over his lips. "Thank you," he said. Frowned, searching for the right words. "For seeing me."

Sadie swallowed hard.

They were quiet for a few beats, both apparently fascinated by their laps. He glanced at her. "What do we do now?"

"Now we find the treasure," she said. Without letting herself think about it she took his hand and pulled him toward the radiator.

He laughed, following her. "What treasure?"

"The one James stole from the Pharmacist."

"You mean there really was a treasure?"

Sadie nodded. "I'm pretty sure. And Bucky sent you the key."

"Bigfoot?" Ford pulled the bill out of his pocket.

"Radiators always get left behind, you said it yourself," Sadie reminded him. "I think the radiator is the safe, and the numbers on that bill are the combination."

"You mean where it says '#41 of 120'?" Ford asked.

Sadie pointed at the thermostat on the radiator. "He said it was for safekeeping. Try it."

It was the third combination that hit it, 4-11-20. With a sigh the thermostat slid to one side, revealing a large space behind it.

Filled with hundred-dollar bills. A lot of hundred-dollar bills.

"How much is there, do you think?" Ford asked Sadie. "Thousands?"

"Maybe hundreds of thousands. I guess the Pharmacist did pretty well."

Ford stared at the money. "This is where I make a crime-does-pay joke, but I'm in shock."

Sadie laughed. "Me too."

"Do you think I can use it?"

"I'm not going to tell anyone. But I think you should move it. Hide it somewhere only you know about."

"I trust you."

"It's not that," she said. She was having trouble meeting his eyes. "It's just that it's time for me to go."

"Go?" he repeated as if the word was unfamiliar.

She laughed, trying to make it seem light, easy. Pretend to be her old self. "I came to meet you because I needed to understand what happened and answer some questions. But there are rules, and—" She put out her hand and was horrified to see it was trembling. "Goodbye, Ford Winter."

He took it, but instead of shaking it, he held it. "I don't want you to go."

"It's really better if I—"

He said, "You're breathtaking."

Sadie's voice caught in her throat. She searched for anything to say, what her old self would have said. But she had only the truth. "You too," she whispered.

"There was one night, in the tree house." He looked at their twined hands. "I don't know how to put this."

She let her thumb brush his wrist. "I know. I was there. With you."

"In the mirror. It was like we, you and I were—"

Her hand slid out from under his so that only their fingertips were touching. "Together," she finished.

He nodded, and his eyes found hers. "It was extraordinary." They stared at one another. "I want to touch you. For real."

"I want you to." She was breathing hard, unable to look away.

He dropped her hand and cupped her cheek in his palm. He looked at her, into her, locking his gaze onto her eyes. "Meet me at the lake. Pirates' Cove."

"That's impossible," Sadie told him sadly.

"Do it anyway," he urged. "The first Saturday in August."

"I won't be there."

"I will," he promised.

She let herself have one last glance at him. "Goodbye, Ford."

He brought her hands to his lips and kissed them both. "Goodbye, Sadie."

She inhaled quickly and turned, not wanting him to see her cry. She stumbled back through the ruins of Bucky's lair, tripping over everything, the lump in her throat making it hard to breathe, tears rolling down her cheeks. *He'd said her name. He'd kissed her hands, and he remem—*

Her name. Sadie froze. Willy's killer had thought, "Watch

this, Sadie," before pulling the trigger. But Ford didn't know her name when she was in his head.

It couldn't have been Ford.

She laughed out loud with joy. She'd been right about him. Only she'd had one thing backward: He wasn't the one who'd been out of his mind. It was her. She had watched someone else kill Willy and thought she was still in Ford's head.

She'd been blind but it was so clear now. Only a Mind Corps employee could have switched her out of Ford's head. And, as she pushed open the door and stepped outside, she realized there was only one person at Mind Corps capable of pulling that off. It had to be C—

She felt a sharp jab and, pitching into the arms of the Serenity Services officer in front of her, lost consciousness.

CHAPTER 33

"Good, you're awake," Curtis said, standing up as Sadie opened her eyes.

She was on her back, staring up at a matte gray ceiling, her wrists bound together. It was windy, and turning her head she saw blue sky and the tops of buildings, unobstructed by glass.

"Is this the Barrington Building?" she asked.

"Yep."

"How did we get up here?"

"I had them turn on the freight elevator. I know the owner." He chuckled.

"MRP?"

"Exactly." He bent and slashed the cable ties on Sadie's

wrists. "Those were just for transport." He flashed her a gun. "This is to make sure you behave now."

Sadie's heart was pounding. Her mouth had a bitter taste, and her lips were dry from whatever had been used to drug her. "I thought Serenity Services took me."

"I asked to borrow you. I'm a patron of theirs." He pulled her to her feet and stood her with her back to one of the squat square columns that lined the floor. "Don't move."

"What are we doing here?" Sadie's eyes left the gun to scan the area the way Ford would, taking in the square columns, curled-up scraps of carpeting, and an empty water bottle rattling around. Nothing useful.

"I'm going to tell you a story," Curtis said. He radiated restless anticipation, pacing back and forth in front of her, the gun in his hand. "Once upon a time there was a girl who saw a boy commit murder. By law and, even more important, by contract, she should have turned him in, but she didn't. So now she has a choice. She can either call and report his crime to the police. Or"—he pointed the gun at the open side of the building—"say goodbye."

All the gears in Sadie's mind clicked into place, and she saw her chance. She looked from the side of the building to him and said, "Okay. Can I use your phone?"

Curtis handed it to her with a reassuring smile. "It's the right thing to do, Sadie."

Sadie shivered, staring at the screen. "I don't know. Turning him in will destroy him. Destroy his whole family."

Curtis became paternal. "You know you're not doing his family any favors if you shield them from the truth of who he is. I'm not asking you to do anything but obey the law and the rules of Mind Corps."

Sadie continued to stare at the phone screen. "Ford isn't guilty."

"You have no proof to the contrary." His voice was soft, almost apologetic. "You really do have to tell them what you saw, Sadie."

Sadie dropped the phone to her side but held it tightly in her hand. It was her only weapon, and she didn't want to lose custody of it. "What if I say I wasn't in my right mind?"

Still apologetic, Curtis said, "They'll think it's a metaphor."

"But it's not. I did see Willy get killed, but I wasn't watching Ford do it. Willy knocked Ford out and while he was unconscious Catrina switched me from Ford's mind to the killer's." She looked at him. "Yours. Tell me, Mr. P, did you enjoy knowing I was in your mind?"

"I did." Their eyes met, and Sadie was repulsed. She couldn't believe she had once found him so attractive.

Talking fast, so he wouldn't see how she really felt, she said, "It was genius. You waved the truth about your identity in front of everyone's eyes the whole time, but no one saw: MRP, Mr. P, Curtis Pinter. The true brains of the City Center operation. That's how Willy got the information from the chips for his incentive program. He was nothing, a pawn. The Pharmacist is just a smoke screen. You were the only one who could have pulled this off."

He smiled benignly. "You're flattering me."

Now it was Sadie's turn to be apologetic. "I didn't mean about the brains. I meant because everyone at Mind Corps is a Minder, so I couldn't have been in their heads. Everyone but you. You're just a chippy."

For a moment his composure slipped, and he snapped, "Don't use that word."

"That's why you'd never been in Syncopy," she went on, stepping toward him. "Claustrophobia is just an excuse."

He leveled the gun at her, motioning her back toward the column. He was in control again, calm and understanding. "What a busy mind you have. Unfortunately you can only tell what you witnessed. Did I mention it's the law? Now make the call."

"You'd really kill me?" Sadie asked.

He nodded. "I would. Revolution requires sacrifice."

Sadie hadn't expected that. "Revolution? What kind of revolution?"

"The end of crime and corruption."

"Wouldn't that be putting yourself out of business?" Sadie asked.

He gave her a wry smile. "The Pharmacist isn't only a money making scheme. He's a pilot program. A boogey."

"A boogeyman? Like Bricolage deals with?"

"Exactly." Curtis was suave now. He slid the gun into a hip holster and used his hands while he talked. "With the Pharmacist we created the ultimate boogeyman, a mysterious figure who's powerful and vindictive and has the magical ability to read thoughts. By using information obtained through Syncopy we were able to radically increase the speed at which he gained power, until he was at the center of nearly all the criminal activity in City Center." He paused, his eyes alight with excitement.

"We're now poised to turn City Center into a criminal nexus where researchers of every stripe can run experiments in a real-world setting *on subjects who don't even know they are being studied.*" He was watching her and her reaction, closely. "We don't have to stop at knowing what gets subjects' attention, we can learn their *intentions.* This is the beginning of a new era in social research and aggressive philanthropy: the living laboratory."

"A living laboratory," Sadie repeated, trying to mirror his enthusiasm. If she could get him to think she was an ally, she might be able to get close enough to get the gun from its holster. "That's why MRP bought so many buildings." She remembered the guys unloading the truck that night in the alley behind Plum's club. "You were setting up discreet research facilities in City Center."

"Exactly." His face lit up and he stepped closer to her. "You understand now, don't you?"

"Yes," Sadie told him. Three more steps, that was all she needed. "It's an amazing vision. I can see why you couldn't let peons like Willy or Ford interfere."

He looked at her cautiously. "Do you mean that?"

She nodded. "This is bigger than individuals. I'd thought you killed James because he stole your treasure, but I now see it was because that kind of recklessness has to be contained."

"And I'll get the money back," Curtis added.

Sadie was contrite. "By treasure I meant Plum. Your sister. How they were going to run away together." She shook her head. "After everything you've done for her. To support her. You promised when you were children to give her everything, and you have kept your word." She reached a comforting hand toward his arm, just out of reach. "It must have been upsetting when James threatened to steal her from you."

Curtis smiled down at her, moving a little closer. "It was a betrayal. And it showed a worrisome lack of judgment on her part. But we dealt with it. It's over."

"You left James's phone in her apartment so she would know what you'd done," Sadie said, understanding it now. "What you were willing to do for her." *And what you'd do again, over and over, if she ever tried to leave*, Sadie thought, remembering the look of fear on Plum's face. "Is that why you kept Ford's watch? To use the same way?"

"Exactly. I wanted her to know that I would do anything to take care of her." Curtis said it simply, as if he were talking about taking out a loan, not murdering people.

Sadie sighed. "She's lucky to have you." She shifted, stepping slightly away from the column. She held his gaze, moving her hand toward the gun. Her fingertips brushed it—

"You're pathetic." The voice came from behind them, and they both swung around to see Catrina storming across the floor toward them.

Curtis seemed surprised and not entirely pleased. "What are you doing here?"

Sadie had the gun halfway out of its holster when Catrina batted her hand away.

"Cleaning up your mess," Catrina said, and with one neat motion got Sadie by the back of her neck and began shoving her toward the edge of the roof.

She talked as she did it, squeezing Sadie's throat for emphasis. "'Trust me,' you said, 'I can control her. She likes me, she'll do what we want. If he has the money, she'll tell us. Think of it as protection, a way to guard our assets.'" Catrina was quoting Curtis, Sadie realized. The conversation she'd overheard had been about *her*, putting her into Ford's mind. *She* was the protection.

Sadie was pushing back against Catrina, making their progress erratic, but they were unquestionably moving closer to the edge of the floor.

"It worked," Curtis protested behind them. "We learned he knew more than we wanted him to. We learned he was a liability and had to be eliminated."

Catrina twisted Sadie's arm behind her back painfully. They were now a foot from the edge of the roof. "You said there was no chance the Committee would send her back, that as soon as she was gone we could kill him. But you didn't get sent home, did you?" Catrina asked, jerking Sadie's arm up and making her yelp. "So it was left to me to figure out how to fix it. Just like today."

Sadie remembered being in the same building on her school trip. Remembered the wind. Remembered Pete shouting to her, "Hey, babe, come check this out," and how he grabbed her and pulled her behind a column and started kissing her. How she'd kept her eyes open, staring at the space beyond the empty windows and thinking how easy it would be to just . . .

Let . . .

Go.

Not anymore. Now she wanted to fight. "If you kill me, it will all come out," Sadie said as she struggled against Catrina's strength.

"What will come out?" Catrina said, pressing forward, using Sadie's arm as a lever. Her tone, her actions were chillingly deliberate.

They were less than a foot from the end of the floor. "The texts. From Curtis to you, ordering you to switch me in and out of his mind." Catrina's pressure let up slightly. "And the one you sent about how you couldn't find Subject Nine and you were initiating emergency removal protocols." Sadie nodded her head behind her to Curtis's phone, which had fallen to the ground. "I forwarded them. If you kill me, someone will find them."

"You idiot," Catrina hissed at Curtis. She jerked Sadie's arm up higher and pushed her right to the perimeter. "But it doesn't matter. No one will believe it. You'll be the girl who committed suicide. Too crazy to take seriously."

The toes of Sadie's shoes had air beneath them. *Do not panic*, she told herself as her heart began to pound and her throat closed. *You're not going to jump. You have to fight.* Spots danced in front of her eyes and her knees rattled. "Bye-bye," Catrina said.

And pulling Sadie with her, collapsed backward to the floor.

Sadie rolled off her and staggered sideways, gasping for breath. She stared at Catrina, who was lying on her back with one foot dangling off the building's edge and something bright orange sticking out of her neck.

Curtis stood next to her. "I told you Miranda was a good shot," he said, as Miranda Roque, sporting an elegant cream pantsuit and a shotgun under her arm, appeared from behind one of the columns.

Miranda looked at him sadly. "Go wait in the car."

"But Moth—"

"Go," she said harshly, and just like that, he went.

"Thank you," Sadie said.

Miranda smiled. "I couldn't let her kill the only person in

five years to get into the subconscious." She gestured with the gun. "Would you mind checking her pulse? Don't want a murder on my hands."

"Another," Sadie couldn't keep from saying.

Miranda rolled her eyes. "Yes, yes."

Sadie bent. "It feels slow but strong."

Miranda's gaze rested on Catrina fondly. "I used the kind for antelopes, not cheetahs. She's more prey than wild cat, I think, despite her nickname." She looked up. "Interesting about names, isn't it? We don't realize how they define us. Your subject, for example. Ford *Winter*. Did you notice how many of his memories and emotions, especially the important ones, involved ice and snow?"

"They were linked to specific events," Sadie pointed out.

"There's a reason they resonated for him."

"That's—" A shiver swept over Sadie. "How did you know? And that I'd seen his subconscious? Have you been in his mind?"

"Always like to do a quick walk-through after a cleaning to make sure it looks okay. I'm afraid we had to remove all traces of you. Not just the past two days; we did a complete detailing to make sure there wasn't any foreign matter inside. Emergency protocol."

Sadie had been ready for that, knew they would have wiped Ford's mind of her, but it still gave her a sharp pang of sadness. Nothing remained of what they'd shared, what he'd said or maybe felt when he was with her. She was gone from his life, irrevocably and completely, forever. "I expected that."

"I figured," Miranda said drily. "Don't blame me. You knew the rules."

"I did. But by those same rules, you know I have to report the murder I saw. And I have proof it was Curtis."

"That's why I'm here. I thought maybe we could come to an understanding."

More gaps were filling in Sadie's mind. "*That's* why you went against the Committee and sent me back. To protect Curtis. You didn't want me to report what I saw—just the opposite. You knew I'd never turn him in if I thought I was turning Ford in. Somehow you knew how I felt about Ford before I did."

"It came off you in waves. You're lucky. Not many people experience that."

Sadie didn't feel lucky. "Curtis was one of the Perfect Garden orphans, wasn't he?"

"'Thing of darkness I acknowledge mine,'" Miranda quoted. "He and Plum were. Babies, the last two. When the state closed down the Perfect Garden they didn't even count to see if they had gotten everyone. And I was the one endangering children?" Her eyes had sparks in them. "They were such a delight. So curious and determined."

"You implanted both of them with chips." Which was why Willy hadn't been able to find Ford when he spent the night at Plum's, Sadie realized.

"Of course," Miranda said. "How could I do it to someone else's child if I wouldn't do it to my own? And it seemed only fair to have a Subject running Mind Corps."

Sadie thought of how many of her friends' parents made exceptions for their own children without blinking. Sadie admired Miranda's code, even if she couldn't agree with its substance. Keeping her eyes on Miranda's still handy gun, Sadie said, "You mentioned a deal."

"Simple. You don't hurt what I love, and I won't hurt what you love."

"Meaning I don't turn Curtis in, and you leave Ford and the Winters alone forever?" Sadie considered it. Thought about Miranda's version of justice, about how she was willing to go to any length to shield Curtis. "Substitute 'protect' for 'not hurt' and you'll have a deal," Sadie said. "You protect what I love, and I protect what you love."

That earned her a flash of a smile. "Sadie, short for Sophia," Miranda said. "The goddess of wisdom. Your parents named you well."

"Now what happens? To Curtis?"

"He'll take a vacation abroad. And of course all the killing and whatnot will stop. I never thought he was capable of—" She swallowed hard, and Sadie thought she was genuinely upset. "Mind Corps is still valuable. I'm not giving up on that."

Sadie nodded. Pushed herself off the pillar and said, "Well, goodbye."

Miranda tilted her head to one side. "For now. I have a feeling we'll be working together in the future, Ames."

Sadie shook her head. "I can't imagine the circumstances."

"It's never a bad thing to have a good shot on your side."

Sadie made her way to the freight elevator and paused before getting on. "How did you know where to find me?"

Miranda laughed. "You don't think Subjects are the only ones who can be tracked, do you? Someone's got to mind the Minders."

EPILOGUE
FIRST SATURDAY OF AUGUST

She went.

She knew it was futile, but she went anyway. The first year it was a sunny, picture-perfect day, the water on the lake sparkling, endless double rows of footsteps in the sand as couples roamed up and down the beach. She thought at one point she saw him but was wrong, and she'd gone home aching, swearing not to try again.

She went the next year too. There was a freak rainstorm, and seeing she was the only person on the beach, she'd taken off all her clothes and lay down in the sand just to see how it made her feel. She wished he'd been there. She wondered what he was doing and if he ever dreamed of the tree house.

The year after, back from her first year as a psych major in college, Decca made her come to a performance of a new play she was starring in instead. The play was in an open-air theater, and when Sadie arrived she'd almost fainted. It was Bucky's theater, still overgrown and lovely, but restored enough to be usable.

Sadie's vision felt like it was vibrating between past and present—that's where Ford and Bucky had stood, that's the catwalk they ran over, there's Ford with a group of people and a pregnant woman, that's the—

Her eye moved back. It was him. With his arm around a pretty dark-haired woman who was definitely having a baby. *Good for him*, Sadie told herself, looking for a place to hide.

Mason loped over to the group, grabbed the woman, and kissed her in a way that made it clear she was his and no one else's. *Good for Mason*, Sadie thought, *good for everyone, my god, it's him.*

He looked 200 percent better than even her best imagination had painted him, the same but a little more lived in, more rugged. His smile hadn't changed, though, the capacity to be mischievous or boyish, a dimple that could tease you coming and going.

"Are you going to say hello?"

Sadie turned to see a girl with impish blue eyes and blond chin-length hair. "Lulu?"

"Mostly Louisa now," she said with a smile that started bold but ended shy. "So? Are you?"

Sadie shook her head, her lips pressed together. "No. I don't—"

"He dreams about you," Lulu said.

Sadie swallowed a lump. "How do you know?"

"You'll have to talk to him and find out," Lulu said, wiggling her eyebrows.

"I really don't think it would be—"

"Lulu, are you handing out programs or picking pock—" His eyes met hers, and it was like there was no one else there, no one else in the world.

Sadie couldn't find any words. She couldn't breathe. Neither of them spoke, just stared at each other.

"Did you design this?" Sadie asked finally, seeing the picture of him on the back of the programs Lulu was holding.

"A friend of mine did," he said, still staring at her. "I just restored it."

"It's beautiful." Her eyes didn't leave his.

"Breathtaking," he said.

Lulu said, "Please meet, because I want to invite Sadie to my birthday party. Sadie, this is Ford, my brother. Ford, this is Sadie."

"Sadie," he repeated, savoring it. He glanced at Lulu. "How do you two know each other?"

"We met a few years ago," Lulu told him. "She helped a friend of mine."

"Will you come to Lulu's birthday party?" he said. "It's going to be about a hundred fourteen-year-olds and me."

"Mom's in Paris on a painting course," Lulu explained. "With her boyfriend."

Sadie blinked back tears. "I'd love to."

"We're having it at our house on Ladyvine Street," Ford put in. "It has a tree house—"

"—with a rocking horse head on the wall," Sadie said.

ACKNOWLEDGMENTS

I owe enormous thanks to all my friends and family for being so understanding when I disappear for weeks at a time in writer's jail, surfacing only to gulp coffee and snarl. Super special thank you's go to Meg Cabot, Benjamin Egnatz, Sigmund Freud, Susan Ginsburg, Peter Jaffe, Rebecca Kilman, Jaques Lacan, Nespresso, pizza, Laura Rosenbury, Santa, Ben Schrank, Georges Seurat, Carlyle Stewart, and Jennifer Sturman; without your support and guidance, I would have long gone out of my mind.

Susan Ginsburg's mixture of wisdom, kindness, intelligence, and generosity continues to dazzle, inspire, and fill me with wonder. She is a marvel. I don't know how I got lucky enough to have her as my agent, but I am grateful in a hundred ways every single day.

Rebecca Kilman and Ben Schrank, my braintrust at Razorbill, went above, beyond, through, and around the call of duty for this book. What's good in it is theirs; the flaws are mine.